By the same author

The Hengest and Horsa Trilogy
A Brothers' Tale
A Warlord's Bargain
A King's Legacy

The Rebel and the Runaway

Lords of the Greenwood

Novellas
The Visitor at Anningley Hall (a prequel to M. R. James's 'The Mezzotint')
Old Town
Whispering in the Cypresses

https://christhorndycroft.wordpress.com/

As P. J. Thorndyke

The Lazarus Longman Chronicles
Through Mines of Deception
On Rails of Gold – A Prequel to Golden Heart
Golden Heart
Silver Tomb
Onyx City

Celluloid Terrors
Curse of the Blood Fiends

https://pjthorndyke.wordpress.com/

Lords of the Greenwood

BY
CHRIS THORNDYCROFT

Lords of the Greenwood
By Chris Thorndycroft

2018 by Copyright © Chris Thorndycroft

All rights reserved. This book or any portion thereof may not be reproduced or used in any manner whatsoever without the express written permission of the publisher except for the use of brief quotations in a book review.

https://christhorndycroft.wordpress.com/

For Gwen.
For introducing me to the greenwood.

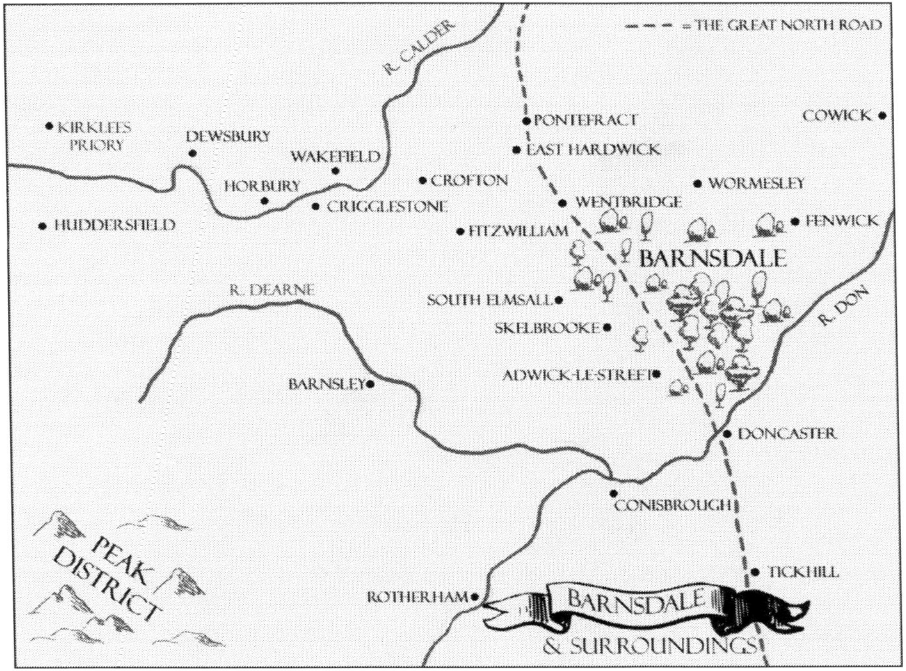
= THE GREAT NORTH ROAD
R. CALDER
KIRKLEES PRIORY
DEWSBURY
WAKEFIELD
HORBURY
CRIGGLESTONE
HUDDERSFIELD
PONTEFRACT
EAST HARDWICK
CROFTON
WENTBRIDGE
FITZWILLIAM
COWICK
WORMESLEY
FENWICK
BARNSDALE
R. DEARNE
SOUTH ELMSALL
SKELBROOKE
ADWICK-LE-STREET
BARNSLEY
R. DON
DONCASTER
CONISBROUGH
TICKHILL
ROTHERHAM
PEAK DISTRICT
BARNSDALE
& SURROUNDINGS

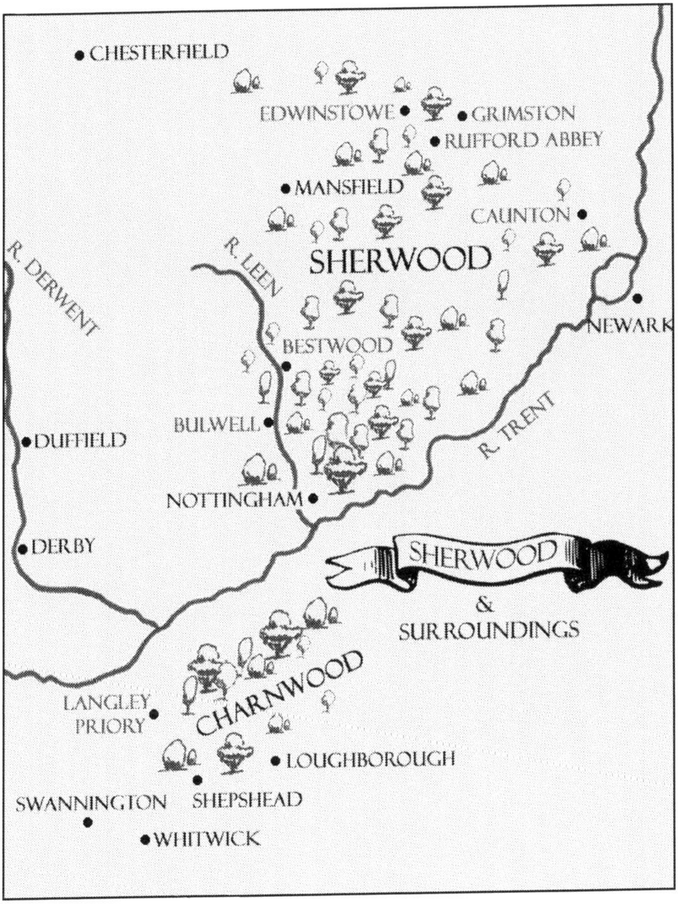
CHESTERFIELD
EDWINSTOWE
GRIMSTON
RUFFORD ABBEY
MANSFIELD
CAUNTON
R. DERWENT
R. LEEN
SHERWOOD
NEWARK
BESTWOOD
BULWELL
R. TRENT
DUFFIELD
NOTTINGHAM
DERBY
SHERWOOD
&
SURROUNDINGS
CHARNWOOD
LANGLEY
PRIORY
LOUGHBOROUGH
SWANNINGTON
SHEPSHEAD
WHITWICK

FITT I
ARROWS IN THE GLADE

"Lythe and listen, gentlemen,
That be of freeborn blood;
I shall you tell of a good yeoman,
His name was Robin Hood."
- A Little Gest of Robin Hood

Yorkshire
Summer, 1320

ONE

The rabbit looked up from the long grass, its ears pricking at a noise only the most sensitive of ears could hear. It chewed thoughtfully and then ducked back into the grass, disappearing for a moment. It reappeared a few feet away, hopping along to find greener pickings. The sunlight, filtered through the gently rippling leaves above, dappled its fur.

Thunnk!

The arrow nailed it to the earth, piercing it above the left shoulder. It struggled briefly and was then still as its short life was extinguished.

Robert Hood, a fifteen-year-old lad from Wakefield, dropped down from the tree he had spent the past hour or so sitting in, bow gripped in his left hand. It was his father's great hunting bow left behind when Robert Hood the Elder had departed the previous September to fight the Scots who had been making raids into England as deep as York. He had not returned and the general belief was that he had been one of the many Englishmen who had drowned in the River Swale, ridden down by the Scottish light cavalry.

Robert plucked the dead rabbit from the ground and drew the rest of the arrow through its body. He inspected the iron tip. It was unbent and the bloody shaft was in good order. He wiped it on the hem of his tunic and replaced the arrow in his quiver. He tried to save them when he could as he had no coin to spend on fresh arrows.

He tied the rabbit's feet together and slung it over his shoulder to join the one that hung there already. *Two coneys for the pot.* Not a bad morning's work but he wouldn't risk trying to bag a third. This wood was on Shacklock land and the Shacklocks were no friends of the Hoods.

Robert delved back into the shadows of the oaks and yews, enjoying the comforting seclusion of their thick trunks and splayed branches. He had always felt at home in the woods. The mouldering leaves muted his footsteps while the silence sharpened his senses making him feel invisible but at the same time keenly alert. And the deepest woods always held that air of ancient mystery that thrilled him.

These trees were older than any man alive and their wizened faces made him think of mythical elves like Hobhood or Hob the Robber as he was sometimes known. His grandmother had told him of such forest creatures when she had been alive. The toothless old dame on his father's side had rarely been taken seriously by anybody and even her suspiciously pagan yarns did little to raise excitement in anyone but young Robert. He had listened intently to her tales of the hooded hob; an impish demon that dwelled in the forests and waylaid travellers, robbing them or sometimes turning them mad so that they wandered around in circles and were never heard from again.

Hobhood had come with the English from Saxony and the little elf had taken root in England's forests, robbing travellers long before the Conqueror and his Norman barons arrived. Robert's grandmother had also told him of real hedge robbers who had used the name as an alias to obscure their traces, thus becoming mythic themselves. It was said that there had been one in the Lionheart's time but the most recent one was Roger Godberd; a soldier who had been outlawed for taking part in Simon de Montfort's rebellion against the old King Henry. The minstrels regularly sang of his exploits in Sherwood Forest at the head of a band of rogues, of his capture and subsequent daring escape from Nottingham Castle.

It was with a touch of pride that she had spoken of their own ancestor – Robert Hood of Wetherby – who had taken the name three generations ago when he turned outlaw before the law caught up with him and hanged him. The phonetic similarity between 'Robert Hood' and 'Hobhood' had become something of a family joke amongst the Hoods, evidenced by the frequent naming of their eldest sons 'Robert' partly in honour of their scandalous ancestor.

Robert made his way towards the track that led to the Wakefield road. The familiar trees told him the direction and he could never understand how people got so lost in woods. To him, each tree was unique, the warped bark and gnarled bulges every bit as distinguishable as the features on the face of a person.

As he joined the track he saw three figures up ahead and froze, cursing his boldness. *The retreat from the wood must always be as subtle as the entrance*, he reminded himself, thinking back on his father's tutelage. He dove for cover but it was too late. They had seen him. From between the branches of the juniper bush that screened him he could see the three youths approaching, each carrying a quarterstaff. It was the Shacklock brothers and their faces were gleefully determined.

Robert drew an arrow from his quiver and nocked it to his bowstring. His fore and middle fingers pulled on the string and he checked himself. Did he really have it in him to kill over two coneys? No, he decided. But would he kill to avoid whatever the Shacklock brothers might do to him if they caught him?

He slowly drew the bowstring back but it was too late and he knew it. The Shacklock brothers were upon him. He was dragged from his hiding place and the bow and its arrow were snatched from him.

"What have we bagged ourselves here?" said John Shacklock, the eldest of the brothers. "A weasel?"

"I hear weasels give birth through the ear," said Ralph, the middle brother, drawing the knife at his belt. He held the blade to Robert's ear. "Shall we open it up and find out if there are any weasel cubs in there?"

"Look at this!" said Will, the youngest brother who was of a similar age to Robert. "Two coneys pinched from father's land!"

"A poaching weasel, eh?" said Ralph. "What do foresters do to poachers?"

"They cut their right hand off," said John.

"I heard they blind them," said Will.

The middle brother removed his blade from Robert's ear and pointed its tip at his right eye.

"They don't do that anymore," said Robert through gritted teeth. He desperately tried not to show his terror at the poised blade. "Besides, this isn't a royal forest. And you three aren't foresters."

"Bit of a chatty weasel, isn't he?" said Ralph. "We'll add insolence to the list of charges against him."

"It's Hood, isn't it?" said Will.

Robert said nothing. Will knew full well who he was. The enmity the Shacklocks bore the Hood family was well known. A couple of years ago, when Robert's father had been a forester for the manor, a local knight had enclosed an area of common woodland near Crigglestone and erected a fence, barring other tenants from gathering firewood or grazing their livestock. Enraged by the loss of common land, a group of tenants tore down the fence and trespassed on the knight's land. The Shacklocks' father had been the ringleader.

As forester, Robert Hood the Elder had confronted the tenants. They had tried to persuade him to see their point of view. Enclosure was a common source of distress for the poorer franklins and yeomen who needed all the firewood and pastures they could get their hands on. But Robert's father had been a strict upholder of the law. That had been his only fault, Robert's mother had said. He had done his duty and as a result the Shacklock family had been fined heavily. It was a slight they had not forgotten.

"But what's to be done with him?" said Will. "If we can't blind him or cut his hand off, what other punishment would fit? After all, we can't let town scum poach on our land."

"It'll just have to be a good old-fashioned beating, then," said John.

"Righto," said Ralph and he sheathed his knife.

The blow from Will's quarterstaff caught Robert in the belly before he had time to react. The wind was knocked from him and he doubled over in agony. A second blow from one of Will's brothers landed across his shoulders and felled him. He bit leaves and spluttered for breath.

The quarterstaffs rained down on him and he balled up, protecting his head. He felt at least one rib crack and he writhed in agony, leaving his face unshielded for a moment.

A blow caught him above the right eye and split the flesh. Blood filled his eye socket and he brought his arms up to shield his face, sacrificing the rest of his body to the savage beating.

When it was over, all he could do was lie still and listen to the jeers of Will Shacklock and his brothers. He could see nothing. Blood swam in his eyes and his head rang like the parish church bell.

"Good bow, this," said one of the brothers. "Nicely made. You need a new bow don't you, Will?"

"Let me have a look," said Will. He gave a low whistle. "Not bad at all. And a quiver of arrows too. A profitable morning!"

The sound of leaves squashed underfoot told Robert that they were leaving and he turned his head slowly, bringing his hand up to wipe the blood from his vision. He saw the three youths walking away, the shortest – Will – held the bow in his hand. *His father's bow.*

Robert staggered back into Wakefield, wincing with every step that sent searing pain up his left side. Ribs were broken for sure and his left eye had swollen horribly shut. Every part of him screamed with pain. As he passed through the southern gate he could feel eyes upon him, examining his injuries, and he remembered why he loved the seclusion and solitude of the woods.

Wakefield was situated on the River Calder and was surrounded by a wooden palisade. The thatched and shingled rooftops of the fifty-odd households were clustered around All Hallows, the parish church, from which extended the four muddy roads that led to the town gates.

The river was the source of most trade. Wool was brought in on barges and the mills situated on the banks supplied flour for the bakeries. The famine of the previous years had abated and there was finally enough bread to fill Wakefield bellies but also enough dead to bury in its cemetery.

The current lord of the manor was Earl Thomas of Lancaster; the king's own cousin and second most powerful man in England. His seizure of the northern territories of Earl de Warenne was the result of a long and complicated feud between the two earls. In the spring of 1317, de Warenne had abducted Lancaster's wife, Alice de Lacy. Never a happy marriage, it was said that Alice had gone all too willingly; a wound with a fistful of salt rubbed into it in the form of a rumour that Alice and de Warenne were lovers.

In retaliation, Lancaster began a hostile takeover of de Warenne's properties including his residence of Conisbrough Castle, much to the condemnation of his seemingly powerless cousin, the king. Early last year Lancaster had taken Sandal Castle which could be seen across the river from Wakefield's palisade on a clear day. With Wakefield Manor under his control, Lancaster had replaced all de Warenne's officials and foresters with his own men and Robert's father had found himself out of a job.

Honesty and duty, it seemed, were not worth a wooden penny in such times.

Lancaster's new steward, foresters and bailiffs strutted about the manor confident that they were the whole of the law in a portion of England that was rapidly slipping from the king's grasp.

As Robert passed the inn at the foot of Bichill, Old Stephen the beggar hailed him from his regular seat on the stoop. "Been in the wars, eh?" he said, looking him over with concern.

Robert liked Old Stephen. He had to be nearing seventy; an unfathomable age in a world where a lad like Robert could expect to reach forty only if he was lucky. Old Stephen had been a soldier in his youth and had fought in Simon de Montfort's rebellion against King Henry III. He was full of stories and excelled in the telling of them. The landlord of the inn let him beg on the street outside and occasionally gave him ale and bread as his tales of war and butchery brought in customers.

"Been a little too bold in your woodland activities?" said Stephen, nursing his jack of ale. The hood of his tattered cloak half masked a knowing smile beneath his wispy white beard. Robert said nothing, not wanting to admit that he was a poacher on the street in broad daylight. "Don't mind me, lad," said Stephen. "I've seen you bring back the odd coney or two and I won't tell. It's your lack of meat and bow that tells me you've had real bother, not your bleeding face. What happened?"

"I was set upon," said Robert. "The Shacklock brothers."

"Ah, they're rough lads Adam Shacklock's boys. Took your bow, did they? That's too bad. It was a fine bow."

"I'll get it back," said Robert. The pain of its loss still stung more than the pain in his body and he was determined to avenge the theft.

"A smart man might say a bow, no matter how finely made, is a fair trade for a dozen or so coneys and the odd pheasant."

"A smart man, aye," said Robert. "But not one with balls."

Old Stephen laughed. "I hoped you would say something of the sort! So, what's the plan? March into Shacklock Hall and demand your bow back?"

"I think I'll have to be subtler than that. But I'll get my father's bow back, don't you worry."

"I look forward to seeing it back over your shoulder. Now you run home and get your mother to look at that eye of yours. It'll probably need reopening to relieve the swelling but I never heard tell of a wound or malady that Matilda Hood couldn't remedy. She's a good woman your mother. If I were a score of years younger…"

"I have no need of a stepfather," said Robert, mustering a grin. Old Stephen regularly alluded to his admiration of his mother. "Take care."

"Take care yourself."

The Hood household was on Bichill where merchant houses had hinged shutters that turned into trestle tables to display their wares during market hours. Robert's home was modest in comparison; a cob-plastered dwelling of five rooms, thatched over with a loft with wooden bars at the windows. His father had built it himself after they had moved here from Wentbridge. Robert had never minded its simplicity. To him it was warm, honest and happy.

Little Mary, the middle child of the Alayn family next door, was carrying a pail of water from the nearby well when Robert rounded the corner. She wasn't so little anymore being no more than two years Robert's junior, but the name had stuck. She was a lively girl with bouncing blonde ringlets and a face as sweet as a rosy apple. Upon seeing him she dropped the pail with a slosh, her pretty mouth forming an 'O' of shock.

"What happened, Rob?" she exclaimed, running over to him. "Your poor face!"

"Nothing that won't heal," Robert replied, proudly.

"And you've lost your bow! Were you robbed?"

"In a manner of speaking. Although I *was* on their land. It's an occupational hazard; getting caught by the men you're poaching from." He tried to laugh it off but his body ached too much for him to be convincing.

"You'd better go in and see your mam. She'll fix you up. Does it hurt?"

"Nah," lied Robert as he headed towards the doorway. "Those Shacklock brothers can't hit half as hard as they pretend!"

"The Shacklock brothers! They're dangerous!"

"Hardly, otherwise they wouldn't have let me walk away!"

"Oh, Rob! Don't jest! Look at the state of you!"

He had to admit, he didn't feel well at all. He entered the house, seeking the refuge and warm care of his mother.

TWO

That summer, the bailiff of Wakefield Manor opened the muster roll at the manor hall to summon young men to fight for Lancaster. There was much grumbling as the summonses were read out in the market place. Robert was on the list as were the three Shacklock brothers and many more of Wakefield's young lads besides.

"How many bloody men does Lancaster need?" demanded Philip Damyson the potter one late afternoon in the thatched lean-to of the inn. Robert liked to sit and listen to the men talk over their ale once business had closed for the day. "Defending his territory against the Scots is one thing, but we all know he's not as opposed to them as Earl de Warenne was."

"Aye," said another man. "Who's to tell what our sons will be used for once they attend their summonses? Fighting the Scots? Or fighting the king?"

There was a hush at this and another fellow piped up; "Watch your tongue, William. Talk like that can get you into trouble. You can't be too sure who might report you to Lancaster's bailiff."

"Bugger the bastard!" said William, his drink getting the better of him. "I liked de Warenne's old bailiff. He was a man you could reason with, a man with his ear to the ground. Lancaster's fellow is only interested in drumming up recruits for his lord's army. Mark my words, we are Lancaster's men first and the king's second these days!"

"Our William has a point," said Old Stephen from his perch on the step. "Lancaster envisions himself as a second Simon de Montfort but for all his talk of upholding the Ordinances and speaking for the king's subjects, he has shown a remarkable interest in building his own kingdom here in the north. Take Sandal Castle, for instance."

"What of it?" asked a merchant from Sowerby who was staying in town on business.

"You have no doubt seen its scaffold cladding. Our good earl is strengthening his control over his new territory. A stone keep? Fortified walls? These are not the works of a man known to be on good terms with the Scottish lords, nor are they suitable reinforcements for a country supposedly at peace with itself."

"What does an old beggar know of such things?" asked the Sowerby man who did not know Old Stephen as the other men did.

"A great deal, friend," Stephen replied. "I fought under de Montfort in my youth and know a landgrabber in the guise of a hero when I see one."

"Some of de Montfort's apologists would take issue with those words, Stephen," said somebody. "Those who revere de Montfort as a saint consider it blasphemy to even suggest he was a mortal man."

"It's blasphemy to suggest he was anything but," replied Old Stephen. "And he would have been the first to admit it. But mark my words, our king has his work cut out for him in Lancaster."

The deteriorating relationship between Lancaster and King Edward II was most troubling for the northern populace. Lancaster had been one of the barons who had orchestrated the murder of the hated royal favourite Piers de Gaveston; the king's most beloved companion. The king had never forgiven Lancaster for this. For his part, Lancaster accused King Edward of lavishing gifts on new favourites such as Hugh le Despenser and his son; both political maneuverers who had amassed vast wealth and power under the king's benevolence, not to mention the envy of their fellow nobles.

Lancaster's increasing hold on the north and the swelling of his army rivalled the king's own power so much so that during the king's progress from Nottingham to York three years previously the royal caravan found the roads through Pontefract – Lancaster's seat – blocked by armed troops. The king had raged impotently but the unspoken truth was known to all his supporters; the north was fast becoming an independent kingdom.

Treason permeated the air and towns like Wakefield felt torn in two directions. Should they obey the orders of Lancaster and dance with treason or remain loyal to their king and lose their lands? While far from a kind and compassionate man, Earl de Warenne had been devoted to his king and there was a feeling in Wakefield that they had come under the boot of a foreign oppressor who was in league with the Scots he was supposed to be protecting them against.

There were even rumours that while the king had desperately tried to retake Berwick the previous summer, Lancaster had informed the Scots that

Queen Isabella was residing at York. The Scottish king, Robert de Brus, had eagerly sent a detachment to capture her. The queen's escape to Nottingham and the lack of any real army to protect her resulted in the Archbishop of York forming a hasty militia made up of priests, clerics and anybody else who could be pressed into picking up blade or bow.

Including Robert's father.

Robert gazed at his ale while the complaints of the other men continued around him. His father had hated the Scots as much as the next Yorkshireman but he had hated the Earl of Lancaster equally. Rumours of Lancaster's friendship with their northern neighbours did little to raise the patriotic fighting spirit in his tenants and Robert Hood the Elder had been fined threepence for not obeying a summons the previous year. Talk of the queen in danger and the increasing rough-handedness of the new manor bailiffs had dissuaded Robert's father from avoiding his duty a second time and he had joined the Archbishop of York's doomed militia never to return.

Robert had as little love for Lancaster as anybody in Wakefield and he'd be damned if he'd take up arms for a traitor.

He got up to leave the inn. He'd had his fill of grumbling old men who, when it came to it, would do just as their lord told them. He increasingly felt like he was cut from a different cloth than his fellow townsfolk. It wasn't just his feeling of freedom whenever he stepped outside the town palisade and saw the soft colours of the greenwood. All his friends had been apprenticed in trades that would see them and their families living comfortably for many years. He had no trade and his family scraped by on what he could poach.

Until a few years ago he had assumed he would become a forester in his father's footsteps but that road had been closed to him with Lancaster's seizure of Wakefield Manor. What then for Robert Hood the Younger? Take up a trade? Few tradesmen would take on an apprentice who was so old. Soldiering seemed the only viable trade and he was determined that if his father had been too good for Lancaster's service, then it would never do for him.

The first really important decision of his life had been suddenly thrust upon him yet he felt as if he had no choice in the matter. As soon as he had been told that his name had been read out in the town square he had known that he would refuse his lord.

"We don't have threepence to spare," said his mother when he got home and explained his dilemma to her. "And there is talk of an increase in the penalty for refusing a summons."

"I know," said Robert. The family's financial trouble was real but his mother had not for a moment tried to convince him that he should attend. He loved her for that.

"We've already had to let the maid go and this little one is getting bigger by the day, though the Lord knows how on thin pottage." She bounced Eleanor, Robert's three-year-old sister, on her knee.

"We'll find a way," said Robert. "*I'll* find a way. I'll get out and earn somehow."

She touched his cheek with affection. "You're your father's son and no mistake. He'd be so proud. Just promise me you'll stay off Shacklock land. I couldn't bear to see them give you another beating or worse."

"Who said anything about the Shacklocks?"

"I know you, boy. And I know what's going on inside your head. I've never minded your poaching. It keeps us fed and every man has the right to feed his family the best way he can. All I ask is that you're careful."

"Careful as a mouse, mother."

"You'll have to lay low. That bailiff will be looking for you. Walter next door has the same idea as you. He won't attend either. Maybe you could help each other out?"

"I think we'll all have to help each other out if it really comes to it," said Robert, grimly.

Robert tried to ignore the inevitable in the days that followed. Many of the town's lads reported to the manor hall and were sent off to Conisbrough or across the river to Sandal Castle. The town began to resemble a town at war; stripped of its young males.

Robert poached with traps, sorely missing his father's bow. He sold his goods to people in the town and stayed well off Shacklock land. Most of his customers paid him in kind; eggs, cheese, leather and cloth which served his family well but he did amass a little coin. He had enough to pay the fine but a sense of outrage made him hide his purse under a loose floorboard in the loft. Why should he pay a fine when Lancaster had more than enough troops for whatever scheme he was planning?

On a Monday morning a further blow was struck to the town's pride. It was Mary who brought Robert the news. He was returning from selling a couple of rabbit pelts to somebody near the southern gate when she ran up to him in the street, her face wet with tears.

"Oh, Rob, you have to get away! Hide!"

"Why?" Robert asked, immediately fearing that his poaching had finally caught up with him. "What's going on?"

"They've taken our Walter! The bailiff and his men!"

"Taken him? What for?"

"For not attending!"

"They can't do that! They have to summon us to a manorial court and give us a chance to pay the fine."

"The rules have changed! The bailiff is rounding up all the lads who didn't attend the summons and taking them over to Sandal Castle. Our da made a right fuss and the bailiff struck him and threatened to arrest him for disturbing the peace! You should have seen our mam weep!"

"The bastards!" said Robert. "They can't get away with this!"

"Well they are and who's to stop them? You must stay away, at least until the bailiff has moved on. They say he's off to Horbury next. Lay low somewhere until he's gone and then you must get gone yourself! Don't wait around for him to return."

Robert's head swam. He didn't know what to do. He kissed Mary on the forehead and made for the inn. It was the only place where friendly faces knew him.

"You're not the only lad looking to bury your head this afternoon," said Old Stephen. "The bailiff has been rounding up this town's boys like hens in the yard."

"I'm for the woods," said Robert. "Until this whole thing blows over."

Stephen's face soured. "I'm surprised to hear that, lad. You always struck me as a man not afraid of a scuffle."

"This is more than a scuffle. If I hang around here I'll be pressed into service. What do you suggest? That I take on the bailiff and his men singlehandedly?"

"Not singlehandedly, no. It's time this manor put its petty squabbles behind it and did something about that bailiff and his lord."

"A fine thing that would be; the manor rising against Lancaster! As well rise against the king!"

"Why not? It's been done before. And not all of Wakefield's lads are as keen to take to their heels as you, Hood. Those Shacklock brothers were in here not an hour past. Young Will had your bow over his shoulder."

"My father's bow?" Robert said. He had thought of little else since the day the Shacklocks had beaten him black and blue and stolen his bow. He'd seen

Will Shacklock around town plenty of times but he had never had the bow with him.

"I don't know what they're planning but it can't be good," Stephen went on. "The older ones had blades on their belts. They stopped in here for a bit of fire in their belly for whatever task they've set their mind to."

Robert barely heard him. All he could think of was his father's bow and how he might get it back. "Did they return to Shacklock Hall?"

"I'm guessing not, considering their weapons and hushed voices. They discussed some things at great length over their ale and they didn't want to be overheard. All I could make out was that the elder two were pressing Will into going along with it. He was as white as a sheet and I believe all he wanted was to return home. They went out the west gate. Take care, Hood. There's something fishy afoot and you've no shortage of trouble yourself. Make sure that whatever you do now has a reason behind it and a good reason at that."

Robert didn't bother to decipher Old Stephen's warnings which were more cryptic than usual and bolted from the inn towards the west gate.

THREE

Robert followed the River Calder south west. The road to Horbury was in good repair but the foliage grew close. There was a statute that required manor lords to keep two-hundred feet clear on either side as protection against hedge robbers but, as with many things since Lancaster's takeover, it had been neglected. That suited Robert. He did not want the Shacklock brothers to notice him approaching and the bracken provided good cover.

He had no idea where they were headed and no idea how he would get his bow back but they only had an hour on him and, if he moved fast, he could catch up to them before they reached Horbury. There was a mill on the outskirts of the village with a small inn on the other side of the road that serviced the travellers coming up from Huddersfield. Robert knew the miller's son, Much, who was the same age as him and occasionally traded flour for rabbit or pheasant.

There was a wagon in the yard and a couple of armed men loitering by it. By their boiled leather armour and tatty maille he recognised them as the bailiff's men and remembered Mary telling him that Horbury was due a visit from the bailiff soon. Did that mean he was nearby too?

The air was still, broken only by the gentle creaking of the mill's waterwheel and the sloshing water against its slimy green paddles. Robert assumed the bailiff and the rest of his men were refreshing themselves at the inn, leaving two to guard their wagon. By the entrance to the inn he could make out a third figure. It was Will Shacklock. He was alone and carried Robert's bow over his shoulder.

It would be relatively easy to take the bow from Will as long as his brothers didn't suddenly appear. Will was no bigger than Robert and Robert's rage and damaged pride would give him an edge in any scuffle. But he could hardly assault somebody within a few yards of the bailiff's men.

As luck would have it, the pot boy emerged from the inn bearing ale and bread for the two guards. They took the victuals greedily and sat down on the rims of the cart's wheels, facing away from the doorway. Robert saw Will turn his head and give a low whistle. He assumed the other Shacklock brothers were inside and Will seemed to be throwing them a signal of some sort.

Robert crept along the bank and made his way around the back of the inn. The foliage was thick and grew close to the stone walls so he had to struggle through, the brambles catching his tunic and tearing his hose. He made his way around to the front and came upon Will like a bolt from the greenwood.

Will tried to cry out but was muffled as Robert clamped his hand over his mouth. He didn't want Will's brothers storming out of the inn to his defence. The bow clattered to the hardpacked ground and they fell beside it, rolling and grappling. Robert squirmed into the position of superiority and rained blows on Will's face, spattering blood from his nose and mouth.

"Oi! What's all this, then?" called a voice and Robert cursed. The guards at the cart had either seen or heard them and were striding over to break up the scuffle. "Ought to be ashamed of yourselves, brawling in a tavern yard!"

Robert and Will were pulled apart by the two burly men. Will struggled more than Robert, his face streaming with blood and panic in his eyes. There was the sound of further disturbance coming from within the inn and one of the guards poked his head through the doorway.

"Christ! They're attacking the bailiff!"

Robert and Will were released as the two men drew their blades and rushed in to save their master. Will was up on his feet in an instant and dived for the bow as the sounds of clashing swords could be heard from within. Robert scrambled to his feet and tried to catch Will but was grabbed from behind as one of the men returned. Will bolted for the treeline.

"The little bastards were acting as lookouts!"

"Where's the other one?"

"Shot into the woods like a spooked lark, the sod!"

Robert seethed with rage, powerless in the grip of his captor who held a mace threateningly. The bailiff and the rest of his men emerged from the inn, red-faced and wide-eyed. Between them they carried Ralph Shacklock; the brother who had threatened to take out Robert's eye. He glared at Robert with rage.

"Hood, you bastard! What did you do?"

"Hood?" said the bailiff, raising an eyebrow. "Not young Robert Hood of Bichill by any chance? Quite the band of rogues, eh? You thought you could murder me and your names would magically vanish from the muster roll. Idiots! Now the charges against you have leaped from the avoidance of a summons to attempted murder. One Shacklock lies dead indoors by my men's blades and another has fled. He'll not get far. After the next manorial court, I'll have two Shacklocks and a Hood dangling from the gallows oak!"

An arrow whistled out of the woods and pierced Robert's captor through the neck. It was a fine shot; skewering the larynx and lodging there while the shocked man choked and coughed blood. He released Robert and the mace fell from his hand as he lurched forward, clawing at his neck. The bailiff and the rest of his men dived for cover as a second arrow thudded into the side of the cart.

The soldier who had held Ralph sank to his haunches and looked about desperately for the nearest cover. He debated the risk of a dash to the cart but Ralph seized the mace dropped by the other soldier and brought it down upon his head with savage force.

He was wearing a maille coif but no helm and the edges of the mace bit deep, crunching through his skull. He tumbled forward, blood pumping through the maille.

Robert wasn't going to let a second chance for escape pass him by and he was up and running for the treeline before the bailiff's men gathered the courage to emerge from their hiding places.

Up ahead, partially screened by the leaves, he could see Will nocking another arrow to his string. He turned his head and saw Ralph following close behind. He also saw the bailiff's man emerge from behind the cart with a crossbow in his hands.

Robert ducked as the bolt was released but it did not find its mark in him. He heard Will cry out and risked another look back. Ralph stumbled, the bloody point of the bolt emerging from his left breast. His legs gave out and he tumbled headlong to lie motionless in the dirt.

Robert leaped into the foliage, relief at its cover coursing through him. Will had vanished, not waiting around for the vengeance of the bailiff to catch up to him. Robert ran and ran, not stopping until his heart felt like it would burst.

He emerged from the woods on a bend of the river and panted for breath. Sweat made his tunic cling to him and ran down his forehead in rivulets. It was a cold sweat borne of terror. He had just seen two of the bailiff's men killed and he was as good as an accomplice, however unwilling. The bailiff knew his name and would be after him with a hot vengeance.

There was no way he could explain that he had not been part of the Shacklock brothers' plot and his avoidance of the summons only spoke against him. He would be strung up as a murderer if the bailiff caught him.

He had to get gone and be gone for good. *Mary had been right.* He had been a fool to loiter in town.

And going after Will all because of my father's bow? I must have been mad!

He supposed he could hide in the woods or even Barnsdale if it came to it. He had the skills to survive, at least until winter. He didn't know what he would do when the cold and the rain set in and all the trees grew bare but that was a problem for another day.

He couldn't leave without saying goodbye to his mother and Eleanor. It was risky to return to Wakefield now but if he hurried he could be gone by the time the bailiff got back and gave up the hue and cry.

As he entered the west gate he wished he had a mantle and hood to obscure his face. He was too well known about town and before the day's end these people would know him as a criminal and a felon. The very people he had grown up with and traded goods with would be ordered to hunt him down and deny him shelter. He tried not to let the tears break from his eyes as he thought of all he was leaving behind. Right now, he had a job to do. There would be time for tears once he was alone in the greenwood.

His mother was picking herbs around the side of the cottage. Eleanor tottered about, clutching at the hem of her skirt. As Robert watched them from across the street, he found that he didn't know how to tell her that he was going away. How could he break the heart of this woman who was so recently widowed? How could he tell her that she now had only one child left to look after and no man to support them at all?

He decided that some things were better left unsaid. He would leave a message with Mary next door and somehow, he swore by the Virgin, he would get food and coin to his mother and sister. They would not starve because of his actions. They would see him again, he was sure of it but for now it would be better if he just left.

Mary was not so easy to convince.

"You have to explain yourself to the bailiff!" she pleaded once he had caught her attention and explained his plans. "Otherwise you'll be hunted for the rest of your life!"

"It won't matter!" he protested. "Two men are dead. They think I was in on it with the Shacklocks! They'll never believe me."

"But how will you survive?"

"There is nothing I need that I can't get in the forest. And I'll send food to my family. But I need your help. Promise me you'll help?"

"Rob, we've known each other since forever. Of course I'll help."

He could have kissed her full on the lips right then. She had always been a loyal friend and he found that he loved her for it now.

"What do I have to do?"

"I don't know yet. Meet me by the giant's rock one week from today. I'll make some plans in the meantime."

The giant's rock was a huge boulder by the river that the local children knew well. It was far enough from Wakefield's palisade but not too far that Mary couldn't get there and back without arousing suspicion.

"I'll be there, I promise. But what about your poor mam? You'll break her heart!"

Robert felt his guts twist into a knot. "I know. But there is nothing I can do about that now. What's done is done. Just tell her that I love her and that I'll not be far away. And convince her that I'm innocent?"

"Oh, Rob, she'll know that. As soon as word gets out that the Shacklock brothers were involved nobody will believe you were anything but an innocent bystander."

"Thank you, Mary. Now, you don't happen to have any food about that wouldn't be missed?"

"Stay here."

She ran indoors and returned several minutes later with a small sack containing half a loaf of dark bread, a hunk of cheese and a couple of small onions. She took her purse from her belt and handed it to him. It contained a few silver pennies.

"I can't take your money, Mary," he told her.

"Yes you can. You might be able to get all you need from the forest but just in case you need something that doesn't grow on trees, you'll at least have a little coin to your name."

"You're the best, Mary. Tell my mam there is a purse hidden under the loose floorboard next to my pallet. She can pay you back out of it. And I'll bring meat for your family too."

"Just get going, Rob. And be careful!" She reached up to kiss him on his cheek.

"God be with you, Mary."

"And you, Rob."

He headed for the south gate and kept to the shadows cast by the jetties of the nearby buildings. As he approached, a figure lurched from an alley and seized him by the shoulder. He gasped in fright and his hand instinctively reached for the knife at his belt. He relaxed when he saw that it was only Old Stephen and noticed with a little fright how quick he was to go for a blade to defend himself now that he was a wanted man.

"You need to get gone, lad," said Stephen, pulling him into the shadows.

"That's what I'm trying to do!" said Robert. "Let me go!"

"You can't just wander out of the gate. They're watching for you. There's only one guard but more will come soon."

"How do they know to look for me? And how do you know about it all?"

"The bailiff sent one of his men running back. He's raised the alarm and there are soldiers on their way to your cottage. They came to the inn to tell us to look for you so we all scarpered and tried to look busy. It's all a bit half-hearted. Nobody can believe that you and Adam Shacklock's boys tried to murder the bailiff."

"It was nothing to do with me! I was just trying to get my bow back!"

"I guessed that might have been it. And it's partly my fault for telling you about Will and his brothers setting out. Had I known what they were planning..."

"I need to get out of here, Stephen!"

"Quite right. Take this." He removed his tattered old cloak and draped it across Robert's shoulders, drawing up the hood and pulling it low. "That won't fool anyone with a mind to look close so you'll need a diversion. Walk steadily and slowly towards the gate. Don't run, no matter what you hear. Keep your face dead ahead and don't look about. Skip now."

Robert found himself pushed gently back into the street. The gate was open up ahead, guarded by a man in maille holding a quarterstaff with a sword at his belt. He could never fight his way past and prayed to God that Old Stephen's plan would work.

He trod slowly as carts lurched by, their iron-shod rims squelching in the mud. People pushed past him, oblivious to the fugitive beneath the beggar's cloak in their midst. The guard turned to look at him and then had his attention diverted by a loud crash as several empty barrels tumbled over.

"Bloody drunkard!" somebody yelled and Robert moved behind a wain loaded with empty chicken baskets that was making its way through the gate.

The guard was still amused by the old beggar that had tumbled a stack of hogsheads and didn't pay Robert a glance as the wain rumbled out of the gate.

FOUR

Robert headed southeast towards Crofton and then cut across country. It was thickly wooded here and if he avoided the villages of Nostell and Fitzwilliam in the south and the town of Pontefract with its castle in the north, there was little chance of being found, at least for several days.

These were the woods his father had taught him to hunt in when they had lived at Wentbridge which lay some five miles to the east. He knew where the streams ran and followed them deep into the gloom of the trees. He squeezed through mossy rocks where the ferns brushed his knees.

He would have to make his camp near water; that was a basic necessity. He needed a place where it pooled and yet had enough current so as not to stagnate. He thought he remembered the perfect spot and when he reached it he suddenly flung himself on the ground.

Somebody was there, by the water, drinking.

Robert parted the ferns and peered across the pool at a boy his age, scooping up water to his mouth with a cupped hand. He cursed and felt as if God was playing a big joke on him. It was Will Shacklock.

The fool was still wearing his garish franklin's clothes of red and blue making him highly visible in the greenwood. Robert always favoured earthy greens and browns to conceal himself when hunting. He then decided that he was the bigger fool for thinking that this pool was a safe place to build his camp. If Will Shacklock could find it in a day, then so could the bailiff's men.

He rose from his cover and strode over to Will, steeling himself for the confrontation. The matter of the bow – which lay unstrung next to Will – would be resolved for good and all. No interruptions this time.

Will saw him and leaped up in alarm. Robert broke into a run and slammed into him, knocking him to the ground. They rolled in a fury of fists and elbows. Robert gasped as Will kneed him in the groin and then felt a searing pain as an elbow connected with his forehead.

He rolled off Will and came up swinging but his opponent had stepped backwards, drawing his dagger. Robert seized his hunting knife and for a moment the two boys stood and stared at each other, each poised to strike.

Robert could see in Will's eyes that he did not really want to plunge his dagger into him and he found that he had no desire to knife Will either, however much he hated him. Both had seen too much bloodshed that day and it was violence that had landed them both in this situation.

"We're evenly matched, Will," he said. "Neither of us would come away looking pretty. Let's not do the bailiff's job for him."

Will studied him. "Aye. Drop your knife then."

Robert was hardly going to disarm himself just to make Will feel comfortable so he compromised by slowly sliding his knife back into its sheath, keeping his hand on its bone handle.

Will did the same and they continued glaring at each other in silence.

"Bastard," Will muttered at last. "Sticking your nose into our business and wrecking everything!"

"I was trying to get my bow back," said Robert. "I had no interest in what you and your brothers were up to. What the hell were you thinking, anyway? Killing the bailiff wouldn't solve anything. Your names would still be on the muster roll."

"Which the bailiff takes around with him in that cart of his. John and Ralph were supposed to kill the bailiff and his two men while I stood lookout to make sure they weren't interrupted. Then we were going to take on the remaining two men together. Then we'd torch the cart and all its contents. But you had to stick your nose in. Bastard! Now my brothers are dead!"

"I am sorry for that, Will. Really. But it couldn't have worked. Somebody would have told; the innkeeper or his potboy or anybody else inside the inn."

"The inn was empty, we made sure of that. Do you think my brothers were stupid?"

"What's done is done. I advise you don't make camp here. The manor's foresters will quickly follow the stream to its choicest part just as we did. We need to move much further east. Maybe as far as Barnsdale."

"We? You're going in the opposite direction to me, Hood."

"Perhaps it might be better if we were to stick together. Safety in numbers, that sort of thing."

Robert had no desire for any of Will's company but at least he was somebody to share the loneliness of exile with. Besides, two sets of hands were better than one when it came to building a shelter, gathering firewood and hunting game.

"You just want your bloody bow back," said Will with a snarl.

"Aye, there is that too."

"Well I'm keeping it. And I can manage well enough on my own."

"Suit yourself." But Robert could see that Will was unsure and was too proud to admit it.

"What's your plan, then?" Will asked. "Live off nuts and berries for the rest of your life?"

"Hardly," snorted Robert. "I can trap and hunt and whatever else I need I can get from town."

"How? They'll lock you up as soon as you set foot in there, ratty beggar's cloak or no. Where did you get that thing from anyway? Your foul old friend Stephen?"

"Yes, as a matter of fact. He's one of my contacts. I have others I can call upon."

"Like who?"

"I'm hardly going to tell you, am I? Not unless you agree to let bygones be bygones and agree to team up."

Will sniffed and gazed across the pool at the greenery that enclosed it on all sides. "I suppose we can share a fire for tonight, but in the morning, we go our own separate ways."

"As you wish. But not here. We drink our fill and then we head east."

"Fine."

They drank and washed the sweat and grime from their faces before setting out. It was close to dusk and they knew they wouldn't get far before night descended but away from the stream was good enough for Robert.

"How far is the Great North Road?" Will asked. "Will we reach it tonight?"

"No," said Robert. "It lies beyond Wentbridge, several miles in that direction." He waved a hand at the woods ahead.

"How do we even know which direction we're going in? All these woods look the same. We could be wandering around in circles!"

"Don't you know that moss grows on the northern sides of most trees?"

Will eyed him sceptically. "Really?"

Robert nodded. "As long as you don't look at the base of the tree where it's always damp. Look higher up. If there is moss in the middle then it's a good bet that part of the tree is in the shade at midday."

"Where did you learn all this woodsman stuff, anyway?"

Robert gritted his teeth. "My da was a forester, if you recall."

Will said nothing and they continued in silence for a while.

"We should stop soon before it gets too dark," Robert said. "No fire. We're not deep enough to risk somebody seeing the smoke. Besides, it's a warm enough night."

"What about food?" Will asked. "I'm starving."

"I'm not about to set traps of stalk beasts at this time of night. No fire."

Will cursed and Robert chose a thick trunk to sleep against.

"Start looking for some brush for bedding," he instructed Will. "Fern leaves are good too."

They foraged about, Will swearing under his breath, and soon they had two small piles of leaves and brush to make comfortable pallets. They slumped down facing each other and watched the shadows creep in around them.

Robert opened the sack Mary had given him and drew out the bread. Will gaped at it. Robert sighed. He broke it in half and tossed a portion to him. Will bit into it eagerly and nearly wept when Robert produced the cheese and onions.

The meal was over all too quickly and Robert wrapped Old Stephen's reeking cloak around himself. Will took his time making himself comfortable, always keeping the bow close to him.

"If you touch this while I'm asleep," he warned Robert, giving the bow a protective pat, "I'll stick my knife in you and won't think twice about it."

"That's a fine way to talk to the man who's just fed you," said Robert.

Will grumbled. "I just don't trust you yet, that's all. You're a sneak."

"Guilty," said Robert with a shrug.

Will looked about. Stars had begun to appear above the creaking branches. "What are you really going to do?" he asked. "I'll go mad living out here with no hope of return. Can we clear our names?"

"Unlikely," said Robert. "Maybe things will quieten down after a while. There'll be other things to take up the bailiff's time. But a full pardon? I wouldn't count on it."

"Then we're finished," said Will in a quiet voice. Robert could see that he was frightened.

"Look, I don't know what the future holds. Sooner or later that bastard bailiff will move on or die and Lancaster too for that matter. The way he's been carrying on it could be all out war with the king before the year is out. Then, who knows? All we must do for the present is survive and provide for our families. I have friends in Wakefield. They'll help us."

"Who?"

"Mary, the daughter of the family next door to us for one. She's the one who gave me the food. Wonderful girl. Old Stephen of course. He's the wisest man I ever met and he's got no love for Lancaster. And I was thinking of Much over Horbury way."

"The miller's son? What use is he?"

"A great deal I believe. He's a solid lad and I trust him. He can give us flour in exchange for whatever we can trap or shoot for him and he won't let on to anybody. We can get him to buy us things from town too. Arrows, for a start. And clothing and blades and all the other stuff we might need. Mary gave me a bit of coin too so that will get us started. What about you? Have you anybody you can trust?"

Will looked away. "No," he said softly. "Nobody. My brothers are dead and I was the least favourite of my father. The only attention he ever gave me came with a beating. Now that John and Ralph are gone he won't stand to see my face."

Robert felt a sudden pity for him. As the youngest of three brothers there had always been something of the runt about Will Shacklock.

"We'll be alright, Will," he said. "There's plenty to organise and we've all the time in the world to do it. But right now, all I want is a bit of kip. It's been a hell of a day."

They left each other to their own thoughts and, with the stars peeping through the treetops, they drifted off to sleep.

The following morning, they continued eastwards into the Went Valley looking for game. Their bellies rumbled painfully and the handful of blackberries they had found did little to satisfy them.

"What are you hoping for?" asked Will. "Coneys? Partridges?"

"Venison," replied Robert.

Will seemed on the verge of saying something but held his tongue. Robert knew that he had been about to tell him that all deer in the forests belonged to the king and to kill one was a serious offence. England's forest laws meant little to them now.

"There is a meadow up ahead," said Robert, indicating the thinning of the trees. It was still early and mist showed white between the trunks. "The deer will be grazing there. But you shouldn't get any closer. Your clothes are a little too garish for the forest. That's something we should ask Much to get us; a tunic and hose in earthy colours for you."

Will regarded him sceptically. "You wouldn't be trying to find an excuse to take my bow, would you, Hood?"

"You're a fine shot, Will. I saw that when you killed the bailiff's man. But I've been hunting since I could walk. It would be better if I bagged us a deer. And it's *my* bow."

Will sighed and handed Robert the bow. He took it with a grin and placed the bottom tip against the inside of his foot, pushed down and strung it. "Go and gather berries," he told Will. "Find water too. I may be some hours. Just don't get lost, whatever you do."

Robert found a suitable spot at the treeline and waited while the morning sun slowly evaporated the mist. He breathed the deep, earthy smell of dew and damp leaves and contemplated. He was getting along surprisingly well with Will. The man was an insufferable complainer and knew nothing about how to survive in the greenwood but considering that they had been ready to gut each other the day before, things weren't going too badly.

Robert saw in Will a brash youth who had been forced to strive for acceptance in a harsh household. His aggression and competitive nature had perhaps been his only way of measuring up to his older brothers who had always been quick to knock him back into his place no matter how hard he tried to rise in their esteem.

Robert almost hoped that Will would remain with him so they could continue to help each other. He was prepared to teach him all he knew about the greenwood if he was a willing student. He would never admit it to Will but he was terrified of being alone.

He didn't know how long he had sat there until the small herd of fallow deer emerged from the woods on the furthest edge of the meadow, their white spots and single stripe winking at him. He ignored the buck for it was too large to eat or carry and he never wasted any meat he poached. There were a few fawns but he wanted a sizable leg of something to give to Much. It would be a way to convince him to help them. He settled on a small doe that had begun to graze near his position.

Silently, he nocked an arrow to his string and waited. The doe was oblivious to his position and wandered closer. In a single, smooth movement, Robert drew back the arrow's fletching to his cheek and let the shaft fly.

It struck the doe behind the shoulder bone, piercing her lungs. She reared and flopped about, startling the rest of the herd who took to the woods at a gallop. Robert leaped from his cover, drawing his knife. She was already dead when he got to her and he shouldered his bow and hefted the animal to rest across his neck.

He found Will stuffing berries into his face by a small brook.

"Ready for a real breakfast?" he asked him.

Will's eyes widened at the sight of the doe and Robert set about stringing it up. Once this was done, he sliced its abdomen open and began to gut and clean the cavity. Will watched in awe as he skinned the beast, pulling the hide off with a clean rolling motion.

"Don't just stand there watching me," he said to Will. "Get a fire going. I want to be eating roasted doe before midday."

Robert jointed the meat and wrapped the choicest parts in the skin. The smaller parts he skewered on sharpened sticks and they set about roasting them over Will's fire.

FIVE

Succulent meat, although not properly cured, blackened and crispy on the outside but tender and juicy on the inside was heaven for the two fugitives. Their bellies bursting with venison, blackberries and cool stream water, all they wanted to do was snooze in the afternoon sun but Robert would have none of it.

"It's a good ten miles back to Wakefield and I want to get this meat to Much while it's still fresh. Let's get going."

They buried the offal and kicked out their fire before setting off, taking turns to carry the joints of venison. Robert kept his bow and Will said nothing about it. It had become symbolic of an unspoken truce between them and Robert felt like their companionship had taken an important step forward.

They even began to talk on the long walk westwards. Robert promised to help Will make a bow of his own and there was no more talk of them going their own separate ways.

It was late afternoon as they approached Crofton and dusk by the time the mill on the River Calder could be seen through the trees that lined its southern bank.

"We must be mad coming this close to Wakefield," said Will as they crossed the bridge and cast nervous glances along the length of the road.

"We'll have to occasionally," said Robert.

"Where will we sleep tonight? You're not suggesting we trek back east once darkness falls?"

"No, we'll camp south of the river and head out at dawn."

The yard was empty of carts and horses as they made their way over to the mill, steering well clear of the doorway to the inn. It was a strange feeling coming back to this place where all the trouble had started. The blood on the dirt showed dark beneath the straw somebody had thrown over it.

Much the miller's son was a short, stocky lad with thick forearms and curly black hair. Despite his youth, he had a powerful chest from heaving about sacks of grain and flour for much of his life.

The mill had shut up its business for that day and, with the other labourers returned to their homes, Much was busy setting all to order for the night.

"Your da about, Much?" Robert said from the doorway.

"Saints alive, Rob!" said Much, whirling about to face them, his broom gripped like a quarterstaff. "You didn't half give me a fright! What are you doing creeping about so close to town? And who's that with you? Will Shacklock?"

"Aye, Will and I have decided that some things are so much water under the bridge."

Much scratched his curly locks in puzzlement. "I've not the faintest idea what's going on, Rob. Your two families have been at loggerheads the past few years then you team up to murder the bailiff right across the yard. Then you vanish leaving four dead in your wake, hunted by the bailiff's men who can't find hair nor hide of you. Now you wander into our mill, thick as thieves."

"It's been a confusing time for all of us, Much," said Robert, "but we need your help."

"And your silence," warned Will.

Much glanced at Will uncertainly.

"We don't want to put you in any danger," said Robert, "but you're the only one who can help us. We can make sure it's worth your while. You see, we have a business proposition for you."

"A business proposition?"

"People come to you from all over the manor to mill their grain for them. You meet all sorts and you're in a good spot to know who's trustworthy and who isn't."

"And who might want a bit of cheap meat now and then," added Will.

"Meat?"

"We can get it for you," said Robert. "In fact, here's a couple of legs of venison to whet your palette." He hefted the doe skin onto the mill floor. It opened, revealing the slippery meat within.

Much's eyes widened.

"We can get you more," Robert said. "Venison, coneys, pheasants, you name it. Interested?"

"You want me to sell the meat for you?"

"And take a cut for yourself, obviously. Of either the meat or the coin."

"But you'll have to keep a buckled lip on it," said Will. "Our lives depend on it."

"Are you jesting?" said Much. "You lads have just killed one of the king's deer. I'll be in as much trouble as you if I'm caught selling game."

"But will you help us?" asked Will.

Much gazed at the glistening venison, its white webbing of fat promising sizzling meat and coin in the purse.

"Much!" bellowed his father from the recesses of the mill. "If you haven't got that place spick and span within the hour I'll belt you!"

"I might be able to help you lads out," Much told the fugitives. "But even my da can't know. He's a hard man but a law abiding one. This will have to remain between us."

"Even better," said Robert.

Much seized the joints and carried them to the storeroom where he hung them behind a sackcloth curtain.

"Now for the other matter of business," said Robert. "We need supplies. I've a little coin although I hope you'll be generous considering that we are now business partners."

"Name it and I'll see what I can do."

"Arrows. Broadheads with peacock feathers the way William the fletcher does them. We'll need at least two dozen. And a tunic and hose in less garish colours for Will. He sticks out like a sore thumb in the greenwood." He counted out a few coins from the purse Mary had given him and handed them over to Much. "If it costs more, I'll pay the difference."

"Gladly done," Much replied.

"Could you let me have some salt and flour? I'll pay extra for that."

"Of course. Where are you boys planning on sleeping tonight?"

"South of the river."

"I won't hear of it. Not with a perfectly good storeroom I won't. Just as long as you are gone with the lark tomorrow. Our customers come in early to get their flour."

"Very generous of you, Much," said Robert.

They slept on the hard floor of the storeroom with sacks of grain for pillows. It was warm and comforting to have a roof over their heads and they both knew that this was to be a seldom luxury in the days to come.

The following morning, they returned east and set about looking for a place to build a camp. They chose a spot on a wooded rise, well covered and with a bubbling brook at its foot. They built a shelter from ash staves layered with fern leaves. Brush would serve as bedding until the deer hides Robert intended to cure with the salt he bought from Much were ready. He also found a flat river stone and hauled it into camp to use as a baking stone upon which he turned out some passable loaves of unleavened bread.

They set about trapping and hunting with a vengeance. Robert didn't know how much meat Much would be able to sell for them but he hoped it would be a lot. The list of things they needed from town grew longer the more he thought about their future in the greenwood and his thoughts constantly dwelled on his mother and sister. He was determined to give both the Alayn family and his own enough meat and coin to live in comfort.

Two bows were better than one and work on Will's bow began in earnest. It took some searching to find a fallen yew tree as they had no axe with which to cut one down. Once a suitable trunk had been found the lengthy process of shaping the rough wood into a smooth and lethal tool began.

Robert had forgotten about the string which was usually made from hemp or silk and reminded himself to tell Much to visit the stringfellow. They also started work on deerskin quivers for their arrows which would be carried over the shoulder forester style rather than at the hip for ease of movement through dense undergrowth.

Once they had shot and dressed a fair bounty of venison and pheasant and trapped four or five coneys, they headed back to the mill to hand their goods over to Much. He had done his bit in sussing out buyers who would hold their tongues as to where the meat came from. The two venison joints they had given him already had sold for over a shilling which was more than they had hoped for.

With a bit of coin to their name, things were looking up and they came back a couple of days later to find that they were now part of a booming trade in illicit game. As they left the mill, Robert's pouch jingled satisfyingly.

A week had passed and it was time to meet Mary at the giant's rock. Robert sent Will south of the river to prepare for their journey back to camp. It would be late by the time they got back and he didn't have much time to spare.

Mary seemed more beautiful than he remembered and upon seeing her he found himself wanting to crush her to him and kiss her sweet face. He wondered what exile and loneliness was doing to him. He had never felt such warmth towards her before. But friendly faces – especially female faces – were rare for him these days. Will, companion though he was, was surly company and he longed for the sweet words and pleasant gaze of a woman.

"How is my mam?" he asked her.

"Coping. I saw her weeping the other day. Times are hard for her with no man about the house. We've given them some food but we have little enough for ourselves."

"I can't thank you enough, Mary. And I promise you, better days are coming. Here." He gave her a purse of coin. "For my family. And this is for yours." He handed her a slightly smaller purse. Her eyes widened.

"How did you come by coin in the greenwood?"

"It's the best place to get it," he replied with a wink. "If you have a good bow you might say it grows on trees."

"We'll eat well for this! Thank you, Rob."

"There's more coming. I've got plans in motion that will see us all through the bad times. Outlawry won't mean a thing. If only... If only I could see them. And little Eleanor? How is she?"

"Missing her big brother. I play with her when I have the time. Look," she handed him something bundled in sackcloth. "Your mother wanted me to give this to you."

Robert unwrapped it and gasped at the sight of horn banded by dull brass. A green baldric was attached to it by hooks. "My father's horn!" he exclaimed. He well remembered the day of his father's leaving. He had taken with him his sword, his dagger and his buckler, leaving behind only his hunting bow and forester's horn. Now both were his.

"Thank you, Mary. Give them my love, eh?"

"Of course. But Rob," her face was worried. "Where will this all end? They're still looking for you. You're in too much danger to meet me so close to town."

"Don't you worry. Will and I have got it all sussed out. We've got a great camp eastwards and friends here in the manor. We'll be alright."

"Will Shacklock. I still can't understand that."

Robert laughed. "Neither can I some days. But we work well together. He's alright. Just grown up in the wrong family is all."

"Just be careful, eh, Rob?"

"Always, Mary. Now, I've got to get going if we're to make camp by nightfall. Same time next week?"

"Yes."

"You're an angel fallen from heaven, Mary."

He made to kiss her on the lips and she didn't shy away. Their mouths met and they held the kiss as long as they dared. Robert burned to run his hands all over her and whisper sweet things into her ear but he wasn't stupid. This would have to do until next time. He left her, knowing that many nights of dreaming of her pale skin and soft lips awaited him with only Will's snores for company.

SIX

The following weeks were ones of great industriousness and the little camp on the rise in the Went Valley became more sophisticated with each trip to the mill. The game they sold through Much earned them good coin with which they purchased useful tools to make their lives in the greenwood easier. They even bought a cast iron cauldron and chain so they could make pottage and stew meat.

Will's bow was finished and Robert taught him how to hunt. Will was used to shooting at the butts on his father's land but knew nothing of stalking. Soon they had doubled their bounty of game. Much had attracted customers from as far afield as Dewsbury and Huddersfield. Most were merchants who passed through the manor on a regular basis and were keen to take some good, cheap game home with them.

They slept at the mill whenever they made a delivery and would be gone the following morning before the first of the customers came for their flour. Will would wait south of the river while Robert went to meet with Mary.

Those meetings were the highlight of every week for Robert but they were short and sweet. Once Mary had told him how his family were doing they would steal a few kisses before he disappeared back into the shadows of the woods, ever fearful that somebody would recognise him and bring word to the bailiff. He wasn't overly concerned about his own safety but the thought of anything happening to Mary because of him was more than he could bear.

One evening, in the heat of high summer, Robert and Will approached the mill, as was their wont, from the bridge as dusk was falling. The road was empty under the darkening sky and the shadows were deep in the trees on either side.

A stone, thrown by somebody unseen, skittered across the dry dirt a few paces from them and Robert immediately nocked an arrow to his string. It was Will's turn to carry the meat and he staggered about nervously with no free hand to grab a weapon.

"Get off the road, you fools!" hissed a voice to their left.

Robert peered into the gloom and saw a figure standing there, limned against the light from the river at his back. It was Old Stephen.

Robert replaced his arrow in his quiver and hurried into the trees, beckoning Will to follow. "What's up, Stephen?" he asked.

"Trouble. Up at the mill."

"What's the old fool babbling about?" asked Will, staggering under the weight of the meat.

"Heed my words or not, young masters," said Old Stephen. "But the bailiff and a company of his men are waiting up at that mill. Waiting for you two."

"He's found out!" said Robert. "Somebody told!"

"They didn't need to," said Stephen. "Much the miller's son has been spotted about town buying things a miller's son seldom has use of. Dozens of arrows from the fletcher's for example. That information reached the bailiff's ears and he decided to search the mill. Imagine his surprise at finding a storeroom full of poached meat!"

"But Much!" cried Robert. "Was he taken? What did they do to him?"

"Calm yourself. How do you think I know so much as to warn you of the trap that awaits? I have keen ears as well you know and I learned of the bailiff's interest in the mill before he set out with his men. I sent Mary to warn Much."

"Mary?" asked Robert. "What's she got to do with all this?"

"More than you would have me believe," said Stephen with a wink. "I have keen eyes too, young Hood, and I have seen her slip out of the east gate the same time each week. I have also seen your mother and sister looking reasonably well fed for a family that has no means of providing for itself. If Mary did her task well Much will be waiting for you at the bridge beyond Crofton. I don't know where you boys have made your camp but I thought you might take him with you. It won't be safe for him to return. Did his father know of this poaching business?"

"No," replied Robert. "Much wanted to leave his da out of it."

"Just as I thought. Anketil would have nothing to do with so bold a scheme. That's good. The bailiff will seek to punish him for owning a cellar of stolen meat but he'll have a hard time proving that Anketil had any knowledge of it so long as he protests his ignorance and his son remains in hiding."

"What of Mary?" Robert demanded, a horrible thought coming to him. "What if the bailiff found her at the mill or learned that she warned Much? She'll be in great trouble!"

"Nothing for it, lad," said Stephen. "She's a keen girl with more than an ounce of wit. I daresay she got out in time and let nobody see her."

"You daresay? I must find out! If the bailiff has her I have to rescue her!"

"You boys can't be anywhere near this place!" Stephen protested. "You have to be off. I'll find out if Mary is alright and get word to you somehow. The bailiff won't harm her. He wants you boys, not her."

"But he'll use her to get to us!" said Robert, drawing an arrow from his quiver as he set off towards the mill.

"Hood, get back here!" hissed Stephen but Robert paid him no heed.

Robert crouched low as he ran and kept to the shadows of the trees so no one at the mill would see his approach. He didn't begrudge the others for not following. Old Stephen was of no use in a fight and, although he got on with Will now, he could hardly expect him to charge into a trap to rescue a girl he did not know.

As he scrambled over a low wall he could see a single light burning in a window of the inn across the yard. He crept down the bank to where the water gushed, kicked up by the great churning wheel. There was a small, barred window that looked in on one of the storage rooms.

Squatting, with his back to the wall, he peeped over the sill. There was a brand burning somewhere and he could see the backs of several figures in the room beyond. Maille glinted in the light. Old Stephen hadn't been lying. The bailiff and his men really were waiting for them.

He made his way around to the front of the building. The door was closed and he hurried past it to a second window that looked in on the mill floor. Through it he saw the faces of the men he had seen from the other side. The bailiff sat at a table taking fistfuls from a loaf of bread. At the same table sat Much's father Anketil, his face bruised and cut.

Robert seethed at this mistreatment of his friend's father but he could see no sign of Mary. Maybe she really had got away before the bailiff had arrived. Else she would be sitting there with Anketil, awaiting Robert and Will to fall into the trap.

He ducked back down and made to leave but his movement caught the eye of one of the bailiff's men. There was a cry of alarm and Robert bolted for the road. The door to the mill burst open behind him and a crossbow bolt clattered off the stone wall as he vaulted over it.

Up ahead, Will stepped out into the road, bow drawn, and Robert ducked as an arrow shot by and struck a soldier in the chest behind him.

"Make for the bridge!" Stephen hollered. "Leave the meat!"

Bitter at having to abandon what had taken them most of the week to poach, the two outlaws and the old beggar clattered across the bridge towards the woods that crowded the road to Crofton. Still pursued by the bailiff's men who had naked blades and curses on their lips for the killers of their comrade, they dove into the woods and cut a southerly direction.

The crashing of feet through bush and snapping of twigs behind them told Robert that they were being hotly pursued and he turned and drew an arrow from his quiver. "Don't wait for me!" he bellowed to his companions and he drew back the bowstring, took aim at a helmed figure fast approaching, and loosed.

The arrow struck the man in the face and there was a sharp cry as he went down. Robert blinked.

I just killed a man. I just killed a man.

It had been so easy.

His hands shaking, he turned and ran. He could hear the shouts behind him calling for all to proceed with caution. Two of the bailiff's men had been killed now and they weren't going to risk a third by tearing blindly into the woods.

Robert caught up with Will and Stephen. Darkness was all around. The trees masked everything and for the first time in his life he was disorientated.

"That was foolish of you, boy," said Stephen. "You need to be smarter than that if you're to survive. Towns and mills are not your friends. The forest is your friend. You must lead your enemies to it not engage them on their turf."

"Right now, I have no idea where we are," Robert admitted.

"West of Crofton. Come on, I'll take you to Much."

They plunged onwards, following the old man's lead.

"Was she there?" Will asked Robert.

"No, not that I could see," Robert replied. "They had Anketil and they were waiting for us. I pray to God that Mary got away without being seen."

They reached a small stream over which a crude bridge of timbers had been laid and packed with earth. Someone had made camp by it and rose up from their blanket at their approach. It was Much. His face was grim at seeing his two comrades.

"Old Stephen squirreled you out of that mess then, did he?" he said. "I wasn't so lucky."

"You're here, aren't you?" Stephen said.

"But my father?" said Much, his face sour. "Our livelihood?"

"Your father is unharmed," said Robert. "Besides a few lumps. As for your livelihood, I'm sorry, Much. I thought I had it all planned out. I truly am sorry."

He felt terrible. Much couldn't go back now, not unless he wanted to face charges for selling poached meat. With a sinking feeling Robert realised that he had become a liability to everybody he knew. His mother. Mary. They were all in danger because of him.

"My da will lose his employment for this," said Much, glumly. "The mill isn't his, you know? It belongs to the manor."

"We'll see that he's all right, Much, I promise you."

Much glared at him, his eyes livid in the moonlight. "How? How can you when you have no money and no way to make any?"

"I don't know," said Robert feeling helpless. Once again, he was desperately making promises he didn't know how to keep. How would any of them survive now? How would his family? How would Mary's?

"There's always robbery," said Stephen.

They were silent, not sure if the old beggar was jesting or not.

"Listen, old man," said Will. "You have our gratitude for warning us about the bailiff's trap, but we'll keep our own council on what to do next. We don't need wild ideas."

"He's right," said Robert.

They all turned to stare at him.

"Crime is the only road left open to us." He felt as if his entire life had been heading towards this particular fork in the road. His old nan's tales of Hobhood had never left him. All his life he felt as if that little green-faced imp was squatting in his mind, forever poking him with a sharp claw in the direction of the greenwood. He was the greenwood and the greenwood was him. They were a part of each other, he realised that now.

"There is a high ground about half a mile south east of Wentbridge," he continued. "It's called the Sayles and it gives a good view down into the Went Valley. From it we can see all travellers coming down the Great North Road. It would make a good lookout point."

"Aye, that it would," said Stephen.

"You've really thought this through, haven't you?" said Will and Robert realised that he had. "Never thought I'd hear Robert Hood so casually discussing robbery."

"Oh, I'm not talking about robbing honest franklins or yeomen. They have little enough as it is. I'm talking about barons, knights and bishops. Fat merchants. The ones who jingle with wealth while those who till their lands starve."

"That's the spirit, lad," chuckled Stephen. "Strike a blow for the common man! But robbing folk isn't as easy as aiming an arrow at some fat bishop and asking him politely to hand over his purse. You need discipline, intimidation and nimbleness on your side. You are three and that's a good number for small robberies but you can't get over ambitious. Most wealthy folk travel with hired guards and with good reason. You'll be up against men not particularly keen to release their purse strings."

"How do you know so much about it all?" Will asked him.

"Because I learned with the best," the old beggar replied.

"You were a robber?"

He laughed at this. "Aye, though I've done my best to hide my past. When I was your age I was part of the most feared gang of thieves in all England headed by none other than Roger Godberd."

Robert started suddenly. "You knew Roger Godberd?"

"As a brother and as a friend though he was not an easy man to like." Stephen's eyes seemed misty in the moonlight as he thought back on days long gone. "I miss him," he said quietly. "I miss all my brothers. I'm the only one left."

"But... how?" asked Robert, eager to know more. "How did you wind up with Godberd's gang? Did you meet him when you fought under Simon de Montfort?"

"I knew him before that. It's a long story and my old bones are tired. I cannot tell you everything now. I need rest."

"Aye, we all do," replied Will. "Here's a good a spot as any. Much has been safe for a few days at least. I say we get a bit of kip and head back to camp first thing tomorrow."

"But your story!" Robert protested, keen as a child for a bedtime yarn.

"I'll tell you a little of it then," said Stephen. "But I must sit down. I could do with some ale and bread for talking on an empty belly is hard work but I suppose I'll have to manage."

They all made themselves comfortable and, like four spectres beneath the moonlight, they listened as Old Stephen began his tale.

FITT II
THE ROAD TO LEWES

"The Sheriff dwelled in Nottingham,
He was fain that he was gone;
And Robin and his merry men
Went to wood anon."
- A Little Gest of Robin Hood

Nottinghamshire
Winter, 1264

SEVEN

I was once Stephen de Wasteneys of Colton in Staffordshire. My uncle William was a lord of the manor; a sorry collection of villages and hamlets on the northern bank of the River Trent where the proudest monument to our family was a rather shabby mill. My father had died during my infancy and my uncle, having no sons of his own, took my brother and I into his household.

My older brother, William, was the soldier of the two of us. Always a rigid bastard without an ounce of fun in his brittle bones, he had been sent to join the garrison at Nottingham Castle when he came of age. Being a bookish child who showed no interest in hunting or warfare, I was destined for the church.

My uncle had given a parcel of land to the Augustinian priory of St. Thomas and it was into those cold cloisters that I was sent to begin my novitiate when I was younger than you are now. I have never been a particularly Godfearing fellow and obedience has rarely come easy to me, so you would be forgiven for thinking that a career in the church was a poor choice for me. I have however, always been keen for knowledge.

On the whole, I took to my lessons well for I had learned my letters at my mother's feet and had always enjoyed reading. I was also possessed of green thumbs which aided me no end in the herb and vegetable patches. Why these particular skills convinced the prior that I would make a good manservant I have no idea, but I found myself plucked from the ranks of freshly-tonsured youths to serve as his personal lackey.

The prior had a great deal of administration to handle with tithes and rents to collect and little time to spend journeying across the considerable extent of his lands. Perhaps my knowledge of Staffordshire's nobility as the youngest nephew of a local lord stood me in good stead or perhaps the prior saw in my restless spirit and bored demeanour the makings of a man ill-suited to life cooped up within the priory walls. Either way I was given a fast horse and a messenger's satchel and sent on my way with sealed letters to distribute.

This was a role I rejoiced in. Once I was beyond the priory walls I considered myself a free man, my order and my duties be damned. The ale shops, colourful merchants' houses and comfortable haylofts of Rugeley, Cannock and Lichfield beckoned with promises of all the vibrant life and comfort I had sorely missed since entering the priory. It was in one of these ale shops, while listening to a bawdy tale about a reeve and a miller's wife, that I heard my real calling, or at least I thought so at the time.

A man entered wearing a monk's habit with many dangling adornments that hinted at a life on the road. He carried a stout ash staff the top of which was fashioned into a crucifix inlaid with silver. His satchel was stuffed with rolls of parchment, his cap had at least a dozen pewter badges of various saints pinned to it and at his neck was a cluster of pendants, charms and talismans in which I could see bones, rabbits' feet and locks of hair in various hues.

As the traveller sat down at a far table and supped his ale I inquired of a neighbour as to the nature of his business.

"He's a pardoner," said my companion. "Charlatans, most of 'em, but you do get the occasional chap with a proper dispensation. They go around selling absolutions for sins; those are the rolls he carries in his satchel. They do a good by-line in reliquaries and talismans too, though you never know if what you buy from them is a real saint's toe or a bit of old pig's knuckle."

My imagination was captivated by the thought of selling absolution to sinners. Surely such things were between God and man and not a matter of coin but my companion put me straight.

"The church serves God but God doesn't pay for their monasteries or hospitals, does he? That requires coin and coin has to be got from the public somehow. There's plenty of sinners about and so long as it's all sanctioned and approved by some canon or bishop, most folk don't mind handing over a bit of coin in return for a fancy certificate in Latin and a conscience that lets them sleep at night."

I immediately saw the profit in such a scam and decided to set myself up as a pardoner immediately, wholly without the authorisation of the prior of course. I thieved vellum from the priory stores and, in my cell by candlelight, I wrote up my own absolutions complete with impressive illuminations. I had no idea what an absolution should contain in its scrawling text but I figured that the majority of my customers would be illiterate anyway so I could most likely write a filthy rhyme on each so long as it was prettily set out with fancy letters and plenty of crucifixes.

I have always been cursed with a smart mouth and a trustworthy face and even at a young age I was aware that women found me attractive. These gifts aided me no end in selling clean consciences to the public and I earned good coin in doing so whenever the prior sent me out on an errand. I earned something considerably better than coin from Jane the vintner's daughter.

I lodged with her family whenever I was in Rugeley rather than endure the expense of an inn and they let me sleep in their undercroft which was cool and smelled tantalisingly of wine. I had not touched a drop of the stuff since leaving my uncle's household and the thought of its sweet sting was almost as intoxicating as the sight of Jane's bosom bulging against the top of her dress and her flaxen hair that was plaited into cornettes on either side of her blushing cheeks.

Word eventually got back to the prior about my scam of course and I was summarily apprehended for my crimes. It probably didn't help my case that they found me in Jane's bedchamber in a state which no man of the cloth should be found in.

Back at the priory I was flogged with a length of knotted rope and while my back was re-growing its skin the prior visited my uncle to discuss my future as a man of God. It was decided that I required further discipline the like of which the church was unable to provide. I was to be sent to Nottingham and delivered into the tender cares of my brother William.

So ended my brief career in the church.

I first set eyes on Nottingham Castle on a cold, misty day which seemed specially brewed by God to intimidate his wayward ex-servant. Its square keep seemed unreachable atop the castle rock which was ridged by the toothed curtain wall. We wound our way up from the town to cross the drawbridge, passing into the shadows of the great barbican. As we entered the outer bailey I felt as if I was leaving sunlight and song and all pleasant things behind me and entering a world even more harsh and cold than the priory I had just left.

Iron clanged from both the training yard and the blacksmith's hut and the mud that caked my boots seemed intent on sucking me down. Steam from horses' dripping mouths and my own breath drifted on the chill air.

I feel at this point I should take the time to remind you of your history. As I was entering Nottingham Castle in that cold winter of 1264, King Henry, the third of that name, was still in France where King Louis IX had just arbitrated a settlement in his favour against the English barons. Led by Simon de Montfort, the barons had been pressing the English king to uphold the Runnymede Charter and the Provisions of Oxford which tried to curb the political influence of his French in-laws and rein in his wild spending.

Once great friends, the relationship between de Montfort and the king had soured after de Montfort had married the king's sister without asking the monarch's permission. De Montfort's attempts to form a parliament that held a check on the king's powers further drove a wedge between the two and it was to de Montfort the barons of England rallied, holding him up as a figurehead of freedom and release from tyranny.

One of Simon de Montfort's strongest supporters was Robert de Ferrers, the 6th Earl of Derby, whose lands had been held in custody until he came of age by the Lord Edward, the king's eldest son and heir. When Robert de Ferrers had reached manhood not all of his lands were relinquished to him by the Lord Edward, including Nottingham Castle. With all the chaos caused by the baronial unrest, de Ferrers snatched the castle with the minimum of effort, replaced its castellan and reorganised its garrison.

When news of the French king's support of King Henry reached English shores the barons immediately began preparing for war. They headed for Wales and attacked the estates of the Marcher Lords who supported the king. While I was being shown to my quarters in a disused stable where the straw looked none too fresh, Robert de Ferrers was continuing his vendetta against the Lord Edward, snatching three of his Welsh castles in quick succession.

I had little cause to be interested in politics at that stage for a new chapter of my life had begun. I learned that my brother had progressed to Master-at-arms of the Nottingham garrison and oversaw the training of new recruits. My lessons began almost immediately and it was made clear that I was to receive no preferential treatment from my sibling.

I had been given my own sword by my uncle on my seventh birthday and had received some rudimentary tutoring in its use which I had found dull and heavy going. That was nothing compared to the rigorous repetition of stances, high-guards, low-guards, advances and counter attacks my brother put us through each morning when the frost was still furry on the posts of the training yard.

The other lads were of my age and hailed from a variety of backgrounds both highborn and low. We sweated, cursed and bled together in those first weeks, enduring broken fingers, skinned knuckles and weary arms that screamed for relief at the end of each day. I hated every minute of it and I hated my brother even more for he seemed to harbour a special disgust of me.

"Keep your bloody end up, Stephen!" he would bellow with increasing frequency as the end of each session drew near and my weakened body struggled to heft the dulled long sword against another attack from one of my comrades. "You're supposed to be fighting, not sweeping the stables although judging by your sword-work that's all you're good for!"

He doled out similar niceties for all of us and I suppose I was fortunate that he did not spare me for my comrades never begrudged me for being his brother. It must be said, I was a poor swordsman. I did not gleefully hurl myself at my opponent, swinging and chopping as some of the other lads did.

I was more interested in defending myself, figuring that should I ever find myself truly fighting for my life, I would be much more inclined to defend or run rather than try and make a hero of myself. This earned me the further sneers of my brother.

Once, when Richard – a molecatcher's son from Grantham – came at me with a cut from the side, I caught the blade in my armpit and held it fast. I winced as the energy of the blow nearly lifted me off my feet, its force dissipating through my padded gambeson. Without overly thinking, I swung my blade at Richard's face and caught him a fine blow on the helm that dented the metal and sent him reeling backwards.

Clutching my bruised armpit, I knelt by Richard's side. He groaned and removed his helmet. Blood ran down from a gash in his forehead and for once, my brother had nothing disparaging to say.

"Are you all right?" I asked Richard.

"I'll live," he replied. "But you don't half catch a man off guard, de Wasteneys!"

"Off guard?" my brother snapped. "Says it all, really doesn't it? I don't know why I bother teaching you lot how to defend yourselves. You all seem intent on getting yourselves killed. If that had been a real battle Stephen's blade wouldn't have been dulled and he might have split Richard's skull. Score one for Stephen de Wasteneys."

"Although not exactly a chivalrous move," said a voice from the other side of the posts. It belonged to a young knight in fine armour who was leaning against the fence watching us. We had all seen him about the castle and none of us liked him very much. He smacked of arrogance and clearly revelled in a birth that was higher than any of ours.

"How so?" I asked of him.

His grey eyes fixed on me and his mouth curled into a mocking grin. "Catching an opponent's blade as if you were a man overboard clutching at a bargepole is hardly clean fighting."

"Clean fighting?" my brother snorted. "No such thing, de Grey. There's no clean or dirty fighting once you're on the battlefield. There is just bloody red slaughter and the desperate fight to stay alive by all means necessary."

"Perhaps that's the way of it in the footman's melee but a knight is honour-bound to uphold certain standards."

"Been in many battles yourself?" I demanded of the spectator. My brother's words in my favour had made me overconfident and the sheen of the young knight's armour and his clean face made me angry. "Or have you just read about them in courtly romances?"

There was an audible intake of breath from my comrades. I had overstepped the mark. The nephew of a minor lord did not speak to a knight in such a manner.

"Mind your tongue when addressing me," the knight replied with a dangerous flare in his eyes. "My family has as much experience with warfare as yours has ploughing fields."

"Be off with you, de Grey," my brother told him. He was a knight too and the remark about our family had touched a nerve in him also.

The knight grinned and shrugged before heading towards the stables.

"Who was that?" I asked my brother.

"Reginald de Grey. You've no doubt heard of his family."

"Those de Greys?"

"There's only one de Grey family although you might be forgiven for thinking there are several as they breed like bloody coneys. The de Greys of Codnor Castle have served the king for years and Reginald's father is currently with him in France. It gives young Reginald a somewhat overinflated sense of self-importance."

"Didn't Reginald marry the Longchamp heiress?" asked Wyotus, another of my comrades who hailed from Sandiacre and had a nasty case of facial boils.

"Aye," my brother replied. "He married Maud, the daughter of Lord Fitzhugh and Hawise de Longchamp giving him Wilton Castle among other possessions. The bastard's not lifted a sword outside the training yard and has more land due to him than all of our fathers and uncles have combined."

"What's he doing at Nottingham?" I asked. "Why isn't he playing lord of the manor at Wilton or wherever?"

"Old William Fitzhugh has a few more years left in him. Reginald has to wait for his father-in-law to be in the ground before he can strut the corridors of Wilton Castle as its lord."

But enough of Reginald de Grey for I'm afraid there is more than our share of him to come. You will have learned from all this that I was not the greatest swordsman in my youth and, although I did eventually achieve some form of professional adequacy with a blade, I still cannot claim that title. I did however do better with a bow.

We practiced at the butts as much as we did with blades between the posts. We mostly used crossbows but I have always had a preference for the humble power of the long bow. Most of us were good as even franklins and yeomen teach their sons to hunt but I am proud to say that I outshone my companions.

My brother said nothing and, as always in such rare occurrences, I took that as the highest compliment of my skills. In fact, as our training came to an end he seemed to run out of criticisms for me entirely. Although there was never anything resembling brotherly love between us, I did begin to feel that I fitted the part of a grateful student and he a satisfied tutor.

I may have been a mediocre swordsman at best but it was to be my keen eye and steady hand with a bow that brought me to the notice of the man whose appearance in my tale you have so patiently awaited.

EIGHT

Not half a month had passed before we were assigned to our watches. I was pleased to be on the same watch as Richard and Wyotus for we had formed a close bond and, as we waited eagerly in the courtyard that morning to be introduced to our sergeant, we trembled with a mixture of excitement and fear.

My first impression of Roger Godberd was one of intimidation. He was a big man, nearly six feet, with a thick nutbrown beard and massive fists. He wore a dark green gambeson into which had been sewn many iron rings and a skull cap of boiled leather which he always wore untied so that the strings dangled down on either side of his face. He did not waste words on niceties and I quickly learned that he was a man always keen to get down to business.

"You three have been chosen due to your proficiency with the bow," he told us. "I have need of archers in my watch as I place more stock in strong English yew and strong English arms than the other sergeants do. While I'm on the matter of the other sergeants, I should tell you this. I demand only two things of my men. They do what they are told and they keep their mouths shut. Each sergeant has his own way of doing things and if you want to remain on my watch, or indeed alive, you'll keep your lips buttoned about what you see and hear in my company. Is this clear?"

All we could do was nod vigorously and hope he believed us.

The watch was a good body of men. They were hard and coarse but not brutal or unkind. Roger's brother Geoffrey served as a second-in-command and there were two knights in the company; Robert le Lou and Ralph le Boteller. I also learned that my brother was a good friend of Roger's. This was revealed to me by Roger himself that night in the Great Hall which was where we received our daily ration of black bread, weak ale and meat or fish depending on the day.

"He's a good man, is William de Wasteneys," Godberd told me around a mouthful of bread. "He vouches for your trustworthiness and swears you are cut from the same cloth."

I was surprised by this. William and I had never been particularly close as children and when he was sent to Nottingham I assumed that was the last I would see of him. He had shown nothing but contempt for me during our training.

"I imagine he holds blood in higher esteem than friendship," I told Roger, "for he knows me little."

"Are you saying that he was overgenerous in his estimation of you?"

I grinned sheepishly. "I won't say that, sir. It's just that my brother and I have drifted apart in recent years. In truth, I don't know what he thinks of me."

Godberd nodded thoughtfully as he dipped a crust of bread in his pottage and pushed it into his mouth. "Churchman, weren't you?"

"Very briefly."

"Don't hold with them myself. Land grabbers most of them. Money lenders and debt collectors. Vultures."

I kept quiet about my own entrepreneurial escapades during my time at St. Thomas's Priory and I later learned the reason for Godberd's hatred of the church but that is something I will get to later.

Garrison work in a castle is pretty mundane although nothing like as dull as life in a priory. It was our duty to patrol the battlements, night and day, keeping a weather eye out for anybody approaching from the town to the east or the River Trent to the south or Sherwood Forest to the west and north. Should we ever come across one of our comrades asleep at his post, we were encouraged not to wake them, but to steal something from them or cut away a piece of their clothing as proof of their negligence.

It became something of a game for Richard, Wyotus and I and we were constantly trying to catch each other out. Once I came across Richard snoring softly against his spear and I nearly made off with a length of cord from his gambeson but my chilled hands disturbed him and he woke with a snort.

"Bugger off!" he snarled, patting himself down to make sure nothing was missing.

"Nearly had you, Richard!" I said with a laugh.

"You won't really hand me in, will you?"

We often joked about catching each other off guard but now that I was faced with the decision I found it a hard one. Richard was one of two friends I had in the whole castle, the whole world for that matter. I didn't want him to lose a day's wages but on the other hand, not reporting a sleeping watchman could get you expelled from the garrison.

"Relax," I told him. "I didn't get proof anyway. Just keep your eyes open in future. I don't want a knife in my back because somebody managed to sneak over the wall while you were kipping."

Richard hawked up a glob of phlegm and spat it over the battlements. "Not much chance of that. I'd welcome a bit of action. It would liven things up a bit around here."

"Be careful what you wish for, Richard," said a voice behind us. It was Wyotus, joining us from the stretch of wall that led from the postern gate. "We live in dangerous times. With all this talk of civil war the pendulum could swing either way."

"The boil-faced philosopher speaks," said Richard. "What do you know about it all, anyway?"

Wyotus shrugged. "With de Ferrers and the other barons sacking royalist properties and the king gathering support in France, who knows what will happen? Nottingham might fall under the Lord Edward's thumb again if things don't go well for our lord."

We stared over the dark green carpet of treetops to the west that was Sherwood Forest. Wyotus, for all his appearances, was a well-learned man. He was a clerk's son and had been sent to Nottingham by his father after some disagreement. It was a common joke in the garrison that it was made up entirely of bastards, criminals and those who had displeased their fathers.

"It might not be as bad as all that, Wyotus," I said, trying to lift the mood. "War hasn't officially been declared yet. It's just a bunch of barons fighting over their inheritances."

"Only a matter of time, Stephen," he replied. "From what I've heard, de Montfort isn't the type to back down and the barons who follow him have too much to gain. Greed drives men to great extremities."

Before the end of our first week on Roger Godberd's watch, he called us aside in the Great Hall and spoke to us in hushed tones.

"You lads are coming with us tonight."

"But it's not our night on the walls, sir," I said.

"This is a private matter. But don't worry, you will find it worth your while. Leave your bows and arrow bags against the wall by the entrance to the cellars and come back after compline."

This was all that was said and we were left to our imaginations as to what was planned for that night.

"I bet they're sneaking off into town," said Richard, his face lighting up with hope. "I bet they've each got a favourite whore in some brothel down there who gives them what they need regular! We've landed on our feet here, lads!"

Wyotus and I shared a look. Richard seemed to be born of a greater libido than the average man. He constantly made lewd references to the female anatomy and his very presence at Nottingham Castle was due to his overzealous sexual appetite.

She had been a franklin's daughter and he had many complimentary things to say about her fine clothes and the finer things beneath them. They had been in love – so he said – although what a franklin's daughter saw in the grubby son of a molecatcher I have no idea. This was also a puzzling question for her father when they were discovered in a hayloft together.

Terrified of her father's anger, the girl did nothing to dissuade the notion that she had been assaulted and Richard decided that perhaps a career in the military would be a prudent step. He fled Grantham before the sheriff could apprehend him and entered the garrison of Nottingham Castle just as Robert de Ferrers claimed it from the Lord Edward.

Bastards, criminals and disappointments, the lot of us.

We did as our sergeant bid and, after getting up off our knees from the final prayer of the day, we retrieved our bows and headed for the entrance to the cellars beneath the Great Hall. We made our way down the stone steps towards a faint glow of candlelight that shone between the dusty casks and hogsheads of ale and pipes of wine.

A small group of men had gathered around a single stump of dripping tallow. Roger and Geoffrey Godberd were there, as were Ralph le Boteller and Robert le Lou along with their squires who were both called William. I was surprised to see my brother also loitering in the shadows. The whole thing had the air of something illicit about it and the idea of my brother – who had once reported me to my uncle for urinating against a churchyard wall – doing anything illegal both appalled and thrilled me in equal measure.

"Are we all set, then?" Godberd asked.

There were nods all around.

"You new fellows are to keep your mouths shut about what goes on tonight, is that clear?"

"Yes, sir," we assured him.

"Then let's head off."

A small trapdoor was hidden in the deepest recesses of the cellar and would never be noticeable to anybody not conducting a full search of the underground rooms. This door was heaved up and a steep stairway led down into the blackness. Godberd lit a torch from the candle that had been brought along and went down first.

Nottingham Castle is built on a sandstone outcrop above the bluffs that descend into the Trent floodplain. The porous sandstone is easily carved and many caves and tunnels have been cut into the rock over the centuries by the people of Nottingham. They use them as crude dwellings and tanneries as well as cool cellars for wine, ale and fish. Every castle, I suppose, has secret passageways leading beneath its walls and it was along Nottingham's dark, secret passage that we trod, heading in a north-westerly direction.

Stairs at the furthest end led up to a cave bathed in moonlight. Godberd extinguished his torch and we stepped out beneath the night sky with the castle rock at our backs and the vast expanse of Sherwood Forest before us.

As we headed down the bluff into the trees, Godberd set about dividing us up. "Geoffrey with me, we'll go west. Le Lou, le Boteller, take your squires and head north. De Wasteneys, you take your brother and his friends. Show them what's what but don't stray too far. We'll meet back at the cave at dawn."

A pale fence was visible beneath the splayed branches of the oaks and we scrambled over it and entered the forest.

"When do we get to know what it is we're doing?" I asked my brother.

"Venison, put simply," he replied.

"Poaching?"

"Well we're not going to ask them to come along quietly, are we? Just stick with me and don't ask too many questions. You're not expected to shoot a deer on your first trip out."

As it happened I did shoot a deer on my first trip; a fine buck with antlers still velvety with youth. We waited for several hours at a spot William had picked out previously where deer were known to graze. It was bitterly cold. There was little snow but the ground was frozen hard and we kept warm by swigging from a wine skin, taking care not to get drunk as a keen aim would be required before the night was through.

The sky was just beginning to pale in the east when the herd meandered through the trees. Keen to impress, I begged William to let me take the first shot. I blew on my fingers to warm them, willing away the tremble caused by chill air and taught nerves. I drew and loosed, striking the buck in a good spot, felling it instantly. As the herd scattered, William followed up my shot with one of his own, taking down a doe which thrashed and kicked and had to be finished off with the knife.

We were dead beat and the others yawned as we made our way back to the cave but I buzzed with excitement. The Godberd brothers were already dressing a hart inside the cave when we got there and once William had told them of how I had made the first kill I was rewarded with hearty compliments and thumps on the shoulders. We did not have to wait long before le Boteller and le Lou returned, each bearing a doe.

We finished off the wine while we skinned and dressed our kills and I enquired as to what was to be done with the meat.

"I have a man in the castle kitchens who can help us with that," replied Godberd. "He'll take the meat off my hands and pay me for it the next week. You'll all get your cut. Extra for you, Stephen as you managed to bag a buck on your first trip!"

By the time we emerged from the trap door in the floor of the cellars, it was almost time for us to begin our shift. That was a day from Hell itself, so tired I was. Once our shift was over I hit the hay like never before and didn't move until morning.

So it went for many days. We treasured our sleep like it was sand in the hourglass for every fourth day or so we would meet in the cellars beneath the Great Hall, bows in hand, and return as dawn was creeping over the battlements, our hands bloody, our bodies tired and our minds on the handsome coin we would receive for our efforts.

There was the constant danger of being found by the foresters who reported to the High Sheriff of Nottinghamshire, Derbyshire and the Royal Forests. Sheriffs were appointed by the king and, although de Ferrers had taken Nottingham Castle, he had no jurisdiction outside its walls. The High Sheriff's word was law and should we be caught there was nothing anybody in the castle could do to save us.

As well as the foresters, there was a colony of hermits who had made their chapel in one of the caves to the south of where we exited the hidden tunnel. Roger warned us not to stray too far in that direction for fear that we might come into contact with them.

One morning after one of these nightly excursions, I made my way to the stairs leading up to the wall, scratching my head and yawning ferociously. Somebody hailed me and I turned to see Reginald de Grey in his spotless armour at the foot of the wall.

"It's a hard shift that is built on no sleep."

"Beg pardon?" I asked.

He smiled. "Godberd shows his men a good time, roistering in the cellars all night. I'm surprised any of you are able to climb the wall at such an early hour. Unless it is plotting rather than winebibbing that goes on these nights you lot hide yourselves away amongst the barrels."

I didn't know how to answer him. He had obviously noticed us sneaking into the cellars and not for the first time either. I turned from him without giving answer but he seized my arm and held it in his mailed fist.

"Perhaps I am not making myself clear. I do not make idle chat. Tell me what you and the rest of Godberd's rats are up to."

I couldn't shake myself free of him without roughly using him and I wouldn't survive the week if I manhandled a knight. I struggled to think of an explanation but my usual quick wit and fast imagination was dulled by lack of sleep and irritation at de Grey's arrogance.

"You'll have to ask Godberd. It's nothing to do with me."

"Very well. Set up a meeting between Godberd and myself in the cellars. I don't want curious eyes associating me with you lot."

I assured him that I would but when I told Godberd, he flew into a rage and slammed me against the support of the blacksmith's hut.

"I was starting to trust you!" he roared in my face.

"You can, sir!" I explained. "But he cornered me and pressed me for answers. I didn't know what to say!"

"Then lie, you halfwit! What am I supposed to say when I meet with de Grey? What do I tell him?"

I had no answer and I felt that my wits, which had served me so faithfully up to that point, had utterly deserted me.

The meeting took place that evening by the light of a candle a good distance from the trapdoor. I was surprised when Godberd told de Grey the truth. I had been trying to think of a decent explanation for our night-time activities but couldn't come up with anything believable and doubted that Godberd would have listened to me anyway.

"I want in," said de Grey, once our poaching exploits had been explained to him.

"We're enough men as it is," said Godberd. "Any more and we run the risk of detection."

"You'll be detected soon enough if you don't let me in," said de Grey. "I'll see to that."

There was grumbling in the room from le Boteller, le Lou and the others. Godberd fixed his steely gaze on de Grey and the arrogant young knight appeared to pale a little but still held firm. "I mean it, Godberd. You've got something good here and I want in on it."

"Very well," Godberd replied, his voice a low growl. He knew he was beaten. He couldn't push around or threaten a knight. If de Grey wanted in then they would have to let him in. "We head out in two days. Dress inconspicuously if that is at all possible for you. And bring a bow."

"I'll look forward to it," said de Grey. "And you won't regret it, Godberd. I've a finer aim than most of you clods, I'll wager!"

NINE

I felt as if Reginald de Grey had stripped away all the trust and admiration I had so gradually earned with my sergeant and I hated him for that. In fact, we all hated him. He joined out little hunting parties but we did not treat him as a friend and we were loath to admit that he was a good shot.

His skill did little to impress Roger Godberd who was still incensed by the extra and unwanted member of our company. Any outsiders knowing of our activities made Roger deeply nervous and Reginald would always be an outsider as far as he was concerned. His arrogance made him a poor man to follow orders and several times he strayed too close to the hermits' chapel which enraged Roger. There was little any of us could do. We had to keep Reginald sweet for he knew our secret and had the means to destroy us all.

The worst of it was that he knew this and it only added to his detestable personality. He flaunted his power over us and took liberties that would have been beyond the pale for any of us, knight or no. Eventually he went too far and that was the beginning of the end.

Warin de Bassingbourn was a knight and friend to Reginald's father who regularly ate at the king's table. He visited Nottingham that spring and Reginald, always keen to curry favour amongst his father's royalist friends, took it upon himself to play host in his usual nauseating manner. We did not know it at the time but part of this hosting included a bit of poaching in the royal park.

Even the king's staunchest supporters are rarely above helping themselves to the royal deer and when de Bassingbourn returned to his manor he took a couple of dressed stags, killed with greyhounds no less, with him. Somebody evidently grew wise to this and reported it to the High Sheriff.

They were waiting for us that night. We hadn't even split into our usual groups before they were upon us. We had crossed the pale fence and had strung our bows when they came charging out of the forest, arrows nocked and blades drawn. I suppose there must have been a dozen of them; far too many for a usual forester patrol and we knew then that we had been betrayed.

The notion of surrender never crossed Roger's mind for a heartbeat. He just wasn't that kind of man and I have spent the rest of my life praising and cursing him for that trait. We ran about in a mad panic. A voice bellowed for us to halt in the name of the king and several arrows thudded into earth and bark, missing us by inches. William took off in a westerly direction and I desperately tried to keep up with him while Roger and Geoffrey headed north. I did not see what happened to the others.

Voices and shouts were gradually drowned in the foliage behind us as we plunged deeper and deeper into Sherwood. Eventually William slowed to a stop and placed his palms on his knees, panting for breath.

"Somebody sold us to the sheriff," I said. "They were ready for us."

"Aye. We'll turn north and try and meet up with Godberd. Come on!"

We jogged off in our new direction but an arrow soared from the bushes and struck William in the back. He fell with a cry and I ran to his side.

The wound was mortal. He coughed blood. I could hear the foresters approaching behind us and I wished I had my sword with me for the man who had taught me to use it lay dying by their hands. He could not speak but I could see in his eyes that he wanted me to run rather than fight.

That I did not avenge my brother is a pain I carry with me to this day but I decided in that moment that the best way to honour him was to survive that night so that I might use what he had taught me against our enemies and not throw my life away needlessly.

Tears in my eyes, I ran. I ran swift and in a roundabout way so that even the foresters had trouble keeping up with me. After heading north for a time, I turned back towards the castle rock where I found Roger and the others waiting for me at the cave. When they saw that I was alone they knew what had happened.

"By Christ, someone has done for us!" said le Boteller.

"Where's de Grey?" asked Roger.

"Taken," Wyotus replied.

"Taken?" Roger said. "That's bad that is. If there is one of us who should not be taken it's that bastard.

He'll squawk at the first opportunity." His eyes burned with anger although he refused to pay me a glance. I knew that he still held me responsible for bringing Reginald into our party and it was only that my brother had been the one slain that saved me from his rage.

We headed back to the castle and our beds knowing that our world had changed entirely. We each had our own thoughts to sleep on. I had my brother to bury and I swore I would recover his body at the first opportunity. The others were no doubt worried about the trouble that would come and come it did the very next day.

I was atop the middle bailey gate when the High Sheriff approached astride his roan stallion with its blue and black trapper. His son, who was undersheriff at the time, rode by his side and a score of men-at-arms rode behind, some bearing crossbows on their backs.

We later learned that, in addition to letting Warin de Bassingbourn have a couple of stags and getting himself captured, Reginald de Grey had spent the night drinking wine with the sheriff and had told him everything, including our names, in an effort to save his own skin.

"Open in the name of the High Sheriff of Nottinghamshire, Derbyshire and the Royal Forests!" called up one of his men.

I looked to the guards who had no knowledge of the previous night's activities in Sherwood. They shrugged at each other and began opening the portcullis.

"Send for the castellan," I said. All night I had thought of the complicated situation regarding jurisdiction between my lord Robert de Ferrers and the sheriff. I could only hope that the castellan would protect those under his own authority and not give us up to one of the king's highest agents during this time of civil unrest. The most we could hope for was a postponed trial.

The sheriff and his entourage trotted into the middle bailey and did not dismount, ignoring the stable hands who had emerged to accommodate their horses. The castellan had appeared on the Bridge of the Tower and stared down at the group, his hands resting on the wooden railing. The sheriff drew a scroll from his satchel and unfurled it.

"By the authority given to me by his majesty the king, I am ordered to take into custody the following members of this castle's garrison for poaching the royal deer. Roger Godberd, Geoffrey Godberd, Ralph le Lou – knight, Robert le Boteller – knight, William de Mungumry, William de Maysum, Stephen de Wasteneys, Wyotus de Sandiacre and Richard de Grantham."

I felt eyes upon me and I looked the length of the battlements to see if any of my comrades were also feeling the scrutiny. I spotted Richard on the west wall but had no idea where Roger or the others were. All the sentries were looking down at the sheriff and a tense feeling of disquiet had fallen over the castle.

The castellan did not descend the wooden steps to greet the sheriff. He kept the high ground and I was encouraged by this. I did not know the castellan personally but he was de Ferrers's man and showed no sign of backing down to an agent of the king.

"My lord is currently away," said the castellan at last. "I am afraid this business will have to wait until he has returned."

The sheriff's lip curled. "Yes, Earl de Ferrers is currently sacking English towns in the name of this godless rebellion against our king."

There had been reports that de Ferrers had besieged Worcester with much burning and looting particularly in the Jewish quarter which handily nullified his rather extensive debts. He had since moved on to Gloucester where the baronial camp had captured the town and penned the royalists within its castle's walls.

The castellan made a slight shrug. "The king is in violation of the Provisions of Oxford and until this whole sorry business is put to rest his authority and, I am afraid, yours is a matter of debate."

The sheriff visibly seethed. He clearly considered every man within the castle a traitor and no doubt would have liked to have seen us all hanged from the walls but his paltry score of men-at-arms was useless against a full garrison.

"Then let us debate, by all means," he said. "Come down from your perch, Lord of the Keep!"

"Until your men have checked their weapons I am quite comfortable here, thank you," said the castellan. "But if you would like to do so and wait for me in the Great Hall, I will arrange for refreshments to be brought to you and I will gladly come down to discuss the matter man to man."

The sheriff had nothing left to play and reluctantly allowed his horses to be stabled, his men's weapons to be checked and the sorry little group headed over to the Great Hall.

The rest of our shift passed like a slow torture while the negotiations continued and it was with no little trepidation that we filed into the Great Hall for our ale once the guard had been changed. The sheriff's men sat at benches looking uncomfortable. Even the ale and bread provided by the castellan failed to make them feel welcome. Roger, Geoffrey and Wyotus huddled in a corner and Richard and I joined them.

"If this goes bad for us then we need to get away," said Roger quietly. "I've sent le Lou and le Boteller with their squires to procure some horses. We can't all trot out of the gate at once. We'll have to take the passageway and meet them on the road south."

"Desert?" I exclaimed, almost forgetting to keep my voice down. "Will that really be necessary?"

Roger nodded grimly towards the closed door behind the dais. "Our brave castellan knows his authority will be overruled eventually. He's just buying us some time."

"Where will we go?"

"Gloucester. Earl de Ferrers is reinforcing de Montfort's sons there and the royalists are held up in the castle. It will be the site of the first great victory in this barons' rebellion. De Ferrers will be in high spirits and will no doubt give us his protection."

"We will plead our case to him?"

"Perhaps, or perhaps it will not be necessary. We are at the dawn of an interesting new age. All will soon change and the petty complaints of a sheriff about the king's deer will be naught to those who lead de Montfort to victory."

The door behind the dais opened slowly and the two men entered the hall. The castellan's face was grim whereas a faint smile of pride had tightened the features of the sheriff. We shared a look and Roger said; "Time to go. Quietly now."

The castellan gave orders to a sergeant and, though we could not hear them, we knew that he was giving the order for our arrest.

We each headed off in different directions to gather our things, retrieve our weapons and fill our pockets with whatever food we could lay our hands on. The word spread throughout the castle that we were to be handed over to the sheriff and we suddenly felt like the criminals we of course were.

Richard and I plundered arrows and crossbow bolts from the armoury and headed back across the bailey towards the cellar door. The sergeant who had been given the order for our arrest had climbed the wall to get an overview of the buildings. He spotted us and cried out, the wind whipping away his exact words although he bellowed them loudly enough for two men-at-arms at the foot of the wall to hear.

They hurried towards us, spears at the ready. We bolted for the cellar door, all subtlety thrown to the wind, knowing that there was no longer time for it. The door was open and we stumbled down the stairs.

"Wait!" I called. "We have to hold them or they'll discover the passage!"

Richard helped me heave the door shut and I slid the iron bolt home.

Roger was waiting at the trapdoor, a burning brand in his hand. "The others have gone on ahead," he told us. "You two are the last. Get moving!"

Slamming the trapdoor behind us, the three of us pelted down that sandstone tunnel for the very last time. My heart hammered in my chest, not knowing what might be waiting for us in the cave beyond. Once more, my life was being turned upside down and shaken and all I could do was hold on and hope that not too many of the familiar things I loved would tumble out beyond my reach.

One of those things was forever lost to me and my rage writhed inside me for I knew that I would never get a chance to bury the brother I had so recently learned to love again.

TEN

We met up with le Lou and le Boteller outside the cave and, climbing into the saddles of our stolen horses, we headed south to war and glory and all the hope and heartbreak those things bring.

We stuck to the Fosse Way for the most part and few paid us any heed. Armed troops were no strange sight on England's roads in those days, or these for that matter, and there were enough of us to deter robbers. We shot game and plundered storehouses to keep ourselves fortified but the closer we drew to Gloucester the closer the landscape resembled one stripped by war. By the time the spires of St. Peter's Abbey came into view, our bellies were aching with hunger.

The town itself was heaving with people but few of them were its original inhabitants. Men-at-arms strode through the streets in groups, their surcoats showing the devices of Robert de Ferrers, Henry de Montfort and the other baronial commanders. Most of the townsfolk had fled, leaving their homes and cellars open to the invaders who gladly enjoyed their wine and salted meat. A fug created by the smoke of cooking fires and the steam from cauldrons of pitch hung over the shingled roofs like mist, ghosting the banners of the distant occupying force.

Through the spectral drifts we could see the castle on the bend of the River Severn, the Lord Edward's own banners fluttering from its keep. The bridge that led from the castle to the barbican on the other side of the river was little more than blackened posts protruding from the scummy water. The burned hulks of a few fishing boats and barges lay on the mud like rotten carcasses.

We got the story of what had happened from some soldiers. They told us that the barons had taken the town via a sneaky ruse. Two knights – John de Giffard and John de Balun – gained entry by disguising themselves as Welsh wool merchants. Once past the gate they had wrestled the keys from the porters and admitted de Ferrers, Henry de Montfort and their armies.

Desperate to retain control, the Lord Edward himself had ridden for Gloucester and crossed the River Severn in a boat borrowed from the Bishop of Tewkesbury. Fighting his way past the baronial forces, Edward gained admittance to the castle and there he remained, untouchable, unreachable but ultimately trapped. The battle was not over yet.

We made our way to the part of town that showed the highest concentration of men bearing the red and yellow of de Ferrers. We found the earl himself at an inn, bellowing in a voice like an enraged bear; "Tell that bloody landlord that if he doesn't open that cask of Gascon wine right now, I'll have the hide off him!"

Robert de Ferrers, 6th Earl of Derby was a large, thickly-bearded man. He was only in his mid-twenties but had an impressive gut that strained against his surcoat, daring it to burst asunder. I often imagined him as a fierce warrior like the great jousting champions but life had cruelly held him back from such achievements. The agonising gout that ran in his bloodline had rendered him little more than a cripple wholly dependent on the use of crutches that leaned against the table next to his wine goblet.

"My lord," said Roger, striding up to him. "We come to you from Nottingham. My name is Godberd and in my company is Robert le Lou and Ralph le Boteller, both knights."

"Good lord, Roger wasn't it?" said de Ferrers, examining him. "You were the chap who persuaded the prior of Tutbury to tell us where the silver was buried."

Roger's face was touched by a rare smile. "Yes, my lord."

I hadn't realised until that point how far back Roger and his lord went. De Ferrers had sacked Tutbury Priory as soon as he came of age nigh on four years previously in a desperate attempt to ease the crippling debt his father had left him.

"Well, why aren't you holding Nottingham Castle for me?" de Ferrers went on. "I can't believe you are deserters for why should you come here?"

"There's been some bother, my lord. We were betrayed. By Reginald de Grey."

The earl's face creased into a frown at the name. "De Grey? I had forgotten one of those worms was at my castle. His father is keen for him to prove his mettle leading garrison troops rather than risk his neck on the battlefield. Has him earmarked for the job of a castellan or High Sheriff I'll wager. What's the bugger done?"

"Invited himself into our hunting party and then, when his own foolishness led to his arrest, turned us all in."

"Spineless wretch! Hunting, eh? Poaching more like, by the sound of it. Royal deer park was it?"

"Yes, my lord."

I was surprised by Roger's honesty.

"Ludicrous forest laws. That's what we're fighting for, de Montfort and the rest of us; an end to the king's monopoly of the lion's share of the land. It's a poor state of affairs when a man can't hunt in his own backyard."

"The High Sheriff came for us," Roger continued, "and we barely got away. We were hoping that you might mediate in the matter."

"No need for it, man. I've more use for you here. We're in the middle of a siege in case you haven't noticed. The Lord Edward is holed up in that castle like a coney in its warren and we await only the final push to take the castle and him as well. That bastard's ransom will wipe my slate clean with my money lenders and I want to see him squirm on my hook into the bargain! No, your place is here, Godberd. And I have a little errand for you already. "

"My lord?"

"There's a widow in a fine house over by the docks. Husband was a draper killed last week. She's sitting on a pretty pile and John de Giffard, damn him, has claimed her house and wealth as his under the terms of war."

"De Giffard?" said Roger.

"A baron. One of Henry de Montfort's chums. One of the lads who snuck into Gloucester in disguise. He's got half a dozen of his men guarding that place although he has no idea what's inside. He can't get in, you see? His trickery won't work on that widow!"

"Can't get in?"

De Ferrers's face split into a grin. "That widow has a dozen armed guards within its walls and has the place bolted up like Kenilworth keep. They send a volley of arrows over the walls every time de Giffard's men get too close! De Giffard knows he's onto something good but has no idea what it is because he can't set foot within the courtyard!"

He roared this last bit and all in the room joined in the mirth. I got the feeling that there was little love lost between de Ferrers and de Giffard even though the latter was something of a baronial hero for gaining the town.

"So, here's the job for you and your boys," said the earl, wiping a tear from his eye. "Go over to that widow's house and convince her that you are willing to protect her. Say that you'll get rid of de Giffard's lads for her. Then, once you're inside the walls, send for me and I'll come and show the good woman how a real man takes care of business."

I wasn't so green as to believe de Ferrers's words. I knew that he wanted to turn the tables on de Giffard and claim the widow's wealth (and body most likely) for himself. It sat ill with me but what could I do? We were a band of landless rogues wholly dependent on the earl's good will and employment. We had to take whatever job he handed us.

We persuaded him to give us a good breakfast before we set out and, under grey skies that threatened rain, we headed towards the docks on foot, our bows strung and our arrow bags replenished from the earl's stores.

The house had a courtyard with a thick oaken door that faced the street. At its rear was a quay that hung over the mud. As we approached, the heavens opened and we drew up our hoods against the downpour.

"This will work to our advantage," said Roger.

None of us asked him what his plan was to get into the house. As usual he was keeping everything to himself.

Several armed men were passing a wineskin about beneath a house's jetty on the other side of the street, sheltering themselves from the rain.

"John de Giffard's men, I assume?" said Richard.

Roger nodded. "Keeping themselves dry. Our road will be a little damper, I fear."

He peered up into the rain at the houses and seemed to be looking for something. He led us further down the street and, well out of sight of de Giffard's men, clambered up onto a stack of poultry cages so that he could reach the lattices of the jetty above. His cloak and muddy boots swaying about, he scrambled up onto the roof and bade us follow.

From the shingled rooftops we had a good view of Gloucester. It was grey and desolate under the rain. Even the smoke seemed dampened and quashed. Southwards, the monolithic towers of the castle loomed on the hill.

We followed Roger along the slippery rooftops towards the draper's house. With a mighty leap that put the fear of God into me, we landed, one by one, onto the roofs that ringed its courtyard. Taking care not to slip, we clambered up on to the ridge and peered down.

There was no sign of any guards and I assumed they were huddled indoors, confident that nobody would be so mad as to leap onto the roofs from a neighbouring building. We slid down into the courtyard and landed with heavy splashes. There were pillared cloisters on either side and a pair of guards were toasting their hands by a brazier out of the rain.

At the sight of us they reached for their arms; one for a crossbow and the other for the sword at his belt. We were quicker, and, with drawn blades, we persuaded them to throw down their arms.

"Where's the lady of the house?" Roger asked them, droplets of water standing out on the oiled surface of his sword.

"Inside," the terrified guard said. "Great Hall."

"Take us to her."

We were admitted through a studded door that led along a dim passage and emerged into a cosy hall with a roaring log fire and garish tapestries on its whitewashed walls. A lady in black sat at a table by the fire and eyed us coldly. Two grand fauves of Brittany lounged at her feet and lifted their shaggy heads as we entered. They growled softly, awaiting their lady's command.

"I suppose I should be flattered," she said, "that some men are so keen for an audience with me that they force their way past my guards. And those were not cheap guards, I can assure you."

I wasn't fooled by her cool, calm demeanour and neither was Roger. The palms of her hands were pressed down on the table top to stop them from shaking. I both admired and pitied her.

"We are in the service of Robert de Ferrers, 6th Earl of Derby," said Roger. "And we have been sent to offer you our protection."

"Your protection?" An eyebrow was raised in false surprise. She saw through this whole charade just as I did.

"Yes, madam. My lord is aware of John de Giffard's intentions on your property. We saw some of his men waiting out the rain across the street."

"Those oafs? My men killed two of them yesterday. If they set foot on this side of the street they'll be riddled with crossbow bolts from the upper windows. Come to think of it, how exactly did you fellows get in?"

Roger ignored the question. "They'll keep trying. And eventually they'll gain entry. We ask no fee unlike these mercenaries of yours."

"Just doing it out of the goodness of your heart, eh?" sneered the guard who had let us in.

"Silence, Wymer," said the lady in black. "You and your men are obviously not worth the coin I paid you so why should I not accept free help when it is offered?"

"Then you will accept our help?" Roger asked.

She glanced at our naked blades. "You have stormed in to my home and have my brave guards trembling like whipped pups. Have I a choice?"

Roger did not answer and that was answer enough. We set about garrisoning the house, bullying and threatening Wymer and his men into doing our bidding. Roger posted one man at each window and marshalled the rest of us in the courtyard. The rain had let up and de Giffard must have got wind of our takeover for a mailed fist was soon hammering on the door.

"Head back to de Ferrers," Roger told me. "Tell him the house is his."

I glanced at the lady in black who was within earshot. Either she didn't hear us or she did not care. As she had put it herself; she had no say in the matter.

I was to exit the way we had entered and Richard and Wyotus helped me up on to the roof.

"Is de Ferrers coming here in person?" Wyotus asked.

"How should I know?" I replied.

"Can't see him making the walk. Not with those crutches of his."

"He'll be carried in a litter, you dolt!" said Richard.

"Not according to what I heard," said Wyotus. "He can't abide the things. Doesn't even own one by all accounts."

"Why not? If I was an earl I'd be carried in one of those things to the privy and back."

"You an earl!" Wyotus scoffed.

I left them to their bickering as I heaved myself up on to the shingles and made my way over the top to slide down to the street on the other side.

I hurried back the way we had come and had not got more than a few streets away before the first chunk of masonry exploded into the roof of a nearby house. At first, I thought it had somehow come from de Giffard's men but it was not long before I learned the truth.

Gloucester Castle had siege engines. Had I been on higher ground I would no doubt have seen the arms of the trebuchets hurling their payloads over the battlements. The Lord Edward's famously thin patience had worn out. He was attacking the town hoping to pound the barons into submission and I was caught right in the middle of it.

The inn where de Ferrers was lodged was several streets away and the stones and masonry tumbled down with devastating frequency. I ran from cover to cover, shielding my face and head from the dust and sharp stones that cut at me in a hellish whirlwind, knowing that should one of those larger stones land on me I would be killed instantly.

I experienced a sudden resurgence in my faith as the sign of the inn appeared through the dust. It was within range of the trebuchets and I could see de Ferrers's men stumbling out in a panic, carrying as many barrels and sides of meat as they could between them.

The earl himself was being helped up into the saddle of a frightened mare that swayed about beneath him under the control of two squires. His crutches were held by a third.

"My lord!" I cried.

He glanced at me and for a moment I thought he did not recognise me or indeed recall the mission he had sent us on. Then he frowned and said; "Ah, Godberd's man. Did you gain entry?"

"We did, my lord. De Giffard's men were hammering on the door when I left though I suppose they will have fled by now. Godberd and the others are in the midst of this hellfire!"

"Nothing for it now," the earl said. "We can't stay in the town. We're heading for the outskirts."

"You're not going to relieve them?"

"Their best bet is to batten down the hatches and wait it out. And your best bet, my lad, is to come with me."

He turned his mount and headed off at a fast trot towards the north gate. I was at a loss as to what to do. It felt like a vile betrayal to leave my companions in the hell that had engulfed the town but de Ferrers had a point. I wouldn't help my friends by charging into the raining death and getting myself killed. All I could do was wait it out and hope that they survived and did not bear me too much of a grudge.

ELEVEN

The trebuchets stopped their barrage a little before compline that night. We watched the dust settle over the shaken town and while de Ferrers and his men dined on looted stores, I wandered through the camp looking for our horses. I had no luck and, promising myself that I would find Roger and the others at first light, I bedded down and caught a few hours of sleep.

There was a commotion at dawn. People were crowding around the north gate and I pushed my way through to where de Ferrers and a man I assumed was Henry de Montfort were astride their horses having a heated debate.

"You do realise that Edward is as trustworthy as a snake?" de Ferrers was telling him. "He'd lie to the Pope himself if he stood to gain anything by it."

"We have no choice, de Ferrers," said the young de Montfort. "The royalists damn near flattened the town yesterday. We must parley!"

"We have Edward as good as captured! With the bastard under our control we could end this war before it even begins! Your father will have a hard time accepting it should you chose to release the king's eldest son."

"My father wants to avoid war at all costs. And you forget that Edward is my own cousin. This dispute is tearing more than one family apart."

"What's going on?" I asked a man-at-arms beside me.

"The Lord Edward has left the castle," he explained. "He wants to discuss terms. The Bishop of Worcester is offering to mediate."

I was all for peace for it meant that I could get back into the town and look for Godberd and the others, but I could see de Ferrers was not impressed by such a notion.

Henry de Montfort held the higher authority and his argument won out. The peace talks were to take place in the chapter house of St. Peter's Abbey and, as the baronial delegation trooped in through the northern gate, I followed in their wake before cutting southwest towards the river.

I heaved a sigh of relief when I saw that the draper's house was still standing and once again thanked God for his mercy. A house across the street had not been so lucky and was half-demolished. There was no sign of de Giffard's men and I assumed they had fled as soon as the first stone had landed.

Le Boteller saw me from an upper storey window and hailed me. "De Wasteneys, you lucky bastard! We thought you had been flattened for sure!"

"De Wasteneys?" cried a voice from within and the door to the courtyard swung open. Roger stormed out. "I don't know how you survived, but God must hold you in his favour! Did you reach de Ferrers?"

"I did. He's currently entangled in peace talks. The Lord Edward left the castle this morning. They are discussing terms up at the abbey as we speak."

"Terms? So, de Montfort is caving in the face of those siege engines. We've as good as lost the town then. De Ferrer's can't be too happy."

"He didn't seem it, no."

He was even less happy when we saw him later that day. We waited in the draper's house and ate and drank from its stores, attended by the widow's servants. There was a loud tramp of hooves in the street outside and le Boteller called out that he could see the earl's colours approaching.

We barely got the gate open before de Ferrers came storming in on his horse, his great wide mouth foaming with curses enough to blister the air.

"Stupid, trusting bastard!" he bellowed, then seemed to notice us for the first time. "I suppose you've heard the news; what that blind ass has done?"

"I'm afraid we have been a little in the dark here, my lord," said Roger.

"De Montfort. Henry, that is. He's handed this town over to Edward on a silver platter!"

"He's surrendered Gloucester?"

"Aye, and spat in the eye of every man who drew blade for it."

"What were the terms?"

"Oh, that both sides are to retreat and leave the town to bury its dead. If Edward keeps his word I'll eat my crutches! Anyway, we have to get out and sharpish. And to think that we had him pinned inside his castle this time yesterday!"

"He does appear to have fixed his siege engines, my lord," said Roger. "That would stack the odds a little in his favour."

"Oh, don't you start, Godberd! I've had a morning of it from Henry and I'm sick to the back teeth of cowardice and excuses. Well, his lordship has spoken and we have to get moving. Start emptying this property of anything of value and load up the horses outside. We won't be able to take any wine with us unfortunately so look for silver, gold that sort of thing."

"So, you are just looters then, no better than John de Giffard," said the widow at last. She had been watching the discussion with an indifferent gaze.

De Ferrers paid her a quick glance and then forgot her as he went about ordering his men to strip the house.

"Did you have us down as anything other?" Godberd asked her.

She gave him a cruel look. "Not for a second. But as you said, what choice does a widow have against armed men who have taken her town? It matters little to me who rules Gloucester; royalist or baron. I'll be robbed either way."

We made for London after that; a great baggage train of knights, squires and soldiers and their loot. Henry de Montfort departed for Kenilworth to explain his actions to his father while de Ferrers led the baronial forces through Ludgate.

I had never been to London nor have I been there since. I was not prepared for its size or the suffocating press of people. The colours, smells and noises all competing for space between the colossal buildings was oppressive and both awed and frightened me.

"Have you ever seen such a sprawl?" said Wyotus. "We'll have to take care not to get lost."

"I thought you had been here before?" I said, recalling that his father had taken him to London once on business.

"I was but a boy," he replied, "and saw little of the city. I wouldn't know the wharves from Westminster Palace."

"Never mind Westminster, I want to try some of that Flemish cunny down at the stews in Southwark," said Richard with a leer.

Wyotus rolled his eyes. "You have never been to London and yet you know where the brothels are. I swear, Richard, you'd find your way around St. Peter's Basilica if there was a whore within sniffing distance."

The city welcomed us as heroes and they turned out in droves as we headed down its broad streets. Common Londoners were wholly in support of Simon de Montfort and his reforms so much so that the queen had been pelted with refuse from London Bridge when her barge had tried to escape the city the previous July. The king himself had skirted London on his way from Rochester to Oxford where he was currently rallying supporters.

We were given quarters in the Ropery along with many other soldiers and the gulls and the shouts of the dockworkers threatened cruel awakenings should we enjoy ourselves overmuch the night before. Our celebrations did indeed lead us to Southwark where I found the brothels to be cleaner than I had imagined, and the women too, although Richard later swore his had less teeth than his old mother did.

Roger did not come with us and I commented on this, thinking it passing strange that a man so obviously interested in the spoils of war should spurn wine and women.

"He's not much of a one for the ladies," said Wyotus. "And when the mood does take him, which is rare, he never pays for it."

"Legendary tight-arse," said Richard. "He won't spend a penny when he doesn't have to."

"Those are harsh words, Richard," said Wyotus. "You know his reasons."

"Aye, I was only jesting. Poor bugger."

"What are you two not telling me?" I asked. "What's Roger's story?"

"He had a family once," Wyotus explained. "A wife and a son and daughter back in Swannington. We never did find out exactly what happened but it was some crime or other that landed him in hot water. He received a massive fine and had to lease most of his lands to the Abbot of Garendon to pay it."

I nodded grimly. I had heard similar stories during my time at the Priory of St. Thomas. Usury was strictly prohibited for Christians but the Church always found a way around things.

"That's when he left to join the garrison at Nottingham," Wyotus continued. "He sent his wife and children to live with relatives. His wife died several winters ago and his only hope of seeing his son and daughter again is to ransom a knight or raise enough loot to buy back his lands. A landless soldier makes for a poor father."

Later, while I was enjoying the company of Saskia from Flanders and some very good wine, Wyotus shambled into our room in a state of excitement.

"I've just been talking to some of de Montfort's lads in the other room," he said, slurring his words for this was late in the evening and we were all a little the worse for wear. "You'll never believe what that bastard Edward has done!"

"What's that?" asked Richard, emerging from behind a curtain, tying the laces of his hose.

"He's reneged on the deal the Bishop of Worcester brokered! His troops have occupied Gloucester, ransomed its castellan and hanged the guards who let de Giffard and de Balun in from the west gate!"

"De Ferrers may dislike Edward for his own reasons," I said, "but his judgement of his character can hardly be questioned."

De Ferrers was predictably furious the following morning and his booming threats and curses rattled our aching heads.

"De Montfort won't stand for it!" he bellowed. "By God he won't take Edward's treachery lying down! It'll be war by the end of the month, mark my words!"

"Will it really come to all out civil war?" I asked Roger when we were alone.

He shrugged. "The monarchy has been at odds with the barons ever since King John's hand was forced to the Runnymede Charter. This war has been a brewing storm cloud but it has taken its sweet time in breaking. Fortunately, we live in such times that see the likes of Simon de Montfort and Robert de Ferrers; resolute men who favour action over ceaseless discussion."

"You wish there to be war!" I said, surprised.

He seemed equally surprised at my own words. "Of course! Peace is a poor companion for men such as us, de Wasteneys. Give me a chance at plunder and the cheer of men revelling in what they do best over endless years of monotonous peace any day."

I could see why Roger's bravado had made him a popular leader of hard-bitten soldiers. He appealed to their basest instincts. But I knew that his lust for loot was grounded in a desire to buy back his lands, to see his children again and for that I could not blame him.

Simon de Montfort arrived in London at the end of the week further convincing us that war was but a matter of days away. He was carried in a specially designed carriage as he had broken his leg when his horse had slipped on ice that winter. Despite not being able to see him in person, all London spilled out into the streets to witness the arrival of a man who was on the verge of being deified by the commoners.

"Can't understand it," said Roger as we watched the pandemonium from the rooftops on Tower Street. "Look at those fools. Bakers, tanners, night soil men. They act as if de Montfort were sainted before death but nothing will change for them. The barons may win and get a say in how the country is run or the king may crush us all but for those fools life will go on; hard and toilsome as it ever was."

"He represents change," I said. "Gone are the days when a king's ruling was as good as the word of God. The Runnymede Charter and the Oxford Provisions changed all that. De Montfort is fighting for a future of reason, of cause that amounts to more than the whim of a fickle monarch."

"And yet the common man still won't get a say in anything."

"And he does not expect to. All he can expect from all of this is that his superiors can speak for him and protect his rights against a king who sees him as little more than chattel. That is the most the common man can hope for and that is what de Montfort represents."

Roger looked at me, a smile touching his lips. "You're a young lad," he said, "and have the right to a little naivety not to mention principles. You'll lose both soon enough."

I ignored Roger's cynicism and felt secretly justified when de Montfort ruled against de Ferrers in a case brought before him by John de Giffard. The country was not officially at war and looting was strictly forbidden not to mention frowned upon by de Montfort. De Giffard had the gall to portray himself as a protector of the people and claimed that de Ferrers had ruthlessly despoiled a poor draper's widow in Gloucester.

We were all called before de Montfort who held council in the Tower. We were escorted to an upper chamber where several barons sat in discussion. As soon as I entered I noticed how young they all were. Few were over the age of thirty and I was struck by the notion that this was a young man's rebellion; generation pitted against generation in a bid to change the status quo upheld by the king and his friends.

De Montfort was a comely, slim man with dark wavy hair that had just started to grey in parts. He had the appearance of an active man and, were it not for his leg which was bound between two splints, I had no doubt that he would be pacing the room in irritation. Opposite him sat de Ferrers, his own swollen leg bound in bandages. Both men had crutches to hand and I was alarmed by the symbolism. This rebellion may be a youthful one but it was an injured one; outnumbered and disabled.

As the charges were read out, de Ferrers raged and called de Giffard all manner of obscenities but the gist of his argument was one that we all agreed with. De Giffard had been attempting to rob the place himself and we had simply got there first. That's all there was to it.

De Montfort was not impressed. "These are our own people, de Ferrers!" he said, slamming his fist down on a side table and making his wine cup spill. "We are not waging war in foreign parts nor are we suppressing rebels. These are honest citizens who have no power in this game of barons and kings. And this is not the first time I've had to warn you against looting!"

"Simon, you must not believe de Giffard's lies!" de Ferrers said. "He would have you believe that he was a defender of lonely widows when really he lusted after that woman's valuables even more than I did!"

"Irrelevant!" de Montfort snapped. "Whether or not what you say is true, the fact remains that de Giffard's men did not plunder that poor woman into ruin! Yours did!"

We stared at the ground and I felt no little shame at being raged at by a man whom all of London revered. Only Roger kept his head held high in support of his lord and I knew then why de Ferrers remembered the name of Roger Godberd and why he prized him above most of his followers.

In the end de Montfort demanded that de Ferrers make amends to the widow in Gloucester. De Ferrers seethed in silence and I knew how he would rage that night at having to fork over money to a mere widow, knocked down another rung in his constant battle to climb out of the depths of debt. I also caught a faint smile on the face of John de Giffard as the verdict was read. It was clear that de Giffard had never hoped to get anything out of this other than seeing a blow delivered to our lord. De Ferrers had plenty of enemies on both sides of this conflict.

Talk in the chamber turned to other matters and I was surprised that we were not dismissed. The presence of our lord, being a commander in de

Montfort's army, was naturally required and we gladly sat in on this pre-emptive council of war.

"The king draws supporters to him daily," said the Earl of Gloucester. "He's cleared Oxford's students out to accommodate his swelling ranks. It is obvious his mind is bent on war."

"Perhaps he says the same of us," said de Montfort. "Have we not rallied ourselves in London? Do not the commoners train every day in Cheapside? If the king is guilty of preparing for war then we are no less guilty."

"Surely you do not doubt our cause, father?" said Henry de Montfort.

"I do not doubt our cause, son, only our sense in not pursuing a peaceful path to achieve it."

"There is no other way, sire," said Gloucester. "If the royalists wanted to avoid violence as we do then Edward would not have gone back on his word and seized Gloucester. If that was not an act of war then I do not know one. They wish to destroy us. We are fighting for our survival now as much as for the Provisions of Oxford."

"And they claim all this activity is in preparation for war in Wales," said Henry. "They hold Llewellyn ap Gruffudd up as an excuse to marshal an army but they do not send to us for help. Not a single baron who has pledged allegiance to you, father, has received a summons."

"And why has the king appointed John de Lovel as castellan of Northampton Castle?" said a young knight whom I later learned was called Nicholas de Segrave. "When a king appoints a castellan to a castle that still belongs to you, sire, his intentions are only too clear. Northampton will be his next target, I have no doubt as to that."

The fears of the barons were shared by the commoners and there was a tension in the city as that of a bowstring drawn taut. Every messenger who rode into the city with news of another knight arriving in Oxford with his retainers to bolster the king's army added a little more weight to the string. By the end of March, the tension had reached breaking point. The string snapped and all London fell into chaos.

The mob attacked the townhouses of William de Valence first; the hated relative and foreign favourite of the king. As fire glowed beneath the clouds over the city, the rioters turned to the Westminster properties of Earl Richard of Cornwall; the king's brother. A small detachment of the mob broke away and headed towards Isleworth and laid waste to Earl Richard's orchards and prized fish ponds.

As always in such riots the Jewish district suffered terribly with looting and murder rampant as people let their hatred of the money lenders and infidels have free reign. I had heard the rumours; that the Jews were plotting against de Montfort, that they had made copies of keys to London's gates, that they had dug secret passageways beneath the city and had reserves of Greek fire hidden in cellars. There was a paranoia building in the city like a kindled flame which was fanned by every new lie, every new outrageous claim and in late March the flames grew unquenchable and they burned for many days.

Simon de Montfort was driven to an uncharacteristic fury by the riots. This earl who saw himself as a protector of the common man's rights and who harboured a personal disgust of looting could not believe what was going on in his name. He demanded arrests of the perpetrators but ultimately, he was powerless to halt the riots.

The royalists were likewise outraged, and the king imposed sanctions on London instructing the castellan of Windsor Castle to halt all supplies from entering the city by boat or cart. As hunger set in, the people's anger turned to desperation. There was talk of terms once again although few on the baronial side were keen to trust the royalists after the Lord Edward's recent treachery.

Talks took place in early April at Brackley in Northamptonshire and Simon instructed the bishops who spoke for him to compromise on all items but the appointment of foreign ministers by the king. The entire conflict rested on this point. The barons were determined to see the backs of the likes of William de Valence. This was the one point they would not back down on and Simon, ironically a Frenchman by birth, was bound to stay resolute to their wishes.

But the king refused to compromise on a single issue, perhaps this one most of all. No peace was reached. The representatives departed and the following day it was reported that the royal standard could be seen fluttering over Oxford. The king had unfurled his colours; a symbolic act the meaning of which was known to us all.

War had officially been declared.

TWELVE

As de Segrave had predicted, Northampton was the first to fall. It had always been the obvious choice. It stood between London and de Montfort's primary residence at Kenilworth and, if captured, would effectively cut him off from his support in the Midlands.

We received word of the attack two days after the king unfurled his banner. Royalist siege engines had hurled their loads against Northampton's southern gate while the rest of the army broke through the north-western wall which, we were later told, had been undermined by a traitor within. De Montfort's second son, Simon the Younger, was captured when his horse stumbled and tossed him into a ditch.

There was panic in London. The first I knew of it was when I was awoken by Roger's boot in my ribs. "Come on!" he said. "Don't you hear the horns? They're calling us to muster!"

Richard, Wyotus, the others and I stumbled out of the ropemaker's to find a torrent of armed men rushing down the street to marshal on the green north of the Tower. We bundled our gear together, strapped on our helms and arrow bags and hastened to find our lord.

It was a chaotic sight. The banners of de Segrave, de Ferrers, the de Montforts the Earl of Gloucester and others wobbled and wavered as men thronged to them and tried to organise themselves. I could see Simon de Montfort's carriage up ahead with the rebel leader himself struggling to make himself heard as he addressed his army. He was clearly eager to get away and we could not blame him when we learned that his own son was now in the hands of countrymen we had quickly begun to call 'the enemy'.

We fell in behind de Ferrers and it was only when the horns blew for us to move out that I suddenly realised that I was heading off to my first battle. As London grew ever distant behind us and our unknown fate loomed ever closer, I began to panic. I may have been a garrison guard, an archer and a poacher but a seasoned warrior? As well pretend to be a bishop!

An archer was far from the worst type of soldier for a coward like me and I could only hope that we would remain well back from any real danger. I could drop arrows onto an enemy host as well as the next man, but I dreaded being made to heft my sword against an enemy and my thoughts turned to my brother once more; poor William who was surely naught but bones and cloth in Sherwood hundreds of miles away.

You can imagine my relief when we reached St. Albans and received word that the battle was already over. Disheartened by the capture of Simon the Younger, the baronial garrison had surrendered to the royalists. Northampton Castle was in the hands of the king and more than fifty minor barons and knights had been captured.

De Montfort and his barons spent the morning in debate. Finally, the decision was made to return to London. Nothing could be gained by marching our outnumbered troops against a castle with a royalist garrison and, with the gloomy clouds of defeat hanging over us, we turned and headed for home. I kept my joyous relief well hidden from my comrades and from Roger in particular who seemed thoroughly disappointed at our failure.

While de Montfort and his barons debated what their next move was to be, we were put to work in Cheapside training raw recruits in the use of blade and bow. You will remember that I was no swordsman, so I spent most of my time teaching them to at least hit the butts with an arrow while Roger and Geoffrey taught them the basics of holding a defensive line and which parts of a man's body to thrust a dagger into or to hack with an axe.

Before long, worse news arrived. The king had not rested idly on his laurels after his victory at Northampton and had marched north to clear up the rebel opposition. Leicestershire and Warwickshire felt the hot vengeance of a furious monarch keen to assert his authority over a part of the country that had defied him for so long. The smoke of burning manors belonging to de Montfort's supporters blackened the skies and by far the most ruthless of the royalist leaders was the king's own son.

We could only watch helplessly as de Ferrers raged at the news of Edward's pillaging of his estates. His castle of Tutbury was destroyed and Derbyshire and Staffordshire were robbed and extorted to the point of ruin. It was hard to believe that the contention between de Ferrers and Edward surrounding the former's inheritance played no part in the young prince's brutality.

Nottingham Castle apparently offered no resistance to the royalists and the king took up residence there for Easter. When we learned that Nottingham's new castellan was John de Grey we did not wonder who had let them in.

"Reginald probably rolled up the portcullis for them himself," said Richard.

"De Ferrers made a gross error when he did not hang that weasel for a royalist sympathiser when he took the castle last year," said Roger.

De Ferrers, undiplomatic oaf though he was, would never have hanged the son of one of the king's staunchest companions during peacetime but I wholeheartedly shared Roger's sentiment. My loathing for Reginald de Grey had not lessened one bit since we had left Nottingham.

The failed march had put the city in a sour mood. The people sought an outlet for their frustrations and there were further attacks on the Jewish quarter. Similar reports reached us from Canterbury where the Earl of Gloucester had captured the city in preparation for an attack on Rochester Castle.

I remember the lies and excuses and I remember believing them. It was only years later that I realized the truth; that there was a cold logic behind the persecution. In attacking the Jews our brave lords could not only relieve themselves of their own debts but finance their armies into the bargain by a system of legalised theft. De Montfort, for all his talk of commoners' rights, conveniently forgot about the Jews who had no legal power to recover their property once the likes of Robert de Ferrers and the Earl of Gloucester had stripped them bare and turned them out of their homes.

We remained in London while de Montfort took his troops east to reinforce the Earl of Gloucester at Rochester. De Ferrers had not got over his falling out with his lord and we were left to train new recruits while the ones we had already trained headed out with the rest of the army.

De Montfort suffered another failure. The king, skirting London, had swept south of us and headed into Kent to counter de Montfort at Rochester. The approach of the royalists had called a halt to the siege and de Montfort had pulled out, terrified of losing London. Stragglers from his army were captured by the royalists and, with the brutality we had come to expect from our enemy, had their hands and feet cut off.

The situation seemed hopeless as de Montfort's forces slunk into the city from a second failure to capture a key castle. The feeling in the city was one of impending defeat. The north was lost, Rochester, Gloucester, Northampton and most other towns of note were in the hands of the king and we had not forgotten that Queen Eleanor was still in France, desperately trying to rally an army to support her husband. We were not thrilled when de Ferrers came to us one hot afternoon and told us that our presence was required at the Tower a second time.

"We're being sent out," said Richard. "On some damn-fool mission that will probably get us all killed."

"How can you be so sure?" I asked.

Wyotus answered for him. "Because de Montfort is desperate. The royalists are pressing in on all sides. It's only a matter of time before London falls. He's willing to try anything, throw his men away on any reckless gambit that has the barest chance of tipping the balance."

"I'd rather be training recruits," I admitted. "Surely that's important too?"

"Lighten up, you lot!" barked Roger. "Anyone would think I was leading a band of craven villiens who would rather be hiding in haylofts than marching out to make their fortunes! I'll tell you this much, I'm pig-sick of training clods who barely know which end of a sword to hold. I'm pig-sick of this stinking city and I'm pig-sick of sitting on my arse while others get drunk on blood and glory! I don't care what de Montfort has in mind but as far as I'm concerned it can only be an improvement on the last few weeks."

We found the upper chamber of the Tower less crowded than on our previous visit. De Montfort sat with a couple of barons I did not recognise. He sipped wine slowly and his recent failures clearly weighed heavily on him. His shoulders were stooped and his eyes were sunken.

"You are no doubt aware of the queen's attempts to raise an army in France," he told us. "The Cinque Ports are, by the grace of God, still ours and in holding them we prevent being blockaded or indeed invaded should Eleanor's fleet land. If those ports should fall the war will be lost. The king is well aware of this and is currently at the village of Battle, less than ten miles northwest of Hastings. Through bribery or conquest, he will attempt to turn the commanders of the Cinque Ports against us. This cannot be allowed to happen."

"What would you have of my men, sire?" asked de Ferrers.

"When I meet the king's army on the battlefield I want to meet them with the full force of every man under my command," de Montfort replied. "And I want it to be for the last time. We are running out of chances and I will not waste more lives on small battles that cannot win us this war. There is not the time to mobilise my entire army to counter the king's advance on the coast but he must be stopped regardless. That is why I need men like those you have under your command; men who are swift of foot, good with a bow and can conceal themselves well. This will be hit-and-run warfare. We are vastly outnumbered and need to wear down the king's advance by slow abrasion. Knights are no good under such conditions. They are too concerned with chivalry and honour."

I saw the corners of de Ferrers's mouth curl. "In short, you require stout lads with no interest in honour who don't mind getting their hands dirty."

"That's more or less it, yes. I know we've had our differences, Robert, but we need to patch those up. Now is not the time for quarrels amongst allies. We must present a united front to the king at all costs and I need those ports saved by whatever means necessary."

"Well, sire, you couldn't do better than Roger Godberd here," said de Ferrers, slapping Roger on the shoulder. "He's a cunning bastard and deadly as a viper at long range. I'll vouch for any man under his command too."

And so, we were sent into the thick woods of the Weald to wage war on the king.

Those days were some of the worst of my life. There were some three-hundred of us that set forth from London under different sergeants. There was a large contingent of Welsh archers – the result of a blossoming friendship between de Montfort and Llewellyn ap Gruffudd – and we distrusted them as we distrusted all Welshmen. The imminent alliance between our leader and the self-styled Prince of Wales was clearly borne of a common hatred for England's king and few had much faith that such an alliance would long outlive the war.

There was little cooperation and we soon fell to squabbling over food and routes. Everything we ate had to be foraged, hunted or trapped and the passing of the king's army had all but stripped the land of berries and game not to mention firewood.

It would have been counterproductive to march in a great shambling body of men so we had to split into groups with each sergeant leading his own men off in a different direction. The Weald was poorly mapped and we easily got lost on those thickly wooded track ways as we tried to catch up with the king's forces. Worse, we often blundered into another raiding party and more than once these encounters led to blows, especially if the other party was Welsh.

To add to our misery the weather was foul. Spring rains pelted us relentlessly and even the thick canopy of the trees could not keep us or what meagre firewood we could scavenge dry. We were muddy, hungry cold and, when we finally began our attacks on the enemy, in fear for our lives.

We struck them hard and fast, sending a volley of arrows into a camp or a convoy and then retreating before they knew what had hit them. I don't know how the other sergeants did things but Roger was determined not to get entangled in a melee if it was at all avoidable. We were archers and we were to wreak as much damage as we could, then fall back before the enemy had a chance to respond.

Gradually our own hunger outweighed any strategy. We targeted small camps that promised good stores and little resistance. As a result, we dined on barrels of salted pork and mouldy herring more often than game. Our attacks on these camps were simple but effective. First, we softened them up with a volley of arrows and then we rushed in to finish off any survivors with our blades.

We were like ghosts in the shadows; invisible and deadly. At least that's what we told ourselves to bolster our courage and I suppose the enemy saw us in these terms too for they were clearly terrified. In any case they acted with atrocious brutality whenever they caught one of our number.

It was a boisterous, boastful lad called Baynard who was taken first. He was one of the Londoners who had joined us and I wasn't alone in disliking him. His vulgar threats and loutish bravado were clear attempts to mask his fear and, whenever we fell back after our single volley, he always sent a desperate second arrow which usually went wide before he bolted to catch up with us.

It was not far from Winchelsea that we came upon a moderate encampment of a hundred men or so, cooking their meat after a day's march. Gold and scarlet banners showing three lions fluttered above the tents.

"Christ, that's Edward's standard!" said Wyotus as we peered through the leaves at the camp. "Why does he have so few men?"

"He must be leading a reconnaissance mission himself," I said. "You know how he likes to play the knight rather than the prince."

"Who cares?" said Roger. "Let's just hope a lucky arrow skewers that particular bastard's arse."

We sneaked around to the western side where there were fewer tents and more soldiers.

"One volley and then we run," Roger warned us. "They are too many to risk a second. Pick your marks and then fall back."

We nocked our arrows, picked out easy targets and loosed. We were running before the cries from the camp reached our ears and were well into the gloom before the enemy had mounted their horses. We had done this before; attack a large camp and draw some of them deeper into the forest where

Roger had posted more archers who would pick off a few so that no more dared go deeper into the forest. It was a good strategy as it was low risk and put the fear of God into the enemy.

This time Baynard's audacity betrayed him. His absence was noted only when Roger did a head count once the raid had been successful. Some of the other lads said they thought he might have been ridden down by Edward's troops as they pursued us into the woods.

That night we heard screams coming from the enemy camp. We plugged our ears for although Baynard was little liked, it did not sit well with us to hear the torment of one of our number while we were helpless to aid him. The following day we edged closer to the camp and found that the royalists had departed, leaving only smoke and ash drifting from their campfires.

We found Baynard's body in a shallow grave they had only half filled in. We found his head in another part of the camp – at least we assumed it was his head – for it had been savaged by the camp hounds and was little more than a bloody, featureless ball of meat.

"How can they treat the dead with such indifference?" I exclaimed, my stomach churning. "Are they not Christian?"

"And are they not our countrymen?" said Richard.

"Civil war strips men of all sense of patriotism," said Roger, polishing his bow. "All that counts now is which camp you are in. We might as well be Saracens as far as they are concerned."

We gave Baynard as Christian a burial as we could muster and I was called upon to say a few words over the hastily erected cross we had fashioned.

We heard further tales of royalist savagery from the other companies. Three stragglers we ran into were all that was left of one company which had been lured by the promise of a truce and then put to the sword, sergeant and all. Their headless bodies had been tossed into a mass grave and left open to scavengers.

We grew even more reluctant to attack the enemy knowing what fate awaited us should we be captured but the king's army seemed to be drawing back from the coast and heading west. We learned from the towns and villages of how they had been looted of food and wine by the royalists. When the king's attempts to bribe the commanders of the Cinque Ports had failed, Edward had taken hostages back to Battle leaving demands that the coast provide ships, men and supplies for his father's army.

Time was running out for de Montfort and on the 7th of May we received word that he had finally set out from London, emptying the great city of all its soldiers, and was en route to confront the king once and for all.

THIRTEEN

The baronial army had made camp at Offham and we learned that the king was headquartered at Lewes; a town roughly eight miles to the south.

"The king is enjoying the comfort of the priory in the town," said le Boteller after speaking with some of the other knights. "The Lord Edward has the castle."

"The king dares to sit in the open like that?" exclaimed Roger. "With nothing but a priory's walls between us and him?"

"Are you really surprised?"

Roger shook his head. In truth none of us were. King Henry had never been known as a military genius. He was a very pious man and preferred the company of monks to soldiers. It was his son and heir who was the military mastermind and we knew that it was Edward who truly led the royalist army.

"Besides, he is hardly a sitting duck," said le Lou. "He must have nearly ten-thousand men under his command all told. The town is infested with them and Edward will ride forth from the castle with every knight he can muster at the first sign of an attack."

"Then de Montfort really means to attack?" I asked, feeling the old sickness in my gut I had felt on the abortive march to Northampton.

"His bishops are discussing terms with them up on the downs as we speak," said le Boteller. "De Montfort is still desperate to avoid bloodshed."

"Aye, but he won't back down if he's pushed to it," added Roger. "He's been pushed too far as it is."

We tried to find de Ferrers but were dismayed to learn that he was not with the army. His disillusionment with de Montfort had run deeper than we had feared and the friction between them had grown unbearable during our time in the Weald. De Ferrers had departed with his men and embarked on a campaign of pillage against Edward's estates in the Welsh Marches and the Midlands. His hatred of the king's heir burned brighter than any loyalty to the baronial cause and we found ourselves part of de Montfort's army without our lord to lead us.

"Foolish ass!" exclaimed Roger in the first display of contempt for his lord that I had ever seen him show.

"At least he's attacking the enemy," said le Boteller. "It could be worse."

"Oh, he's attacking Edward alright. Under the guise of fighting for de Montfort's cause. But any fool can see that he is using this war as an excuse to get back at Edward. He's filling his coffers with the prince's gold while we are stuck here on the eve of battle!"

"We could always run and join up with him," I suggested, hoping that Roger would mistake my cowardice for a wish to join in the looting.

"We have no horses," he replied. "It would take days to find him. And I doubt we could slip away unnoticed. Our return has been cheered and de Montfort needs every man he can get his hands on. Face it, lads. We're in this battle whether we will it or not."

We climbed the downs to where most of the army was enjoying the sun and the view of rolling green hills and wooded dales. The downs descended in three spurs reaching the banks of the River Ouse which ran north to south, cutting through the town of Lewes. There we waited out the day while the talks continued in the shadow of a windmill further down the hill. Beyond that stood a leper house built in honour of St Nicholas and beyond that lay Lewes and its castle sitting atop a hump on its north-western side.

The bishops returned with sour news. The king flatly refused to compromise with the barons. It had been expected. He had refused terms before and since then he had taken several castles that had previously been held by the barons. Now he was negotiating from a position of strength and was confident in his superior numbers.

We returned to Offham and de Montfort and his barons discussed tactics and formations late into the evening. We ate some stew that was being cooked up in great cauldrons and began scavenging and bartering for equipment. Le Lou and le Boteller were determined to enter the battle mounted and desperately sought horses. I suppose they were successful for I saw little of them and their squires after that night. Roger met with several other sergeants and minor lords.

"We're under de Segrave," he said on his return. "He's been put in charge of all the Londoners de Montfort brought with him. They've barely got a sword between them and no experience of battle.

We're supposed to cover them when the fighting starts, the poor bastards."

"What about the Welsh companies?" I asked. "I haven't heard a Welsh voice since we set foot in this camp."

"They're not here," Roger replied. "Either they're still in the Weald or they've gone back to their prince. There'll be precious few arrows sent into the enemy host once the battle starts and we'll be shooting most of them."

"When do we attack?"

"God knows. De Montfort doesn't strike me as a man to mount a night attack. He has more honour than that. More fool him. We need as much surprise as possible on our side. Oh, here you are."

He handed us each a scrap of white cloth that had been cut into the shape of a cross.

"What's this?" I asked.

"De Montfort wants every man under his standard to wear them. A sign of God being on our side."

I tried to sleep but spent most of the night begrudging my companions their snores. It occurred to me to run away. I was confident that one man could slip away unnoticed. But where would I go? Who would take me in? I resigned myself to the attitude of a man about to tread the boards of the scaffold and surprisingly that made it easier. I was wholly in the hands of God and nothing I could do would change my fate. Sleep came but it did not stay for long.

We were kicked awake and before I was fully conscious of what was happening we were marching down the road that led to Lewes. The whole army was on the move and dawn had not yet broken.

"So, we are attacking at night after all," I said to Richard and Wyotus.

"Not according to what I just overheard," said Wyotus. "Apparently it is but a few hours before matins."

It was to be a dawn attack and we turned off the road and headed up a wide pathway that led to the top of the downs. We were hastily arranged into battalions and ours was on the northernmost spur, closest the river and directly before the castle. To our right we could see the banner of Gloucester and beyond that the banners of de Montfort's two sons, Henry and Guy. At our rear de Montfort himself led the reserves, his leg apparently healed enough for him to sit astride a horse.

It was an awe-inspiring sight. I had never seen, nor have I since, so many mounted men at once. It was a sea of nodding heads, tossing manes and jingling bridles. The faint glow of dawn before us set armour, helms and spear tips aflame with gold. The colours of the knights' trappers and fluttering banners was almost blinding in their vivid purity amidst the yellowish green of the downs.

We must have made a terrifying sight from Lewes. Already we could see activity below us. Troops flooded out of the town and formed two battalions at the foot of the downs. We could see the Lord Edward's banners above a sweeping horde of knights as they made their way from the castle through the town's west gate, forming a third battalion directly facing us. If I had thought our numbers were impressive I was immediately corrected in my assumption by the sight of our enemy.

"Shit, I'm going to fill my hose!" said Richard in a quiet voice next to me.

We were at the rear of the Londoners. They put us to shame with their bravado which I could only assume was borne of terror. It had kindled a delirious sort of courage in them. They whooped and jeered and sang a lewd song about Edward's mother. They were poor city folk for the most part. Few helms could be seen; only boiled leather caps and their weapons were crude hunting implements rather than tools of war. Before them were the few knights de Segrave had under his command. I struggled to see if le Lou or le Boteller were with them but could see only the backs of helms and horses' arses.

A horn blared somewhere and we found ourselves moving forward in one earth-trembling slither. I craned my neck and saw that the other battalions were beginning to lag behind. The baronial line was angled in a south-westerly direction and we had less ground to cover meaning that we would meet the enemy lines first. It made sense. Send in the poor, untrained fodder first, expendable wretches that we were.

The royalists moved forward and Edward's battalion, eager for blood, broke into a charge.

"Hold!" shouted Roger and we staggered to a halt while the rest of the battalion thundered forward. "Nock!" he commanded.

With shaking hands, we nocked arrows to our strings and drew them back. I felt as if I had no strength in my shoulders but somehow, I made the fletching reach my cheek.

"Loose!"

We let fly and our arrows sailed over the heads of our comrades and into Edward's ranks. We did not see how they fared for our own front line obscured that of the enemy. The two lines met in a sudden, jarring explosion of horseflesh, iron and wood. The blunt force of the enemy mass broke our front line immediately, hurling horses and men end over end to land on the infantry behind, crushing them. The screaming was unbearable and I could not tell horse from man.

"Keep shooting!" Roger bellowed over the howling, screech of death.

We loosed volley after volley into the hazy mass of the enemy which kept pressing forward. Our knights were more or less obliterated in seconds and then came the awful hacking and trampling of mounted men against infantry.

The Londoners were powerless against the descending axes, maces and swords and the grass turned pinkish with spilled blood and entrails. Our men began to fall back and before we could comprehend what was happening, the battle had turned into a rout.

The Londoners charged at us, their terrified eyes livid as they desperately trampled one another to avoid the deadly press of the enemy at their backs.

"Christ, fall back!" Roger yelled.

There was no point staying. We would be trampled by the panicked Londoners and then hacked down by Lord Edward's host. We turned and bolted up the hill. Most of the Londoners headed north up the narrow valley between the downs and the river towards Offham in a mad break for the trees that might offer some sanctuary. The enemy followed and we loosed arrows in their wake.

Others climbed the hill and drew some of the knights after them. There was nowhere to run. We flung ourselves flat as they crashed into us and I felt the gust of a blade passing over my head. I buried my face in the ground and prayed and wept.

I did not know it was over until I felt a hand on my shoulder. I rolled over and saw Roger looking down at me, his scalp bleeding. "They've passed," he said. "Vanished into the trees on the other side of the downs. Come on, get up."

I was almost too fearful to rise and look upon what was left of my comrades. I nearly wept anew when I saw that Richard and Wyotus had survived and were gazing about in as much of a daze as me. But many faces I had come to know during our days in the Weald lay before me, bloodied and glazed over, never to speak again.

We crested the northern spur of the downs and looked upon a sight that made what we had survived seem like a petty skirmish. The Gloucester and de

Montfort battalions had slammed into the royalists and for as far as the eye could see was colour and dust and blood and slaughter. It was difficult to see who was winning as we were too far off to see any white crosses but there was a definite feeling of movement from west to east which spoke in our favour.

More horns blared and the reserves led by de Montfort brought up the rear. That was enough to break the royalists and they turned and fled, hotly pursued by the baronial cavalry. It was an appalling scene. The grass was dark with bodies and thrashing horses. Royalists who had lost their mounts stumbled forward, leaning on their kite-shaped shields for support, determined to continue the fight on foot, only to be hacked down by baronial knights.

"They're heading back to the town!" Roger said. "We've all but won! Come on! Or there won't be a tun of wine or a gold ring left for us!"

We hurried to keep up with our sergeant as he pelted down the hill towards Lewes where the first of the retreating royalists were already staggering in through its gate. The road led past St. Anne's Church and a second windmill around which many knights and men-at-arms had gathered. There was much merriment and they were singing something about the 'wicked king of the millers'. We asked one of them what was going on.

"Duke Richard of Cornwall, the king's own brother, has barricaded himself within!" the man exclaimed. "The mighty King of the Romans is hiding behind sacks of flour like a wretched miller!"

We shared the laughter but we could see that Roger's heart was set on more tangible trophies so we continued on towards the west gate. As we passed under the portcullis we were instantly overwhelmed by the sounds of a doomed town. Most of its inhabitants had fled as soon as the king had commandeered the priory but he had billeted the houses and inns with royalist soldiers and it was the screams of those pitiful souls that filled the early afternoon air as de Montfort's men came for them with bloodied swords.

"Get on that rooftop and see what you can see," said Roger to me and I scrambled up onto the shingles of a nearby house.

The castle commanded most of the view. It was terrifyingly close and was made all the more ominous by the fluttering lion banners of the Lord Edward proclaiming that, even though Lewes was lost and Edward had vanished over the downs, the castle remained royalist and impenetrable. The baronial forces steered well out of range of its arrowslits until a more coordinated attack could be planned, instead heading south through the town towards the priory. I could see the spires of the priory in the distance. Its sprawling rooftops and high walls were the second largest obstacle in de Montfort's way.

I clambered back down and we threaded our way through the streets. There were shouts and the clang of blades up ahead and we stumbled upon a skirmish at the meeting of two side streets. Some men-at-arms bearing Gloucester's livery had been set upon by some royalists. We got stuck in and pierced several of the king's men with our arrows before Gloucester's men mopped them up with their blades.

"Thanks for the help, friends," their leader said. "Who are you? De Montfort's reserves?"

Roger shook his head. "Archers under de Segrave although I suppose we are our own men now."

"Christ! We didn't think anybody from our left flank survived! We saw them put to the rout by the Lord Edward, curse his name."

"Where is the king?" Roger asked.

"Barricaded within the priory. It's a miracle he made it back alive. Reports say that he had two horses killed under him and still he managed to slink away without being taken. We're trying to press through the town but royalists lurk around every corner. It's good that you ran into us; we need cover if we're to break through to the priory."

"Well you'll have to find it elsewhere," Roger replied. "We're not going to the priory."

"What? De Montfort needs every man there to convince the king to surrender."

Roger shook his head. "We've sacrificed enough for de Montfort in this battle. I've seen good friends ridden down by the royalists and now we seek payment for our efforts."

"So, you'd trade honour for loot?" said the man-at-arms with a sneer. "I suppose no more can be expected from common archers. Listen, stringfinger, I'm ordering you to accompany us!"

"Ordering me?" Roger snarled. "I don't take orders from Gloucester or his men."

We might have come to blows with them but there was a great commotion coming towards us. Men on horseback galloped down the street with reddened blades and foaming mounts. Some bore the arms of Edward and I knew then that our greatest enemy had returned to the fray.

They scattered us like pins and I saw two of Gloucester's men hacked down where they stood. I dived for cover and watched as Roger was pressed into a doorway by a knight swinging a mace. He had discarded his bow and was deflecting blows with his sword.

I nocked an arrow and took aim at the spot beneath the right shoulder where the breastplate and backplate met. I loosed and skewered the knight's armpit, disabling his weapon arm. As he reeled in his saddle Roger thrust upwards with his sword and caught the knight under the rim of his bucket-shaped helmet. Blood gushing down his breastplate, he fell backwards out of his saddle and lay choking on the street.

Another knight had been taken down by arrows from Richard and Wyotus and the rest had galloped off down the street, apparently persuaded we were more trouble than we were worth.

"Why are Edward's knights heading south?" Richard asked. "Why not make for the castle?"

"He's probably trying to re-join his father in the priory," said Wyotus.

I gazed at the mess in the street. Several of Gloucester's men had been killed including their officious leader and the rest had fled. We did not head further south but struck out eastwards, determined to avoid any more cavalry charges for the rest of the day.

We spent the afternoon foraging in houses for food, drink and anything of value. Most of them had had their doors kicked in either by de Montfort's forces or by the royalists when they had first taken the town. We managed to find cheese, stale bread and a tun of wine which we tucked into in a deserted brickyard with the sun on our faces. It was a delightful reprieve but Roger would not let us rest for long.

As we set out a number of fires broke out in the northern part of the town. We learned that de Montfort was attacking the castle and the royalists were responding with fire arrows which lodged in the thatched roofs of the closest buildings creating an inferno that prevented de Montfort's troops from getting too close.

As the fire spread, the attackers fell back and we found the streets filled with rivals looking for plunder while the north of the town was engulfed in flame and smoke. Roger cursed our ill fortune.

We returned to the brickyard as night fell and ate some more of the stores we had found. We watched the glow of fire in the north which turned the night sky as orange as an autumn sunset before dropping off to sleep, exhausted.

The following morning the king surrendered. We made our way to the priory and watched as he and Edward emerged to the uproarious cheers of the victors. King Henry was a tall man but thin and hunched over as if pressed down by many worries. His shoulder-length hair was dark and flecked with grey and all about him was the aura of weakness and defeat. I truly pitied him.

De Montfort's supporters were delirious in their victory. We had done the impossible. We had defied our king and the Pope himself. We had stripped a God-appointed ruler of his power. Our actions would reverberate throughout Christendom and future generations would judge us accordingly. As I watched the king and his son being led away to Simon de Montfort's headquarters in the town I remember praying to God to forgive us for what we had done.

FITT III
SWORDS OF VENGEANCE

"Knowest thow Robin Hood?" said the sheriff,
"Potter, I pray thee tell thow me."
"A hundred torne I have shot with him,
Under his trystelltree."
- Robin Hood and the Potter

Yorkshire
Autumn, 1320

FOURTEEN

The vintner was a slim, pasty man with a short black beard clipped into a point. His clothes reflected a bustling trade and suggested that he was one of the wealthier wine sellers who operated from York. He rode with two hired swords; tough, burly lads from Haxby.

He always brought along armed help when his trade drew him south. He had buyers in Doncaster and Rotherham and to get to them he had to pass through the vastness of Barnsdale. A slow wain groaning with casks of wine was a tempting target for any hedge robber and the forests of England were known for hobhoods, woodwoses and other terrible forms that preyed upon lonely travellers.

The vintner, his two guards and the carter made them four but still, the vintner's heart always thumped in his chest as the stifling greenery closed in on him and it never slowed until the towns of his destination appeared through the trees to the south. It was the silence of the woods that unnerved him the most.

They had crossed the river at Wentbridge and now faced miles of dense foliage in which anything might lurk. They had barely travelled an hour when an arrow whickered out of the greenery and thudded into the dirt a few paces from his horse's hooves. Startled, the mare reared up and he patted its neck to calm it.

Two men stepped out onto the road up ahead. Both had bows with nocked arrows. They wore the coarse, earthy garments of poor yeomen but their faces were hard and keen with the energy of youth sharpened by hunger.

The vintner tried to keep his composure as the sell-swords at his back drew their blades. It was an encouraging sound. Two against two, not including himself and the carter. And what chance did two ragged robbers have against armed professionals?

"Stop where you are, good sir," said one of the robbers. He was a lean pup with dark brown hair that fell almost to his shoulders. He would have been considered comely but for his rough clothes and general dirty appearance. "I'm sure you know what we want so hand it over and there'll be no unpleasantness."

The vintner was angered by the young man's arrogance. "What makes a pair of forest-spawned whelps so foolish as to think they can rob me when I have two seasoned warriors in my retinue? You are hopelessly outnumbered but I am willing to be merciful. Turn tail and flee immediately and there will be no bloodshed."

"You misjudge our numbers, friend," said the robber. "I have a dozen men concealed in the trees. I have but to give the word and you and your friends will be riddled with shafts."

The vintner glanced from side to side. He saw nothing but leaf and bush but he dared not take his eyes off the two robbers for long in case they were trying to divert his attention. The robber who had spoken seemed a reasonable type but his surly companion had the angry look of a killer.

"You're bluffing," he said, feeling the sudden need to be decisive. "You haven't any more men than I have, else they would reveal themselves."

Without warning an arrow sailed out of the trees to his left and embedded itself in the side of the wain. His mercenaries looked about in alarm, their horses sidestepping nervously.

"Shall we start again?" asked the robber. "Tell your men to throw down their swords."

The vintner began to panic. How many men did these rogues truly have? And what good were swords against bows anyway? He quickly resigned himself to defeat. "Do as they say," he told his mercenaries.

His men let their swords slip from their hands to land on the soft earth. The chief robber shouldered his bow, replaced his arrow in his quiver and drew a long knife at his belt. With his companion covering him, he came forward and seized the purse at the vintner's belt, severing its cord. Pocketing it, he scrambled up onto the wain and cut the ropes securing a butt of wine. It rolled free and landed on the road with a heavy thud.

"Get moving," said the robber, jumping down from the wain.

The vintner looked astounded. "You're not going to take all my wine?"

"If I ruin you now then I won't have a chance of robbing you again the next time you pass through Barnsdale!" he grinned at his own jest and plucked up the swords, shoving them under his arm. His companion heaved the butt up onto his shoulders and the two of them wandered off the road into the foliage which quickly obscured them.

Not wanting to test his luck further and still not sure how many bowmen were watching them, the vintner hurriedly signalled the carter to move onwards, considering his losses slight and thanking God for surviving the encounter.

Much burst from the bushes as Robert and Will passed by, casting his bow aside and leaping up to grasp Robert around the neck in a playful grapple. The three of them whooped and wrestled with one another, the tension of their encounter dissolving into exhilaration. They had done it! Their first robbery had gone off without a hitch and, with the wain and the three riders heading south, they were left to examine their profits.

Robert emptied out the vintner's purse into the palm of his hand and counted the money. It amounted to several pounds and was more coin than any of them had ever set eyes on in their lives. They also had two swords and a butt of wine to their names.

"We should have stripped the bastard of every cask he had," said Will.

"And how would we have carried it away?" said Robert. "Besides, I do not intend to ruin honest businessmen. Just relieve their purses of a little weight. This butt will do for now. We'll sell it and give the money to Much's father. It might go some way in paying his fine and retaining his job at the mill."

They headed back to camp where Old Stephen was keeping a fire going. They were hungry from spending all morning atop the Sayles keeping watch for a suitable target heading south on the Great North Road.

As they chewed their venison Will eyed the butt of wine longingly. "Oh, but for a drop of that stuff," he said. "I haven't had a good drink since we turned outlaw."

"We'll remedy that soon enough, Will," said Robert. "But there's no sense in wasting our first profits. We have to be smart with how we live out here. There'll be other vintners passing through Barnsdale."

"Not just vintners," said Old Stephen. "All sorts of goods. Meat, cloth, iron, pots not to mention large sums of money. The Great North Road is one of England's arteries and all traffic between York and the Midlands passes up and down its length. You lads could be as rich as kings as long as you keep to your charter."

Robert nodded. "Don't get over ambitious."

"And spend your profits wisely," said Will, rolling his eyes.

Old Stephen had drummed this mantra into them over the past few days and they accepted his advice gratefully. His tales of his days with Roger Godberd had thoroughly impressed them and even Will had developed a liking for the old man. His company was well worth the meat they gave him.

Winter came hard and fast and Robert felt suddenly unprepared. He had always planned to winter with family in Wentbridge but as the trees began to grow bare he realised he needed to make the arrangements fast.

His cousin, Simon Hood, was at least five years older than him and had sired a small brood in a thatched house north of Wentbridge. He was a woodcutter by trade and his property was surrounded by trees, secluded with plenty of storage space that could shelter three outlaws quite comfortably.

Robert paid a visit one Sunday when Simon and his family had returned from church.

"Robert!" Simon exclaimed upon seeing him. "I almost went and fetched my quarterstaff for I didn't recognise you! You've grown two feet at least since I last saw you!"

"I had a hard time deciding if I had come to the right cottage myself," Robert replied. "For this can hardly be the same family I saw four years ago. Your children were but babes in arms. Now look at them!"

Simon's boy and girl were cheeky and hale and peeped at Robert from behind their mother. He threw them a wink and they vanished behind her skirts.

"What's up, Robert?" asked Theresa Hood. "You look as if you've seen some rough living. Look at your clothes!"

"Aye, and why are you here alone?" Simon added. "Is your mother well?"

"As far as I am told," said Robert. "I haven't seen her these past few months."

"What?"

"You haven't heard?"

Their faces were blank.

"I'm an outlaw."

"Oh, Rob," said Simon. "You'd better come indoors."

Robert told them everything; the attack on the bailiff, the flight into the woods, Will, Stephen, Much and his killing of the bailiff's man by the mill.

"Whatever you need," said Simon, "just say the word and we'll do our best."

"We need shelter," Robert said. "Winter is coming. There are four of us; myself, Will, Much and the old man. Is there any chance of putting us up? We'll keep you in meat and firewood."

"Don't say another word," said Simon. "You're family Rob, and as for the others, well, if they're all right with you then they're all right with me. And besides, Lancaster is far from popular, especially here in Pontefract Manor. Those thugs he calls bailiffs have rounded up nearly all of our young fighting men and anybody who plies a trade that can feed warfare has been pressed into service. Blacksmiths, carpenters fletchers and bowyers from across the manor have been making weapons and siege engines for a pittance of pay."

"He's building an army," Robert said.

"Aye. To fight the king when it comes to it. God help us."

Robert thanked his cousin and left to make the final preparations for winter. They shot and hung deer, smoking some of the meat to make it last. On their final trip to Wakefield for the year Robert gave Mary enough money to see both her family and his own kept fed and warm until spring. Mary had grown ever more concerned at the amount of coin he was able to hand over.

"Don't you worry about it, Mary," he told her. "It was my actions that placed you all in danger. I take full responsibility for your upkeep. I can spare it, really. It's a drop in the ocean, I promise."

"Christ Jesus, how much more coin do you have?"

"Enough," he said with a grin.

"Have you robbed every poor carter passing through Barnsdale?"

"Of course not. Only the wealthy ones and even those we didn't strip bare. We let a vintner keep his wain of casks but one not a month past. And a knight was allowed to keep half his purse after running into us last week. We don't take everything from them. It's more a form of tax for passing through our forest."

She was still not convinced and he realised he had mistaken her concern. In truth it was not guilt at accepting stolen coin but fear that he was growing too bold, too ruthless that troubled her. It had gone beyond robbing out of necessity to stay alive. They were positively hauling the wealth in and Robert had to admit that this robber lark had turned out to be surprisingly easy.

"I feel like I knew you once, Rob but those days grow ever more distant to me," Mary said. "I don't know this robber who comes to me with bulging purses and jests about his life of crime. Where will it all end? I thought maybe you might come back to us once all this horridness was over but the longer you travel this path the further you wander from us."

He held her and kissed her gently. "It's still me, Mary. My circumstances may have changed but I swear that I have not."

She looked up at him, her eyes damp. "Will we ever get you back? Will your mother and little Eleanor ever see you again?"

Her words dragged his mood down and he bit his lip. "I don't know. I pray to God that it will be so, but... I just don't know."

With the first of the snows Robert and his companions trooped out of the forest, all their gear over their shoulders, and bedded down in one of Simon's storage huts which they had insulated with deerskins.

The winter passed slowly but comfortably. They took their meals with the family in the cottage and they were good times full of cheer. Old Stephen entertained them with stories and their frequent trips out into the snow-laden woods ensured that food was plentiful. Robert gave Simon enough coin to see that they did not want for anything else.

They were forever watchful of anybody from Wentbridge passing by the cottage and on the rare occasions that somebody did, they hid themselves away and prayed that they had not been spotted. The snow piled up around the storage hut and the four outlaws were toasty warm within as the cold winds moaned outside.

Only Robert felt any discomfort. He felt like a hen cooped up and he yearned for the freedom of the forest again. While the other three snored through the night his thoughts dwelled on Mary, the slumbering greenwood and what spring would hold for all of them.

FIFTEEN

Simon de Warde, the High Sheriff of Yorkshire, peered at the letter with concern. It had been sent from Tickhill Castle by the hand of William de Aune, castellan of that castle and close confident of the king.

"Christ Jesus," he muttered under his breath. "Not de Audley too!"

"What's that?" asked Constance his wife who had just entered the room to accompany her husband to supper.

"The Marcher Lords are paying the north a visit," said Simon, indicating de Aune's letter. "Hugh de Audley, Roger de Mortimer, Roger Damory and plenty more besides. They've tried to be inconspicuous but de Aune's spies have spotted them easily. They're heading for Pontefract."

Constance raised her eyebrows. "To be Lancaster's guests?"

"Hard to believe, isn't it? But ever since our wise king wrenched the Gower Peninsula away from the Marcher Lords and handed it to Hugh le Despenser, they have been wringing their hands with jealousy and speaking openly of revolt. They'll even put their hatred of Lancaster behind them if an alliance with him might add some weight to their punch."

"So those former favourites, who once called you traitor, allow their jealousy at having been usurped in the king's affections by the young le Despenser drive them to treachery!" said Constance, a smile curling her thin lips. "And Lancaster, whose determination to see de Audley and Damory removed from court so ruined them two years ago, is the one to offer them an alliance? Passing strange, do you not think, for two parties who so loathe each other to meet in secret? What's in it for Lancaster?"

"I believe he sees in them a valuable distraction. If he can promise them his support he might convince them to attack le Despenser's lands in the Welsh Marches. And if that happens..."

"The king's attention will be turned away from the north..."

"Leaving Lancaster free to put into effect whatever it is he has been planning."

"Do you suspect rebellion?"

"I wouldn't put anything past Lancaster. He's an arrogant fool but there is nothing more dangerous than an arrogant fool with an army at his back."

It was late February and the moat around the sheriff's manor house at Guiseley had begun to lose its skim of ice. The snow on the drawbridge had melted and the hooves of the approaching horsemen could be heard from the Great Hall.

The sheriff strode out into the courtyard to see who came to his gates. A small company of armed men wearing Lancaster's sigil on their surcoats were dismounting in the yard. He sighed as he recognised the face of Wakefield's bailiff.

"Welcome, bailiff," he said. "What can we do for you?"

"It is more what I can do for you, my Lord Sheriff," said the bailiff. "I come bearing news that could be a great boon to you."

"I suppose you'd better come in and warm yourself then."

"Very kind of you, sheriff. It's a long ride this early in the year."

The sheriff led the way into the Great Hall where the fire crackled merrily. He went directly to the side table where William de Aune's letter lay open. He doubted Lancaster's thick-skulled bailiff could read but he took no chances and quickly folded it. He poured some wine into a pair of goblets and handed one to the bailiff.

"I know you're a busy man, sheriff, so I'll get right to the point."

"That's very kind of you."

"I heard you've had a spot of bother with robbers on the Great North Road as it passes through Barnsdale."

"There was an increase in robberies on that stretch of the road before Christmastide, yes."

"Well, I have reason to believe that the culprits are already known to us. In fact, I'd go so far as to place a wager on them being Robert Hood and William Shacklock."

The names drew a blank for the sheriff. "Beg pardon?"

"I don't suppose you remember all the names brought before you at the County Courts but I certainly won't forget these two. They were outlawed in September. They plotted my murder and killed two of my men in attempting it. A further two of my lads were killed during an altercation outside one of the manor's mills where they were fencing poached game. We have reason to believe that the miller's son joined them and fled with them into Barnsdale."

"Dozens of outlawed wretches vanish into Barnsdale every year," the sheriff said. What makes you think these in particular are responsible for the increase in robberies?"

"A potter passed through Wakefield recently. He was a loudmouthed braggart who spouted many tall tales but the one that credits an ounce of truth was of his escape from three men who had tried to rob him in Barnsdale. He claimed that he had talked them into letting him keep his purse. Nonsense most likely for who ever heard of a hedge robber who wasn't a villainous scoundrel out for all he can get? Anyway, this potter knows the people of Wakefield as he regularly sells his wares at market and he swore he recognised one of the robbers as William Shacklock; a young lad whose father has land near Crigglestone."

"And what good does this information do me?" said the sheriff, refilling the bailiff's goblet which had been emptied with vulgar haste. He was beginning to lose his patience. Lancaster's man was a tiresome fellow who took too long to say very little.

"The potter said there were three of them. If Shacklock was one then it's a good wager the other two were Robert Hood and the miller's son. Hood has family in Wentbridge. I imagine he has wintered with them and, now that the worst of the cold is over, he will no doubt return to the woods and his thieving ways. The Hoods of Wentbridge are well known. You could easily apply requisite pressure on them to give up their wayward member."

"Well, I thank you for your help, bailiff," said the sheriff. "But tell me truly, why do three outlaws operating in Barnsdale draw your eye so keenly? Does your lord not have more pressing concerns?"

The bailiff looked confused and the sheriff considered the possibility that he had not been subtle enough. The question had been intended to tease out some acknowledgement of Lancaster's plans but instead he might have aroused the bailiff's suspicions. He did not want word to get back to Lancaster that he knew about the meeting of the Marcher Lords at Pontefract.

"Shacklock and Hood tried to kill me," said the bailiff. "A man tends to take that personally. Shacklock's two brothers were also in on the plot but they were dispatched by my men. I will not rest until I see William Shacklock and Robert Hood dangling from the gallows oak. The wretched miller's son too for that matter."

The sheriff smiled. *So, it is a personal matter.* Vengeance was easy to understand, especially where a simple oaf like Lancaster's bailiff was concerned. His fears had been unfounded.

"I must thank you for your help, bailiff," he said, "and I can assure you that these three villains will feel the swift hand of justice as soon as I am able to apply it."

Robert had hated the winter. It had been too long, too dark and too cold. Under close confinement his companions had begun to irritate him. He had yearned to be free under the greenwood canopy and to hear the song of birds around him.

Now that spring had arrived and they had said their farewells to Simon Hood and his family, he beamed at the warmth of sunshine and the smell of new growth. But his first visit to Mary that year was one that shook him to his foundations and tore away his joy.

It had started as it always did with the exchange of purses for news of his family. His mother and Eleanor had borne out the winter well thanks to his efforts and so had the Alayn family. They did not discuss the concerns Mary had expressed before winter but Robert could see that they still bothered her. He bent to kiss her and she turned away from him.

"What's wrong?" he asked her.

"We can't do that anymore, Rob. I'm sorry."

"What do you mean we can't? You're still my girl, aren't you?"

"Rob... please understand."

"Understand what?"

"That this cannot go on. It never could. It was always a doomed thing; a delightful but wretched and doomed thing."

"You don't love me anymore? I know we've never spoken of our feelings for each other but believe me when I say that I love you with all my heart."

"Don't make it harder, Rob! You must see that we have to end it! We are just fooling ourselves by carrying on like this. I'll always be there for your family for I love them as much as my own. I'll find a way to get your money to them but you have to understand that this can go no further. You're an outlaw with no hope of being pardoned, not in the near future at any rate."

"Who knows what the future holds?"

"Try to see things from my point of view. I am a woman now and there are certain expectations of me. I want to go on loving you, believe me I do, but we live in a harsh and brutal world that has no time for foolish love like in the ballads. If I do not marry then people will begin to suspect..."

"Marry?" said Robert with a sinking feeling in his gut. He could barely believe his ears.

"My father has promised me to the son of a wealthy merchant. It was arranged over Christmastide."

He choked on his words, struggling to get them out. "Mary, how can you go along with this? Your father is not a brute, he would not force you..."

"He's not forcing me, no. It's my decision. I have to think of my future, Rob. You'll always have a piece of my heart but you have vanished down a road I cannot follow."

"I'm right here, Mary."

"Here in this moment, yes. And tomorrow you'll be gone and I'll be left wondering if I'll ever see you again, waiting for that awful day when I hear that Lancaster's men have caught up with you. Don't you see that God has left nothing for us? No future, no children, no possible path that we might walk together. We have reached a fork in the road and if you love me as I love you, you'll learn to accept that."

Robert couldn't bear any more. Tears brimmed in his eyes and he fought them back. Anger gripped him. "How can you say that you love me and then reject my love out of cowardice? By Christ's cross I would never let danger keep me from you! Our love is our own and neither Lancaster's men, nor the king himself can take that from us!"

"That's the difference between us, Rob. You have so much courage, more than any man I've ever met, but you're living in a dream world. The leaves of the greenwood blind you from the reality I am forced to live in."

"Then come with me! Come with me to the greenwood! We could find a clerk or monk to marry us so it would be holy in the eyes of God. We'd be happy there. There are no laws in the greenwood. We could rule it as king and queen!"

"Listen to yourself! King and queen of the greenwood? I can't believe you think it's all that simple. Men are looking for you, Rob. Probably the High Sheriff himself wants to see you hanged. What sort of a life is it to be hunted? What sort of a life is that for children? Your world is one I can never be a part of. I'm sorry, Rob."

"Fine. If that is what you wish."

"It is. And don't be petulant. If you refuse to see sense then I'm wasting my time."

"And I'm wasting mine." He turned to go.

"Rob, stop," she said.

He turned and they stared at each other for a time.

"God forgive me," she whispered and she went forward to kiss him.

They held the kiss for a long time, knowing that it was to be their last. Finally, with tears streaming, she turned from him and was gone.

SIXTEEN

There were six members of the party but from what Much had seen from his spot on the Sayles, none of them were sell-swords. The party included two women in fine veils and flowing gowns of rich cloth. The four men wore doublets, padded and cut fashionably. This was a wealthy group and, although they certainly had swords and probably knew how to use them, they did not look like seasoned warriors.

"Probably think they're too big a party for robbers to attack," said Will from the bushes where they crouched, waiting for the group to reach them. "Soft town folk. Stupid too. Anybody could tell them that they need an armed escort through Barnsdale. Fools."

"Six of them, three of us," said Robert. "Think we can handle two each?"

"Two of them are women," Will reminded him.

Robert peered down the length of the road. He could see the six riders approaching, talking gaily, oblivious to the danger they were in. He felt a contempt for them that was more in keeping with Will's usual attitude. He had felt little joy in life since Mary had spurned him; only the lust for more coin and a desire to be feared and hated as much as he feared and hated the world beyond the greenwood.

"We'll all step out to meet them this time," he told his companions. "Their numbers don't matter. Scare them witless and they're ours."

Long before the party got close to them, there was a great whoop and roar of voices as several people charged out onto the road. The horses were spooked and began to rear and whinney frantically.

"What in the name of God?" Will exclaimed.

"Someone's beaten us to it!" said Much.

They walked out onto the road and watched as a gang of six peasants assailed the party, some dealing the men blows with quarterstaffs while others hung back, trying to find a mark with their bows. There was a cry of pain as the sword of one of the riders caught an attacker on his unprotected head. He went down like a sack of flour.

"The stupid bastards are bungling it!" said Robert. "Watch out!"

Two of the men had broken free of their attackers and led the women out of the danger. They charged down the road towards Robert and his companions.

"They've seen us!" said Will.

The look on the face of the lead rider was one of furious anger. The three outlaws turned and bolted for the trees. The rider's sword swung down in an arc and caught Much on the shoulder, sending him sprawling with a cry of agony.

"Much!" Robert yelled and nocked an arrow to his bowstring.

Will ran forward to drag Much to safety as Robert let the arrow fly. It struck the rider in the side and he yelped in pain, reeling in his saddle.

The other two riders had caught up and the group wheeled and turned about in confusion. Robert nocked a second arrow.

"Come on! Let us be off!" cried one of the riders. "It's not worth the fight! Protect the women!"

The man Robert had struck leaned forward, gasping. His bloody hand clutched the shaft that had sunk deep into his body. One of his companions seized his reins and the group thundered off down the road and out of bowshot.

"Is he all right?" Robert asked Will who squatted by Much's side.

"Don't know. It was a glancing blow but a nasty one."

Much's brown tunic was soaked with blood at the shoulder and a deep gash in the cloth revealed an ugly wound. He gasped and tried to sit up.

"Rest, Much," Robert commanded him.

"I'm all right," said the miller's son, clutching his wound. "Just need stitching up, that's all. It's only a flesh wound. Bloody hurts though."

"We'll get that seen to as soon as we get back to camp," Robert assured him. "But first..."

He turned his furious gaze to the group of would-be robbers further down the road. They were busy attending to their own fallen man who appeared to be dead.

Will helped Much to his feet and he and Robert put arrows to their strings. Much, one arm useless, drew his sword and hefted it clumsily in his left hand.

"What kind of an ill-prepared, incompetent band of fools are you lot?" Robert bellowed at the strangers. They might try and kill him but his rage could not let it go. "You were evenly matched and two of them were bloody women!" he continued.

"Two of us are bloody women, what of it?" snapped a voice and Robert noticed a female with greasy blonde hair piled up in a knot on the top of her head. She carried a bow. The other woman in the party was a slight girl with coppery hair that had been chopped short. He presumed it was supposed to make her pass for a boy but there was little chance of that. Her elfin face was too pretty. The men were a collection of scruffy villagers in coarse garments. They glared at Robert through dirty faces and gripped their weapons, spoiling for a second fight.

"And you three fools let them slip by you," said a familiar voice. "Is this truly the great Robert Hood we have heard so much of?"

Robert noticed his cousin for the first time. "Simon! What the devil are you doing with this lot?"

"I happen to be their leader," said Simon Hood with a grin. "Elected, of course."

"But you're an honest woodcutter," Robert protested. "What are you doing robbing people on the Great North Road?"

"I'm a woodcutter no more. And after hearing of your great success in Barnsdale, me and this lot decided to seek you out. We've spent days looking for you. Sorry about letting those bastards loose on you. And sorry about your wound, Much, but if it's any consolation, they killed one of ours. Poor Walter. We'll take his body back to his family."

"What's been going on, Simon?" Robert asked. "Don't tell me you've been outlawed too."

"I suppose I will be sooner or later," his cousin replied. "Some of this lot already are. Meet Wat Coward and Rob Dyer. The lasses are Katherine Coll and Anna Cawthorne. They're good honest folk fallen afoul of Lancaster's men."

"And yourself?" Robert asked him. "Did Lancaster need a woodcutter and you refused to offer your services?"

"No. I just saw a group who needed a leader and I thought that leader might be you."

"You brought them to me? What am I supposed to do with them?"

"Listen, Hood," said the blonde woman who was called Anna. "If you don't want us then say so and we'll be on our way. It's no skin of our noses. I don't know why your cousin dragged us out here after you anyway. You don't seem all that great."

"Better than you lot at least," Will snapped. "I've never seen such a shambles made of a robbery."

"Care to have a contest of something other than words to settle it?" she asked, drawing an arrow from her quiver.

"Ha!" Will scoffed. "It would hardly be a fair contest!"

"All right, enough!" barked Robert.

"You see how they lack discipline?" said Simon. "I thought they might swell your ranks nicely with a bit of training and a foot up their arses now and then."

Robert ran his hand through his hair and sighed. He had never considered taking on any strays. Will and Much were good enough for small robberies and there was Stephen back at camp making them a nice gang of four. On the other hand, if Simon could vouch for these rogues, a larger band would make more profit.

"Let's talk it over back at camp," he said. "It's not safe to stand around on the road."

As they headed through the forest Robert said to Simon; "You still haven't explained your part in all this."

"How do you mean?"

"Will you be going back to your family or will you stay with us and help me control these friends of yours?"

"I thought I might join you."

"You'll be outlawed. What of Theresa and the children?"

"What of your mother and little Eleanor? You provide for them, don't you?"

"Simon, this isn't a decision to take lightly. Every day I wonder if I did the right thing in running from the law."

"How can you say that? You're wealthier than you ever would have been in Wakefield and your family eats well for it. If you'd stayed they would have hanged you. Then where would your mother and sister be?"

"Maybe I didn't have a choice, Simon, but you do."

"Rob, we're dirt poor. And things are set to get worse thanks to Lancaster. It might be civil war before the year is out. What chance does a woodcutter and his family have with bands of knights roving the countryside helping themselves to whatever they want? If I can just get in on some of the action you've been seeing, I can provide for Theresa and the children better than I can chopping logs."

Robert said nothing. He saw the truth in Simon's words but hated to be the one responsible for such a rash decision on his cousin's part. He remembered Mary's words to him on the day they had parted. He had lost so much in becoming an outlaw but it wasn't too late for Simon.

When they reached camp, Stephen saw to Much's wound. He smeared a nettle salve on it and bound it in clean linen.

"It's a nasty one, Robert," he told him in hushed tones. "I've done all I can but the infection might have beaten me to it. I've seen men survive worse but I've also seen them die from less. You can never tell for the first few days. If it begins to burn he'll need extra help."

"We'll cross that bridge when we come to it," Robert said, patting the old man on the arm.

They made an occasion of the night and feasted well. By the light of the campfire they talked and sang and grew merry on stolen wine. The newcomers were a good bunch, scarred and toughened by hard lives of poverty but it had not dampened their spirits, only sharpened them. Each had a tale to tell that spoke of England's troubles and its injustices.

"Wat Coward here used to be a fish merchant in north Lincolnshire," Simon explained, indicating the surly man with the black moustache. "He regularly ferried his goods down the River Trent to Nottingham until brigands from the Isle of Axholme attacked his ship and stole forty pounds worth of goods. That was enough to ruin him. The thieves were in the employ of John de Mowbray; one of Lancaster's dogs."

"How did you come to know each other?" Robert asked.

"Wat met me through our mutual friend Rob Dyer here. A cartwright by trade, Dyer has a daughter who was on the cusp of womanhood when she was raped by a sergeant wearing the sigil of Roger de Clifford; another of Lancaster's friends. Rob had hoped to marry her into a good family but Lancaster's friends put an end to that. Rob came upon the sergeant at an inn and stabbed him six times in the neck. Can't say I blame him."

"Outlawed, eh?" Robert said, looking to Dyer, an older man with greying hair but visible strength in his powerful arms.

"Aye," he replied. "And my only regret was that the bastard died too quick."

"Outlaws don't last long on their own, everybody knows that," said Simon. "So, I thought I'd introduce them to you and see what you thought of them. I led them into Barnsdale in February to look for you though you're a bastard to find. Anyway, that's when we ran into these lovely ladies."

Robert glanced at the two women. "So, what are your stories?"

"Not much to tell," said Anna. "A couple of petty thieves on the run from men who want to rape us, beat us and kill us. Not always in that order."

"Are you sisters or what?" Will asked.

"Do we look like sisters?" asked the small redhead who was called Katherine.

"In truth, no," said Robert. They were about as different as he could imagine two women being. Anna was tall, rangy and had a hard face that had clearly taken a few knocks in its time. Katherine was short, compact and pretty with greenish eyes and a petite mouth that looked like it still had a few smiles left in it.

"I ran into Anna outside a tavern near Ackworth," said Katherine. "Some men caught me trying to steal from a franklin's saddlebags. They were going to give me a pretty thorough hiding but Anna stepped in and together we managed to make a break for the woods. She saw that I wasn't really a boy and I think one or two of the men did too and planned to give me something other than a beating."

"You can imagine that they weren't too interested in joining us," said Simon, "but I convinced them that they'd be safer with us than wandering the woods alone."

"Bollocks you did," said Anna with a sneer. "And that's not how it happened. You three practically begged us to keep you company for all the good it'll do you." She glanced at Robert. "I made it clear to them that if they were looking for a couple of whores to keep them warm at night they could keep on walking and the first one to put his hand on either one of us would lose all it is to be a man."

"You two seem like you can handle yourselves," said Will with a grin. "Although your aim needs work."

"We'll see how yours is on the morrow," Anna replied.

"Anna has been my guardian angel," said Katherine. "She taught me to shoot a bow and kill a man with my bare hands. Although I haven't had the chance to try that one yet."

"You will in time," said Anna, spitting a lump of gristle into the fire where it hissed.

As they carried on talking the stars began to appear in the darkness above the treetops. Robert liked these new companions because he recognized himself in them. They had been wronged in more ways than one and were keen to seize the world by the throat and shake it for all it was worth. There was a ferocity in them that he felt he could use and in the morning, he did not even need to announce that they were now part of his band.

SEVENTEEN

As Stephen had feared, Much's wound grew inflamed within days and the miller's son became feverish.

"He needs help," Stephen told Robert. "Though God alone knows who will help us without turning us in."

"Kirklees Priory," said Robert.

"How's that?"

"I know the prioress. She's my cousin."

"Your cousin? I never knew you had family in the clergy."

"I only met her once or twice. Her name is Alice de Scriven and she is the daughter of my mother's older sister."

"Kirklees is quite a trot from here."

"We can make it in a couple of days. We'll purchase a pony in Wentbridge so Much will be spared the walk."

"Then we'd best leave immediately. Much grows sicker by the hour."

Robert explained his plans to the band.

"You can't take him alone, Rob," said Will. "And Stephen's not up to the walk. I'll go with you in case of trouble."

Robert took Will to one side. "I need you to remain here," he told him. "I don't want to leave our camp in the hands of Simon's friends."

"You don't trust them?"

"I hope I can but one of us should stay with Stephen just to be sure. Simon should stay too, he's their real leader. I'll take a couple of our new companions. Maybe they can prove themselves on the road."

He decided on the company of Wat Coward and Katherine Coll. They strung their bows and Robert belted on one of their stolen swords. Wat and Katherine took turns in helping him carry Much as far as Wentbridge. They found a secluded spot within sight of the town and lay Much down on a bed of long grass.

"You two stay with him," Robert told Wat and Katherine. "I won't be long."

"Let me come," said Katherine. "I'll watch your back."

"I don't need a girl to watch my back," he said.

She set her jaw. "If somebody had watched Much's back then he wouldn't be in this situation at all."

"Fine," Robert grumbled. "Leave your bow. We can't look like a couple of poachers strolling out of the forest. Keep your mouth shut and let me handle things."

She bristled at this. "I handled myself well enough long before I met you, Hood."

"Even so, I'm in charge and I don't want complications."

It had been years since Robert had walked those muddy streets but even so, he was worried somebody might recognize him. He still wore Stephen's cloak and he tugged the brim of the hood down to shade his face.

"You used to live here then, did you?" Katherine asked, looking around the town with interest.

"Yes, until we moved to Wakefield when I was eleven or so."

"Does it seem familiar?"

"Like I left just yesterday."

"Where was your house?"

"A couple of streets over. We don't need to go there."

"Big place?"

"No. Small. We were poor until my father became a forester. It was just big enough for the three of us."

"I can't picture it."

"Why are you trying to picture my childhood?" He glanced at her and was surprised to see that she looked suddenly flushed.

"I didn't grow up in a town," she said. "I just wondered what it was like. I grew up in the middle of nowhere."

"Daughter of a charcoal burner, wasn't it?"

"Aye, in Knaresborough Forest. There were only three of us too, until my mam died, that is. Then it was just me and my old man. I suppose I was the same age you were when you moved to Wakefield. Funny how everything changes when you reach that age, isn't it?"

"Is that when you ran away?"

She nodded. "My da always had a weakness for the drink. After my mam passed he was at a loss with what to do with me. He used to make me watch the charcoal heaps and lay on heavy with his fists at the slightest excuse. I had to stay awake and dig draughts if the smoke changed colour and Heaven help me if I ever fell asleep. Do you know how long those heaps burn for? Days and days. Sometimes he was gone for the whole of the burning, drinking away our money and snoring in an alehouse yard.

"I used to sit by those smouldering heaps and imagine that the curling smoke was my life drifting away on the wind. That terrified me. All I knew was that I had to leave him. I couldn't spend the rest of my life as a charcoal burner and I hated him more than anything. So, one day I just got up and left. I suppose that lot of charcoal was ruined. Serves the bugger right."

Robert glanced at her and saw that a tear had formed in the tail of her eye. She rubbed it away and pretended she was scratching at a louse in her tufty red hair.

They managed to buy a pony without incident and were soon on their way west with Much slumped in the saddle, the sweat standing out on his brow.

Kirklees Priory was situated on the northern bank of the River Calder, closer to Huddersfield than Wakefield. The gatehouse and hostelry was a stone and timber-faced building set in a quiet glade near the priory's fishponds. Robert knocked on the door and a small hatch opened revealing the elderly, pointed face of the hostler. She peered out at them with suspicion.

"Our friend is hurt, mother," Robert told the hostler. "He needs the tender attention of you good ladies."

"You are armed?"

"Aye,"

"Then you'll have to leave your weapons. I will speak with Domina de Scriven."

The hatch slammed shut and Robert and Katherine unbelted their blades and stowed them with their bows on the pony.

Domina de Scriven was a woman of middling years although it was often hard to tell with nuns as any grey hair was kept well hidden beneath veil and wimple. She did not recognise Robert and this came as no surprise. He recalled seeing her once or twice as a child and the woman who stood before him did not resemble the one in his faded memories. She regarded him with cautious suspicion but her eyes softened when she saw Much slouched over the pony's neck and in those eyes Robert finally saw the kind cousin he had known a lifetime before.

"I know you do not recognise me," he said, "and that you have little reason to trust the word of a shabby, armed man at your gate, but I am the son of Matilda Hood who was born Matilda le Harper."

Her eyes widened. "Robert? Saints preserve us! What has the Lord dealt you these past years? You look like an outlaw!"

"I'm afraid that is more or less the shape of it."

"And your mother and sister?"

"Both well, but alone and reliant on my help."

"You can tell me all about it at as soon as I've seen to your companion."

A timber stair led up the outside of the guesthouse to the quarters above and they carried Much up to a sturdy cot in one of the bays. A young laysister came to clean and treat his wound under the guidance of the prioress.

"He needs rest now," the prioress said once the wound was bound and Much lay slumbering on his cot. "Rest and prayers. But before you see to the latter, tell me what evil has befallen my aunt's family."

They sat at a table in the hall downstairs and food and drink was brought. The outlaws tucked in hungrily but graciously. The prioress eyed Katherine suspiciously as if trying to work out if the scruffy, shorthaired urchin at her table was a woman or a particularly effeminate boy. Over the meal, Robert told his estranged cousin all that had occurred since his father's death in the September of 1319.

"We were hoping," Robert said, washing the last of his bread down with a mouthful of ale, "that seeing as we are family, you might be gracious enough to temporarily neglect your duty to the agents of the law and forget that we had been here."

"I think under the circumstances I would be willing to do just that," she said. "Much will have to remain here until his wound heals and you three are welcome to remain with him here in the guest house."

"Thank you," Robert said.

She smiled briefly. "Now, I must leave you and attend to my duties. Pray for your friend. Pray to the Blessed Virgin for his life."

They remained at the priory for over a week and slept on pallets in the room opposite the one that held Much. Several other lodgers were squeezed into the same space and Robert found himself sharing a pallet with Katherine. He was intensely aware of her female form against him all night even if all the other men in the room were oblivious besides Wat. He kept thinking of Mary and the hours they had spent in each other's arms and wondered if it would feel as good to wrap his arms around Katherine, scruffy tomboy though she was.

He prayed for Much at every opportunity. Wat and Katherine did too but he could see that they were growing anxious. They did not know Much as he did and he could not blame them for wanting to leave. They were all in danger with every minute they spent at the priory. Robert trusted his cousin but what of the other nuns, laysisters and guests? Any one of them might betray them to the authorities.

Katherine, more so than the others, was afraid of discovery for some of the other guests were eyeing her suspiciously. Her disguise only held up without close scrutiny and quarters were cramped inside the guesthouse. The biggest problem was urinating in privacy. All the men in the dormitory pissed into a communal chamber pot which was emptied each morning. Katherine took to sneaking off into the nearby woods and it was on one of these occasions that one of the men came upon her squatting against a tree and swore loudly at the revelation.

Robert, who had been nearby, had heard the man's exclamation and entered the woods to find Katherine hurriedly tying her hose while the spectator gawked and snorted with laughter.

"Always thought you were too pretty to be a boy," the man said. "How old are you anyway? Old enough for a man to make a woman of you, I'll bet! Or maybe those lads you came in with have already done the deed. Can't say I blame them."

Robert slammed his fist into the side of the man's face and knocked him flat. "Any more of that talk and I'll break every bone in your face," he told the man as he writhed on the ground, clutching his throbbing cheek. "And if you breathe a word of what you've seen here today to anybody then I'll consider it a grave offence. It won't be a thump in the head you'll get, but a knife in the dark."

"Mad bastard!" said the man as he struggled to his feet. He hurried off and Robert was confident that he had made his point well enough.

"Thanks for that," said Katherine. "Taking a piss has always been the hardest thing about this lark. It's the one thing I can't fake."

"When we get back to the greenwood you won't have to carry on this charade," said Robert. "You can grow your hair and be a woman freely."

"Believe me, it's easier to be a boy."

"Anna doesn't seem to have any problems."

"No, Anna's more the type to cause problems for other people, not the other way around," Katherine said. "Anyway, I'm not as tough as she is. If I was then I wouldn't have been so dependent on her help when she found me."

"You really look up to her, don't you?"

"Toughest bitch I ever met. She's saved my skin more times than I can count. You don't know how hard it is to be a woman without means, without family. In the eyes of men, you're either a whore or something dangerous they don't understand. Either way they'll treat you like dirt."

"None of my band will treat you like dirt, I promise you," he said.

"Aye, you are a different breed of man than most of them."

"How so?"

"Most men cause chaos and reap the benefits, but you, the chief of a band of outlaws, you have forged order out of chaos. Where would your followers be without your leadership? They wouldn't stop at just robbing travellers passing through Barnsdale. They'd be burning farms, thieving crops, raping and looting."

"Oh, they're not as bad as all that," Robert protested. He didn't like her assumption that all men were, at base, lawless brutes.

"But for your leadership," she said. "Simon brought us to you for a reason; because we needed you. You lead and inspire while others would exploit and corrupt."

Robert was flattered by her perception of him but felt it was misplaced. He was no great leader and his band were no rapers or looters. But Katherine had lived in the chaos created by worse men than him all her life. Small wonder she was surprised to find a man who was prepared to treat her as an equal.

To Robert's delight their prayers were eventually answered and Much's fever died down. His wound began to close and Robert promised his cousin that he would leave a heavy donation to the Blessed Virgin at the next opportunity. Waving aside her pleas for them to remain another week, the outlaws gave her their thanks and began the long journey back to Barnsdale.

EIGHTEEN

"I know a draper in Featherstone," Wat Coward said. "He can probably give us a good price for it."

"Don't know what possessed you to thieve this lot anyway," Will said to Robert, peering at the cloth with distaste. "It hardly seems worth the effort of hauling it about."

"When a merchant doesn't have much coin in his purse it makes sense to take some of his goods in kind," Robert replied. "It's not the first time we've found ourselves with some odd gear to fence. Remember the pots?"

They had taken twenty-two ells of cloth from a merchant's cart earlier that morning. The carter had been heading to York from the dyers in Lincoln who were famous for their scarlets and greens. Unfortunately, the cart had not contained any scarlet which was phenomenally expensive due to the use of crushed insects imported from the Mediterranean. Instead the outlaws found themselves in possession of six ells of sky blue and sixteen ells of green.

"We'll sell the blue to your draper, Wat," Robert said. "The green... I have a mind to fashion some garments for us."

"Garments?" exclaimed Will. "If you think I'm prancing about the forest in green hose and cap you can think again."

"Relax, Will. I was only thinking of a simple mantle with a hood." He turned to Stephen. "Didn't you say you used to tie bits of brush and leaf to your tunics when you roved with Roger Godberd?"

"Aye," said the old man with a grin. "It obscured our outlines when we were lying in wait for a mark to rob. Some of the lads had maille and plate armour which is easily spotted in the woods. We used to lash leafy sprigs to our limbs to blend in better."

"Camouflage?" said Katherine, touching the fabric.

"And hoods to hide our faces," Robert added.

"Trying to live up to your name, Hood?" said Much with a grin.

"Well camouflage is all well and good," said Will, "but who's going to stitch the bloody things? I'm no seamstress, I can tell you that much."

The men turned their gazes to Katherine and Anna.

"Fuck off," said Anna.

Will laughed as if the whole scheme was a mad one but Stephen spoke up.

"I'm no poor hand with a needle and thread," he said. "I used to patch up clothing for Godberd's gang although my hands have grown a little shaky in my old age. Let me see if I can't fashion something passable from these bolts. I don't contribute much to this venture of yours other than a bit of firewood and the odd story."

"Thank you, Stephen," Robert said. "We'd appreciate it."

It took Stephen the best part of a week to cut and stitch eight hooded mantles of the green cloth and on the band's next robbery they looked like jade phantoms striking from the greenwood. They felt invisible as they moved through the forest and the ease of their escape made them feel so free and at one with the forest that even Will thanked Stephen for his efforts.

Robert had taken to meeting Mary's brother Walter on the outskirts of Wakefield once a month to deliver the coin for their families. Another member of the band who made similar visits was Rob Dyer whose family lived at South Elmsall. He returned from one of these visits in late July with news that caused great discussion in the band.

"They've captured Great John of Holderness and have him caged at South Elmsall," Dyer said. "My Greta says they're going to take him to York to stand trial before the end of the week."

Great John of Holderness was a well-known criminal in Yorkshire. An unusually large man, he had once been a servant in the High Sheriff's own household until he had a dispute with the sheriff's steward. The steward had denied John victuals as punishment for some slight and, being a man with a quick temper, John had helped himself to food and drink from the sheriff's stores. When confronted by the steward, John dealt him such a blow with his fist that the man never recovered and remained a halfwit, the sense forever dashed from his brain.

Great John turned outlaw after that and worked for various gangs who robbed travellers and households across Yorkshire. A rough and argumentative man quick to anger, John had never been able to keep the same company for long, always some dispute or slight forcing him to move on, usually leaving a body or two in his wake. He often operated under the alias 'Reynold Greenleaf' but there was little disguising his massive size and ferocious temper.

"What of it?" Much asked. "Good riddance to him, I say. I heard he killed the horse of a man he robbed because the beast looked at him funny."

"A horse?" sneered Will. "He must have killed a dozen men and you're troubled by a horse?"

There were chuckles at this. Much was known for his kindness towards animals; a kindness most of the other men considered a weakness of the feminine variety.

"They'll hang him for sure," said Simon. "Does that set your mind at ease, Much?"

Much was silent.

"Mayhap we could postpone his appointment with the hangman," said Robert.

"Postpone it?" Simon asked. "What for?"

"He has a fearsome reputation. And a mighty pair of fists. He could be an asset to us."

"You want Great John to join our band?" said Will. "Have you lost your senses?"

"He'll murder each and every one of us!" said Simon.

"I hardly think so if we are the ones to rescue him," Robert replied. "He'll owe us a debt. That's a powerful debt to call in."

"We don't need his sort of trouble, Rob," said Much.

"Neither do our enemies," said Katherine, "or the people we rob. Life would be a lot easier with a man like that on our side. Most travellers would simply hand over their purses just at the sight of him. And once word gets around that Great John is one of our number we'll be all the more feared."

"Is that what we want to be?" Much asked. "Feared?"

"Yes," said Robert. "Fear is a powerful ally, isn't that right, Stephen?"

The old man nodded. "It can be sharper than swords and decidedly less bloody. If you lot can avoid violence and still make off with people's purses then all the better."

"Even if he decides not to join us," Katherine continued, "just the rumour that we freed him would give people something serious to think about. We'd be feared either way."

"I'd rather people feared my blade," Will grumbled but nobody listened. Even Much and Simon were half-won around to the idea of rescuing Great John and Wat and Rob Dyer were decidedly for it.

"How is it to be done?" Simon asked. "He'll be well guarded."

"We need to get creative," said Robert. "And we need to fell a couple of trees."

The lofty nave of the York Minster still held the last echoes of the choir, its vaulted stone ceiling ringing with a steadily dissipating song in worship of God. Mass was over and the footsteps of the congregation thudded softly as they exited through the portal.

William de Melton, the Archbishop of York, walked down the nave, his white and gold robes a stark contrast to the green tunic and black-trimmed mantle of the High Sheriff of Yorkshire who strolled by his side.

"Something's got to be done about these Barnsdale outlaws, de Warde," he said. "They're getting bolder and bolder. Last week a monk of St. Mary's was robbed on his way to Doncaster. A monk, by the rood! Are these men just godless?"

"I fear so, Your Grace," the sheriff replied. "They live like animals out in the woods and so their souls have degenerated to the state of beasts. I have sent patrols into Barnsdale but to no effect. It is too wide and untracked, its trees too thick. I must lure them out with a ruse somehow."

"Then do so!"

"I assure you, Your Grace, I will stop at nothing to see them hanged."

"We have enough trouble in Yorkshire without robbers plaguing all trade and correspondence."

The sheriff knew the archbishop referred to Lancaster but did not dare speak his name, even within his own minster. Lancaster had spies everywhere.

"The man's got to be stopped," said the archbishop in a hushed tone. "His support of the Marcher Lords is little short of outright treason! Their ravaging of le Despenser's lands in Wales has the king frantic."

"His supporters here in the north have been stirring up all kinds of trouble too," the sheriff replied. "They are as bad as the robbers in the forests."

"Would that we could deal with them as harshly as those pagans, but the earl's foothold is too strong, his forces too numerable."

"And yet the king is not without his own supporters in the north."

The archbishop grunted acknowledgement of this. "You, de Aune and I perhaps but all the powerful landowners have thrown their support behind Lancaster, convinced that he can rid England of the king's foolishness and the tyranny of the le Despensers."

"There is also my colleague, Andrew de Harclay."

"The Sheriff of Cumberland? He has voiced support for the king in the past but his proximity to the Scottish border is not something to be ignored. Being so close to those savages may have corrupted his mind, that is if Lancaster has not turned it against the king already."

The sheriff met his wife on the steps of the minster and they rode back to Guiseley. The afternoon was fair and warm. It was early evening when they reached the manor house and there was a letter waiting for Simon. Once again, it had come from Tickhill Castle. He opened it and read.

To his dearest friend and lord High Sheriff, greetings. You ought to know that my spies have reported the movement of a strongbox containing a large amount of silver heading northwards from the Isle of Axholme towards Pontefract. This strongbox is the property of John de Mowbray, Lancaster's detestable supporter and sent with the clear intent of funding Lancaster's burgeoning rebellion. My aim is to take this strongbox in the name of our Lord King and I require your help in doing so.

I will send six men-at-arms to you as soon as you are ready. They will aid you in securing the chest. Once it is in your custody, you are to conduct it to Birkham Grange where I will post more men to bring it to me at Tickhill. Naturally you will be sufficiently rewarded for your part in this.

"Are you coming to bed, husband, or does your duty keep you up into the small hours?" Constance said, setting down her goblet which was drained of the posset she was accustomed to drinking before bed.

"It's from William de Aune," he explained.

She sighed. "I declare, that fellow is like a bee; constantly buzzing about some snippet of information or whiff of nectar. What is it now?" She took the letter from him and read it.

"Silver. What else could be that bee's choicest nectar? So, he fancies thieving from Lancaster and his friends now, does he?"

"It does strike me as an easy way to hit Lancaster where it hurts and isn't that something worth doing?"

"Indeed. And fill de Aune's coffers into the bargain. You are not really naive enough to think that he makes this request of you merely out of a sense of duty to the king?"

"No, I am not as naive as that," the sheriff replied. "But how is it to be done? The strongbox will certainly be guarded by a heavy escort and I can hardly be seen to act like a common brigand, no matter how well the lords in the north play that part."

"Then why not send real brigands?" Constance said. "Ones with nothing to lose and who might shield your good name."

"Just ask them, I suppose? And hope they don't slit my throat?"

"They'll do nothing of the kind as long as there's a profit to be made. You yourself have said that they are slaves to coin."

"Aren't we all?" he replied with a smirk. He tried to appear flippant but within his head plans were sprouting like shoots in spring. *Hire robbers to do his dirty work? Wakefield's renegades perhaps?* And when he was done with them they would be within his grasp, helpless, exposed and easily dispensed with. *Two birds with one stone.*

He smiled. Perhaps it was time to look this Robert Hood and his companions in their villainous faces at long last. *But how to contact them?*

NINETEEN

Will could hear the clop of hooves on the hardpacked dirt road long before the train came into view. From their hiding spot in the bushes, it sounded like a lot of riders but Will told himself that sounds could be deceiving.

"How many do you reckon?" Anna asked him.

He shrugged. "Rob said there wouldn't be more than five or six mounted men in the vanguard. There'll be crossbowmen with the prison wagon but those are not our concern."

Will sat in wait with Anna, Simon, Wat and Rob Dyer. Their nervous breathing was hot and heavy in the closeness of the bushes. Anna was close enough to him that he could see every imperfection in her blue eyes.

"Pick your targets, but don't be too long about it," he told them. "Knock off a few of the bastards if we can but it's not the end of the world if we don't. Our job is to draw the vanguard away from the wagon."

"We'll need to let them see us," said Rob Dyer. "Probably have to step out onto the road, at least a little."

"Aye, but don't *look* like you want to be seen. We need to be a whiff of honey in the bear's nostrils. No more, no less."

"I'll give the buggers some honey," said Anna as she inspected the tip of one of her arrows.

"Quiet," Will hushed. "They draw close."

The vanguard was made up of six riders. They wore hauberks and simple iron helms. They had no sigils or surcoats and were probably just local lads on the sheriff's payroll.

As they passed, Will nocked an arrow and motioned to the others to do the same. Bowstrings creaked as they drew in unison; a deadly sound in the muffled forest.

The arrows struck the vanguard like a hail of feathered death. Horses reared up and screamed. Two of the riders had been struck; one fell dead to the ground while the other roared in agony and clutched the shaft that had skewered his shoulder. The other arrows had been deflected by maille or helms but one had lodged in the flank of one of the horses making it buck and snort in pain.

The riders drew their swords and looked about frantically. Will led the company out onto the side of the road where they would be visible should anybody look their way. He drew another arrow and loosed it at the vanguard.

A rider caught it on his shield. They had spotted them.

"Run!" Will yelled to his companions.

They turned and fled back into the woods. The enraged vanguard followed in hot pursuit, keen for vengeance. They hacked aside foliage with their blades and pushed their mounts onwards into the gloom of the woods.

Further down the road the prison wagon had ground to a halt. The driver stood up in his seat and peered at the road ahead. "We've come under attack!" he cried.

"Robbers?" asked one of the crossbowmen who walked beside the wagon.

"Can't say. The van just chased them into the trees. They'll give 'em what for! Should be safe enough to continue."

"No! Hold here until we know the way ahead is safe," replied the captain of the group.

Robert heard their distant voices from where he huddled in the undergrowth with Katherine and Much. "Now!" he hissed.

The *cheval de fries* was a heavy construction that required the strength of all three of them to carry. Fashioned from a single tree trunk, sharpened stakes had been lashed to it making it a prickly barrier which was long enough to cover the width of the road.

The soldiers with the wagon had spotted them and began loosing their crossbows. Robert and his companions ducked and the bolts either went overhead or struck the roadblock.

They unslung their bows and returned the offensive. The shortcomings of the crossbow in the face of the ordinary bow were well demonstrated in that brief skirmish. While the soldiers were struggling to reload, the outlaws sent a second volley and killed two of them. The remaining soldiers dived for cover either behind the wagon or in the undergrowth on either side of the road.

Robert, Much and Katherine shouldered their bows and drew blades. Making for the wagon, Robert cut down a soldier who ran forward to halt them, battering aside his blade and shearing his neck open.

Much ran around to the back of the cart and slid his quarterstaff between the lock and the jamb. With several heaves, his muscles straining, the lock broke and the man within the cage rose to his feet.

Much's eyes goggled at him and for the first time Robert noticed the man they were trying to rescue. He was immensely tall and had a long mane of shaggy, dark hair. His clothes were of rough-spun wool and he wore a sheepskin jacket that looked like it had been made from the entire animal.

Much stumbled backwards as Great John booted open the cage door and stepped down onto the road. Robert approached the giant.

"Robert Hood at your service," he said. "I hope you will be at ours in finishing off your captors."

John turned his head to glare at a soldier on the other side of the wagon who was desperately trying to reload his crossbow.

"Try stopping me," he growled.

In four strides he was within reach of the unfortunate soldier. He swept aside the crossbow with a mighty paw and knocked the helm from the man's head with the other. Seizing the terrified soldier's skull within his two big hands, he began to squeeze.

The solider squealed and Robert, Much and Katherine winced as they heard bone crack. The man's legs thrashed and then went slack. Great John let him tumble to the ground like a ragdoll.

"These bastards have been giving me grief and poking me with sword points since we left South Elmsall," John said.

The soldiers who had fled into the woods had marshalled beyond the tree line and were pressing the offensive. Crossbow bolts thudded into the side of the wagon as Robert and his companions took cover. They tried to find marks in the dense foliage but found themselves shooting at shadows.

"The vanguard is back!" said Robert, hearing angry voices further down the road.

The *cheval de fries* proved a worthy obstacle to the returning riders and their horses slithered to a halt just short of its spikes. One of the riders yelled an oath and hacked at it with his sword but to no avail. The others dismounted and began trying to move the barricade.

"We're pinned down!" Much yelled. "We can't fight them on two fronts!"

"Where the hell are Will and the others?" Robert said.

"Maybe dead," Much replied.

"If only I had a bow," said John with a snarl.

"There's nothing for it," said Robert, looking to the barrier. The riders had managed to shift the obstruction from the road. "They're upon us. We have to flee!"

"What about the others?" Katherine demanded.

"Much may be right," said Robert. "They might be dead. We must retreat into the woods. Follow me!"

They turned and fled into the trees. The riders had seen them and pursued, crashing into the undergrowth, hacking and slashing.

The outlaws plunged onwards with no direction in mind but away from the road and their mounted pursuers. Robert noticed that John was no longer with them and Much had gone too. He and Katherine were all that was left of his band.

He cursed himself. He had been so foolish to think that this would work. They had rescued Great John but for what? The giant had taken to his heels at the first opportunity and how many had been killed in securing his release? Will? Simon? All of them? And now Much was gone too with little hope of escape for any of them.

He could hear the riders gaining on them and they emerged into a grassy glade. There was no cover and they would be ridden down in seconds. Robert drew his sword and turned, seizing Katherine's wrist and forcing her behind him.

Two riders thundered into the glade. Their companions had evidently pursued John and Much into a different part of the woods. Robert gripped his blade and stared into the eyes of the nearest rider. They were fiery with rage. Katherine had drawn her sword too and was tense by his side, ready to die with him. Robert decided that as far as having somebody to die alongside went, he could do a lot worse.

The rider spurred his horse and came at them, his sword arm swinging. Robert deflected the blow and felt pain in his elbow as the vibrations rang through his forearm. Before the rider wheeled his mount for another pass, the second came at them, striking at Katherine. She batted the blade away and took an optimistic swing at his leg but missed.

The riders turned and pressed in on them, hemming them in like fish in a barrel. Their faces split into grins and Robert knew they intended to take their time with their prey.

Sword points lunged at them from both sides and Robert and Katherine fought back to back, blocking and fending them off with a clash and slither of steel, knowing that it was only a matter of time before one of them found its mark.

The head of one of the riders suddenly exploded in a shower of blood and teeth as a large rock connected with it, crumpling the helm and knocking him from his horse. His companion wheeled in his saddle to look for the source of the attack.

Great John strode from the woods, his bulging forearms flexing with deadly power. The rider turned and rode at him, sword held high to cut him down.

John was too quick and too powerful. He ran at the rider head on and leaped up to grasp his sword arm before he could use it. With a mighty wrench he heaved the man from his saddle, cracking the bone in the process. The man grunted in pain as he hit the ground. John seized the bloody rock that he had hurled at the first rider and slammed it down into the second rider's face, splintering the jaw. He struck again and again, pounding the man's face into a bloody ruin until his body stopped twitching.

Gasping with exertion, his sweat-soaked shirt clinging to his enormous chest, he rose and let the dripping rock fall from his reddened fist.

"Thank you," Robert said, his eyes wide at the awful violence they had just witnessed. Katherine had her hand clasped over her mouth as if she was forcing back the vomit rising in her gut.

John nodded at him. "I always pay my debts, Robert Hood. You may consider us even now."

"I should think so."

John sensed further danger and spun to face the woods. Several figures lurked there and Robert tensed for further fighting. He recognised Will and heaved a sigh of relief.

"Don't move," Will commanded Great John, an arrow pointed at his chest. Simon, Anna, Wat and Rob Dyer emerged behind him, their own weapons ready. Much was there too.

Robert was exhilarated to see them all alive but John was ready to kill anybody who pointed a weapon at him.

"Easy, Will," Robert said. "He's a friend."

"Is he?" Will grunted, not taking his eyes off Great John. "How can we be sure? I've never seen bloodshed like it. He looks like a wildman to me, Rob. A woodwose. Probably kill us all as soon as our guard is down."

"Why don't you lower your bow and find out," John snarled. "Or are you too craven to face a man without pointing an arrow at him from ten paces?"

"Will, put away your arrow," Robert commanded. "He just saved our lives."

"He's right," said Katherine. "I trust him. You should too."

Anna placed a hand on Will's shoulder and he seemed to relax. His bowstring slackened and he slowly lowered his weapon, still keeping Great John fixed in his unblinking eyes.

"Just so you know," he told John, "I'm as quick with dagger as I am with a bow. If you so much as give any of my friends a dirty look, I'll kill you."

"Try, if you like," said John. "And you can join the ranks of forgotten fools who also thought they had what it took."

"All right, enough horseshit!" said Robert. "We're all friends here. There'll be no violence. Let's round up the horses, gather what gear we can and head back to camp. John, you're welcome to join us for tonight and for as many nights as you wish."

"I'm not quite sure I understand you, Hood," said Great John. "Why did you spring me?"

"Prestige. Notoriety. And to recruit you if you're willing."

John looked around at the band. "So, what are you lot? A rebellion in the making?"

Robert shook his head. "Just a band of poor outlaws trying to survive. Like you."

John shrugged. "Well, never look a gift horse in the mouth, that's what my da used to say whenever he was sober. I'll sup with you tonight and then see how I feel in the morning. Let's take a look at this camp of yours."

They made their way back to camp with a good deal of maille and blades along with five horses. The one that had been lamed by Will's arrow was put out of its misery. The prize of the haul was a snow white palfrey that looked fit for a lord and which Robert claimed as his share of the booty.

As they had done when Simon and the others had joined the band, they feasted and made merry. Great John was a surly, argumentative man but his brashness was matched by his mirth and his capacity to drink staggered them all.

"We'll have to hope more vintners and ale merchants pass through Barnsdale," said Old Stephen to Robert as the outlaws prepared to bed down for the night. "Our new friend has all but emptied the last butt of our stores."

"I'm sure the forest will provide as it has always done," Robert replied.

"Do you really think he'll join us?" Katherine asked him.

"He certainly seemed to enjoy himself tonight."

"But will he be just as jovial with an aching head in the morning?"

Robert shrugged. "We've done all we can for him. If he chooses to go his own way then there is nothing we can do. God has a plan for all of us."

"You really have faith in God's will, don't you?"

He blinked at her. "You don't?"

She looked away. "I don't know. My childhood was probably the worst there is. Do you know how charcoal burners are treated by town folk? There isn't a trade in the world that is more secluded and shunned. Spending days and days awake in a haze of wood smoke far from any habitation doesn't exactly inspire trust and friendship in people. Accusations of drunkenness, sodomy and even devil worship plague all in that damnable trade. Only one of those things was true of my childhood but it was enough to make me run and never look back."

"Still, at least you got away, eh?"

"But I ran from nothing to nothing; to a life of crime that has caused me to be hunted like a dangerous animal. All I ever wanted was food in my belly and a life free from beatings and isolation. I fought to get away from that and I'm still fighting. Is this God's plan for me? People say that God loves us all but I honestly have never felt loved by anybody in my life."

"Katherine, I had no idea," Robert said and he placed a hand on her arm.

She pulled away from him. "I don't want your sympathy. I don't know why I even told you all that."

His expression must have looked hurt because she said; "Sorry, Rob. I've drunk too much wine tonight. Goodnight."

Robert watched her leave and felt a pity for her that he would never admit to her. Small as she was, she was a tough fighter with no small amount of pride. But tonight, she had let her mask slip just a little for him to see the hurt child beneath.

He must have fallen asleep for he did not notice that she had entered his shelter until he felt her arm around his chest. She had lain down on his pallet behind him and was holding him close.

He rolled over to face her. The moonlight that peeped in through the woven branches of his shelter illuminated every detail of her face; every feature and shadow rendered into perfection. Her skin was smooth and pale, her lips dark like wine.

He opened his mouth to say something but she pressed a finger to his lips. "Don't say anything," she whispered. "I didn't come here to talk."

He wondered exactly what she had come for. He found himself longing to hold her close, kiss her even. He had struggled with his feelings towards her of late. Until recently, his thoughts had been so preoccupied with Mary that he felt he had been blindsided by this woman who now lay next to him, her hands on his chest.

He decided to kiss her. She did not shy away as he feared she would. In fact, she held the kiss and moved in closer to his body. He felt something soar in his chest; a revelation, a release of all those desires he had felt for Mary but had never been realised due to all the barriers the world had placed between them. Those feelings suddenly embraced this woman beside him; this woman who was not concerned about reputation or marriage but who was an outcast, a fighter like him who might die tomorrow and had to seize these rare moments of happiness or lose them forever. In a perverse way, the threat of death made them as free as the birds in the sky. Katherine was part of his world in a way that Mary could never be and in that moment, nothing had ever felt so right.

TWENTY

The sheriff could detect the potter's reek from across the hall. His manor house was not accustomed to receiving peasants and neither were his nostrils. He preferred to hold audience with the lower elements of society in more open and airy places.

The potter was a sweaty little man with bare arms and rough hands. His apron was caked with layer upon layer of crumbling clay. The bailiff of Wakefield stood by his side, his eyes upon the decanter of wine which stood on the side table. He licked his lips hopefully.

"You have my deepest gratitude for bringing this man to me," the sheriff told him. "I will not bore you with our conversation; my wife will accompany you to the kitchens and see that your belly is filled for the return journey."

"Oh, I don't mind," the bailiff said. "I am really quite interested in hearing how you intend to use this potter in apprehending the outlaws."

"I have told my steward to open a pipe of that wine you expressed such fondness for on your last visit," the sheriff added.

The bailiff's eyes lit up. "Oh, well… it would be a shame to waste it if it's already opened…"

Constance ushered him in the direction of the kitchens. The sheriff had requested the potter be brought to him on the pretence of using him in a plan to arrest the outlaws and that was as far as he was prepared to let Lancaster's bailiff in on it. The potter looked about the hall in bemusement, not quite sure what was expected of him.

"I am led to believe that you have met the hobhoods of Barnsdale," he told the potter, using a curious bit of folklore to appeal to the commoner.

"Oh, aye, sire," the potter replied. "Tried to rob me blind but I made 'em laugh with a few jokes of mine – very good ones they were too – and they let me keep half my purse."

"Not as disastrous a meeting as it might have been, then."

"No sire."

"Still, they stole half your purse. That must have stung somewhat."

"That it did, sire, that it did. Many a day's work was lost on that meeting. They took some of my pots too, the buggers."

"Indeed? Then you, as a law-abiding Englishman, would feel no pity for them should they meet with some swift justice? In fact, I would go so far as to say that you might be willing to help arrange that meeting."

The potter considered this. "Aye, I would at that. If the chance presented itself."

"Excellent. Then I have use for you and shall see that you are properly rewarded for your cooperation."

"What would you have of me, sire?"

"I need you to take a journey through Barnsdale. You will take with you a large load of pots to tease the outlaws into robbing you again. You will also take with you a representative of mine disguised as your apprentice. This man will carry my seal and a message for the outlaws."

"What message?"

"That is beyond your concern."

"This representative of yours," said Constance who had returned from the kitchens having seen the bailiff seated at a table with a wine cup in his hand. "Who are you planning to send?"

"Oderic, my sergeant," the sheriff replied.

"And what is to stop the outlaws from killing him, husband? This potter might be able to buy his way out of trouble with his purse but Oderic has but your seal and that is as likely to condemn him as it is to save him."

"They are unlikely to kill a man carrying a message that promises them such a deal as I am offering, Constance," said the sheriff. "My message will have their undivided attention, I assure you of that."

"And yet Oderic is not exactly a diplomatic man. What if he bungles the delivery of your message? What if he makes the outlaws suspicious? Insults them?"

The sheriff felt his ire rising. He knew very well the root of his wife's interest in his scheme. She enjoyed fine gowns as much as he enjoyed fine wines. She had even helped him plan the whole scheme. But now she was showing signs of diminishing confidence in it. The potter glanced from husband to wife in confusion, not sure what sort of marital conflict was unfolding before him.

"Do you have another candidate in mind?" the sheriff asked his wife.

"Yes," she replied. "Me."

Both the sheriff and the potter gaped at her. "You jest, Constance," the sheriff said.

"I do not. I can carry your seal as well as any man. Better even, for as your wife I carry a little of the authority it holds. And the outlaws will not see me as a threat or an arrogant soldier to be taught a lesson in manners."

"They may mistreat you on other grounds," the sheriff replied. "They are outlaws after all. Little more than savages."

"Then I shall have to appeal to their base instincts."

The sheriff's eyes widened at this.

"Oh, don't look at me like that, husband. You know I will only ever be true to you. But these outlaws will be unaccustomed to the wiles and soft tones of a female. It may grease the wheels of the negotiations."

The sheriff considered his wife's words and the potter spluttered a protest.

"Sire, you can't seriously be considering this!"

"Do you presume to tell me my own mind?" the sheriff snapped.

The man paled. "No, sire, but I cannot be held accountable for your wife's safety should you go through with this plan. Sending her to meet with outlaws?"

"Are they not as jolly and as quick to laugh at a jest as you previously claimed?"

"Well, the banter of a fellow yeoman perhaps, but who is to say what they will do when a noblewoman comes across their path? I can't guarantee her safety."

"I assure you, potter," Constance said, "My safety is my concern and mine alone. You just worry about getting me to them. I'll handle the rest."

The outlaws were pleased to see the potter again for he had been a jovial enough fellow who did not let a simple thing like robbery spoil an afternoon's exchange of gossip and banter. That did not mean that they planned to let him slip through Barnsdale without robbing him a second time. This time they were surprised to find a woman in his company and a pretty one at that. She was dressed in a simple hooded cloak befitting a peasant woman but there was no disguising her fine graces and well-fed complexion.

"Have you taken a wife, good potter?" asked Robert as he laid a hand on the reins of the carthorse.

At his back his band bared their weapons but with little conviction. They saw no danger in the situation and all hoped for a quick and congenial transaction.

"Him, a wife such as this?" Much said. "Impossible!"

"Aye, she's too beautiful for you, potter!" said Robert. "Which lord did you steal her from? Tell us quick and we might not beat you too thoroughly before we return her to him."

"She's not my wife, you fools," said the potter. "But she is a noblewoman and she carries a message for you."

"A message for us?" asked Robert.

"The good potter speaks truth," said the lady.

Great John pushed his way forward and peered at her face. "By all the saints!" he exclaimed.

She smiled. "Hello, John."

Robert looked from the noblewoman to Great John. "Did you fail to mention that you had been a lordling in your youth, John?" he asked.

"No, but I was a servant," he replied. "In this woman's house."

"You don't mean to tell us that she is..." Robert began.

"Constance de Warde, wife of the High Sheriff of Yorkshire at your service," the woman replied.

Robert stepped back, his hand falling to the hilt of his sword. The rest of the band suddenly looked more alert and glanced up and down the road as if expecting a company of knights to be upon them at any moment.

"It's a trap, Rob," said Katherine.

"Aye," said Will. "Let's away."

"Wait until you hear what I have to say," said Constance. She produced a seal from her cloak and handed it to Robert. "My husband's. Proof of who I am but the presence of John here will hopefully render it redundant. I carry a proposition from the sheriff. Might we talk a while in private?"

"I have no secrets from my band," Robert replied.

Constance looked at them. "There are more of you than I was given to believe." She glanced at Katherine and Anna. "And women too. You may trust your followers but I trust only their leader. Is that fellow you?"

"Aye," said Robert. "I'm the leader. Very well." He helped her down from the cart.

Katherine placed her hand on his arm and spoke quietly in his ear. "This is a trap Rob. I don't know what they're planning but it's a trap."

"There can't be any harm in hearing what she has to say," he told her.

As he led Constance off the road and into the woods Will called out; "Don't wander far!"

"And we'll be watching and waiting!" added Katherine, her words directed towards Constance. "The slightest hint of treachery and we'll spare neither you nor the potter!"

"Your band truly revere you," Constance said to Robert when they were alone.

"We are as brothers and sisters here in the greenwood," he told her. "The world has left us nothing but each other."

"A simple but romantic arrangement," she said.

"You'd better tell me what you have to say. My band won't wait forever. They already think you mean to murder me."

"How could I do that?" she said, a wry smile curling the corner of her mouth. "An unarmed woman against a hardened forest outlaw? Very well,

I'll say my piece. We live in confusing times, Hood. Loyalty is not always a cut and dry matter of those on the side of the law verses those who have fallen afoul of it. My husband understands this and he hopes that you understand it too. The king has many enemies and if he is to defeat them he must find allies in the unlikeliest of places. Some of those allies might be criminals whom he would reward handsomely if they should assist him."

"You're talking about Lancaster, aren't you?"

"In a way. How do you feel about the man?"

"It was his actions that caused me to be outlawed," Robert replied. "He and his friends are a curse on the land. Many of my followers suffered similar injustices and lost their homes, their families and their freedom as a result."

"Then you would be willing to aid my husband? You would show no qualms in robbing Lancaster and his friends of a large amount of silver?"

"Rob Lancaster? Gladly but for the chance. His men do not travel in small numbers and we are few."

"But if my husband were to provide you with some valuable intelligence about their movements, you might be able to strike them when they are vulnerable."

"That would depend on how good the intelligence is. I don't risk the lives of my band recklessly."

"Very good. There is a strongbox of silver on its way to Pontefract from Lord de Mowbray's lands on the Isle of Axholme. The wagon carrying it will be escorted by a company of soldiers, both knights and footmen. They plan to stop at Birkham Grange four nights from now. Now the grange consists of two buildings; the barn and the brewery. The brewery is a small building half a mile to the northeast of the barn. It is surrounded by a wall. I have it on good authority that the strongbox will be stored there overnight with a small guard while the rest of the men will bed down in the barn."

"Whose authority?"

"You have heard of William de Aune?"

"The king's spymaster?"

"Good enough authority for you? De Aune has a man in de Mowbray's guard who passed us this information. This isn't the first time de Mowbray has sent coin to his master at Pontefract."

"Why would they keep the strongbox at the brewery with such a small guard and so far away from the rest of the men?"

"De Aune's man says it is to remove it from the one place potential thieves will look for it. A barn full of sleeping soldiers must house something worth stealing. Nobody will think to raid the brewery."

"So, your husband wants my band to steal this strongbox from the brewery without arousing the dozen or so knights slumbering nearby and carry it off into the greenwood, presumably to a prearranged destination where he will be waiting to receive it."

"Yes. You are to bring it to our home at Guiseley where you will receive a handsome cut of the strongbox's contents as well as full pardons for you and your followers."

"Full pardons?"

She nodded. Robert's head span. He had never thought that this could be possible. *A pardon?* He could return home! He could return to his mother, to Eleanor. *And to Mary?* The scent of freedom was bittersweet. Had this offer been made to him at the beginning of spring he could have been saved so much heartache. But even the pain of losing Mary that had plagued him for weeks on end seemed distant to him now. *Because of Katherine.*

She had helped ease him of it and he felt suddenly ashamed for jumping at the chance to leave the greenwood and return to his old life. What would that mean for her? Their relationship was like a fresh shoot in poor, rough soil. It was strengthening day by day but it was used to the clear sky and the everchanging elements. Could it survive the restraints of freedom?

Constance was confused by his hesitation. "Surely such a reward is worth a little risk?"

"Just how much silver is in this box?"

"De Aune estimates that it is equal to five hundred pounds or near enough."

"And our cut will be?"

"Five pounds per head. Plus your freedom."

The money was modest for running such a risk but Robert knew that he could not refuse. He could not deny the others their chance of freedom even if his own heart was undecided.

When they returned to the road they found Katherine, Will and the others in exactly the same positions they had left them in, as if they were statues, immovable in the absence of their leader.

"Then we have a bargain, Hood?" Constance said as he helped her up into the cart.

"Aye," Robert replied. "I'll discuss the details with my band."

"Very good. It is imperative that you steal the strongbox four nights from now. It is the only chance we have of getting it. Use the utmost discretion in conducting it to us at Guiseley. Don't fail my husband, Robert. Don't fail me."

As the cart rumbled off down the road, Robert explained the plan to his band.

"You can see that this is a trap, right?" Will asked.

"I agree," said Katherine. "Promising us pardons for breaking the law for them? I don't believe a word of it."

"The north has almost become a separate country under Lancaster," Robert explained. "It's hardly breaking the law if we help the king take back his own land. Why wouldn't he reward us for helping the sheriff?"

The others grew more receptive to the idea and even Will's distrust of the sheriff's wife had been softened by the promise of living out the rest of his days as a free man. All pondered the merits except Katherine who remained unconvinced. Her concerns did little to ease Robert's own. She seemed as reluctant to grasp freedom when it was offered as he was. *What if this is all a horrible mistake? What if she doesn't want her pardon? What if she wants only to live in the greenwood with me?* He wanted to discuss it with her but did not feel ready to reveal his feelings for her; it might ruin everything.

As they wandered back to camp, Robert asked Great John of his relationship with Constance.

"She's a good woman, is Lady Constance," John replied. "Always treated the servants right though she has a wicked tongue if she's crossed. It was because her that the steward and I fell out."

"How so?" Robert asked.

"He was a lecherous pig with no respect for women or his employer. I came across him in the buttery making lewd remarks about the sheriff's wife to one of the other servants. I told him what I thought of him and he threatened to have me thrown out. I said I'd like to see him or any other bugger try and our heated words reached the ears of the lady of the house. She demanded to know what the fuss was about so I told her which earned the steward a lengthy spell in her bad books. He hated me with a passion after that."

"Is that why he refused you victuals?" Robert asked.

"Aye. He said that if he couldn't throw me out he'd starve me out. Well, I thought I'd prove him wrong and helped myself to what was rightfully mine. That had him in a state, I can tell you. Until that point he'd only ever hurled his sour words at me but seeing me in the buttery with my mouth full of game pie and a flagon of wine at my elbow made him angry enough to lay his hand on me, the fool. So, I cracked his skull for him."

"And became an outlaw," said Robert in awe. The story was a touching one and cast Great John of Holderness in a wholly new and not entirely unsympathetic light.

The band said nothing in response to his story. They walked the remainder of the journey in silence, each of them reassessing their new comrade. Of all his band, Robert couldn't see John being outlawed for protecting a woman's good name. But that was what had happened; another act of injustice that had turned a good, honest man to a life of crime and brutality.

And now there was hope of a pardon for all of them.

Robert made up his mind there and then that he would do whatever it took for his companions to gain their freedom. He might love Katherine but he also loved Will, Much and all the others and he could not be the one to hold them back from their freedom.

TWENTY-ONE

Constance hated these impromptu visits from the archbishop. The task of getting the household in order, ensuring that the buttery and pantry were stocked with enough food and instructing the cook to prepare some of his grace's favourite dishes was a mammoth effort barely recognised by a man who likely saw his visits as informal occasions and not inconvenient in the least.

It might not have been so bad if he didn't insist on travelling with a great retinue of followers. It wasn't as if Guiseley was all that far from York but the archbishop was a fearful man and all the more so since the increase of robberies in south Yorkshire that year. This time he had brought four canons and ten men-at-arms on loan to him from Thomas de Furnival who held the lordship of Sheffield. These fourteen men sat at table in the great hall and ate and drank their considerable fill while her husband and the archbishop sat at the head table, their heads bowed in close talk.

It was late afternoon and the meal had been going since noon. Constance was tired and fed up with the way long dinners and too much wine stretched the business of politics.

"You fellows may see to our horses," the archbishop said at last to his men. "I wish to leave before dusk and the sheriff and I have important matters to discuss."

The hint was taken and the canons and men-at-arms rose as one, emptying their goblets and, one or two stuffing their mouths with the last of the bread, filed out. Constance oversaw the clearing up of the dinner things. Her husband called for more wine and a servant hurried to refill their goblets.

When the last of the servants had departed the Great Hall, Constance loitered in the screens passage. The hall was quiet and motes of dust danced in the light from the high windows. The voices of her husband and his guest carried well in the echoing hall however discreet they considered themselves.

"I must confess, Simon," said the archbishop, "I am impressed by your faith in this scheme."

"Implying that you have little faith in it?"

"I don't say that. Only that it is a bold one. And you even sent your wife to meet with the outlaws! That is boldness in the extreme."

"It was her idea. I was just as surprised as you but she insisted. I don't think she finds life entertaining enough here in Guiseley."

Constance smiled. She was a dozen years younger than her husband and he had always thought her excitable and flighty. He was wrong. In truth her interests were as material as his and she would never have suggested going to meet with the outlaws had it not been known to her that John of Holderness had joined the band. The recent and devastating raid on her husband's prison wagon and the escape of Great John had the nobility in an uproar.

The bodies left on the Great North Road had embarrassed her husband but had pleased Constance. As soon as the news reached her ears she knew that she had a potential ally in the greenwood. John had always been a respectful servant and it was only the actions of that odious former steward that had seen him become an outlaw. Had she been able to intervene, she would have spoken in John's defence but the great oaf had taken to his heels as soon as he had knocked the steward on his backside. Her husband had been forced to raise the hue and cry immediately. A pity, but the good Lord has unseen plans for all the pieces on His game board.

"How exactly do you intend to convince this Robert Hood and his band to hand the silver over to you?" the archbishop continued. "Do you honestly expect them to turn up here with a wagon of coin and their caps in their hands? Why wouldn't they just keep the lot for themselves?"

"They won't be turning up at all," Simon said, "Because it won't be them stealing the silver."

"I don't follow."

"I have dispatched Hood's gang to Birkham Grange under the impression that they will find de Mowbray's men slumbering there. Instead they will find mine and de Aune's for we will have robbed de Mowbray of the strongbox earlier in the day."

"Then why send Hood and his gang to Birkham?" the archbishop asked. "I understand that you intend to trap them but do you not fear that they may overpower you and make off with the strongbox as you instructed them?"

"Their attack on the grange will keep de Aune's men busy. They may be able to kill or capture a few of the outlaws but in truth the attack will serve as a diversion so that two of my men – whom I have given secret orders to – can make off with the strongbox under cover of darkness."

"Leaving de Aune's men to think that some of Hood's gang stole it while in reality it will be on its way to you here at Guiseley with not so much as an ounce of suspicion landing upon your head! My apologies, sheriff. I underestimated your guile! But robbing de Aune? One of the king's most loyal supporters?

"De Aune is as much of a crook as de Mowbray or Lancaster for that matter. He may serve the king like a loyal hound but do not think that this silver he has recruited me into helping him steal will be sent to the crown. It will fill de Aune's coffers and his alone. I have a need of that silver, William. Yorkshire has a need of it. And I intend to get it."

Constance suddenly felt too frightened to move. If the archbishop had underestimated her husband then she had doubly done so. She had been wholly ignorant of his plan and she had even willingly played a part in it; a part that would see John and Robert Hood and all the rest of them put to the sword or hanged.

She couldn't let that happen. It wasn't just her liking for John. She didn't know why but she felt uncharacteristically fond of the brazen outlaw she had met in Barnsdale and was determined to steer him clear of the doomed path she had set him on.

The outlaws sat around their fire and discussed their plan of attack. Much was on lookout, circling the camp at a half-mile radius, keeping a watch for anybody straying from the Great North Road.

"If we leave it until after dark, there won't be enough light to see by," Will explained. "We won't be able to hit a barn door from two paces."

"You can barely do that anyway," said Anna with a smirk.

He bared his teeth at her in mock menace and pushed her with the flat of his boot playfully. Despite several archery tourneys, there had been no definite conclusion on who was the better shot and it remained a point of contention between the two.

"But a night raid will give us the edge of surprise," John said. "And we'll need all the advantage we can get."

"John's right," said Robert. "This won't be an easy robbery. We need to be in and out in a heartbeat else the knights in the barn will be roused to our attack and rush to counter it."

"All the more need for light to see what we are doing," Will protested.

"How are we to make our attack, anyway?" Katherine said. "Go in as one or make a divided attack?"

"Divided," Robert said. "You know the grange, John. Tell us how it's laid out."

"True, I passed by it once when I was roving with the Bradburn gang. The brewery itself is a small thatched building with perhaps a pair of windows looking south. A low wall surrounds it and I've a mind that its north and east sides are part of the brewery."

"Is the wall low enough to scale?"

"Aye, but why scale it when we can walk through the gate?"

"Because the gate will be watched and is the perfect place for a diversion. I want you, Will, Anna, Much and Rob Dyer to try and enter through it and not be too quiet about it. Halt when you are challenged and send a few arrows their way to make sure they know we mean business. Meanwhile, Katherine, Simon, Wat and I will scale the western wall and make for the brewery. We'll enter through one of the windows if the door is too stout. We'll kill anyone inside and when we have the strongbox over the wall, I'll blow my horn and you're to be off at once. Head north and we'll meet on the road."

"If you're company is to be doing the killing," Will said, "why not take little John here? He's more adept at cracking skulls. Why waste him on a diversion?"

There were laughs at the 'little' jest and John growled at Will.

"Because I want you two to work together," Robert explained. "If he saves your life as he saved mine, it might give you a touch more respect for the man."

"If he doesn't go berserk and kill us all, I'll be happy," Will grumbled.

"Much is back," said Simon. "And he's got company."

"What?" Robert exclaimed.

They leapt to their feet and seized their weapons. Strangers approaching the camp, in Much's company or not, could not be good news.

"It's the bloody sheriff's wife!" exclaimed Katherine, her face sour.

Three figures approached the camp; one was the stocky figure of Much and the other two were ladies astride horses.

"My lady," Robert said, placing a hand on the bridle of Constance's horse and offering his free hand so that she might dismount. "What brings you this deep into the greenwood?"

"She was on the road bellowing for Great John," said Much. "I could hear her a mile off."

"I was not bellowing, young man," said Constance testily. "I was merely trying to get somebody's attention."

"Well you got mine, and that of anybody else who might be within five miles."

"You were calling for me, my lady?" John asked. "What's the fuss? Are you alright?"

"I'm quite alright, John," Constance assured him. "But I bring ill news. My husband means to double-cross you all. The raid on Birkham Grange; it's a trap. It won't be de Mowbay's men there but the sheriff's reinforced by a detachment from William de Aune of Tickhill. They will be lying in wait for you."

"I bloody knew it!" said Will.

"But why have you and your handmaiden ridden out here to warn us?" Robert asked. "How can we trust you? How do we know that this is not a ruse in itself?"

"I swear by the rood that I speak the truth, Robert," said Constance. "Have I yet given you reason to distrust me?"

"She speaks truth," said John. "I can vouch for her honesty."

"But who can vouch for yours?" muttered Will.

John turned on Will. "Do you trust anyone at all?" he demanded.

"No one has ever given me enough cause to," Will replied.

"Quiet!" Robert commanded. He turned to Constance. "I believe you, my lady. But what is to be done? The offer of pardons is off the table I take it?"

"It was never on the table, I am afraid. Please believe me when I say that I knew nothing of my husband's treachery when I put the bargain to you. I thought his offer genuine."

"Rest assured that you share no part of your husband's blame. But tell me, was there ever any silver leaving Axholme for Pontefract? Or was that just bait for the trap?"

"Oh, the silver is real enough. That is the cause of my husband's uncharacteristic treachery. John de Mowbray is funding Lancaster's rebellion and William de Aune and my husband have plotted to steal the latest shipment of coin heading north. But my husband has gone so far as to double-cross de Aune. They are robbing de Mowbray's train this very day. The silver will be conducted to Birkham Grange but will much too closely guarded for you to even think of attempting to steal it so please don't try."

"Your husband was to use our assault as a cover for stealing the silver from de Aune's men, wasn't he?" Robert asked.

"Yes. And have you all hanged into the bargain."

"Is he still intending to receive the strongbox at Guiseley?"

"I don't think so. He rode out this morning telling me he had business in the East Riding but I overheard one of his men say something about the chapel at Wormesley."

"He must be intending to receive the stolen silver at Wormesley chapel," said John. "That's a secluded place, sure enough."

"Very well," said Robert. "You should return to Guiseley, my lady, else your absence be noticed. And I thank you for your warning."

She eyed him curiously. "What are you planning, Hood?"

"The less you know about it, the better."

"Yes, perhaps that is true. Come along, Bess, we must away. Do you think you might spare good Much here to escort us back to the road? We should be hopelessly lost otherwise."

"Of course. And we shall be moving camp after today so you need not try to remember your way."

She smiled. "I wouldn't dream of it. Thank you, Robert. Take care. My husband is not to be underestimated."

"Neither am I, my lady."

Once Much had led the two ladies through the woods in the direction of the road, the band turned to Robert, their faces expectant.

"Well?" asked Katherine. "What's the plan?"

"You heard the woman," Will replied. "It's a trap. There is no plan. Not anymore."

"Oh yes there is," Robert replied. "Our pardons may have been nothing but woodsmoke but I'm not about to lose out on five hundred pounds of silver."

TWENTY-TWO

The chapel at Wormesley was an isolated building facing open fields that broke into woodland to the south. A low wall ringed a small cemetery and its guardian was a fussy, thin-faced monk whose constant handwringing was beginning to irritate the sheriff.

"We'll be out of your beard as soon as my men arrive," the sheriff assured the nervous monk.

"It's not that I have no desire to aid the king's agents," the monk replied, "but this chapel is no place for armed troops. I've told your men several times already not to enter here with their sword belts buckled but they don't pay me a blind bit of notice!"

The sheriff rolled his eyes and headed for the door. His men were cooking meat over a small fire in the chapel grounds and the blue smoke drifted amongst the headstones. He found that he could not relax as they could. His nerves were taught to breaking point. Too much rode on whatever was happening at Birkham Grange. It wasn't just the thought of five hundred pounds coming his way that made him edgy. If his plan failed then William de Aune – one of the king's most powerful agents – would declare him a traitor. His career, not to mention his life, would very much be on a downward slide.

"Sire!" cried one of his men near the wall. "The wain approaches!"

"God be praised!" the sheriff exhaled. "And about bloody time too!"

The wain, agonizingly slow, creaked in through the gate and ground to a halt. The horses needed to be changed for the final leg of the journey to Guiseley and the sheriff wanted to make sure that nobody was following them. The two men who had conducted it from Birkham Grange got down from the wain and gladly accepted ale and meat.

"How went the raid?" the sheriff asked them, rubbing his hand over the brass and oak of the strongbox, fighting the temptation to have it broken open immediately so that he might set his eyes on his prize.

"Like a dream," replied one of the men. "The outlaws struck just as we were bedding down for the night. They hit the brewery just as we were told. Not a very subtle lot; we could hear the cries from the barn. Oderic kicked us all awake and marshalled us to reinforce de Aune's men. We hung back as you ordered and were on the road north before the battle was over. I don't know if de Aune's men were able to finish off the outlaws or if they took any alive."

"It is of little consequence," the sheriff replied. "Their death or capture was only ever the sugar on the pastry. This here is my main concern." He rubbed the dark oak longingly. He didn't recognise the two men who had brought it to him but Oderic had been in charge of hiring men for some time and knew how to pick the right ones for the job. These two were young but they had a quickness to them that suggested intelligence higher than the usual oafs Oderic hired for strongarm work.

The attack came suddenly and without warning. Arrows sailed down on the chapel grounds, striking two of his soldiers who fell with bloody shafts protruding from them.

"De Aune's men followed you, you fools!" the sheriff roared as he took cover by the wall. He peeped over it and saw a small group of ragtag figures in hooded green mantles and rough-spun wool approaching across the fields.

"No, it's the outlaws!" he said. "You let the outlaws track you here! Get the strongbox inside the chapel, quickly!"

The two carters hauled the box down from the wain and dragged it into the chapel. The sheriff followed them and shooed away the monk who scuttled off muttering prayers. The sheriff heaved the doors closed leaving the remainder of his men outside to deal with the oncoming outlaws.

It was then that he felt the blade pressed firmly against his Adam's apple.

"Move a muscle and I open your neck," said the man who held the dagger.

The sheriff could hear the intake of breath from the monk at this new outrage.

"You'd not dare spill blood in God's house!" the monk stammered.

Another blade was brandished by the second carter and the monk fell to praying at the altar.

"Who... who are you?" the sheriff managed, his Adam's apple bobbing painfully against the blade which felt like it had already drawn a little blood.

"The name's Robert Hood," said the voice in his ear. "And you are to tell your men outside to throw down their weapons and surrender."

"Watch out!" John bellowed as a crossbow bolt whizzed past and burrowed into earth a few feet away. "They're shooting back!"

"Did you expect them to stand there for a second volley?" Anna asked. "Get your head down, you great fool, and wait for them to finish before we advance!"

"Do you think we'll get to the wall before they reload?" Much asked.

"We'd better hope so!"

"How many are there?" Katherine asked.

"I saw three helmed heads but I bet there's more," said John. "Probably no more than five or six."

The crossbow bolts had ceased thudding into the ground near them and it was only a matter of time before the first of the soldiers would be ready to shoot again. Katherine scrambled to her feet and bolted towards the chapel.

"Hey! Wait!" cried Much.

Anna rose, her face fierce. "Rob and Will are in there," she said, "so stop cowering and fight!"

Much and John looked to each other and then back at Simon, Wat and Rob Dyer. They were being shown up by the women and it stung. As one, they rose and bounded in Katherine and Anna's wake, making sure to keep their heads down.

Katherine reached the wall just as a crossbowman poked his head up, his weapon primed. She slid to her knees as the bolt whistled overhead. Behind her, Much halted and nocked an arrow to his bowstring. He loosed and it struck the crossbowman in the eye, knocking him backwards with a cry.

Katherine cast aside her bow and scrambled over the wall. Two crossbowmen dropped their weapons and went for their blades. A third man loitered by the wain, his crossbow wavering to find a mark.

Katherine drew her sword. Stephen's lessons pushed to the forefront of her mind and she desperately tried to recall some of the more unorthodox advances he had taught her. This was her first real swordfight and she needed every advantage.

"Take 'em nice and slow, lass," said Anna's voice beside her. "I'm right here at your side."

The others had reached the wall and the crossbowman by the wain took aim.

"Watch out!" Katherine cried. "By the wain!"

The bolt loosed and the outlaws ducked. One of them – she later found out it was Wat – rose up quickly, drew back his bow and loosed a shaft which struck the crossbowman in the chest, piercing his maille hauberk and sinking him to his knees.

The swordsmen lunged and Katherine and Anna parried the blows frantically, the dull ringing of iron coursing through their forearms.

We outnumber them, thought Katherine in an effort to calm herself. *There are only two left and we are seven.*

John, Much and the other three scrambled over the wall but before they could join the fight, Anna cried; "Look out! More of them on our left!"

Katherine's saw that three more soldiers had crept around the chapel and were trying to outflank them.

Now they were seven against five and the sheriff's men were seasoned warriors with helms, maille and good swords. The outlaws had four blades between them. Simon, Wat and Rob had but bows and daggers.

Katherine's opponent grinned as he sidestepped her lunge and struck out with his blade, nearly connecting with her shoulder. He missed and the movement set him off balance. Katherine took advantage of his failed attack and slammed the hilt of her sword into his face.

His nose guard caught most of the force but his helm twisted under the impact and blood spurted from his broken lips and flattened nose. He cried out at the pain and in his distraction, did not have time to parry Katherine's swing which connected perfectly with his exposed neck, nearly severing his head. He went down gushing blood.

Old Stephen will be proud, she thought. *And Rob.*

There came shouts from the doorway to the chapel. All heads turned, friend and foe, to see the cause of the commotion.

The sheriff was the first to emerge from the chapel, Robert's dagger at his throat. Behind them lurked Will, the hood of a monk in one fist and a dagger in the other. The monk gibbered pitifully.

"Don't just gawp," the sheriff stammered. "Drop your weapons, you fools!"

The soldiers looked about dumbfounded, not sure how to proceed.

"Do it, damn you all!" the sheriff roared. "They mean to kill us both!"

The soldiers heeded their employer's cries and swords and daggers fell to the mud, belts unbuckled and hands raised in surrender.

"The silver is yours, you brigands!" the sheriff said bitterly. "You've won. I don't know how, but you've won!"

"Aye, we won," said Robert. "But not in the manner you're thinking." He released the sheriff from his grasp. "You've been had, Lord Sheriff!" He wandered over to the wain and produced a key from a pouch at his belt. He unlocked the great strongbox.

The sheriff peered inside. When he saw the fist-sized rocks within, his face paled. The outlaws laughed.

"This box was part of a haul we pinched weeks ago," said Robert. "The wain and horses too. We were even able to dress like your ruffians with all the gear we've been pinching off folk passing through Barnsdale."

"And the silver my wife instructed you to steal from Birkham Grange?" the sheriff demanded. "Where is that?"

Robert shrugged. "On its way to Tickhill for all I know. Without us to provide a distraction at Birkham Grange, your men won't have been able to sneak away with it. We didn't fall for your deception, sheriff, but you certainly fell for ours!"

Katherine smiled. It had been a devilish plan and Rob clearly delighted in taunting the sheriff with its intricacies. He would not, however, mention how they had come to know the name of Oderic; the sheriff's henchmen. That valuable piece of information had been provided by the sheriff's own wife and Rob wanted to keep Constance Ward's involvement a secret. Katherine didn't understand that; to her mind it would be the perfect salt in the wound to tell the sheriff exactly who had betrayed him.

The outlaws set about retrieving the surrendered weapons and cutting the horses from their harnesses. The wain would be abandoned but the horses were too valuable to leave behind.

"What now?" the sheriff asked. "What purpose did this assault on me serve? Neither of us has the silver. Will you butcher us all like the godless rogues you are?"

"Watch your tongue, sheriff," Robert replied. "I intend to deliver you whole. But if you test me, I may consider forfeiting some of the ransom by removing any part of you that annoys me."

"Ransom?" said the sheriff in a resigned but markedly relieved tone. "So that's what you cravens want! Well, how much am I worth then?"

Robert grinned at him. "By my estimate, about five-hundred pounds of silver."

The ransom demand was dispatched to Guiseley Hall and it was Constance herself who set about securing the funds. The trade was made on a small bridge that crossed the River Went upstream. The sheriff was in a foul mood after being roped to a tree all night. He had not been mistreated and the outlaws had even fed him but this had not eased his humiliation and rage.

They stood with him on one end of the bridge while Constance and a tall, sour-faced man-at-arms Robert took to be Oderic, approached on the other side. Two soldiers staggered behind them bearing a hefty chest between them.

Beyond the bridge, under the trees, several horses grazed. Astride one of them was a man in a rich riding cloak that barely concealed the robes of a man of the cloth and a high-ranking one at that. He gazed across the bridge at the outlaws intently as if studying them.

"You really should keep a better eye on your husband, Lady Constance," Robert said. "Luckily we came across him and were able to conduct him to you safely. Heaven knows what trouble he might have got himself into otherwise."

"Is it not enough that you are robbing me blind, must you insult me before my wife as well?" the sheriff grumbled. "Just make the exchange so that we can all return to our respective homes and pursuits."

"Very well, Hood," said Constance, the trace of a suppressed smile on her lips. "Here is your silver. You win this round."

"And don't think I won't forget it!" said the sheriff. "You've made a powerful enemy today, outlaw."

The chest was brought forward and opened. It contained five sacks that bulged promisingly. Will stooped and cut one of them open with his dagger. Coin glinted within.

"Do you wish to count it?" Constance asked.

"I think the word of a lady will suffice," Robert replied. He looked to the churchman in the shade of the trees. "Tell your friend that if he'd like to make my acquaintance he's more than welcome."

"He's happy where he is," Constance replied. "He has no wish to associate himself with outlaws. Paying the ransom of his friend is more than enough to soil his gentle sense of piety."

"Who is he?"

"The Archbishop of York. I had nobody else to turn to. Nobody of such means at any rate."

"William de Melton?"

"The same."

Robert's stare hardened. This was the man who had led his father and a good many others to their deaths at the Battle of Myton. He wished he was but a little closer...

"Let's be off," said Katherine. "Before we are betrayed once more." He eyes were fixed on Constance.

"My dear girl, I assure you that any deception was wholly on the part of my husband and his colleagues," said Constance, meeting her eyes. "I delivered my message to you as I was instructed. I consider my conscience clean."

"As do I," said Robert. "And now that there is nothing else to be done, I believe it is time for us to depart."

They took a roundabout way to ensure that none of the sheriff's men were following before striking south for camp.

With the campfires crackling and the fat of boar and venison hissing, they counted the silver. Lady Constance had been true to her word. It was five-hundred pounds exactly.

"We divide it equally, ten ways," said Robert.

"That's fifty pounds a head," said Little John with a low whistle.

"Rob," said Old Stephen, "I hardly deserve a share. You lot risked your lives for this silver. My days of accumulating plunder are long behind me."

"Nonsense," Robert said. "Everybody gets their share regardless of their role in the acquiring of it. We work as a band and what the band takes, the band shares."

"But what are we to do with such wealth?" Much asked. "It's more coin than I ever expected to see in a lifetime."

"I speak only of my own share," said Robert, "but I've a mind to use it to heal some of the hurts in this land caused by the Earl of Lancaster and his bullyboys. To reimburse men who lost their livelihoods like Wat here or had their families mistreated like Rob Dyer. Not all such people have the means to fight back as we do. A little coin here and there can relieve some of their suffering."

"Well, I'm all for that," said Rob Dyer.

"Aye, and me," said Wat.

"It's hardly my money anyway," said Old Stephen, "so those more unfortunate than us are welcome to it."

Much and Simon also agreed as did Katherine. John and Anna were unaccustomed to sharing anything they had fought tooth and nail for but they were also unused to fellowship and it was that which swayed their hearts on the matter. That just left Will who grumbled and complained as Robert had expected but he eventually decided that it would not do to be the only one who kept his portion for himself.

Katherine kissed Robert as the others began carving off slices of boar meat and passing around a wine jug. "I love you, Robert Hood," she said. "Your heart is as true as the truest arrow. And I'm sorry for harping on so about the Lady Constance. Her fine graces and comely features are things I will never have and I felt threatened by her. I couldn't bear to lose you to somebody else."

"You jest, girl. I'll never love another no matter how fine her airs might be. I'm yours and no other's. Don't ever worry about that."

They kissed, long and passionately. When they were done he asked her; "How do you feel about the Lady Constance now?"

"Forgotten her already," she said with a grin.

"That's good. Because I intend to send her the white palfrey as a gift."

The smile vanished from her face. Her petite features hardened. "What?"

He grinned sheepishly. "She helped us, Katherine. She could have done nothing and we'd have been captured and hanged most likely. She put herself in danger and went against her own husband to honour her word to us. That deserves some reward, surely?"

"She probably has a stable full of fine horses. What does she need with our generosity?"

"It's not generosity. It's thanks for saving our lives. And she did save them, Katherine. You might refuse to see it, but I don't. I shall send her the palfrey and consider all debts squared. We need never deal with her again. Would that please you?"

She folder her arms. "Immensely. But I would have rather sent her her husband's head than our finest horse."

Robert laughed and put his arm around her. He looked around at his band and smiled. He was not the only one. Wine and meat were plentiful, coin was in no short supply and the greenwood offered more freedom than any sealed bit of paper from the High

Sheriff could. They were homeless, lawless rogues but they were happy.

Even Will smiled these days. He sat with Anna, his arm around her as they shared a trencher of meat. It had not gone unnoticed that they had begun to share a shelter at night.

"You and I, Will and Anna," Robert said to Katherine. "We're becoming quite the little family out here in the greenwood."

"How about a story, Stephen?" Much said around a mouthful of bread.

"Aye, time for you to earn your share, old man!" said Robert. "Tell us what happened after the Battle of Lewes. How did you and Roger Godberd return to Nottinghamshire?"

"That's a far-off point in my tale," said Old Stephen. "And much occurred on the road to it." He worked his gums around a bone, sucking the marrow from it. "I'll tell what I can tonight and we shall see how far we get."

And with bellies full and hearts content, Old Stephen continued his tale.

FITT IV
THE VALE OF SLAUGHTER

"Up they started all in haste,
Their bows were smartly bent;
Our King was never so aghast,
He weened to have been shent"
- A Little Gest of Robin Hood

Herefordshire
Spring, 1265

TWENTY-THREE

A year had passed since our victory at Lewes and, although much had changed in the land, little of it is dramatic enough to bother going over in any great detail so I feel that a short summary will suffice.

Simon de Montfort was, to all intents and purposes, ruler of England. He made no public claim to this of course and Henry was still king in name but in name only. He was as a prized palfrey; hauled from court to castle, putting his seal to the new government's demands but it was very much de Montfort who held the reins. Henry was de Montfort's trump game piece; the very thing he had fought against was the very thing that now validated his rule.

The first parliament was held in late June and set about ratifying de Montfort's coup and setting up a new administration of which the king was but a figurehead. Four knights from each shire attended and were allowed to discuss general matters of state; a staggering acknowledgement of the common voice which had tongues wagging nervously in every royal court in Christendom. His position rendered constitutional and legal, de Montfort almost immediately headed west to put down opposition to his rule by the Marcher Lords led by Roger de Mortimer who still held out for their king.

There was still a very real threat of invasion from France. Queen Eleanor was intent on freeing her husband and son from bondage and was doing an impressive job of mounting an army against us in Flanders.

It was this threat that we spent the late summer of 1264 guarding against. Henry de Montfort, who was now lord of the Cinque Ports, ordered all his officials to marshal their ships and men at the port of Sandwich with the dual intent of defending the coast and stopping messages passing between the king's supporters in England and the Queen's agents in Bordeaux, Bayonne and Flanders. Nobody was allowed to enter or leave England without the new government's express permission and trade was badly affected.

We were sent to guard the coast while the fleets prowled the waters looking for rogue traders, spies and messengers. Over three hundred archers were stationed at Winchelsea, ready to rain death down on any invasion fleet trying to land on England's beaches.

We occasionally took to the water with more aggressive intentions. Godberd was eager to join the sailors of the Cinque Ports in their new pastime which can only be described as piracy as they boarded both English and foreign vessels, cutting the throats of those on board and seizing their cargoes. Henry de Montfort did little curb these activities and indeed became something of a pirate lord himself by seizing all wool on its way to Flanders earning the nickname 'the wool merchant'.

These raids weren't especially fruitful and I was glad to leave the coast before winter set in. It wasn't just the seasickness – which I discovered that I am particularly prone to – but seaborne robbery is twice as dangerous as hedge-robbing and I saw many men lose their footing and pitch into the rolling waves either to be dragged down by their sodden gambesons or have their skulls crushed between two listing vessels as they thudded together.

We wintered at Kenilworth; that great stronghold which had been given to Simon de Montfort by the king in happier times. Built of red sandstone, Kenilworth enjoys the reputation of being England's most impenetrable castle. This is largely due to the great manmade lake that surrounds it on three sides dammed by a causeway King John had built as part of his extensive refortifying a generation before.

The garrison's main charge was to guard the Lord Edward who had his own quarters in the keep. He had been transferred from Wallingford Castle to more secure surroundings after a rescue attempt led by none other than Warin de Bassingbourn had failed that November. Wallingford's garrison had threatened to send their captive over to his comrades using a mangonel if they did not disperse, which they ultimately decided would be wise.

But the prince's friends did not give up. The exiled royalists who had fled after Lewes had returned from France in secret and made their way to the west where Roger de Mortimer and the other Marcher Lords threatened Gloucester. The royalist ranks were swelled by the addition of a new ally who posed the greatest threat to de Montfort's rule.

Gilbert de Clare, Earl of Gloucester had fallen out with de Montfort over the division of the spoils. Resentful of the gains made by de Montfort's sons Henry and Simon the Younger, de Clare challenged them to a tourney at Dunstable. The brash de Montforts eagerly accepted and all expected the violence to go beyond the boundaries of sport. De Montfort had feared this too and had called the whole thing off, enraging de Clare who returned to his lands in the Marches and renewed his association with his neighbour Roger de Mortimer.

The threat in the west required urgent attention and de Montfort marshalled his forces once more and set out for Hereford where he intended to form a buffer between de Mortimer and de Clare. Not about to leave his hostages behind, even in England's strongest castle, de Montfort brought the king and Edward with him.

We had recently found ourselves without a lord after de Ferrers's latest and most severe fall from grace. Things had never fully healed between de Ferrers and de Montfort and his absence at Lewes only added to the resentment de Montfort and the other barons bore him. He had been summoned to parliament that January and ordered to hand over Peveril Castle. De Montfort intended to use it as a bartering chip in his negotiations with the papal legate. Having already lost Nottingham after so recently acquiring it, de Ferrers was reluctant to part with yet more of his inheritance which he had fought so hard for and told de Montfort in no uncertain terms of his intention to keep Peveril.

The following month de Montfort had de Ferrers arrested on charges of 'diverse trespasses' and incarcerated in the Tower of London. Since then we had become archers on permanent loan to whoever required our services. Shuttled between coast and castle we were kept fed and paid but it was a meandering, aimless life. Our latest charge was to guard the king and his son and it was in the cellars of Hereford Castle that Roger, Wyotus, Richard and I made merry while one of the most important developments in the Barons' War began over our heads.

"Would that we could get to him!" Richard exclaimed, spilling ale from his leather drinking jack as he perched precariously on a barrel. "But while we sit here in the king's company, our lord sits in England's strongest gaol!"

"Aye, as well consider breaking into Avalon, for its key is no less difficult to procure," agreed Wyotus.

Roger swigged from his jack, droplets of ale glistening on his surly, unshaven face. "It's his own damned fault for wandering into de Montfort's trap. He has precious few friends in parliament and his summons was a blatant attempt to strip him of his lands. It was a lamb to the slaughter, politically speaking. Even John de Grey handed Nottingham over to the new government, knowing that he was beaten."

"If he were to escape or be released," I said, "what would he do? Do you think he would side with the king as Gloucester did?"

"De Ferrers would rather die than sup with royalists," Roger snorted. "He may be a fool and a greedy one at that, but there is no man in Christendom he hates more than the Lord Edward. That hatred alone will keep him on the baronial side, at least nominally. He is no Gilbert de Clare to switch sides out of spite."

"And so, he will rot in the Tower while we sit here scratching our arses and babysitting the king and his whelp," said Richard.

The boredom was taking its toll on all of us and on Roger in particular. Since our return from the Cinque Ports our lives had reverted to the monotony of garrison routine, first at Kenilworth and now at Hereford. We didn't even dare attempt any poaching as the woodland without the castle was unknown to us and forays from the royalists at Bristol to the south and Roger de Mortimer's castle at Wigmore to the north were common.

Roger itched to be away but our brief career as pirates had not made him a rich man and with his old patron in gaol there was precious little for him to do but what he was told. He could not return home emptyhanded, so we remained with our sergeant at the disposal of de Montfort.

There was a constant flow of men and supplies between Hereford Castle and the garrisoned town of Gloucester to the south east. Discipline was lax and there was much confusion. Naturally we flouted the circumstances and it was Margot – a chambermaid I had taken a liking to – who had provided us with the key to the cellars on that hot, lazy afternoon.

"What time of the day is it?" Richard asked.

"I think I heard the bells for none not long ago," Wyotus replied.

"Christ, how ale washes away the day! We'll be up on the walls before long."

"If I never stand atop a battlement again I'll die a happy man," Roger grumbled. "I've had my fill of castles and my lungs yearn for free air." He rose suddenly, as if struck by an epiphany. "Let's ride out! I ache for a good gallop and the feel of the wind on my face!"

"What for? asked Richard. "A raid? A hunt?"

"Desert again?" I asked hopefully, though not believing it for a second.

"Just a ride," Roger replied. "We'll be back before our shift beings. Come! The stables!"

We stumbled out of the cellar and bolted the door behind us. I reminded myself to return the key to Margot at the first opportunity or it would go very ill for her. She was a lovely girl and, although we had only known each other for less than a month, I had developed some feelings for her I could not readily explain.

We tried our best to appear sober as we staggered upstairs and lurched out into the hot sunlight which was blinding after spending the afternoon in the dim and cool cellar. I averted my eyes from the glint of the sun off the helms of the soldiers on the bailey wall.

Roger strode ahead, making for the stables. He was a different man to the stern sergeant I had first met at Nottingham Castle what felt like a lifetime ago. He was fed up with garrison life, fed up with taking orders and fed up with being so far from his home and children, poor and at the service of men he loathed. He was a risktaker and a lusty thief out for all he could take and we loved him for it.

We found fewer horses in the stables than usual and a young groom was leading two beasts – a chestnut rouncey and a fine grey charger – out by their bridles. I caught a glimpse of blue skirts at the far end of the stables and hurried after them.

I caught Margot as she left the building and drew her to me, pulling her into the shade of the eaves. "Hello, dearest," I whispered before kissing her quickly on the mouth. She slapped me but it was a playful tap.

"Stop it, you fool, you'll have us both pilloried! And you reek of ale!"

"My friends extend their gratitude," I said, stifling a hiccup. I pressed the key into the palm of her hand. "What's a chambermaid doing lurking about in the stables anyway? Hasn't the good Thomas de Clare got a chamber pot that needs emptying? Over his head preferably?"

Thomas de Clare was the brother of the turncoat Earl of Gloucester. De Montfort still trusted him despite his close friendship with Edward. The two were inseparable and we thought de Montfort a fool for allowing their friendship to continue. Edward had enough friends on the outside. It was folly to let him have one on the inside too.

"He and the Lord Edward have ridden out this afternoon," Margot replied. "His Royal Highness feels a little cooped up and wished to make sure his horsemanship is not being neglected."

"He enjoys a remarkable amount of freedom for one supposedly under house arrest," I said, bitterly. I had not forgotten the slaughter he had inflicted on the Londoners at Lewes and I loathed being in the same castle as him. "But you have not answered my question. What are you doing here? If I find that you have been carrying on with that groom I just saw, I'll cleave his skull for him."

I was joking but Margot was not in a mood for humour. "I was told to send that groom out with a spare horse. I didn't ask questions."

"Told by whom?" Margot was acting passing strange and my interest was piqued. There was so little diversion within Hereford's walls.

"Stephen, please!" she pleaded.

She was holding something back and I became alarmed that somebody might have been laying some pressure on her. I had become protective of her and the drink made me even keener to prove my bravado. "Tell me," I said. "If somebody is threatening you..."

"No, it's not that..." she began.

"Stephen, come on!" I heard Roger bark from within the stables. "Daylight's wasting!"

"What is it?" I said. "What's going on?"

"De Clare told me to send the boy with the horse. He said to wait until after none. That's what the message said anyway..."

"Message? What message?"

"I can't tell you any more, Stephen, please!"

"Margot, you know that it is my duty to guard the Lord Edward. If you know anything about any attempt to rescue him you have to tell me. I won't let my feelings for you save you if you lie to me now." I was bluffing and I felt ashamed afterwards. I would never have turned her in no matter what she knew. My loyalty to de Montfort only stretched as far as the coin, bread and ale lasted but I was determined to get to the bottom of this.

She looked at the ground. "A man in the town gives me messages to take to de Clare. He pays me well. I swear, Stephen, I know of no plot to rescue Edward!"

"What man is this? Does he say who he is?"

"He's a knight. His mistress is Maud de Mortimer."

"Maud de Mortimer!" I exclaimed. "Roger de Mortimer's wife?"

"That's all I know, Stephen. You won't tell on me, will you?"

"No, I won't, Margot. I promise. Where are Edward and de Clare now?"

"Widemarsh Common."

I kissed her on the forehead. "Now get going and say nothing of this to anyone."

She hurried off and I went back inside to see my companions saddled up and champing at the bit to get going.

"She's a sweet one, Stephen," Richard said. "You're lucky I didn't get to her first!"

I ignored him. "Thomas de Clare has been in correspondence with Lady de Mortimer," I told them.

"What?" Roger exclaimed. "Did that girl just tell you...?"

"I beg you all not to speak of her," I said. "She did her duty in telling me what she overheard and that is where her involvement ends. I want her name left out of any future discussion on the matter. De Clare had her send out that groom with a fresh charger to Widemarsh Common. That's where Edward is riding."

"This reeks of treachery!" said Roger. "Let's be off! If we can prevent Edward's escape, we will be well rewarded!"

We thundered across the drawbridge and headed north through the town. As we came upon Widemarsh Common we could see a cluster of grooms and attendants on the grass some yards from the woods. One of them held the reins of a grey charger. We galloped towards them but before we had crossed half the distance, a group of riders emerged from the trees on foaming and gasping mounts. We could only hear a muffle of voices at that distance but the men were in high spirits. Some of them dismounted and handed their reins to their attendants.

I could spot Edward half a mile off. Even back then people already referred to him as 'Longshanks' due to his tall and athletic frame. He was considered comely by the ladies and his dark hair fell shoulder length in a cascade of enviable curls. I saw him swing up into the saddle of the grey charger and I spurred my own horse.

"Come on!" I yelled to my companions.

Edward wheeled his mount around and several of his companions joined him as he bolted for the trees at a fast gallop. There were cries of alarm from the grooms and knights who had dismounted as they struggled frantically to scramble back into their saddles and give chase. By the time they were away, Edward, Thomas de Clare and several other knights had vanished into the woods.

We joined the chase, more for appearances than anything else. Our presence on the common may be hard to explain and we had to give some show of trying to stop the fleeing prince, however futile it might be. The mounts of Edward's pursuers were worn out and the prince was on a fresh charger.

The day was hot and the horses soon tired. We caught up with the other pursuers in a clearing but the chase had already been lost.

"Blast the bugger!" Roger exclaimed as we slowed to a canter.

There were curses all around for we all knew what this appalling event portended. With Edward free the royalists would have a strong figurehead to rally around. And Longshanks was a cunning strategist who would not miss a trick in organising de Montfort's enemies into a lethal assault on him.

Our world had so recently changed that we could scarcely bear it to change once more. And it was about to change suddenly and decisively for the worse.

TWENTY-FOUR

De Montfort was predictably enraged by the escape of his prized hostage. His anger was no doubt fuelled by the fear that we all shared. Longshanks would descend upon us in a hailstorm of vengeance for every single sight he had suffered since the abuse of his mother as she had fled London to the incarceration of he and his father.

Our presence on Widemarsh Common was investigated and we were summoned to an audience with de Montfort himself. We largely stuck to the truth. We had simply wished to take the air and familiarise ourselves with the lands surrounding the castle. We had heard that Widemarsh Common offered good riding and, upon witnessing Edward's escape, had given chase like the loyal soldiers we were.

We were believed and dismissed but kept under close watch by the castellan who was not so trusting as de Montfort. He knew there was more to our story and, in the absence of further proceedings, he doubled our watches as punishment for taking horses that did not belong to us.

As we had predicted, life at Hereford Castle soon changed. In early June, Edward, bolstered by Gilbert de Clare, Roger de Mortimer and John de Giffard (another recent turncoat), attacked and occupied Worcester, burning the bridge across the River Severn. We all saw the danger; Edward would burn every bridge in order to keep us isolated from the rest of England and cut off any hope of reinforcements. If he managed to pen us on the western bank of the Severn we would be finished.

De Montfort immediately made plans to move his army to Gloucester and escape across the river at the recently rebuilt bridge there. Edward was quick off the mark and besieged the town before de Montfort even got the army up on its feet. With memories of the last siege of Gloucester all too recent in my mind, I was not the only one who saw history beginning to repeat itself.

Our only other hope of crossing the Severn lay at Newport some fifty miles to the south and only then if de Montfort could muster enough boats to carry his army across. Requests for vessels were dispatched across the river to Bristol where, although the castle was royalist, the town's populace were decidedly baronial.

I had seen little of Margot since Edward's escape. As far as my companions were concerned, she had merely overheard some treachery in her master's chambers and dutifully passed the information on to me. I was the only person in the whole castle who knew of her part in the matter.

I found myself unable to blame her for I was not held to the baronial cause beyond its ability to feed and pay me. But I knew few would share my opinion of her – even my comrades who wanted to be long gone from Hereford, de Montfort and whatever new hostilities the coming days might bring. For the lowly soldier, a traitor was a traitor and I feared for her safety, whatever she might have done.

Preparations were well underway for the march south when I saw what I thought to be the last of her.

Roger and the rest of us were given orders to assist in stripping the town of any food and equipment that might sustain the army on the move and to keep civilian protest suppressed. Salted meat, wine and grain were piled into carts and taken into the castle leaving the populace with little to feed themselves. It was on the eastern outskirts of the town that I saw Margot waiting with a destrier, a courser and a packhorse loaded with equipment. She wore a hooded cloak but I recognised her stance and the way she grasped her left elbow whenever she was nervous. Her eyes widened as I approached.

"What are you doing here?" she asked me.

"De Montfort has us robbing the town blind," I replied. "We're moving out in a matter of days. What are you up to?"

"Also moving out. I've found employment elsewhere."

"You were just going to leave without saying goodbye?" I felt crushed and was embarrassed to show it.

"It is for the best."

"I would have been deeply wounded had I never had the chance to see you again."

"You said yourself; you are leaving in a matter of days."

"I would have sought you out first. I would have said goodbye."

"Well, this is goodbye then."

I was hurt by her coldness. "Where are you going? Whose equipment is this?"

"Stephen, you already know too much about me. I beg of you, do not pry further. It would serve neither of us. I thank you for your silence and your love... if it can be called that?"

"It can. Yes, I love you." I kissed her for the last time and we held the embrace for as long as we dared. She pulled away and looked nervously beyond the dipping heads of the horses at a tavern on the other side of the street as if expecting somebody to come through its door towards us at any moment.

While her back was to me I lifted the coverings on the packhorse and caught a glimpse of weapons and a shield emblazoned with a crest I was unfamiliar with. It had three gold cross-crosslets fitchee on a field of red with a gold chief running across the top edge. I replaced the cover as she looked back.

"Go now, Stephen. Don't stay here. Thank you for everything and know that you have my love, always."

I bowed slightly and turned from her, keeping my last glimpse of her beauty in my mind for as long as I could manage, willing it to be frozen in memory forever. When I rounded the corner, I halted and looked back, hidden by the shade of the jetties.

A man had emerged from the tavern and was making his way to Margot. He had dark hair and wore good mail with a blue surcoat that showed no crest. He was a knight, that much was clear and I presumed that the equipment belonged to him.

He helped Margot up into the saddle of the courser before mounting the destrier. With the packhorse in tow they headed off towards the east gate.

"Looks like she's given you the slip," said Wyotus as I re-joined my comrades. "Sorry, Stephen. We could see that you liked her."

"Oh, aye," I replied with a shrug. "Enough for a tumble in the hay. Pay it no mind. I'll find another strumpet in Monmouth or Newport. It will be my last farewell to this bloody part of the country. I'll not return across the Severn again in my lifetime if I can help it."

"Too right, that," said Richard. "I've seen enough Welshmen, grim keeps and sour fishwives to last a lifetime."

When we got back to the castle we learned that we were moving out at dawn. There was to be little sleep, though God knows how precious it is to an army on the cusp of a long march. There was mail to polish, blades to sharpen, armour and helms to be repaired not to mention horses to be shod and wains to be loaded before any of us could get a bite to eat and a lie down. Even then, sleep rarely comes easily to men whose future hangs upon the politics of war.

I made my way to the clerk's quarters in the keep while Roger and the others were bedding down. I took a candle to light my way down the dim stone corridors to a pokey apartment with a fireplace and a great many heavy chests and sturdy shelves. At the rear of the chamber was a small four poster bed where rumpled sheets could be seen behind pale drapes. A sloped desk with two tiers overflowing with scrolls and writing implements occupied the centre of the room and a man in long robes and a silk cap sat at it, his feather making small scratching sounds on the parchment.

"Can I help you?" he said, looking up at me with some irritation. He glanced at my attire and must have wondered why a lowly soldier was coming to visit him late in the evening. It amused me to think that I had once been a man like him; squirreled away in a cell copying texts and dulling my eyes by flickering candle light. I wondered if I would ever have recognised myself as I stood there in a dirty gambeson, a well-used dagger at my side and more scars on my body than I have ever cared to count.

"I hope so," I told the clerk. "I can see that you are busy but I have a simple question I wish to put to you."

He pinched the bridge of his nose and exhaled heavily. "Then I suppose you had better do so, my eyes could do with a rest at any rate." He was what I considered an elderly man back then although his age was nothing approaching mine now.

"You have tomes the heralds use to identify the crests of knights?" I asked him.

"Several," he replied.

"And no matter how lowly the knight, his family crest would be recorded somewhere?"

"That's the idea. What crest is it you are looking for?"

"A red field. Three cross-crosslets fitchee in gold. And a gold chief."

He rubbed his beard and gazed thoughtfully at a spider making is web in the eaves above the door. "Not one I know off the top of my head, although it does have a ring to it. Just a minute."

With a slow, painful movement he rose from his seat and moved across the room to a chest. He opened it and inside I could see many leather-bound tomes and scrolls of yellowed vellum. He fished around inside for a moment before triumphantly bringing out a hefty volume.

"Here we are! I believe this is the one we are looking for."

He pushed aside some scrolls and placed the book on his desk. Crests passed my eyes in bright flashes of colour as he rifled the pages before stopping at one in particular, his ink-stained forefinger hovering over the illustrations.

"Ah! The crest of the de Arderne family."

"Never heard of them."

"Not a powerful family or a particularly well-known one. Their current lord is Ralph de Arderne. He was Sheriff of Exeter back in the 1250s as I recall. Has a son by that name too though I can't tell you much about him."

"You've told me all I need to know, thank you." I left him and returned to my comrades to catch what little sleep I could before the march south.

The following month was one of the most brutal we had yet seen. It was a month of ceaseless marching, uncertainty and constant danger. De Montfort's plan to cross the Severn at Newport faced immediate opposition from the castle that overlooked the River Usk that joined the Severn. There was no way past without coming into conflict with the troops of John de Giffard. De Giffard now held Usk Castle for his fellow turncoat Gilbert de Clare who stood between us and London.

De Giffard did not lead a particularly strong force but it was enough to bar the way to the coast. De Montfort decided on attacking Usk Castle which would have the dual result of breaking through de Giffard's forces and luring de Clare back west, leaving the London road open for Simon the Younger to head west with reinforcements.

We took the castle without many losses but de Montfort was faced with a dilemma; leave a garrison to hold it or abandon it to Edward's forces who would soon be hot on our heels from their recent victory at Gloucester? It was decided that no garrison would remain behind to face Edward's fury alone. Our brief siege had served its purpose – the road to Newport was clear – and de Montfort would need every man ready to fight when we joined with his son east of the Severn.

We reached Newport at the beginning of July. We were sent down to the coast to escort the incoming ships from Bristol but as we reached the silty mudflats where the Usk flows into the Severn, we saw our ships under attack by three galleys carrying archers from upriver.

"Longshanks's men from Gloucester!" Roger said with a curse. "He must have learned of de Montfort's message to Bristol."

The tide was coming in and the mudflats were shrinking. The ships from Bristol struggled to outrun the galleys and reach the mouth of the Usk where the rising tide would carry them in. Fire arrows sailed forth from the galleys, thudding into the decks of de Montfort's ships, setting caulking and sail aflame. We watched with sinking hearts as our potential fleet was sunk, one by one.

"If we can get across to that spit of land yonder," said Roger, pointing across the mud to a grassy peninsular on the eastern bank of the Usk, "we can give our vessels some aid."

We had taken a small boat down to the coast and carried with us our bows and arrow bags. We wouldn't be able to save much of the fleet but we might be able to persuade the royalists not to follow whatever was left of it up the Usk to Newport.

We pushed our little vessel out into the gradually widening river and rowed across. By the time we reached the peninsular the ships from Bristol were just entering the mouth of the Usk and were within hailing distance. Two at the rear were in flames and we could feel their heat over the water.

The royalists continued to shoot as they drifted closer to our position and we strung our bows.

"We'll have a fun time of it if they decide to beach them on this side of the river to see us off," Richard said.

"You're not wrong," said Roger, "but by God we need to save some of those ships or we'll never leave the Marches alive."

We began sending volleys of arrows towards the galleys and I was reminded of those dreadful piratical days after the Battle of Lewes and was glad that I had solid ground beneath my feet this time rather than a rolling deck.

We saw archers fall as our arrows thudded into wood, gambeson and flesh. Some of them shot back at us but the arrows went wide. Our arrow bags grew light as we shot volley after volley and as the galleys drifted closer I began to believe that they would indeed land on the mud and put us to the flight or the sword.

Mercifully, with the remnants of the Bristol fleet winding their way up the Usk towards Newport and the mouth of the river obstructed by flaming wreckage from the two burning ships which had foundered and begun to sink, the royalists decided that they had done enough damage and began to fall back. We hurled jeers and insults in their wake as they turned about, heading back up the Severn towards Gloucester.

Only three ships had survived and it was a crushing blow to de Montfort and every man under his command. Roger spat fire at this latest obstacle. Without a fleet and with hostiles closing in from the northeast, there was only one direction left open to us.

"We're moving northwest," said Roger to us after a briefing the following day.

"What, into Wales?" I asked.

"Aye. Into Wales. Prince Llewellyn won't harm us. Not while he is engaged to de Montfort's daughter."

The proposed marriage between the Welsh rebel and Eleanor de Montfort had surprised us all and yet it is often the way to seal alliances. Still, the thought of traipsing into the Welsh mountains did not fill us with a great deal of hope.

"The plan is to make for Hereford in a roundabout way that will not bring us into contact with Longshanks or de Giffard's forces," Roger continued. "Though what we are supposed to do once we are back at Hereford I have no idea."

"It's a stronger castle at least," said Wyotus hopefully.

"We're going around in bloody circles," Roger grumbled.

On the 7th of July we burned the bridge across the Usk to secure our rear and plunged northwest, making first for Pontypool and then Abergavenny. We marched for ten days on largely empty stomachs. Only the local diet of milk and mutton was available to us and in small quantities that left us aching for good English bread. As we passed into the Black Mountains we felt under constant surveillance. Welsh scouts were spotted on numerous occasions and we were glad to reach the small market town of Gelli on the other side. From there we headed east and made Hereford Castle before the end of the month.

TWENTY-FIVE

Our fears of being trapped at Hereford with all escape routes cut off were eased by a slim but fragile ray of hope. Upon arrival we learned that Simon the Younger was on his way west and had made it as far as Winchester. He had made painfully slow progress but he was finally close enough to pose a threat to the royalists. If he reached Oxford he would be within striking distance of Gloucester but Roger dismissed this notion.

"He'll make for Kenilworth," he said. "Only safe place for him to go. He can't take Gloucester, however much he'd like to. It's a tough nut to crack and Longshanks has left a sizable garrison."

We were drinking ale around a smouldering cooking fire in the middle bailey. Several other sergeants were with us along with a knight – whose name I cannot recall – who regularly sat in on de Montfort's councils.

"With Simon the Younger at Kenilworth and us at Bristol – *if* we ever cross that damned river – Longshanks will be caught between hammer and anvil," said the knight.

"How large is Simon's force?" Roger asked the knight. "Are they strong enough to hold Kenilworth against a siege?"

The knight sucked at his ale and winced a little at its sourness. "Strong enough for that, aye. Let's see. Of the barons he has Robert de Vere, Gilbert de Gaunt, William de Munchensy, Richard de Grey, Adam de Newmarket, Baldwin Wake, Walter de

Colville and Hugh de Neville. There are plenty of knights too..." and he proceeded to reel off a list of knights he knew personally or by reputation. My ears suddenly pricked up at one of them and I started almost violently. "Ralph de Arderne?" I asked, rudely interrupting the knight who looked at me warily. "The elder or the younger?" I added.

"The younger," the knight replied. "Don't know him personally although I did meet his father on one occasion. Let's hope he's as good with a sword as that old warhorse."

I quietened down and felt the eyes of my comrades on me. When we broke up to go to our beds I spoke to Roger in private.

"Ralph de Arderne," I told him. "I am fairly sure that he is the traitor who organised Longshanks's escape."

Roger regarded me in the fading light, trying to read my face. "How do you know this?"

"Margot told me that he was involved, although she did not say how."

"And you're just telling me this now?" His eyes burned dangerously in the dark.

"He left Hereford within days of the escape," I protested. "I thought it not important."

"Not important?" Roger snarled. "Not important that a spy was left to roam free through the ranks of de Montfort's army? Now he's making for Kenilworth where who knows what his next scheme will entail? He could jeopardise the entire campaign!"

I didn't know what else to tell him and decided to keep quiet. I was already finding it difficult to keep track of all my lies. The less said the better. I did not want to put Margot – wherever she was – in danger and yet I could not fail to share my knowledge of a traitor in Simon the Younger's army.

"De Montfort will have to be told," said Roger rubbing his beard. "I don't know how that will go for you, Stephen. He will not likely be pleased by your silence."

"Will you help me?" I asked him.

"Aye, I'll do what I can, even though I know you're still not telling me everything." His eyes refused to leave mine as if he thought he might burn the truth out of me with them. "I'll help you this one time, Stephen because you're a good man who looks out for his comrades. But I swear, if you spin another lie of this magnitude and don't tell me, I'll do de Montfort's job for him and string you up myself."

Roger was absolutely right; de Montfort was not at all pleased. I was invited to present my information to him in the Great Hall of the keep and several other barons were present, their faces unreadable by the flickering candlelight.

"And I must enquire how a common archer came by this information," de Montfort said slowly, his fingers steepled, the tips of the indexes touching his bottom lip.

"It was passed to me by the chambermaid of Thomas de Clare," I said. "She overheard him discussing a spy for Roger de Mortimer. She later learned that the spy was one Ralph de Arderne; a knight in your son's army."

"Fetch this chambermaid to me immediately," de Montfort said.

"She is no longer in employment at Hereford, sire," I said. "She left before we marched for Newport."

"And where did she go?"

"Of that I am not certain, sire."

"Her name? You know that, I trust?"

"Margot, sire. I know nothing more."

De Montfort looked to the castle steward who sat beside him. "Check this man's story. Find out all you can about this Margot." He turned his attention back to me. "The issue of your relationship with one of the castle's chambermaids will have to wait for another time." As he said this, his eyes narrowed and I felt as if I was being judged by God himself. De Montfort was known to be as pious as King Henry. "Right now, I need to act on this information. This morning I received word that my son has entered Kenilworth Castle. This has prompted the Lord Edward to abandon Gloucester and return to his primary base at Worcester. If this traitor – this Ralph de Arderne – is with my son then he is in danger. All England is in danger."

"What can we do, sire?" asked one of the barons. "Stuck on this side of the Severn we cannot march for Kenilworth. Not with Edward's army standing between us and them."

"We cannot cross the Severn, no," de Montfort replied. "But a small company might make it across undetected. They could cut across country and ford the Severn at Kempsey. They could make Kenilworth within a couple of days. Mounted, of course."

He looked at me and the corner of his mouth curled into a slight smile despite the gravity of the situation. "You will have your chance at redemption, archer. Godberd, you will go too along with however many men you see fit. I will give you something to show my son that I sent you. You are to seek an audience with him at once and expose this traitor."

I felt Roger stiffen beside me and knew I would be for it as soon as we were exited the keep. "Yes, sire," he said. When do we leave?"

"Immediately. I will have the quartermaster provide you with the swiftest horses in the castle. Do not tarry, do not stop. Let nothing slow you. Kill the beasts if you have to but get this message to my son quickly at all costs."

Once we had emerged into the middle bailey Roger clasped me around the neck with a powerful fist. I thought he meant to strangle me but he hugged me close and whooped with exhilaration.

"You are a gem, Stephen!" he cried. "By tonight we will be on the other side of the Severn galloping free!"

"You're not angry?" I asked.

"Couldn't be happier! How hard have we all tried to find our way out of this mess? How long have we marched and fought and marched again, around in circles looking for a way out? And now you, through your happy cavorting with the castle staff, have found us one! We can leave this stinking army to its fate in the Marches and make our fortunes back in merry old England!"

The others, to my surprise, were just as joyous at the proposed mission. I suppose I had been too concerned with my own silence about Margot's treachery and had felt the danger of discovery too close for too long that I had not considered the implications of what I knew. But now that all (or almost all) was in the open and a new path had opened before us, I felt a release and was able to join my comrades in their levity.

The team consisted of five men; Godberd and I, Geoffrey, Richard and Wyotus. We had become a tight unit, loyal to each other because of what we had experienced together since we had left Nottingham. It was a loyalty forged in blood.

We set out that afternoon and said not a word to anybody. De Montfort had proven good on the horses; they were fine beasts and we made good time, reaching the River Severn by nightfall. The village of Clevelode in the manor of Kempsey is four or five miles south of Worcester and as we approached the sluggish waters beneath the moonlit treetops we grew uneasy at our close proximity to Longshanks's army. There were undoubtedly scout patrols about not to mention villagers who might turn us in.

With the river spray flashing like diamonds around our ankles, we pressed our horses across the ford and climbed the bank on the other side. Our elated spirits were raised yet higher with the warm dawn that set the sky on fire before us, dazzling in its promise.

It was a hot day and the sun was relentless. We reached Kenilworth late afternoon and could see Simon the Younger's army encamped on the shores of the mere with the great red castle reflected in those still waters. Men bathed and rollicked in the shallows and the sight made us want to join them for we were sweaty, dusty and sore from our journey.

"He must have gathered a great deal of men," said Wyotus. "Too many to house within the castle walls."

We discovered that the encamped army was even larger than it appeared as we wandered between the tents looking for somebody who could arrange an audience with Simon the Younger. As well as the lakeside camp, the baronial force had occupied most the town; commandeering inns and town houses where men lay about drinking, dicing and whoring.

"I don't think much of the discipline around here," said Roger with a frown. "We've just wandered right into their midst entirely unchallenged. No wonder a spy operates here with ease."

We were eventually directed to Simon the Younger and were astounded to learn that he had not taken up residence within the castle. He had set up camp at the priory just as the king had done at Lewes, preferring comfort over security.

"Silly bastard!" said Roger. "God help them all if Longshanks decides to attack!"

We did not find the situation any better within the priory grounds. Simon's quarters consisted of a tent in the shade of the trees and the soldiers who were supposed to be on guard were drunk and had women in their laps.

"Were the blazes is de Montfort?" Roger exclaimed in sheer exasperation.

"Who the hell are you?" asked one of the guards, shoving the whore from him as he stumbled to his feet, stooping to buckle his sword belt.

"I'm Roger Godberd sent from the Earl of Leicester at Hereford. I have an important message for his son and require an immediate audience." He showed the letter de Montfort had sent with us and the guard squinted as he inspected its seal.

Simon the Younger was summoned from his tent and we were received in the open beneath the splayed arms of an oak tree. Wine was provided and we drank gratefully, quenching our dry throats while Simon read the letter.

"This de Arderne character," he said at last. "Do you know him by sight?"

Godberd looked to me.

"I believe I do, sire," I said. "I saw him once at a distance. And I know his sigil."

"Then I suggest you start searching the town for him. Bring him to me when you have him."

Roger blinked. "Don't you know where he is?"

Simon frowned at him. "I don't keep tabs on every minor knight under my standard. He could be anywhere."

"It might take us days to find him," Roger replied. "Can you not rouse the camp? Get everybody looking for him?"

"Look around you, man. My army is currently enjoying a much-needed rest after a hard march. Half of them are drunk and the other half nurse hangovers from last night. It would not go over well with them if I started kicking them into action and spoiling their fun."

Roger tensed and I could see that he was livid. "This spy could be our undoing, sire. I would have thought that our news might have been taken a little more seriously."

"Careful, stringfinger," said Simon dangerously. "I am in no mood to argue with common soldiers. This de Arderne fellow may prove a nuisance, I am sure. But there is very little damage he can do at present. The Lord Edward's army is at Worcester and on the morrow, I shall galvanise my own force into a formidable threat to him. But for the present, I intend to let them recover their strength and distract their minds a little."

"Very well, sire," said Roger and we left the priory to begin scouring the town for Ralph de Arderne.

"That we should have to do his bloody job for him!" Roger raged. "Does he want us to whip his slipshod army into shape for him as well? De Montfort's faith in his reinforcements, not to mention his son, is gravely misplaced. If Longshanks attacked tonight, he could take Kenilworth and decimate that fool's army."

"Longshanks won't move from Worcester yet, surely?" I said. "He'd leave the Severn unguarded and de Montfort would be able to escape into England. Besides, we'd know if the royalists had left Worcester, wouldn't we?"

Roger shrugged. "We don't know how many perimeter scouts Simon the Younger has sent out, if any. We certainly encountered none on the way in."

It was beginning to get dark and the inns were showing more activity as soldiers made their way from the bathing at the mere to the ale shops.

"It's best if we split up," said Roger. "We have more chance of finding him then. Ask around. You all know the name and sigil. If you locate de Arderne, do not try to apprehend him singlehandedly. We don't want him slipping the snare with knowledge that he is a hunted man or else he will become impossible to find. Wait until we can take him together. Clear?"

We all nodded and set off towards different taverns were the bawdy songs and brawls awaited us in a haze of summer evening heat and fumes of sour ale.

It was past midnight when I finally received a tip. Hours of bantering with drunken soldiers, putting questions to valets and squeezing information from whores before they squeezed coin from me finally paid off. I was told that de Arderne had a page who had recently returned from out of town on an errand. This page was taking his supper at an inn two streets over and I dashed out to see if I could catch him before he hit the hay for the night.

The inn was heaving and I pushed my way through the press of sweaty bodies, scanning each table as I went, looking for a youth at his meat. Plenty were eating but they were all either grizzled warriors or youths in polished armour. There was nobody in the velvet jacket and cap of a page. I asked a couple of men-at-arms if they had seen a page recently dining at the establishment and they told me yes, but he had just left.

I fought my way out to the street and looked up and down it. In the dimness ahead, I could see a boy making quick progress before vanishing around a corner. I pounded after him and delved into the shadows.

I must have stepped heavily for he knew that he was being followed and quickened his pace. I gave pursuit. The town's granaries rose up on either side of us, casting all in black shadow. The page made a dash for the gloom and I sped forward, seizing him by the shoulders.

He twisted and brought his knee up into my groin. I gagged and stumbled, clutching my aching parts, but still kept after my quarry. We passed into the light of the moon on the other side of the granaries and I succeeded in knocking him to the ground. His cap fell off and the moonlight illuminated a face I recognised.

The dark hair was clipped short. She passed well enough for a smooth-faced boy but for one who had known her – and loved her – her features were unmistakable.

"Margot!" I exclaimed.

"For the love of Christ, Stephen, why can't you let me be?" she almost pleaded.

"Believe it or not," I said, "I had no idea it was you. I didn't even expect to find you here at Kenilworth. It's your master I'm after. De Arderne."

She looked at me with a touch of cynicism on her beautiful features now rendered boyish by mud and cropped hair. Her eyes told me she did not believe me.

"Oh, very well," I admitted. "I did consider the possibility that you were here with him. But it's him I want. Not you. I swear."

"Are you here with company?"

I nodded. "Roger Godberd and the others from Hereford. De Arderne has to be stopped, Margot. I don't know what hold he has over you but I will help you if you help us."

She stood up slowly and dusted down her jacket. "He's a monster..." she said in a voice little more than a whisper. "There's no limit to his ambition."

"I'll get you away from him," I said. "I promise. You don't have to fear him anymore."

"And do I have to fear you, Stephen? Or Roger Godberd? Will you not be dutybound to bring me to justice?"

"You will be left out of it. I'll see to that. Roger will play along. With de Arderne in chains, nobody will be interested in you."

She smiled. "It's good to see you again, Stephen." She kissed me under the chin. "I must look a fright. Not quite how you remember me, eh?"

"Oh, I don't know, I think you're quite fetching in velvet and hose."

"You're teasing me. Do I truly arouse nothing in you anymore?"

Her hands fumbled at my belt buckle and I felt something very much aroused at her touch.

We made love on a pile of sackcloth beneath a lean-to with the uproarious town a distant hum in the background. The moonlit streets by the granaries were deserted and we lay in each other's arms afterwards and dozed, savouring this brief interlude in the never-ending march of duty and war. I knew it was folly but I had missed her and, with de Arderne's operative rendered helpless in my arms, I knew that there was no further treachery he could accomplish until she returned to him.

But this time, I swore, *she* would lead me to *him*.

TWENTY-SIX

I felt Margot slowly squirm from my embrace and rise. I feigned sleep for a little while longer until I was sure she had left me. Then I got up and hurried after her echoing footsteps.

It was dawn and the revelry in the town had eased into a drunken slumber which made the shouts of alarm all the more audible. They came from several streets over and they fed a sense of urgency in me that briefly overcame my pursuit of Margot.

I passed between the buildings to the street on the other side and saw mounted men waving blazing brands and barking orders to several footmen. The footmen booted down the door of a nearby house and stormed in. They emerged with a knight in a state of undress and set about binding his hands.

A woman I took to be his companion screamed at them and earned herself a sound cuff from a mailed fist that sent her sprawling. The knight was heaved up onto a horse and the mounted group galloped off while the footmen headed down a side street no doubt bent on further mischief.

"Christ Jesus, we're under attack!" I uttered in a hoarse croak.

My pursuit of Margot forgotten, I fled in the opposite direction intending to raise the alarm as soon as I found a body of baronial soldiers. I promptly came across one but they were otherwise engaged fighting a group of footmen who seemed to have set fire to the thatch of a building.

"Whose men are they?" I shouted at a baronial soldier who was cleaning his blade after hacking a man down.

"Not sure, but one of the lads in the market square said he saw Thomas de Clare's sigil on one of the bastards."

I swallowed. It was the royalists who were attacking, most likely Longshanks's entire host. And with half the town drunk, we were all as good as hanged. But there was something not quite right about it all.

"Town square?" I asked. "What's going on there?"

"Same as here. Raiders torching buildings and looting houses. Groups of them have popped up all over the town and they're striking us like vipers."

"That doesn't make any sense. Why attack in small parties when Longshanks could wipe us all out in one fell swoop?"

"Search me," said the soldier.

"Unless it's a diversion!" I exclaimed. I did not wait to hear the man's reply. I had to find Roger and the others. I looked up at the thatched and shingled roofs. If I knew my comrades, they would be up on high trying to pick off the attackers one at a time.

I scrambled up and scanned the rooftops for figures in the moonlight. Orange glows had sprung up throughout the town and I could see fire reflected off the great mere. There were ripples in the water and I could make out boats rowing frantically for the castle.

Towards the priory I saw several figures atop a roof and recognised the distinctive shape of bows bending and springing back. I made my way to them, scrambling up roofs and sliding down thatch, leaping across gaps and sidestepping smoke holes.

"Nice of you to join us!" Roger said as Richard and Wyotus hauled me up to their level. I immediately began stringing my bow.

"It's Longshanks," I said, nocking an arrow. "He's made his move from Worcester but there's something amiss."

"You're telling me," Roger replied as he let fly an arrow that struck a man-at-arms in the street below. "If this is his idea of an attack then his military skills have been sorely overestimated."

"And we all know first-hand that that is not the case," added Wyotus.

"I've never seen such a disorganised mess," said Roger. "As soon as a squad torch one building they flee like coneys and move on to the next."

"That's because it's a diversion," I said. I then described the squad of troops who had dragged a knight out of the house.

"I heard they took Adam de Newmarket too," said Richard. "They'll get a fat ransom for that bugger!"

"So that's it," said Roger. "Snatch squads! Longshanks has sent in groups of arsonists as a distraction while his knights steal our brave barons from their beds. And I don't suppose we have to wonder how he knows where their lodgings are." He glanced at me meaningfully.

I remembered then how de Arderne's page – Margot – had just returned from an errand out of town that night. Had she travelled all the way to Worcester to tell Longshanks that Simon the Younger was at Kenilworth? Had she even told him where his highest ranking barons slept?

In anger I drew my bow and aimed at a royalist who was scurrying for cover below. The shot went wide which only added to my frustration. He scampered off and Roger said; "That seems to be the last of them at least in this area. Come on! We'll be needed elsewhere!"

We slid down to the street and hurried through the town, following our ears towards the highest concentration of cries. We found a pitched battle in the next street over; Londoners against royalists. We found cover and began loosing arrows into the enemy.

Our contribution helped and the royalists fell back, pursued by most of the Londoners. Others began stripping the corpses of good armour, maille and weapons; things that were in short supply amongst the regiments from London.

My ears pricked at a set of footfalls to our rear. Fearing a surprise counterattack, I whirled, drawing my sword. I saw two figures further down the street dart into the shadows of an alley, their forms illuminated by the torch one of them carried. I could make out a man and a youth.

I dashed after them arousing the alarm of my comrades who followed me, their own weapons drawn. A second group of royalists fell upon us from a side street and we engaged them, reinforced by the remaining Londoners who were keen to try out their new weapons.

I left the fight and ran down the alley the two figures had entered. It led to a small stable where the discarded torch lay sputtering on the ground. A destrier and a courser were already saddled with a packhorse waiting patiently behind. The scene was so familiar that I felt as if fate was giving me a second chance to set things right.

And as I watched, Margot bestowed a kiss upon de Arderne that made me determined to not to fail in my duty this time. It was a passionate kiss and de Arderne held it and held her to him as if all the world could not tear them apart. I knew then that I was looking upon two lovers and that I had been a fool of the highest order.

The scene was so perversely ludicrous – a page boy kissing a knight – that I might have laughed aloud had my heart not been breaking beyond repair in that moment. Instead I mustered something between a chortle and a snort of derision. Their heads spun to look at me, wide eyed.

"Not this time, you lovebirds," I sneered. "You'll not escape justice this time. And I'll play the fool for you no longer, Margot."

"Stephen, I am sorry," she said. "I tried to warn you. I tried to tell you not to get involved but you insisted..."

"I was an ass, true," I said, "too head over heels in love to recognise a scheming bitch when I saw one. Are your feelings for this man as true as you once declared them for me? Or are you playing him for a fool too and pocketing Lady de Mortimer's silver and laughing at us both?"

"I've heard about all I'm going to take from you, stringfinger," said de Arderne, drawing his sword.

I gripped my own tightly, ready to kill the traitor and then finish off his accomplice once and for all.

"There's no time, Ralph!" Margot cried. "We must away! Edward's troops will be retreating anytime now and we cannot remain now that we are exposed!"

Ralph lowered his blade and then sheathed it but not because of his lover's words or through fear of me. I felt Roger and the others appear at my side.

"De Arderne?" Roger asked me.

"Aye," I replied. "And our old friend Margot."

"Dressed as a page?" Richard hooted. "That's a rich one! Still fancy her, Stephen?"

"We have to stop them," I said.

They had both mounted their horses and, apparently deciding to abandon the packhorse, made to leave the small courtyard. De Arderne had picked up the torch and brandished it at us menacingly.

We unshouldered our bows and fumbled for arrows. I would rather have skewered him with my sword but to be riddled by arrows was a good enough fate for any traitor.

With a sudden movement, de Arderne thrust the torch up into the overhanging thatch of the nearest building. It crackled and caught alight. Casting the torch aside, he seized the timber support and jerked it sideways.

Burning thatch spilled down, showering us with sparks, forcing us to retreat. The flames burned between us and our quarry and through them I could see de Arderne's grin of triumph before he wheeled his mount and joined Margot as she galloped out of the courtyard.

I never saw Ralph de Arderne or Margot again although I did learn that their love for each other did not last. In the late 1280s de Arderne's loyalty to the de Mortimers was rewarded when he married their daughter Isabella. Margot's fate was forever a mystery to me.

The attack on Kenilworth was over by the time we emerged from the burning courtyard and we spent the rest of the morning helping haul water from the mere to douse the fires.

The whole thing had been a devastating ruse. It was learned that during the chaos, the royalist snatch squads had made off with over a dozen knights not to mention a great deal of stores and loot including several of Simon the Younger's banners.

The young de Montfort himself had escaped capture by being in the first boat to row across the mere to the castle. As we stripped down to our braes and washed off the soot and sweat in the mere, we wondered what his next move would be.

We learned it by noon the following day and if the army had been lax before, they made up for it now with a flurry of activity. De Montfort the Elder had crossed the Severn at Kempsey and was marching east.

"Then Longshanks's entire army must have left Worcester," said Wyotus. "Otherwise they'd never dare cross."

"So where are they now then?" asked Richard.

The question remained unanswered and we felt a sense of unease and dread for de Montfort's army which was surely under surveillance by an unseen enemy as it marched toward us.

Simon the Younger was determined to set out immediately and join his father. We were placed under the banner of a Yorkshire baron called John d'Eyville; a gruff and coarse man who put me in mind of Robert de Ferrers only slimmer and more physically able. We trooped out of Kenilworth the following morning and headed southwest.

The day was grim and storm clouds boiled to the north, creeping ever closer. Looking back, I cannot shake free the sense of symbolism. Of course the sky was leaden with portents of doom. On that black day it could have been nothing else.

The storm broke on the morning of the 4th and the army took shelter at a place called Alcester. The roads turned to muddy deluges and we were sodden and miserable. A scout returned in the lashing downpour and told us that Simon de Montfort's army was camped at the market town of Evesham a mere nine miles to the south of us.

This brightened our spirits even if the weather showed no signs of doing so and we knew that as soon as the rain let up we would head for Evesham. There, the two baronial forces, so long separated, would finally reunite and cement de Montfort's rule of England.

The skies cleared a little after noon and we headed out. We had barely covered three miles before the first of the refugees crossed our path.

"They talk of battle at Evesham!" said somebody up front.

"Battle?" d'Eyville roared. "And they desert! Craven swine!" he galloped ahead to speak with Simon the Younger.

The army halted while scouts were sent out to seek the truth. They returned bearing evil news.

"They say the battle is already over," said Roger. "And that Longshanks won!"

"How could this happen?" Richard asked. "How could they strike so suddenly?"

"Because of that accursed rainstorm!" Roger replied. "Had we not tarried at Alcester, we might have made Evesham in time!"

"But de Montfort!" I said. "Did he escape?"

"No word."

The news from the scouts spurred the army forward and, as we crested the ridge and looked down into the Vale of Evesham, we learned the dreadful truth.

Bodies littered the vale and the ground had been churned up into a horrific mixture of mud, blood and entrails. Already the carrion birds had begun to descend, pecking and clawing at flesh barely cold. The standards that fluttered in rags or lay trampled in the filth told the story; few royalists had fallen here.

"This wasn't a battle," I heard d'Eyville mutter. "It was a bloody massacre!"

We descended into the town looking for answers. Monks from the priory had emerged and, with the help of pale-faced locals, began the unenviable job of arranging the dead for burial.

"The bastards used the banners they stole from us at Kenilworth," said d'Eyville after a council had been held. "Longshanks tricked de Montfort into thinking it was his son's army approaching. By the time they learned the truth it was too late. Simon is distraught. His father and brother Henry were both slain."

"So, de Montfort really is dead then," said Wyotus in a quiet voice. "The dream is over." Nobody answered. We were numb, all of us.

We later learned something that would shatter the young de Montfort's resolve further. His father's body had been brought from the field to the priory and was in a ghastly state. It had been horrendously mutilated. The head, hands and feet were missing and it was little more than a red ruin.

"They say they gave it to the dogs to maul after they beheaded him, just as we saw in the Weald," said Roger with a bitter grimace. "They chewed off the softest parts first; the member and testicles. Praise God he was already dead by that point."

I later learned that Roger de Mortimer had been directly involved in the mutilations and had even sent de Montfort's head to his wife at Wigmore Castle as a grisly trophy. She was rumoured to have dined in its presence. I was not the only one to hate the de Mortimers with a passion from that day forth.

We returned to Kenilworth; one of only two bastions of the baronial movement left, the other being Dover Castle. Simon the Younger concealed himself in his solar and saw nobody.

"He's even refusing food," d'Eyville told us. "Blames himself for the death of his father and brother. Poor bugger."

"Well, what's to be done?" Roger asked. "It won't be long before Longshanks knocks on Kenilworth's door. Do we intend to sit out a siege; one we can't possibly win?"

"Bugger that," said Richard. "I heard talk of falling back to Dover. That's where de Montfort's widow and remaining sons are. They could arrange transport to France but I don't fancy that much either."

"Leave England?" d'Eyville snapped. "Not on your life! Are we not Englishmen? Are we to be bullied out of our own country for fighting for the Provisions? Maybe the de Montforts have plenty of truck with the French, being Frenchmen themselves, but I own extensive property in Yorkshire and Lincolnshire and Longshanks will have to give a better fight to take those from me! The fens and woods of Axholme provide good cover for men in hiding. If we head north the rebellion could continue indefinitely!"

"So now we're a rebellion once more?" said Roger in a weary voice. "Christ Jesus, will it never end? But days ago we were soldiers for the legitimate government!"

"That government is over, I fear," said d'Eyville. "The civil war is over. And we, my friends, are on the losing side."

D'Eyville had the ear of Simon the Younger and, after the parliament of September and the subsequent disinheritance of all de Montfort's supporters in October, the desperate man listened to what must have seemed to him the only strong voice left. In November we headed north to the misty marshes and gloomy woods of Axholme where the ill-fated barons' rebellion entered its final phase.

FITT V
THE WOODWOSE AND THE GREEN MAN

"A sword and a dagger he wore by his side,
Had been many a man's bane,
And he was clad in his horsehide,
Top, and tail, and mane."
- Robin Hood and Guy of Gisborne

Yorkshire
Spring, 1322

TWENTY-SEVEN

The sheriff thought the potter's reek had been bad. That was as roses to the stench of the man who sat on the edge of the table in his Great Hall. It was a rotten smell; of fungus and tree sap and mouldering leaves with a hint of carcasses. He was popping grapes into his mouth and washing them down with wine which he managed to spill with frequency down the front of his already soiled shirt.

He was the most extraordinary man the sheriff had ever seen. He wore no maille or armour of any sort. Simple yeoman's garments long overdue a soak served as his under layer and a patchwork hide cloak hung from his shoulders. It was crudely stitched and poorly cured and the occasional tufts of black hair suggested that it had originally come from a horse. This assumption was confirmed by its hood which had two long ears that hung down the man's back, shrivelled and twisted.

By far the most bizarre part of the rogue's attire was his helmet which he had removed upon entering the hall and placed on the table where its unblinking gaze kept catching the sheriff's eye. It was a battered old thing crested with the skull of a young foal. The bottom tip of it pointed down and formed part of the nasal and, when it was placed on its owner's head, it gave the man a nightmarish appearance that smacked uncomfortably of the pagan.

"I must say, you come highly recommended," the sheriff told the man, not knowing why he felt the urge to flatter him. There was something unnerving about the man that suggested he should be kept on good terms.

"I'm a hunter," said the man, wiping his mouth on a dirty sleeve, "and I keep hunting until I get my kill." He set the wine goblet down on the table and grinned wide. His blackened teeth were not a sight for a weak stomach. "But my services are at a premium, sheriff."

"Yes, as to that, what figure were you considering?"

"Two hundred pounds for Hood's head, body and soul."

The sheriff snorted. "Two hundred pounds? For a simple bounty hunting job?"

"Simple jobs are for simple men. And you have those by the score. No, this hobhood is something special. The name is bestowed upon every fool who finds himself on the wrong side of the law with nothing but the forest to keep him from a hanging but, every once in a while, one comes along truly deserving of the name. I understand he caused you some considerable personal inconvenience."

There was a half-smile on those ugly lips and the sheriff stiffened. He didn't care how much this bounty hunter unnerved him, he would take no cheek from a yeoman-turned-thief taker. The memory of his ransoming still burned his pride sorely. Half the shire was privy to it and his name was accompanied by a chuckle whenever it was spoken from tavern to tannery. But by God, he would rectify that soon enough. There would be precious few chuckles once Robert Hood and his band were dangling in York's marketplace.

"Fifty pounds," he said. "For the whole band."

The bounty hunter sighed and slid down from the table. He was a short man but stout and swarthy. He set down his wine goblet. "I'll come back when you are a little more serious."

"Very well, I'll pay twenty pounds for him dead and fifty for him alive. Plus ten for each of his band, dead or alive, your choice. That's a hundred and fifty for the whole band if all goes to plan."

The bounty hunter considered this. "Done. I'll need men."

"How many?"

"Six should do it. They shall be my hounds to flush out the game bird for my arrow. Their salaries will be paid by you and not subtracted from my bounty."

"Fine. I expect quick work from you, sir. My acquaintance in York says that you apprehended that rogue money lender with a certain degree of finesse and efficiency."

"He was still in the city, it has to be said," the man replied. "And an old Jew does not provide so much sport as a fully-grown hobhood. This chase promises to be most entertaining."

"Just as long as it doesn't take too long. I want Hood hanged as soon as humanly possible. Go now, and wait in my guest quarters. I will have my sergeant Oderic select six men suited to the task. And then you are to be on your way, bounty hunter."

The man grinned wide, retrieved his extraordinary helmet and slunk out of the hall without a word. The sheriff frowned. It was not so much that the man was disrespectful; rather he was indifferent to authority. He clearly saw no reason to bow or 'sire' the sheriff and the whole exchange had been as of one between two equals. That kind of confidence in a yeoman unsettled the sheriff but not half so much as his own reluctance to chastise the man for it.

"Saints preserve us, what a reek your new friend carries with him!" Constance said as she entered the hall.

The sheriff entertained the thought that she had been listening from the screens passage. *Sly wench! How many times has she played that game?*

"I'll have the servants burn some incense if it distresses you, my sweet," he replied.

"No matter, I am riding out shortly with Bess to give alms to the poor at the chapel at Yeadon. Have you your bounty hunter?"

"I believe I have. If he is as good as his reputation he will bring Hood to me by the end of the month."

"Are you so sure that outlaws are your primary concern, husband? After all, your friend William de Aune is in dire need of reinforcements at Tickhill if he is to rebuff Lancaster."

The sheriff grimaced. Under pressure from the barons, the king had reluctantly banished the le Despensers in August of 1321. In January the king had rescinded their banishment and they had returned, enraging Marcher Lords such as Roger de Mortimer and the northern barons. Lancaster had moved on Tickhill Castle and the sheriff had received orders to stop any Marcher Lords who might lend their aid to Lancaster from entering Yorkshire.

"The stalemate at Tickhill shows no sign of breaking," he said. "There is little I can do to help de Aune. I need men to uphold the law and I have few enough to spare as it is. The best I can do is to keep the king's peace in Yorkshire. Civil war is breaking out in our midst and we can't allow criminals to take advantage of the situation."

"Well, not common criminals, of course," Constance replied. "Just the likes of John de Mowbray, Roger de Clifford and their ilk. William de Aune too, for that matter. He has all but stripped Doncaster of supplies."

"Supplies intended to help him withstand the siege," the sheriff replied irritably. "Really, Constance, I sometimes wonder where your allegiances lie. To even mention de Aune in the same breath as those dogs should be punishable as treason."

"And yet I see very little difference in their actions other than in whose name they do them."

"And if I didn't know better, I could swear that you think to turn my mind from hunting down those vile outlaws. Are you sure the presence of that oaf, John of Holderness, in their ranks has not softened you to them? He did cripple my old steward in defence of your name, after all. Or so you would have me believe. Do you feel you owe the man a debt?"

"Husband, you let your injured pride speak instead of your sense. Would you be so insistent on hunting these creatures had they not held you for ransom?"

"My pride is never better, I assure you. Outlaws should be hanged, that has always been my mind on the matter."

"Well, we had better hope that this bounty hunter of yours makes good on his promise. For the safety of the shire, of course. What did you say his name was?"

"Gisburn. Guy de Gisburn."

The outlaws' camp in Barnsdale had weathered the winter admirably. Since Simon Hood had joined them it was no longer safe to winter with his family in Wentbridge so the outlaws had fortified their camp and dug in for the worst of the weather.

Their shelters had been reinforced and insulated with thatch and they slept on pallets of brush covered with deer skins. The horses had been stabled in a thatched covering and walled in with wattle screens along with plenty of feed looted from barns and wains. Fires were kept fuelled and plentiful stores rationed to last the long dark months with the exception of a feast at Christmastide which was a rare break in the monotony of winter survival.

Now that the snows had all but melted and the frost was not so biting in the mornings, the band was stirring and facing something of a crisis of identity.

Since their rescue of Great John and their ransoming of the Sheriff of Yorkshire the previous year, their names had become near legendary in the shire. They were praised in the villages where they were occasionally given aid whenever the band dared approach seeking food and conversation. But with legendary status, discussion inevitably turned to the matter of what was to be done next.

Even the most content of the band felt that robbing merchants and monks was something of an anti-climax after their bold schemes of the previous year. They were rich but they were not free and never would be no matter how rich they became. Wealth was something of an obsolete goal to them now but their leader refused to see it that way.

"This robbery could be the best start to the year we might see," Robert told his band as they sat around the campfire which was banked high to stave off the morning chill. "And it's not even February!"

"Aye, we should be keeping ourselves warm and safe this early in the year, not tearing off on wild errands," Much said.

"And why should we be doing somebody else's dirty work for them anyway?" Katherine said.

Robert sighed. "Is this my band getting lazy from resting on their laurels too long? Are you so much fattened swine from wintering in a warm barn with a full feeder? Spring will soon be upon us and I for one wish to stamp my feet and shake off the cold."

"It's not just that, Rob," Katherine said, "How can we even trust these Bradburn brothers? They're not from around here. Their business isn't ours."

"We can trust them because John here trusts them, isn't that right, John?"

Little John nodded his shaggy head. The nickname dreamed up by Will had stuck although few used it to his face. "I ran with John and William Bradburn for a while after I fled the sheriff's employ. They're not a bad pair as far as outlaws go. I wouldn't marry my daughter to either of them but they're good enough for robbing houses with. Aye, I trust them."

"And this mysterious employer of theirs?" Much asked. "James Coterel. Who knows anything about him?"

"Heard of him," John admitted. "His family runs things over in the Peak District. His father had lands in several manors there but he died nigh on seven years ago. James is his eldest son and inherited his lands but it wasn't easy for him to hold on to them. He and his brothers had to spill blood and the Bradburn brothers did some of the spilling for them. That was before I met them but the Coterel family has grown in strength since then and now looks beyond the Peak for their wealth."

"Aye, our way," said Much. "What if our helping them gives them ideas about moving into Yorkshire for good? Barnsdale isn't big enough for two gangs of outlaws and this James Coterel sounds like a lofty gent who would rather see us out of the way or under his thumb."

"Why care in which direction he looks?" said Robert. "If he has any designs on our turf then we'll fight him off. As it stands he is asking us to rob

Adwick Hall and go shares on the treasure Simon le Lound stole from him. Its easy money and plenty of it."

Simon le Lound was lord of the Adwick-le-Street manor. His son had been betrothed to James Coterel's sister, Berengaria. A quarrelsome family, the young le Lound was killed in a tavern brawl and dashed his father's hopes of securing Berengaria's handsome dowry in any legal sense. Armed bandits stole the chest of precious plate and jewels from one of the Coterel manors and James Coterel had a good idea where the treasure had wound up. Reluctant to strike out on his own, he had sent his lackeys, the Bradburn brothers, to fetch it back using whatever means necessary.

"What do you think, Stephen?" Katherine asked the old man who stirred the fire with a blackened stick while he worked his few teeth around a hard crust of bread.

"Housebreaking?" said Old Stephen with a wrinkled frown. "That's a far cry from relieving those who pass through Barnsdale of a little weight in their purse. And I remember you once saying that robbery was only a means to an end, Robert."

"You yourself have told us of how you robbed abbeys and manor houses when you ran with Roger Godberd," Robert replied.

"Aye, and we all did our penance for those evil days. Godberd eventually renounced his villainous ways before it was too late."

"Well I seek no boon from the law nor forgiveness from God as he did," Robert retorted with disdain. "I'll not live out my days tilling my fields for I have none. We are robbers and this is a chance to rob a manor house! Who among you would turn your nose up at such a haul?"

"It sits ill with me," said Much.

"And me," added Katherine.

"Bugger it, I'm all for it," said Will.

"Count me in," said Anna.

John nodded his assent and there were vague mumblings from Simon, Wat and Rob Dyer but nothing particularly committal.

"The ayes have it," said Robert. "But I press none of you to do that which you would not. The road is open to any who no longer wish to be a part of my band."

Katherine's eyes widened but it was Much who spoke for the both of them. "So, you'd cast out your companions who disagree with you? You'd turn on us over pursuit of coin? Even Katherine here?"

"I have no wish to lose any of you," Robert replied. "Katherine least of all. But I am no tyrant to hold free people in bondage to me. However, a divided band is not a strong one. Our strength lies in our unity and our commitment to a common cause. If we cannot agree then perhaps it is best to part ways."

"That's bloody blackmail!" said Much. He rose angrily to his feet and stomped off to see to the horses in their stable.

The meeting was over and Katherine remained with Robert, sharing the warmth of his cloak but he felt precious little warmth from her. "You'd really ask us to leave if we don't agree to join you on this mad venture?" she asked him.

"Of course not," Robert replied. "Not you at any rate. As for Much, he'll do as he's told like he always does. I had to lay it on thick else what is the good of having a leader? We can't have a difference of opinion in the band, not when danger so often calls on us to trust one another with our lives. They'll all come around, you'll see. Silver has too strong a pull on a man's heart."

"But what of a woman's heart?"

He smiled at her. "Well, Anna's all for it. I'll just have to think of something more tempting than silver to convince you."

"I just don't like it, Rob. We don't need dealings with outsiders. We do alright on our own."

"The Bradburn brothers are outlaws just like us; no better, no worse. They might even have joined us had they not run across Coterel first. Who are we to value ourselves higher than them?"

"I just hope you're right, Rob. I really do."

TWENTY-EIGHT

The screams were muffled by the low thatched roof of the woodcutter's cottage but there was nobody within miles to hear them in any case. The whimpering of the terrified children from the corner mingled with the agonised howlings and acrid stench of burnt flesh to build an unbearable atmosphere within the cottage.

Guy de Gisburn paced the room slowly, showing not a smidgen of discomfort. He was in his element and the soldiers loaned to him by the Sheriff of Yorkshire watched with grim purpose and some degree of trepidation. The stench was truly awful, it had to be said.

"Fascinating thing, fire," Guy said. "I heard tell that some Greek stole it from God and gave it to man. It didn't end too well for that Greek but you won't want to hear about that right now. What interests me is what man did with that fire or rather, what fire does to man. It's safe to say that we have grown dependant on it so that we can't live without it, not with winters like the one we just had. And yet, if not treated with care, it burns through our forests and our homes, killing our families and destroying our lives. It is truly a double-bladed knife so much so that I have to wonder that God did not let us keep it out of a sense of spite. Perhaps it was not that Greek who was truly punished, but man."

The woman screamed again but her voice was weakening. The sweat ran in rivulets from her scalp. It was hot within the woodcutter's cottage but it was rather the agony of searing flame that made the woman sweat so.

"In my experience, the human mind can only take so much pain until it gives in and delivers sweet oblivion," Guy said. "You will be pleased to know that our time is almost up so we must be brief. Your husband, Simon Hood, left this house sometime last year and joined his cousin Robert in Barnsdale Forest. He has been back here to give you coin and to kiss his children; that much has been ascertained. Tell me where he and the other outlaws have made their camp and your relief will come that much quicker."

The woman's teeth ground together but there was no way of knowing if this was her biting down on her words or fighting the pain. For all Guy knew, she could no longer hear him. He looked her up and down and shook his head thoughtfully.

She was stretched out on the cottage floor, her hands bound and held high above her head by two of the sheriff's men. Her gown was bunched up around her waist and her bare, pale legs were held down by a bench with a large chopping block placed atop it. She could not move. Her bare feet lay in the coals of the fire, the skin long since burned away. Fat hissed in the flames. There was little left of the woman's feet but blackened shapes. She would never use them again but she may live a cripple's life if she spoke now.

She did not. Her eyes glazed over and her straining arms went limp.

"She's gone," said one of the sheriff's men helpfully.

"Indeed she has," Guy replied.

"What if she spoke the truth?" asked another. "What if she really doesn't know where the outlaws are?"

"I can almost guarantee that she does not," said Guy. "Why should they tell her? It is much too great a risk."

"Then why all this?" asked the second soldier, his pale face betraying his burdened conscience.

Guy drew his knife slowly and admired its gleaming blade. "To get our prey's attention."

It wasn't until Robert strode into camp that he knew something was terribly wrong. He and Will had been out hunting and they carried a buck between them, dressed and skinned. Simon and Wat had returned from Wentbridge where they had gone to deliver coin to Simon's family.

"Why is Simon on his knees?" Will asked. "Is he wounded?"

"Something's up," said Robert and they laid the buck down on the grass and hurried over to the rest of the band who had gathered around the distraught Simon.

"They came for his family," Wat explained. "The bastards tortured Theresa and then killed her. The poor woman had no information to give so they killed her. Bastards!"

"What happened?" Robert demanded.

"We came on the cottage and saw there was no smoke," Wat said. "The last fire had died out days ago but the stink of Theresa's burned feet still lingered."

Simon let out a muffled howl.

"Her throat was cut so that was probably what finished her after the bastards grew tired of torture."

"We'll find whoever did this, Simon," said Will. "If it takes us one year or ten, we'll find them and make them pay."

"My children," Simon groaned. "What have they done with my children?"

"They were taken?" Robert asked.

"Aye, but by who and where to is a mystery," said Wat.

"It makes no sense," said Robert, gazing upon his cousin with pity. "Why this brutality now?"

"It's that bastard sheriff," said Will. "We stung him just a little too hard when we ransomed him in the summer. He's out for revenge to heal his damned pride."

"And he's going after our families!" said Rob Dyer.

Katherine turned to Robert. "We have to get word to them. To yours in Wakefield and Dyers in South Elmsall."

"Aye," Robert agreed. "But we can't go in person. The sheriff knows who our families are and will have men posted to watch for our return. This all may be a ruse to draw us into the open. Will and Anna, you go to South Elmsall and check on Rob Dyer's family for him. Tell them to get out and stay with relatives. If you see anyone suspicious, do not engage them. Just come straight back to camp. Bring Dyer's family with you if you have to but for the love of God make sure you aren't followed. Wat and Rob, if you wouldn't mind, please go to Wakefield and do the same for Will's family and mine. We're too well known there to go ourselves."

"I've only got my old da left," said Will. "But I still wouldn't want the old bastard tortured on my account."

"Don't you worry about it, Rob," said Wat. "We'll see to it."

"Thank you."

"What will the rest of us be doing?" Katherine asked.

"We have a meeting with the Bradburn brothers in two days. You, John and I will go to Skelbrooke tomorrow as agreed and discuss our plans with them."

"You're not going to try and find out who did this?" Katherine asked him.

"We know the sheriff is behind it," Robert replied.

"He's not the type to torture women," John said. "He doesn't have the stomach. It'll be some thief-taker or bounty hunter he's employed. Somebody new is my guess. Else we would have seen this level of brutality before now."

"We'll find him, whoever he is," said Robert. "But we can't let some thief-taker ruin our plans. We need to ensure the safety of our families and then press ahead with our business. This snake will reveal itself to us sooner or later and then we will cut off its head in one clean blow."

"But Simon's children!" said Katherine.

"We have no choice! We have no idea where he's taken them. It'll do no good tearing about like headless chickens. We have to let him make the next move. Then we will strike, I promise you."

The granary at Skelbrooke was pitifully empty and echoed with the promise of hunger and misery to come. It had been recently looted by Lancaster to feed his army and the faces of the villagers told of the fear they had of the coming months. They remembered the famine of recent years all too well.

The Bradburn brothers knew somebody of standing in the village and used it as a base for their operations in Yorkshire. From what John had told Robert, they were a town gang who ran protection rackets and fenced stolen goods. They preferred to hide behind legitimate businesses rather than trees and foliage.

They were tall, dark men. John Bradburn had shaved his locks while William kept his long and greasy. Their faces were hard and scarred and their clothes were a curious contrast of rich and poor; proof of common stock layered with the profits of thievery. John wore a doublet of red velvet, browned by dirt and William's coarse tunic was held in by a belt studded with garnet and gold. If there was any consistency to their clothes then it was their flavour of the towns. They were not garments to withstand woodland life.

The two brothers stood in a circle of light thrown onto the hardpacked earth through one of the owl chutes. These high openings in the stone walls were designed to tempt owls to nest in the granary and keep it free from mice. They also let in beams of light that gave the cavernous interior a sepulchral atmosphere where dust motes danced in the air like snowflakes.

Several other members of the Bradburn gang loitered in the shadows, weapons never far from hand. They watched Robert, Katherine and John approach as owls might watch mice from up on high.

"John!" William Bradburn called, his voice echoing impressively. "It's been too long!"

"Aye," Little John replied. "It's been many moons since we robbed that widow of her jewels at Barnsley."

"I always said you had a place with us, John," said William. "But you valued your freedom more than the oath of brotherhood. And yet here you are, part of another gang. I wonder at your change of heart."

John shrugged. "I'm getting sentimental in my old age. My days of lonely wandering are over. I'm in good company now, as I was with you many moons ago. Meet Robert Hood, our leader and champion."

"Well met, Hood," said John Bradburn. "Who's the lass?"

"Katherine Coll," said Katherine, before Robert or John could answer for her.

"Never had much truck with women in our gang," William said. "More trouble than they're worth." He approached Katherine and sniffed her as a hound sniffs at an unfamiliar scent. "What makes this wench fit to work alongside men?"

Robert cleared his throat. "This wench is my companion and a damned good fighter at that. She's worth any three of yours."

"Care to test that claim?" John Bradburn asked. The men at his back roused themselves, sensing the opportunity of some sport.

"Put your cocks away," said Little John. "We are associates not enemies."

"My brother has a point, John," said William. "If we are to do business together we should all know with whom we are working. Take these lads, for example," he beckoned the loitering men over to him. They clustered around the two brothers, confident smiles on their lips. "Hard men whose loyalty has been put to the test again and again. Either of you been soldiers?"

Robert and Little John shook their heads.

"I was a soldier," William continued. "John too. We fought the Scots at Bannockburn under Roger de Clifford. It taught us a lesson which we use every day. One man, no matter how good a fighter, can be killed easily. But a man with his brothers by his side can be invincible so long as every man watches his brothers' backs. When the army begins to think like individuals, the battle is lost.

"Wasn't Bannockburn a disaster?" Katherine muttered.

William ignored her. "A gang like ours is very much like a small army. One weak link and we all fall." He patted the shoulders of the men by his side. He kept his hand on the neck of the man to his left; a burly oaf with a slight paunch that bulged against his rough-spun tunic.

"If one soldier thinks only of himself then he endangers the whole army." The hand on the man's neck squeezed tight. Sweat stood out on the man's brow and his eyes darted nervously to William. "But if the brothers are lucky, they can smell out the weak link before it is too late!" William's ugly face split into a grin.

The man at his side made a sudden run for the door. The Bradburn brothers anticipated it and grabbed him between them. "The rope!" William cried to his comrades.

Robert, John and Katherine stood by and watched helplessly as the gang fastened a noose around the neck of their comrade. He began to gibber in terror. The words sounded like some sort of apology but they came out as incomprehensible sobs. The end of the rope was tossed over one of the rafters and the wretched man was hoisted up, his legs kicking frantically and his hands clawing at the cord that dug into his neck, cutting off the air supply.

The rope was tied to a pillar and they all watched the man dance for a while, his awful choking echoing in the granary. It would take a long time for him to die. Robert remembered seeing criminals hanged at the gallows oak in Wakefield when he had been a boy. Sometimes they kicked for hours if there were no kind family members about to tug on their ankles and quicken their passing.

"Now," said William, apparently planning to go on with the meeting despite the jerking man swinging about in the background. "Let's get down to business."

"It couldn't be easier," Robert said as they rode back towards Barnsdale. "Simon le Lound will be hunting at Loxley Chase two weeks from now and will be taking much of his retinue with him. Adwick Hall will be more or less undefended."

"I just hope the Bradburns' man on the inside has his facts straight," John said. "We had trouble with that before. Did I ever tell you of the pig's ear we made of a robbery just outside of Rotherham? We were lucky to get out of that one alive. John Bradburn has a scar on his calf from the hound that bit him."

John proceeded to relate a humorous account of the botched robbery that did not serve to improve Katherine's confidence in the whole scheme at all.

"Rob, these men are not our kind," she interrupted. "They're a town gang. We don't need their acquaintance."

"Are you prejudiced, lass?" Robert asked her. "Town gang, forest gang, what's the difference? Silver is silver however you look at it."

"They just hanged a man in front of us! One of their own! What does that tell you about them?"

"That man was a traitor. They couldn't trust him."

"And so they killed him in cold blood? Would you do the same to any of us?"

"I honestly don't know," he replied. "Depends."

"You can't mean that."

He turned in his saddle angrily. "What do you want me to say, Katherine? That I'm nothing like them? We're no saints either in case that's never occurred to you. We've killed men. Innocent men, in the eyes of some. The church would certainly damn us to hell and the crown would hang us if they had half the chance. Open your eyes. We're no better than the Bradburns."

He rode on ahead leaving Katherine and John on the road behind him.

"They aren't so bad," said John. "Rough bastards but Rob's right. We're no better."

"You're a bad influence on him," Katherine said. "He wasn't like this before we rescued you. He has a good heart but he's too easily led by you and Will.

John laughed. "I suppose him being an outlaw is our fault and all!"

Katherine ignored him and rode off to join Robert.

"Well excuse me for seeing things as they are," John muttered.

TWENTY-NINE

The inn at South Elmsall had a yard at the rear with the stables on one side and the ugly facades of the neighbouring houses on the other. A low archway was the only entrance to the confined yard which was deep in shadow despite the bright square of afternoon sky above.

Several horses occupied the stables hinting at a good day's custom. Will and Anna left their own beasts with the stable boy and entered the inn. It was dim and smoky inside and the deep hearth threw out plenty of heat but not enough light to illuminate its many dark corners.

The inn had several customers sitting in small groups at trestle tables, conversing in low tones, their dress showing a variety of trades, guilds and goods. This was the inn where Rob Dyer had plunged his knife into the neck of Roger de Clifford's sergeant after the man had raped his daughter but there didn't appear to be any soldiers about now. Will picked a table not too close to the hearth and they sat down. He called the landlord and demanded ale and meat be brought.

"Do you think they have straw pallets here or feather?" Anna asked him.

"Straw," he replied. "This place is more alehouse than inn."

"Never mind. Straw is better than brush and deerskin. I can't remember the last time I slept in a bed."

"It'll be brush and deerskin for quite some time, I'm afraid," Will replied. "We're not stopping here. Once we've had a sup and a bit of grub we've got to get back to camp."

"It's late, Will. It'll be dark before we get back. Let's stop here for the night, eh?" Her hand slipped under the table and cupped his member. He removed it hastily. It wouldn't do to draw attention to themselves now. They had done what they came for and every minute they spent in the village was a risk.

Still, there was a limit to how conventional Anna could look. Not many females went around in breeches, doublet and cloak with a dagger at her belt. Anna had been so roughened by an outlaw's life that Will wondered if she had ever been much of a lady to begin with. The idea of her in a dress was laughable. Still, she cut a fine figure in men's clothes and he found the whole dirty, rough ensemble on a woman much more arousing than wispy veils and fine gowns.

"How about it, then?" she persisted.

Will shook his head. "Dyer needs to know that his family are safe. I won't prolong his worry unnecessarily. Not even for a toss in a straw bed with you so you might as well cool off or I'll take you out into the yard and dump the horses' trough over you."

"You bloody try and I'll dump you in it first."

He smirked. He didn't know why but Anna was the only person he could remember that could make him smile. A smile was a rare enough thing for her too and yet she often grinned at him. "What happens after we get back?" she asked.

"We get on with this robbery. The killer of Simon's wife will reveal himself sooner or later, just as Robert said."

"Why is it always Robert making the decisions?"

Will gave her a puzzled look. "I thought you were all for this venture with the Bradburns."

"Oh, I am. I'm just wondering how much longer Rob can keep this band together. He's already facing opposition from Much and Katherine."

"He'll keep it together. Much is a good lad but easily led and Katherine... well, she loves Rob so she won't be a problem."

"I wouldn't underestimate her. She's a sweet girl but cunning as quicksilver. It wouldn't surprise me if she bends Robert's ear into calling the whole thing off."

"Katherine?" Will snorted. "Hard to believe. I still have trouble picturing you both running together; you're as chalk and cheese. Why did you keep her around?"

"She was a good friend when I had none. Anyway, what if I'm right and Katherine manages to sway Robert's mind?"

Will said nothing. He could see that she wanted to change the subject. She never liked to talk about her past and Will knew so very little about it. He knew she was from York and had fallen afoul of the authorities for some petty crime which her refusal to face justice for caused her to be outlawed.

"It should be you leading the band," Anna said and Will wasn't sure he heard her right at first. "You'd be a good leader. Stronger than Robert."

"Maybe," said Will. "But maybe I don't want to lead."

"Why not?"

He shrugged. "Rob's always been the man in the know. I was glad of his company in those early days just as you were of Katherine's. I'm not going to fight him for the leadership now. Anyway, what I really want is right here beside me." He leaned in close and risked a kiss on her lips. They held it for longer than was sensible, causing a few heads in the inn to turn and stare.

A burly man in maille entered the room and strode over to a group of three that were drinking and sharing a capon in the shadows of the stairs. He sat down and whispered something into the ear of a curious man in a patchwork hood. The whole group looked decidedly unsavoury and Will couldn't understand why he had not noticed them before.

He turned back to Anna and noticed that her eyes were fixed on the man in the hood as if she was both intrigued and terrified at once.

"What is it?" he asked her.

"Nothing," she replied, shaking her head as if to wake from the remnants of a daydream. "Where's that bloody landlord with our meat?"

He eventually arrived and Anna wolfed down the food, washing it down with ale and letting her eyes wander everywhere except at the small group under the stairs. Will didn't like the look of things either, especially as the mysterious hooded man kept looking in their direction.

"We'd best be on the road," Anna said, wiping the ale from her mouth with her sleeve. "Daylight's wasting."

"Aye, you go see to the horses, I'll pay the landlord what we owe him."

Will rose and headed towards the bar while Anna made for the yard. As soon as he was on his feet he felt the company beneath the stairs rise with him and follow him to the bar. He tensed and his fingers reached for the hilt of the dagger at his belt. He was hopelessly outnumbered should it come to a fight but at least Anna was out of the room and had a chance of getting away. Then he realised that she would never run. She'd fight to the death by his side. He felt both love and irritation for her in that moment.

"Travelled far, pilgrim?" one of the men asked over his shoulder as Will tossed a few broken coins down on the bar top.

"Do I look like I'm visiting some saint's bloody shrine?" he replied.

"No need to take that tone," said the man and Will noticed for the first time that he wore maille under his cloak. In fact, they all wore maille. *Soldiers. But no sigil.*

"We just haven't seen you around here before," said one of the others. "Or that fine filly of yours. Is it housebroken?"

Will whirled to face the man who had spoken. His life might be hanging in the balance but he'd be damned if he'd let any man talk about Anna that way. "Watch your tongue, blockhead or I'll cut it out after I've cut your throat."

This made the men bristle. Hands reached for sword hilts under cloaks but something stayed those hands. This lot were thugs looking for trouble but they were not prepared to go all the way. *They've got orders*, Will thought.

"Don't tell me you and that fine young woman are courting," said the first soldier. "If she were mine I'd make her dress more like a lady. Even if she ain't one."

Careful, Will told himself. He knew that they were trying to goad him. *But why?* Why wait for him to strike the first blow? It was as if they needed an excuse. *Any* excuse. He gritted his teeth and tried to quench his anger. If he played these bastards right, he might just walk out of here alive.

"What hedge lord has you lot in his employ anyway?" he asked them. "Can't he afford proper livery?"

"Watch it, wastrel," said the first soldier. "Happens we don't care to reveal our employer's identity."

That settled it in Will's mind. These louts had to be in the employ of the sheriff. They were probably waiting here for Rob Dyer to come running to his family so that they might capture him or follow him back to camp. Maybe they had been the ones who had tortured Theresa to death but he tried not to let his mind wander down that road. If he did, he didn't know that he could control himself and then both he and Anna would be dead.

The men put more questions to him and he did his best to fend them off without causing too much offence. It grew into something of a game and Will felt as if they lacked real interest. It was almost as if they were stalling him, buying time. Then it struck him.

Anna.

He bade them farewell and left the inn at a hurry, cursing himself for forgetting about the strange hooded man who was no longer with the group. *If anything had happened to Anna...*

He found them in the yard. Anna had her back to him. The stranger's ugly face was half hidden by its hood and a single eye glinted as he approached.

"What's going on out here?" Will demanded.

Anna spun to face him, her face pale. She seemed unharmed.

"No offence intended, sir," said the hooded man. "I was merely passing the time of day with your delightful companion. I hope I have not overstepped the mark?"

"Are those your men in there?" Will asked him.

"Comrades, yes. I apologise if they have caused insult. They like their ale early in the day and their manners are coarse at the best of times."

"What is your name?" Will asked him.

"Guy de Gisburn. And yours?"

"None of your concern."

"Will..." Anna warned, apparently embarrassed by his rudeness which was uncharacteristic of her to say the least.

"I can see that you are a secretive pair," Guy said with a knowing wink. "And I'll not take offence. The roads are dangerous these days and it pays to be cautious. Especially if one does not have the luxury of an armed escort.

"We'll be on our way now, if you don't mind," Will told him.

"Not at all. Godspeed."

The hooded man wandered back indoors and Will and Anna retrieved their horses and saddled up. They worked quickly and did not speak. Things had taken a decided turn for the risky and they needed to get away as soon as possible.

They trotted out of the yard and headed north. The sun's dying flare cast long shadows over the fields and woodland on their left. Will kept turning in his saddle to look at the road behind them. Once or twice he thought he saw movement in the distant dust and heard the occasional clink of a bridle somewhere far behind them but it may have been his imagination. It was the time of day when the tired mind is toyed with by dim light and creeping shadows. The uneasy feeling did not pass until they entered the comforting shade of the greenwood.

"So, Dyer's family is unharmed and so is yours, Rob," said Much. "Why Simon's then? Why torture and kill Theresa?"

"Because my cousin's family lived in isolation," said Robert. "Both Dyer's and mine live in towns. It was days before Theresa's body was found. It was all too easy to do it with no chance of being come upon. Cowards!" he spat into the ashes of the fire with disgust.

"But we know your families were being watched," said Old Stephen. "Wat and Dyer were followed as far as Crofton."

"Aye, but we managed to throw them off our scent," said Wat. "They won't have known in which direction we headed once we entered Barnsdale. There were two of them. Looked like soldiers but they showed no allegiance."

"And this strange character Will and Anna ran into at South Elmsall sounds like more of the same sort," said Stephen. "What did you say his name was?"

"Guy de Gisburn," said Will.

"Heard the name," said John.

They all turned to him. "What do you know, John?" Robert asked.

"I heard he's a thief-taker. A bounty hunter. And worse. A man with no morals nor limits is what they say. Even the Bradburn brothers fear him."

"They are acquainted with him?" Robert asked.

"Not by their choosing. He apprehended a pair of lads who worked for them as I recall. They swung at Doncaster but that wasn't the worst of it. It was de

Gisburn's pursuit of them that turned the blood of the Bradburns cold. He was brutal. Torture, murder, nothing is too low for him in the pursuit of his prey. If de Gisburn is on our trail then we'd best be cautious. And pray."

"If he's as dangerous as all that then we'd best rid ourselves of him," Will said. "Permanently."

"This isn't some cheap sell sword, Will," said John. "He's cunning and ruthless and has the backing of the sheriff. He'll be a tough opponent to face."

"If only we had some clue as to his whereabouts," said Robert. "His presence at South Elmsall was surely to spy for Rob Dyer's return. He'll be long gone from there."

"He'll be somewhere near East Hardwick," replied Anna.

"How came you by that information?" Robert asked her.

"De Gisburn told me himself."

"That's right," said Will, remembering. "You and he were having a little chat when I came out of the inn. What exactly were you talking about?"

"He was after some cunny, if you must know," Anna replied sharply. "He didn't ask outright, just danced around the matter being a slight sharper in wits than the average man. One thing he did tell me was that he and his lads had recently passed through East Hardwick."

"Probably came from Pontefract then," said John.

"Not if he's the sheriff's man," Robert replied. "Pontefract is Lancaster's seat. The sheriff upholds the king's law, not Lancaster's own brand of justice."

"East Hardwick, eh?" said John. "There's little enough there. Somebody would know something if a viper like had been in their midst.

"Then we set out tomorrow, early," said Robert. "I've a mind de Gisburn holds Simon's children at East Hardwick or nearby and I mean to rescue them and kill de Gisburn too if there's a chance of it."

Simon himself had not taken part in the meeting. He was a ruin of a man since he received the news of his wife's murder and the abduction of his children. He did nothing but drink heavily in the evenings and doze in his shelter all day. He uttered nothing except the occasional howl of grief whenever the horror inside of him broke the surface like a lumbering kraken from the depths.

It was late and Will and Anna retired to their own shelter. As they crawled in and bedded down on the deerskins, Will turned to Anna.

"You never said de Gisburn was sniffing around you like a dog,"

"It hardly seemed worth mentioning at all," Anna replied.

"I didn't see you rebuffing his advances too heartily."

"You didn't see his advances either. I told you he was a deal more tactful than the average inn rat."

"And you think this chivalric of him?"

She eyed him critically. "Are you really so low as to show jealousy of him? Of this murderer and kidnapper?"

"I just think it passing strange that you did not mention your conversation until occasion required it."

"I saw no need to and as I said, he was a talker and said a great deal while I tried to ready our horses. I could have done without his nattering in my ear. All I remember is his comment about East Hardwick."

"All right, I'm sorry. I just don't like the idea of other men speaking to you. I don't like visiting the villages at all. Too many people, too many questions. And you stick out like a sore thumb."

"Meaning?"

"Meaning men have a mind to talk pretty to you."

She kissed him on his cheek. "You don't have to be jealous, I promise you. I've not been interested in a man in years. You're the first for a long time and I mean for you to be the last."

Will folded his arm behind his head and Anna rested her head on it. "I should have killed that bastard when I had the chance," he muttered.

"Aye," she replied. "You should have."

THIRTY

The village of East Hardwick was nestled between the Great North Road and a small stream that ran southeast to join the River Went west of Wentbridge. Woodland surrounded it on all sides and the grass was thick with snowdrops that were on the cusp of flowering.

Robert, Little John and Katherine rode the wain which was loaded with barrels to give them the appearance of ale merchants. The barrels were all empty but one which concealed the band's weapons. The other outlaws rode behind disguised variously as pilgrims, tradesmen and travellers. They had never entered a village en masse before and needed to appear as peaceful wanderers who had met on the road.

Peace was something of a fragile hope for the settlements that lived in the shadow of Pontefract. Many had been stripped of goods by soldiers wearing Lancaster's sigil who were a common sight in the inns and on the road. The roads were busy. Wagons of grain, materials and supplies passed up and down the Great North Road between Pontefract and Tickhill where the ongoing siege summoned the tramp of men and horses like a horn on the hunt.

"That's the third lot of soldiers that have paid our wain a thirsty eye," said John as they approached the village. "I say we ditch it. It's only a matter of time before Lancaster's wolves decide to rob us."

"And then we'll be for it when they find the barrels a little on the light side," added Will.

"Agreed," Robert said and they pushed the wain off the road where it could be concealed by the trees. They carried their weapons deeper into the woods and buried them under foliage. It wouldn't do to march into the village like a small warband. They had to keep up the pretence of simple travellers.

Nevertheless, nine was a group large enough to attract unwanted attention and Robert divided the band in two. "Will, you take Anna, Simon, Wat and Rob Dyer, and head for the alehouse." He said. "See what you can find out. John, Katherine, Much and I will scour the rest of the village and see if we can't get some information from the locals. Watch out for Lancaster's men. We don't want them to see us asking too many questions."

Robert led his detachment into the village first while the others waited. It was a busy place for a small settlement. Soldiers had garrisoned some of the buildings and had pressed the village blacksmith into shoeing their horses and repairing their armour. Robert guessed the alehouse would be crawling with Lancaster's men and did not envy Will and the others their task.

A group of soldiers were dicing on an upturned barrel while their equipment was being repaired at the forge. Robert and the others hung around the hut, hoping for a chance to talk with the blacksmith without being overheard. The hiss of the quenching trough and the clink on the anvil was a continuous noise and the poor blacksmith was kept so busy that the chance of a chat with him seemed slim.

Another group of soldiers came down the street bearing one of their number between them. The man appeared to be dead and blood seeped down the front of his maille from a severe gash in his throat.

"What the devil...?" cried one of the dicing soldiers who was apparently a sergeant. He rose angrily at the sight of a comrade come to harm.

"We were bringing a grain ark taken from one of the hamlets south of here," one of the slain soldier's companions claimed. "We were lured into the woods by a cowardly arrow sent our way and left Thomas to guard the ark. When we got back we found his throat cut and the grain ark stolen."

"Imbeciles!" the sergeant snapped. "To leave one man to guard a grain ark on the road? That arrow was clearly meant as a distraction. They saw you fools coming a mile off, no doubt! I'll report this to Constable Reynold and he'll have the hides off your backs! Where did this happen?"

"Not far from that monastery south of here," said the unhappy soldier.

"The woods hereabout must be crawling with hobhoods," the sergeant replied. I'll see if old Reynold can't send some lads out to apprehend some of the buggers. A few hangings might curb the locals of their thievery at least a little."

The soldiers accompanied the returning party and their fallen member to another part of the village telling the blacksmith they would be back to collect their gear shortly. Robert took his chance and ducked under the thatched roof of the hut.

"Greetings, smith," he said. "You seem to have enough business."

"If its smithing you want done, you'll have to get in line," the blacksmith replied. "Lancaster's men have me working night and day."

"It's information I'm after, not smithing," Robert replied. "Have you heard the name de Gisburn in these parts?"

The smith shook his head as he drew a section of plate armour from the forge and inspected its colour. "Doesn't ring a bell."

"No sign of a hooded man who travels in armed company with no sigil?"

"There are dozens of armed men wandering into East Hardwick each day looking for work in Lancaster's army. If you've no sigil to give me, I can't help you."

"Very well. We heard the soldiers speak of a monastery south of here. We saw no such building on our way here. We're new to these parts, you see."

"It's screened by the woods. Those sods only know about it because they tried to loot it last week. The monks there are Carthusians and want nothing to do with Lancaster and his rebellion but they handed over some grain and mead just the same if only to stave off further visits."

"Carthusians?" Wat said once the two halves of the gang had met back at the wain to exchange news. "I heard tell of their lot. Secretive bunch. They only attend mass once a month, so it's said. Nobody sees them the rest of the time."

"Sounds like a good target for de Gisburn if he wanted someplace to hide," said Robert. "Secluded. Isolated."

"They wouldn't shelter the likes of him, surely?" said Wat.

"Maybe at sword point they might,"

"Do you think he'd dare?" Much asked.

"De Gisburn?" John said with a snort. "He's the devil himself. He'd show no qualm at murdering a monk to get his way."

"Do you think he and his men were the ones who stole that grain ark and killed one of Lancaster's men?" Will asked.

"Possibly," said Robert. "If he's hiding at that monastery then he and his men need feeding. And if the Carthusians lack grain after Lancaster's foraging..."

"De Gisburn wouldn't think twice of thieving whatever was passing by," Katherine added.

They headed south and found the monastery after several forays into the woods. It was a small church of rough stone with a wooden spire protruding from its shingled roof.

"Looks more like a hermitage than a monastery," said Wat as they viewed it through the foliage.

"It must be just a small cell of Carthusians, not a full charterhouse," Robert replied.

"My babes are in there, I know it," said Simon, his hand on his sword hilt. They had brought their weapons with them although they had nothing resembling a plan of attack.

"Stay your hand, Simon," said Robert, placing his own hand on his cousin's shoulder. "If your children are in there, we'll get them out, I promise. But we don't know what's going on inside. There maybe half a dozen monks held hostage with them. We can't risk anything until we scout the place out."

"Let's get going then," said John.

"Only one of us should go," said Robert. "No good in the whole lot of us traipsing about the place."

"I'll go," said Simon."

"No. I will. You're too keen for blood."

"And you aren't?"

"Of course I am. But a cool head is needed right now. There'll be time for bloodletting later."

He unbuckled his sword and quiver and handed them to Katherine. "I'll be back soon. Everybody just wait here and don't let yourselves be seen."

He cut through the woods to where the trees grew close to a low precinct wall. Keeping to the shadows of the trees, he followed the wall around towards the stream. He could see nobody about inside the compound but there were enough buildings to house and feed a dozen monks. The two largest buildings were the chapel and what Robert assumed to be the hall or dorter where the monks slept.

The wall met the banks of the stream and Robert slithered down into the water. It was icy cold but did not reach much above his knees. Following the bank to the edge of the compound where the precinct wall began once more, he clambered up and squatted, dripping, at eye level with the top stones. A small plough field led to the woods and Robert could smell the dung that had recently been spread over the furrows. Within the compound was a byre, a granary a henhouse and a small fishpond. With whatever grain they grew in the neighbouring field, Robert did not wonder that the Carthusians did not lack for outside sustenance. He delved back into the trees and headed full circle to re-join his comrades.

"Nobody about," he told them.

"That could be very good or very bad," Wat said.

"Well what do we do now?" Will asked. "De Gisburn may have a detachment of the sheriff's men indoors but loitering about in the woods isn't going to get Simon's children back. I say we storm the place and face the odds whatever they may be."

"Aye," agreed John. "Enough skulking about. Let's have at the bastards!"

"We must be careful not to put Simon's children in danger!" Katherine warned them. "If de Gisburn feels threatened, he may hold the babes' lives hostage to halt us." She saw the pained look in Simon's eye. "I'm sorry, Simon, but I only think of your children's safety. We must practice caution."

"He's already holding them hostage," said Robert. "Will and John are right. There's no more use in waiting or spying. We should hit them hard when they're not expecting it. It's the only chance we have of getting those children away safely."

"What's the plan?" Will asked.

"Two teams," Robert said. "We hit them from the north and the south. They'll think a bloody storm has opened over their heads. Will, you lead your lot across the field towards the byre and granary. Check those buildings first. Be quick and be silent. No use in giving the game away until we have to. Kill any soldier you encounter but try and squeeze some information out of them if you can first. Find out where the children are. De Gisburn too for that matter."

They split up as they had done before, only this time they carried strung bows and naked blades. Will led Anna, Wat Rob Dyer and Simon towards the dung-smelling field while Robert, Katherine, John and Much cut right. There was no cover that close to the walls but the buildings had few windows and nobody knew they were coming. Robert nocked an arrow to his bowstring and motioned the others to follow close.

They climbed silently over the stone wall and entered the compound. The chapel was the closest building and they hurried over to it and pressed their backs to its plastered wall. Sidling around to the door, Robert motioned Katherine to cross to its other side and cover him as he opened it. Easing the tension in his bowstring, he planted his right boot against the door and shoved it inwards.

It swung in easily and the darkness within seemed to grab at him. He felt helplessly exposed, despite Katherine's arrow tip that swept the open space, ready to fly at any threat that might emerge. As his eyes grew accustomed to the dimness, he could make out low wooden benches and an altar at the far end, draped with a white cloth. The building was one long room and could not hide anybody from sight of the doorway.

"Empty," he told the others. "Let's move on to the hall."

As they cut across the grass towards the hall, they heard the ring of blades coming from the other side of the compound.

"We can come upon them from behind and even the odds a little," said John.

"Hold!" Robert hissed and ducked down, motioning the others to do likewise.

The door to the hall had opened and two men in hauberks emerged, both carrying crossbows. They hurried around the building, clearly planning to reinforce their besieged comrades on the other side of the compound. Robert drew back his arrow and loosed, sending the shaft into the side of the foremost man.

The arrow pierced the maille shirt and the man fell with a cry. His comrade whirled around and loosed his crossbow in the vague direction of the outlaws. They all ducked and the bolt went over their heads. Katherine rose up, bow drawn, and sent an arrow into the crossbowman's face. He went down silently but his comrade still writhed in agony on the grass which was damp from the blood leaking through the links in his maille.

The outlaws hurried over to the dying man. Robert drew his knife and pressed it against his throat.

"Tell us all you know and I will hurry your passing," he said into the man's ear. "Lie to me or refuse and I will prolong it."

The man was white as a sheet and coughed, the motion causing his face to screw up in agony.

"How many of you are there?" Robert asked.

"F... five," the man managed.

"Five soldiers plus de Gisburn?"

The man's wide eyes flitted to him and Robert saw a fear there.

"Speak!"

"Aye! Five plus de Gisburn!"

"The children!" Much demanded. "Where are the children?"

The man coughed some more and his lips showed red. His eyes began to drift. Robert shook him violently. "Where are they?" he repeated.

"You'll not get more from him," John said.

It was true. The man's body had gone slack and there was barely a flutter in his eyes.

"You should have asked him about the children first," Katherine remarked.

Robert said nothing. He drew his knife across the man's throat, finishing him. Then he entered the hall.

"Shouldn't we try and help the others?" Much asked.

"Not until we're sure no more of the bastards can come upon our backs," Robert said, peering into the gloom of the hall.

"There should only be three of them left," said Katherine.

"And de Gisburn," said Robert.

The hall had a central hearth surrounded by plain cut benches and tables. A wooden ladder led to an upper storey which was presumably the dorter. A screens passage concealed the far end and the outlaws crept towards it, their footsteps echoing in the roomy chamber. Beyond they found a small solar. In the solar was a monk.

He wore the white robe and pointed hood of the Carthusian order and was visibly terrified of the outlaws. As soon as they entered the chamber, he fell to his knees and clasped his hands together as if in prayer.

"You are either here to save me or to kill me," he said. "Either would be God's blessing!"

"What are you doing in here, monk?" Robert asked him.

"Praying!" the man said excitedly. "There is naught else I can do!"

"Do the soldiers keep you locked in here?"

"They do. But God will judge them for I may not."

"What of the rest of your order?"

At this the man fell silent. His face showed a great sadness at something of which he seemed unable to speak.

"You're the last one?" Katherine asked, her voice filled with pity.

The monk nodded.

"Where's de Gisburn?" Robert asked him.

The man's face turned from sadness to terror at the mention of the name.

"Do not speak that demon's name lest he should be summoned by it!" he hissed.

"Where?" Robert asked again but the monk did not hear him.

"He's the one who did for my brothers. Only through his cruelty did he keep me alive! Why else?"

"What did he do to your brothers?" Katherine asked.

At this, the monk's eyes drifted upwards to gaze fearfully at the ceiling as if the answer lay in those simple beams, or rather beyond them. Robert moved out of the solar and climbed the wooden ladder to the dorter, his sword drawn.

About a dozen pallets were laid out in tidy rows and at first glance there seemed to be nothing of interest in the vaulted chamber. But something compelled Robert's eyes to drift upwards and then he saw the cause of the monk's misery.

They hung upside down like carcasses in the market square. Their white robes were bound about them and they resembled cocooned insects trapped in a spider's web. Their throats had been cut and the blood from them had pooled and congealed in the pallets below, soaked up by the straw.

Robert clambered back down and the look on his face must have piqued the curiosity of his companions for they filed up, one by one, to see for themselves. None spoke as they descended, their faces pale.

"He's a madman..." said Katherine.

"I never really believed he was that mad," said John. "I thought it was just stories really."

"Where is he!" Robert demanded of the monk loudly. He drew his knife and held it threateningly at the wretched man.

"Rob, no!" said Katherine, placing a hand on his arm.

"Tell me!" Robert said.

The monk closed his eyes and sank to his knees in prayer.

"We'll get no more sense from this one," John said. "We'll find him, Rob. But first let's help Will and the others. They may still be in danger."

THIRTY-ONE

The monk followed them out as they left the hall. The battle was over. Will and the others walked across the grass towards them, their blades red and the sweat standing out on their brows.

"How many?" Robert called out to them.

"Three," Will called back. "The buggers had crossbows and nearly got Wat. Anna killed two of them though." He grinned at Anna with pride.

"Praise be to God!" the monk declared. "We are saved! I must kneel to Him in thanks!" he scurried off, his habit flapping, in the direction of the chapel.

"But where's de Gisburn?" Robert muttered.

"And where are Simon's children?" added Much.

The look on Simon's face showed that he did not consider this a victory at all. There could be no victory until his children were back in his arms and de Gisburn was dead at his feet.

"No sign of them?" Will asked.

"No," Robert replied. "Any luck your end?"

"Fat chance. We had a time of it just trying to stay alive. And my Anna doesn't take prisoners!"

"That bloody monk must know something," Robert said.

"Monk?"

"Aye, we found him in the hall. They'd been keeping him locked up though God knows what for. The rest of his brothers were strung up and bled out like pigs."

They headed over to the chapel and Robert posted Will and Little John at the door as lookouts.

With de Gisburn still about, he would take no chances.

The monk knelt by the altar, his hands together in prayer. The rest of the outlaws crowded into the small chapel and approached the kneeling figure.

"Listen, brother," Robert said. "Have you seen any children about this place? Two of them; a boy and a girl no more than five years of age."

"Children..." the monk mumbled. "The laughter of children is fleeting like the song of spring. Like sunlight over God's green fields it warms us and then is gone all too quickly."

Simon lurched forward and seized the monk by his habit, hauling him around to face them. "Where are they?" he cried. "Where are my children?"

"Gone with God," the monk replied. "Gone to dream amidst the wavering grass and to watch the salmon in the sky."

"The man's raving," said Much in irritation. "There's no sense to be had from him."

"Salmon in the sky..." said Robert and then a cold feeling came over him. "The fish pond!"

The outlaws bolted from the chapel. Will and John joined them from the doorway and they tore across the compound towards the cluster of farm buildings on the other side. Simon ran ahead and didn't stop when he got to the small body of water. He splashed into its shallows, the water lapping around his thighs as he delved deep with his hands, searching, searching.

He gave out a cry and hauled a sodden form up, its golden hair limp like seaweed. The pale skin of his daughter was like lime-wash and Simon's face was twisted into a tortured, soundless grimace. The other outlaws helped him drag her onto the grass and then dove back into the pond to search for the boy. He was duly found and laid beside his sister.

Simon made no noise as he knelt at their sides, his face pressed to their wet forms. He rocked back and forth in his agony.

"The bastards weighted them down," said John inspecting the rocks tied to their feet. "Why do that? Why kidnap them and then kill them?"

"To make us come," Robert replied. "There was never any hope of getting them back alive. It was all a ruse to draw us here."

"A trap?" asked Will. "Well it failed. We finished off the sheriff's men and are still standing."

"Aye, but where is de Gisburn?" Much said.

Anna had remained in the chapel as the outlaws bolted from it. She couldn't leave. Not after the light that shone in from the high window had fallen on the monk's face as Simon had held him by the throat. He smiled at her and it made her sick.

"You've lost, Guy," she told him. "Your hired swords are dead and if you've harmed those children, you'll know a pain you never thought possible."

"And yet you said nothing when you saw me," Guy de Gisburn said, his wide smile blasphemously wicked beneath the white hood of his habit. "You could have told your friends who I was and yet something stayed your tongue. I wonder, what was that?"

Anna said nothing.

"Could it be the man I saw you with at South Elmsall? The one who stood guard outside this chapel just now? What is his name? He was ever so reluctant to give it to me before."

"Will," Anna replied through gritted teeth. "And you're not fit to speak it."

"William Shacklock! Hood's companion from Wakefield! And your bed mate too, if I'm not mistaken. Just as my brother was, once upon a time. I don't doubt your reluctance to see me in the hands of your companions. Not with what I know of you. What would dear Will think of his lover if he knew the truth about her?"

"If you think that will save you, you are gravely mistaken," said Anna. She drew the dagger at her belt. "I'll finish you first and have done with it!"

Guy tut-tutted and parted his habit to reveal a long blade of his own. He still wore his filthy horsehide rags beneath the white cloth. "Let's not fool ourselves, Anna. We are very nearly family after all."

"It may have been consummated but it was never holy in the eyes of God."

Guy laughed. "I know you loved my brother. As did I. Can we really be so hateful of each other when one we both held so dear wounded us both so?"

"It was your wound that killed him," said Anna bitterly.

"Brothers fight. Especially when the leadership of a criminal enterprise is up for grabs. It doesn't mean I loved him any less."

"You don't know the meaning of the word. You never have. And where is your precious criminal enterprise now? All I see is a thief-taker doing odd jobs for the sheriff."

"And you yourself have come a long way from the wife of an alehouse proprietor. We are all of us in a constant state of change, like the seasons."

"You're done with changing now, Guy. When the others come back, you'll be strung up like the filth you are."

"No. I have no intention of crossing blades with your master just yet. I'm having far too much fun to end the game now. You will tell me what Hood's plans are; where I can find him, what he is planning next. You will tell me or I will wait here and die, but not before the truth about you passes my lips. We'll see about your happy ending with William Shacklock then."

Anna looked into those dark and unhinged eyes and knew she was beaten.

They carried the limp bodies of the children up to the chapel. Robert knew that they would have to bury them but it didn't seem right taking them from the pond directly to a dark hole in the ground. They should be laid under the eyes of God for at least a while so that some prayers might be said.

When they got to the chapel Anna stumbled from its doors.

"Anna!" Will cried. "Christ, I didn't notice she wasn't with us!" He ran to her and held her. "What happened?" he asked her as the rest of the outlaws crowded around her.

"De Gisburn got away," she said.

"De Gisburn was here?" Robert demanded. "The monk...?"

"Was de Gisburn in disguise," she replied.

The outlaws were silent as the knowledge that their dreaded enemy had been in their midst all along sank in.

"I didn't get a proper look at him, else I would have known," said Will.

"But you knew, didn't you, Anna?" Robert asked her.

"Not until you all stormed out of here and he turned from the altar to watch in your wake. The light from the window fell on his face and I knew him for the man we met at South Elmsall."

"Did he harm you?" Will asked.

"I tried to gut him but he disarmed me," Anna said, looking down with embarrassment. "Then he was off into the woods. I called for you but you were down at the pond."

"How long since he fled?" Robert asked, his eyes ablaze.

"Rob, he's gone," said Katherine. "You can't go tearing after him. It's over."

"And we've got these little ones to lay to rest," Much said.

They carried the children into the chapel and laid them down on the stone flags. Their wet clothes formed puddles on the stone. They lamented Old Stephen's absence for he might have sung a psalm or said some fine Latin words. As it was they made do with silent prayer while Simon's sobs echoed around the chamber. Afterwards they buried them in a small clearing in the woods and erected two small wooden crosses.

"We should do something for those monks too," Much said.

"We don't have time," Robert said. "If anybody should come upon this place while we're still here we'll get the blame for their murders."

"But we can't just leave them hanging there..." Much protested.

It was agreed that they would cut the monks down and lay them in their beds with their hoods covering their faces. It was the least they could do and, under the circumstances, the only thing.

Little John supported Simon who was too wracked with grief to walk of his own accord and the band of outlaws headed back to their cart and horses near the village's outskirts.

"How is it that it wasn't until we had all left the chapel that you realised the monk was de Gisburn," Robert asked Anna as they rode back towards Barnsdale.

"I told you, the light was dim," she answered. "I didn't get a good look at him until he moved closer."

"But why did you tarry in the chapel? Why you; the only one who could recognise him but for Will who was without the building."

"What are you getting at, Rob?" Will asked, leaning forward in his saddle.

"Just chewing over the events in my mind," he replied.

"If you've got something to say, then spit it out so I can ram it back down your throat!"

"Back off, Will," Robert snapped. "I have a right to question a member of my band if I've a mind too, your bed mate or no."

"Your band? I don't recall any of us electing you leader as it happens."

Robert turned in his saddle. "So, it has finally come to that, has it? You took you time, I must say. Was it when you figured that you no longer needed me to show you how to hunt and how to steal that you found the courage to challenge my leadership? Face it, Will, without me you'd have been hanged by Wakefield's bailiff a day after your brothers tried to murder him!"

"Stop it, all of you!" Katherine said and they looked at her in some surprise. "Look at us! Turning on each other after all that's happened! Is this what de Gisburn has done to us? Haven't we come through enough together to trust one another? Haven't we seen enough bloodshed to forge a bond as strong as family, a bond that even de Gisburn cannot break?"

They said nothing further as they rode on. They were all in a sour mood. The argument had been a distraction from the memory that lingered in their minds of Simon's murdered babes; sodden and pale on the wet grass. Each of them was left to dwell on the events of the day which would haunt them for many days to come.

There was no victory to celebrate that night.

THIRTY-TWO

Simon de Warde sat at his desk, a ledger in front of him, as he totted up the incoming goods intended to bolster the royalist forces. Most had been confiscated from captured Lancastrians as they fled Tickhill. It was an endless list of arms, coats of maille, gambesons, gauntlets, bucklers, pikes, leg guards and plate shoes. Food in the form of pigs, venison, grain, barrels of herring and salted pork and wine and ale seemed like a vast amount of victuals but Simon knew from experience that such quantities rapidly vanished into the bottomless hole of an army's appetite. Then there were the captured horses and equipment; saddles, bridles, lances, cruppers and shafrons. Things of higher value trickled in too, things that had surely been looted from Yorkshire towns by Lancaster's barons; cups of gold and silver, dishes, robes, furs, silk garters, silver chains, pearls, glass buttons and leather-bound books.

The door opened and Constance entered the room, ushering their two-year-old son before her. He tottered about and tripped over the edge of the wolf skin rug and began to bawl. Simon rose and scooped him up in his arms. He sat back down, balancing Simon the younger on his knees, and began to bounce him up and down until the chubby infant's teary face cracked into a smile.

"What news from the queen?" Constance asked as she sat down in the chair opposite. She had seen the royal messenger leave Guiseley that morning and recognised him as the queen's man who had delivered the orders in January to arrest any Marcher Lords heading north. As usual, it was Queen Isabella who took charge of the administrative affairs of her husband's realm in a time of crisis.

"Instructions to rally Yorkshire against Lancaster," Simon replied. "Offer safety to deserters from his army and to amass goods and supplies to reinforce His Majesty's army when it gets here."

"Hence the looting of the shire by William de Aune and yourself."

"Looting? When has it ever been different in times of war? We all have to do our bit, make our sacrifices or else victory will elude us."

"Are things really so desperate? Lancaster failed to take Tickhill and after Roger de Mortimer's surrender at Shrewsbury one might assume that he is running out of friends and luck."

"One should never assume when it comes to men like Lancaster," Simon said reprovingly. "He abandoned his siege of Tickhill because the king's army is mustering at Coventry. He has undoubtedly headed south for Burton Bridge with the intention of preventing the king from crossing the Trent. And with the spring floods, the king is not likely to find a passable ford upriver."

"So, there will be a battle at Burton Bridge and Lancaster will be defeated."

"Again you assume, Constance. What if Lancaster should prevail?"

"Against the king whose following has been bolstered by the return of the le Despensers and their retinues?"

"You underestimate Lancaster's strength. For too long has he held the north and strengthened his army on the fat of the land. He might just prevail and then where would we be? Don't forget de Montfort's victory over King Henry at Lewes fifty-odd years ago however short-lived it was. Kings can be defeated and those who were most loyal to them find their predicaments most dire."

"You think of yourself?"

"I think of all of us. If Lancaster is victorious he will appoint his own sheriffs and men like William de Aune and I will be cast out like tenants unable to pay their rent. What then for you and young Simon?"

The infant squealed with joy, wholly unaware of his precarious future. Constance bent to pick him up and she held him close as if her husband's words had had a profound effect on her.

"Then we must do all that we can to support His Majesty and ensure Lancaster's defeat," she said decidedly.

Simon's steward had been waiting patiently outside the door for an opportune moment to enter and he took it now.

"Guy de Gisburn has arrived, my lord," he said. "I had him shown into the Great Hall."

"De Gisburn?" said Simon excitedly. "Is he alone?"

"Yes, my lord. I did not enquire as to the whereabouts of the troops you lent him."

"Very well, I'll see him now."

"I'll put Simon to bed," Constance said. "I'll not have him in the same room as that bounty-hunting animal."

Simon did not wonder at her disproval of the man he had sent to hunt down her precious outlaws. His mind was all but made up on the matter of her treachery. The final test would be to see how she reacted when presented with Hood's head and perhaps John of Holderness's too. That would spell the end of this nonsensical empathy for hooded robbers.

De Gisburn still wore his extraordinary horsehide cloak but the helmet was missing. The hood was raised and the twisted, dried ears that hung down on either side of his face would have been comical but for the deranged mind that looked out from the depths of the stinking garment.

"How fares the hunt?" Simon asked him. "Do you have Hood's head to show me?"

"The hobhood is a more elusive animal that I gave him credit for," de Gisburn said, not without a flare of admiration in his voice. "The hunt continues but I have the scent of blood in my nostrils."

"Then you failed. Where are my men?"

"It was your men who bungled the trap and let Hood escape. I no longer have need of them. Which is fortunate as they are all dead."

"Dead? All of them?" Simon was astounded. How had the madman managed to lose every last one of them?

"Butchered by Hood and his pack. As I said, it was their own clumsiness that did for them. But pay it no mind, sheriff. I require no further soldiers from you. I shall continue the hunt alone. However, I have information that will entice you to follow close in my footsteps and see an end to Hood personally."

"Personally?" Simon said. "If you think I'm blundering off into the greenwood with you because you're too incompetent to apprehend a robber on your own then you're sorely mistaken. I'm busy enough as it is."

"Yes, amounting wealth and arms to ensure the king's victory against Lancaster." De Gisburn smiled. "I saw your foragers on my way to Guiseley."

"What of it?"

"What if I could lead you to a treasure that would buy a dozen men-at-arms with blades of the finest steel and the fastest horses?"

"Hood has such wealth in his keeping? Surely he has already drunk and whored away the ransom he received for my life."

"Whatever wealth he has he intends to increase it significantly. Have you ever heard of the Coterel family?"

"Mmm, yes. Landowners in the Peak District as I recall."

"Indeed. And perhaps you have heard of Berengaria Coterel's dowry that was recently stolen by Simon le Lound of Adwick Hall."

"I did hear something of the like."

"Well, Hood and his pack intend to steal it with the help of the Bradburn brothers."

"The Bradburns? Here in Yorkshire?"

"They share some wild history with Great John who was once your servant I believe. He uses the name 'Little' now, by the by. Some sort of outlaw joke I understand."

"The Bradburn brothers and the Hood gang in collusion?" said Simon, rubbing his chin. "And such a wealth to be gained if I should apprehend them in the stealing of it! How have you come by this information?"

"I have corrupted one of Hood's followers and turned them to my service. I need you and your troops to surround Adwick Hall on the night of the robbery so that none of the outlaws slip the net."

"Very well. I will marshal my soldiers at a point nearby and form a perimeter once the outlaws are within the manor grounds. We will await your signal. I shall send for wine. We have much to discuss in the planning of this trap."

"There is one condition," Guy said, his voice honed to a fine edge by hate. "Hood's life is mine to take."

"Hood's head on a pike is all I require. How that is achieved I leave to you."

The gatehouse was a timber-framed building that guarded the bridge leading into the cobbled courtyard of Adwick Hall. The still water of the moat that surrounded the hall on all sides was like black glass beneath the clouded moon. The trees wavered gently in the cool breeze and the shadows were deep in the woods that circled the home of Simon le Lound.

Little John rose from the undergrowth like an enormous mushroom sprouting in record time. He stared at the bridge and gatehouse, his features stony in the silver light of the moon. He heard the soft rustle of leaves as Katherine, Much, Will and Anna rose up around him.

It had been a hard fight for Robert to persuade John and Will to take part in what was essentially a distraction. They wanted to be in on the robbery itself, danger and conflict as meat and drink to them. But Robert had been determined not to waste the skills of his best fighters on the simple robbery of a property that, in all probability, was little more than deserted. He wanted them on the outside where the fighting, if there was to be any, would likely occur. Or so he said.

But why then, the others had mused, had he sent Katherine with them? Surely he would want her out of harm's way. John suspected that Katherine wanted no part of the robbery and shared Old Stephen's view that it was a pointless and dangerous exercise in greed. But her reservations did not mean she was not willing to do her bit in the scheme. *Perhaps Robert wanted her in the company of his best fighters*, John thought. *Who better to protect her?* Although none would dare suggest this notion in the presence of Katherine for she loathed such coddling.

The real surprise had been Anna's attitude. She had been as keen as John and Will to rob Adwick Hall but ever since the nightmare of the Carthusian hermitage, she had expressed little interest in the scheme and her reluctance had begun to rub off on Will. Things had soured between them and Rob. They spoke little at camp these days.

Nevertheless, John was glad to have them with him. Robert had given him command of the party instead of Will and that spoke volumes about the bad atmosphere in camp. Will had always been Robert's righthand man.

Their mission was to cause a distraction that would draw the attention of whoever occupied the gatehouse while Robert, Simon, Wat and Rob Dyer slipped into the grounds on the other side.

At a signal from John, the outlaws swept silently towards the bridge, keeping low, like snakes in the long grass. They did not carry weapons save the daggers at their belts. They needed their hands free for the bushels of straw soaked in animal grease they carried with them.

The party split into two with John and Much heading left of the bridge and Will, Anna and Katherine heading right. The two teams slithered down the banks that sloped into the waters of the moat and, clinging to the wooden supports of the bridge, vanished into its shadows.

They stuffed their bushels in the eaves of the supports on either side. This done, Little John fumbled with flint and knife while the others scrambled up the banks and headed for the trees. Sparks flashed brilliantly in the gloom until John finally succeeded in kindling one of the bushels which began to glow and crackle, dropping orange embers to hiss in the waters below.

By the time John had reached the trees, the other bushels beneath the bridge had caught and the foremost portion of the structure was ablaze; a curling bloom of orange flame reflected brilliantly in the waters of the moat.

John and the others watched with smiles of satisfaction from their refuge in the shadows. Their portion of the work was done.

A noise to their left startled the group. The crackling of undergrowth, as of a large body of men and horses passing through the woods, made each of them grab whatever weapons they had brought with them and ready themselves to fight or flee.

Mounted figures could be seen some distance through the trees and the moonlight glinted off kettle helms. There was a great many of them and they were converging on the outlaws, refuting any notion that their appearance was a coincidence. These soldiers had been lying in wait for them; waiting for the right moment to strike!

The outlaws turned and fled. Questions plagued John's mind as he ran. *How had the soldiers known about their plan to fire the bridge and why had they waited until the bridge was roaring merrily to strike?* He pushed these thoughts from his mind. He tried to think on nothing but the desperate urge to get away.

A second column of riders and footmen appeared through the trees up ahead. They were fenced in and, as the two columns converged, the outlaws knew there was no escape. It was hopeless.

The enemy was too strong and too knowledgeable of the outlaws' plans. Capture or death was imminent.

THIRTY-THREE

The windows of the hall were like black eyes set in silver but for a dim glow in one upper storey solar. Robert shook his head disapprovingly. Black windows were a sure sign that a house was unoccupied. A man more sensible than Simon le Lound would have instructed his servants to leave a fire burning in the Great Hall while he was hunting at Loxley Chase. Such a measure was a good deterrent against all who might have designs on the hall's rich contents. But there would be fire enough in a while, if Katherine and John and the others had done their job well.

They crossed the moat on a small raft of timbers lashed together. The water was clean enough this early in the year and free from the green slime that would accumulate in high summer but it was icy cold. They paddled up to one of the windows that looked in on the storerooms and kitchens of the manor hall.

Robert rose slowly from the raft so that it wouldn't rock too much. Water sloped over the timbers anyway and Simon cursed as his feet got wet. Robert pulled back the shutter on the window and, grasping the edge of the sill, hauled himself up and through it.

The storeroom was black as pitch and he fumbled his way around, brushing against casks, dangling joints of dried meat and shelves of jars and pots. Simon, Wat and Rob Dyer dropped down to join him in the blackness.

Robert found his way to the door and pushed it open an inch. There was a light burning somewhere but the house was entirely silent. He pushed the door open wider and they found themselves in the kitchens. The baking oven was cool, the ashes at its door un-swept. Flour lay strewn across the kneading benches as if the preparation of food had been cut suddenly short.

Robert led the others into the Great Hall. It was dim and the shuttered windows let in only enough moonlight for them to see the outlines of benches and tables. There were other shapes too; dark, heavy-looking things strewn across the floor between the tables and the roasting pits. Robert nudged one with his foot and his sharp intake of breath caused the others to turn.

"Small wonder there are no servants about," said Wat in a low voice. "The poor buggers are all here."

There was at least a dozen of them; grooms, cooks, chambermaids and young stable lads. There were even a pair of wolfhounds, their great still forms atop the corpses; grey fur matted with blood. Robert knelt and inspected the body of a large lady with apron and hands white with flour.

"Throat's cut," he said, grimly.

It was a scene that was uncomfortably familiar and Robert wasn't the only one whose mind drifted back to those dead monks at East Hardwick. He cast his eyes around the place and up at the hangings that dangled from the rafters. Some movement in the darkness caught his eye and he flung himself flat as he yelled out a warning to his comrades.

An arrow sailed through the air and embedded itself in one of the long oak tables, missing Wat by an inch as he dove for cover.

"Up in the minstrels' gallery!" Robert said and cursed his lack of a bow with which to shoot back.

"Is it him?" Simon asked, his eyes livid in the darkness.

Robert risked another glance up at the gallery and ducked back down as a second arrow found its mark in the bench he was using for cover. He had seen the patchwork cloak and the pointed hood with its sinisterly pagan ears and knew he could not be mistaken.

"Aye, it's de Gisburn," he said and immediately regretted it. Simon's wide eyes had dulled to a simmering rage and he was off like a coney, bolting for the door by the dais that led to the stairs.

"Simon!" Robert cried and cursed as another arrow almost found its mark in him. While de Gisburn nocked another shaft to his string, Robert took advantage of the delay and tore after Simon who had reached the nail-studded door and was heaving it open.

By the time Robert got there Simon was halfway up the stairs to the minstrels' gallery. Robert seized his cousin by the arm and pinned him to the wall.

"Get your hands off me!" Simon cried. "That bastard took everything from me; my Theresa, my children, everything! You would not dare deny me my vengeance!"

"No, I would not," said Robert. "But we must take care. He is a vicious fighter. There is no good in charging at him alone. We must take him together!"

"Fine! But I make the killing blow!"

They drew their daggers and lamented their shortness. Swords would have been better but they had brought none, not wanting to be weighed down while crossing the moat. They emerged onto the minstrels' gallery and found it deserted. De Gisburn had vanished to another part of the hall. They edged out of the gallery and explored the passage that led to the solars of Simon le Lound and his lady.

A fire burned in the grate of one and Robert knew as they entered it that this was the light they had seen from outside. De Gisburn had most likely been using it as his lair while he lay in wait for them. This whole thing was rotten to the core. How had de Gisburn known that they would be here? Was it the Bradburns? Had they betrayed them? That made no sense. They were supposed to take the treasure to them at Skelbrooke where Robert's gang would be given their cut before the Bradburns would take the rest back to James Coterel. Why would they throw all that away?

The door to the solar slammed shut behind them. De Gisburn stood between them and the passage. His hand slid the bolt home, cutting them off from Wat and Rob Dyer who were making their way up the stairs to re-join their comrades.

De Gisburn drew his own dagger and the three men faced each other, waiting for somebody to make the first move. De Gisburn lunged and drew first blood, opening a gash in Simon's tunic through which blood immediately seeped. Robert thrust at de Gisburn but his short blade was parried and the flat of de Gisburn's boot sent him reeling backwards onto the rug on the centre of the floor.

De Gisburn was suddenly on top of him, his dagger raised for a killing blow but its downwards swing was intercepted by Simon who seized his wrist in one hand and used the other to drive his own dagger into de Gisburn's neck.

De Gisburn grimaced and hurled Simon from him, clawing at his neck from which blood ran freely. He emitted a horrible gargling sound and Robert fancied that his cousin had struck his killing blow but there was enough life left in their adversary to still make him a threat.

He backed away from them towards the open hearth. Before either of them could stop him, he had plucked a burning log from the flames and hurled it at Simon.

Simon ducked and the log hit the wall in a shower of embers. It rolled across the floor and rested beneath a hanging tapestry which began to curl and burn.

Robert and Simon took their eyes off de Gisburn for a moment to see the tapestry catch flame. When they looked back he was halfway out of the window. Robert ran to grab him and clutched at thin air as de Gisburn plummeted into the moat below.

Wat and Dyer hammered on the other side of the door and Simon went to let them in, clutching at his wound which bled terribly. The tapestry was entirely aflame, filling the small solar with black smoke. The rafters above were beginning to scorch and soon enough the whole roof would be blazing.

Wat and Dyer burst into the room just in time to see Robert dive from the sill and splash into the cold waters below.

Will followed Anna as she wove between the trees, on and on, into the night. The sounds of shouting had died away behind them and Will had a horrible feeling in his gut that they had just run out on their comrades who were now in the hands of the sheriff.

Eventually Anna began to slow down. Will caught up with her and they both stopped to catch their breaths; her leaning against a tree and him resting his hands on his knees. The night air cooled the sweat on their backs and made them shiver.

"How did we evade them?" Will managed after a while. "Those two columns of riders closed in on us like a noose drawn taught!"

"Luck I suppose," Anna said, her face pale and damp with sweat in the moonlight.

"I just can't understand how they found us. Do you think the Bradburn brothers turned us in?"

"Possibly."

"Shit! John and Much and Katherine were all taken most likely. Poor buggers. And what about Rob and the others? If the Bradburns gave the game away then the sheriff will know they're in the manor hall.

They'll be next." He wiped the sweat from his eyes with his palms and tried to collect himself. "We have to go back. We have to try and help them."

"What for? It's over Will. Can't you see that?"

"Rob won't go down without a fight and I want to be at his side."

"Why? So you can be captured too? Don't you see, Will? This is our chance, our chance to make a clean break and strike out on our own."

"And where would we go?"

"Anywhere! Barnsdale is wide and it is all ours now. We can run things the way we want to!"

"But the others..."

"We can't change their fate. But we can live on in their names."

Will was silent. He wanted nothing more than to run away with Anna and start a new life but he couldn't shake this nagging feeling of betrayal. Still, she was right. There was nothing they could do to help Rob and the others. To go back would be to join them at the gallows or be cut down by the sheriff's men. They had no choice.

Once their breaths had returned they plunged on into the woods and were consumed by the shadows.

THIRTY-FOUR

Robert didn't feel the cold. His body burned with the heat of the chase and the hot desire for vengeance. His tunic and mantle clung to him, soaked from his swim across the moat, and his feet squelched as he ran through the woods.

He had seen de Gisburn clamber out of the moat ahead of him and had struck for the shore with long strokes. He was pretty sure of the direction he had taken. Besides, de Gisburn was sorely wounded and his strength would ail soon.

The trees sighed above him as he ran and he found their voices encouraging. This was his home, not de Gisburn's. De Gisburn represented all that was corrupt and decayed about the greenwood and his very presence soiled the pure serenity Robert had always associated with it. His advisory represented an infection that must be cut out.

Eventually he came upon him in a glade. De Gisburn had run until he could run no more and was kneeling, his hooded head bowed as if in prayer. Robert approached him cautiously and drew his knife.

"It's time to finish this," he said. "It's time you paid the price for all the innocent lives you've taken. All the pain you've caused." Robert's thoughts were on Simon's wife and children. The slaughtered monks at East Hardwick. The murdered servants of Adwick Hall. He wanted to make de Gisburn suffer for them all if he could.

"And you see yourself as the noble avenger?" De Gisburn said and from his voice Robert could tell he was grinning. "Do you really think we are so very different, you and I?" He rose slowly, and turned to face him.

The tunic beneath his horsehide cloak was soaked with blood and his face was pale beneath its hood. "I too was the son of a forester. Forced into outlawry for a crime I did not commit. Hunted, hated and unloved. Like you, my pain forged me into a being far greater than those who had cast me out. I became the hunter instead of the hunted. Folk began to whisper my name in fear as if speaking it aloud would summon me."

"Don't flatter yourself by thinking that we are anything alike," Robert told him with venom in his voice. "We may have been cut from the same cloth but we chose two very different paths."

"The path through the greenwood is the only path for the likes of us. You really don't see it, do you? We are both the hobhood; the stalker, the hunter, the forest demon. We are two sides of the same coin; I the woodwose and you the Green Man."

"You're a bounty hunter, nothing more. You do what you do for payment."

"And you don't?"

"I steal what I have to in order to survive. You're just a common criminal like the Bradburns who betrayed us to you. There is no honour in what you do."

"The Bradburns? Look to your own, Hood. The betrayal came from Shacklock's woman."

"Anna?" Robert tried to hide his surprise but in truth it made sense to him. It had always made sense only he had never been able to fully believe it.

"We go way back, Anna Cawthorne and I," de Gisburn continued. "It wasn't too difficult to persuade her to turn on you all. Your band is in the hands of the sheriff and he can hang them all as far as I am concerned. They are but small game birds in the great hunt. You were my real prey. Now, I admit that I was in awe of you, of your reputation. There have been hobhoods before but you... *you* changed *everything*. Holding the sheriff to ransom? That act alone lifted your name to the company of Hereward, of Fulk Fitzwarin and all the others who have trod this path before. You are myth, Hood. As am I."

"I don't prey on the weak or the innocent."

"Oh? The people you rob are not innocent? The lives you have taken in your pursuit of silver were justified? They were guilty of being rich perhaps, but that was their only crime. And the treasure at Adwick Hall that the Bradburn brothers are paying you to steal, is that a treasure you cannot live without? Is it worth the price of all the people you have killed?"

"I killed no one in the pursuit of it. The blood of those servants is on your hands."

"I accept what I am. You do not. I seek only to expose your hypocrisy."

As he saw himself through the dark prism of de Gisburn's eye, Robert began to consider the events of the past weeks in a different light. He remembered Mary's words to him, spoken a lifetime ago. She had been right. His actions had gone beyond robbing people to stay alive. Greed had manoeuvred its way into his motivations and gradually taken over. After they had ransomed the sheriff they had all become richer than they had ever dreamed of and yet that had still not been enough. It had not bought their way out of outlawry. They had sought larger profits, needless profits. The robbery of Adwick Hall? Most of the band had been against that. Katherine had been against it. Had he lost his way with her too?

He was furious with himself and he was furious with de Gisburn for making himself see through his own folly. Ironically, everything de Gisburn had said to him had been the truth. De Gisburn was his dark half; what he could have been in another world. *What he might yet become.*

No more.

He lunged at de Gisburn but his enemy was ready for him despite his weakened state. They grappled and rolled on the leafy floor, knives struggling to work their way into a weak spot. De Gisburn drew blood from Robert's shoulder and Robert grasped his wrist and held it, squeezing with all his might. He shook it and the knife tumbled from de Gisburn's grip. He could see in his opponent's eyes that he knew it was over.

Robert's knife slid into de Gisburn's throat and he pushed it in up to the hilt. De Gisburn's lips parted and blood pooled in his open mouth, choking him. He gargled and coughed and eventually died with a smile that curiously resembled satisfaction on his face.

Robert let the body fall from his grip to rest softly on the ground. He panted for air and realised that he had been holding his breath as de Gisburn's life had slipped away. The colours of the greenwood seemed to return to him after a long absence. He could smell the dawn and the mossy smell of his home. The sky was paling in the east; a clean glow through the treetops.

Somewhere the sheriff had his band in irons. For the first time in a long while he knew exactly what he had to do. He looked down on de Gisburn's corpse and his bloody fist squeezed the knife in his hand tightly.

Then he went to work.

William de Aune cut a striking figure in his highly polished armour. Inspired by the armouries of Lombardy, gleaming pauldrons overlapped the breastplate and a gorget protected him from breastbone to chin. His curved bascinet, which could deflect blows far better than the flat-topped bucket helm so favoured by most English knights, sat on the table between him and Simon de Warde and reflected the light of the brazier that burned as they broke their fast.

Dawn revealed the ruin of Adwick-le-Street. The manor hall still burned and the pale morning sky was marred by its black smoke. It was the only stain on an otherwise fruitful venture. Simon had invited de Aune to accompany him on his expedition to capture the outlaws. The promise of treasure liberated from Adwick Hall had drawn him from the reparations of Tickhill with a whetted appetite for reimbursement.

The first part of the plan had gone well. Half of the outlaws were now in de Warde's custody excepting William Shacklock and one of the women who had somehow escaped. The second part of the plan in which Hood was to be allowed entrance to the hall where his fate awaited him, had been bungled badly.

De Gisburn had been supposed to kill Hood and then de Warde's men would storm the hall and recover the treasure along with anything else of value. It was possible that the fire from the bridge had spread to the hall itself, but witnesses had claimed that it had started within the Great Hall or one of the solars above it. With the bridge ablaze, Simon's men had been unable to gain entrance to the manor hall and could only watch helplessly as the place was consumed by fire along with any treasure it contained.

Hood was probably dead, de Gisburn too for that matter. *Never mind*, Simon thought. He was at least saved paying the bounty hunter his fee.

It was the loss of Berengaria Coterel's dowry that had truly spoiled things. De Aune had not shown anger as Simon had assumed he would. Instead he had matter-of-factly stated that he would reimburse himself by looting the village. Tickhill needed replenishing as it may have to withstand a second siege if Lancaster retreated from Burton Bridge. He had to hold the north until the king could chase

Lancaster into his grave and that required food, coin and supplies.

With the excuse of duty to the king waved high like a battle standard, Adwick-le-Street had been stripped of every barrel of salted pork and every tun of wine. Blades and bows were piled up outside de Aune's tent and confiscated horses were hobbled in a makeshift paddock, ready to be taken back to Tickhill.

"Lancaster won't hold out," de Aune said as he poured some weak ale into his cup from the jug on the table. "He has Tutbury Castle but will have no wish to get bogged down in a siege he cannot possibly withstand. He'll come running back north with his tail between his legs and we must be ready for him, de Warde."

Simon broke apart some of the fine white manchet loaf and popped a piece in his mouth. "Will we be able to keep him from entering Yorkshire? A defeated army may still be a strong one."

"He'll try and slip past us and return to Pontefract. From there he may send to his allies in Scotland and that must be prevented at all costs."

One of Simon's men-at-arms poked his head into the tent. "De Gisburn approaches, sire," he said.

Simon swallowed and rose clumsily from the table.

"Your bounty hunter lives," said de Aune. "Perhaps you'll have to pay him after all."

"That depends if he bears news of Hood's death."

Guy de Gisburn bore more than just news. The figure slumped over his shoulder wore the unmistakable green hood and mantle that the outlaws in Simon's custody all wore. It was something of a livery to them. Soldiers turned to stare at the strange bounty hunter whose appearance had been spoken of throughout the ranks with notoriety. None stopped the man in the horsehide cloak from striding into the camp of their master. From what they had heard of de Gisburn, none dared.

The bounty hunter halted several yards from Simon's tent and tossed Hood's body onto the grass.

"You've done your job at last, it seems," Simon called out and he genuinely felt like smiling. The day was getting better and better. He would be rid of both Hood and de Gisburn in a single morning.

"Did you doubt me, sheriff?" De Gisburn called back. He drew his knife. "I have cut off the viper's head and now I wish to see to its body."

"Hood's band is to stand trial," Simon said. "Don't worry, they'll be hanged soon enough, I'll see to that."

"They have tricked you before, sheriff and have caused me no end of inconvenience. I wish to end them personally. Consider it part of my payment."

"Oh, very well," Simon said. "Make it quick and then be on your way. And then I never want to see you again." He had planned to interrogate the outlaws on the whereabouts of Shacklock and his whore but was happy to rid himself of de Gisburn once and for all. Besides, with Hood and the rest of the band dead there was little else Shacklock could do. He would be hunted down eventually.

De Gisburn departed for the heavily guarded tent where Hood's followers were held. Simon ordered Hood's body be brought up to him so that he might inspect it and decide what should be done with it. He had pondered the idea of quartering it and displaying the body parts in various towns in Yorkshire as a deterrent against robbers. *But first I will show Constance the head.*

Katherine had given up straining against her bonds. It was futile and had already earned her a boot to the face which had made her eye swell up. That had almost caused Little John to rise up in a rage and set about the single guard within the tent with his own boots but the other outlaws had managed to calm him down.

Wat, Simon and Rob Dyer had been seized as they had fled the burning manor house. They had dived into the moat from an upper storey window and were quickly ridden down by the sheriff's men who were circling the manor looking for a way in.

They had told her what had happened; how de Gisburn and Robert had fought, how de Gisburn had been wounded and how Robert had pursued him into the moat. That he wasn't bound with them meant that he had not been captured and that filled her heart with hope.

And yet, perhaps it means that he is dead.

She tried not to let her thoughts wander down that dark route. Rob had to be alive. He *had* to be.

She almost cursed God for His cruelty when Guy de Gisburn pushed his way through the tent flap. He wore his disgusting horsehide cloak and its hood was pulled down low over his eyes but it was unmistakably him. He looked as if he had received some rough treatment for his face was lumpy and discoloured. Blood was clotted around his neck from an ugly wound. This brought her some small comfort.

"The sheriff says you are relieved," de Gisburn said to the guard who rose from his seat.

A blade flashed. The guard tried to cry out but de Gisburn's hand clamped over his mouth and all he could do was sink slowly to his knees as blood pumped from under his arm where the knife had punctured him vitally.

De Gisburn raised a hand to his forehead and then something hideously surreal happened. His face slid away like the skim off a vat of cream. What lay behind that mask was a grotesque red thing that grinned at them.

"What by God's grace..." began Little John, his face wrinkled in revulsion, but Katherine had suddenly seen in that gory mask the eyes of the man she loved.

"Rob!"

"Aye, lass! You didn't think I'd leave you all in the hands of the sheriff, did you?"

"Rob, by Christ!" said Much. "But de Gisburn...?"

"Let's just say we have little time before the sheriff discovers that the corpse I brought him has no face."

He began to saw at their ropes with his knife. As soon as he was free, Little John seized the sword of the fallen guard. "What's the plan, Rob?"

"You and I will hold off the guards while the rest of you make a break for the woods. Don't argue, Katherine, we have no time and there are too many of them to make a pitched battle of it. On me, now!"

He bolted from the tent with Little John close behind. The sheriff had discovered the trick and his soldiers were running towards the tent with drawn blades.

"Run!" Robert cried and the others took off towards the woods.

Little John's sword clanged against the blade of one of the sheriff's men and then shattered his breastbone while Robert danced with another, his long knife flashing to find a way into his guts.

"Don't wait for me!" he called to John. "Re-join the others."

"The devil I will," John replied and slew Robert's opponent with one swift stroke.

The other soldiers were almost upon them and Robert and John turned and bolted. They knew they would have a hard time of it losing their pursuers at such close proximity but the greenwood would eventually conceal them. It always did.

THIRTY-FIVE

The men assembled near the bridge over the River Dearne, not far from Barnsley. The sky was clear and the day warm making the stink of sweat-soaked garments and unwashed bodies all the more potent in the close-packed ranks. It was an army of peasants; rogues and wastrels mostly, looking for no payment beyond meat, ale and a chance at plunder. Such was the calibre of men drawn by the sheriff's last-ditch attempt at preventing the Earl of Lancaster from returning to the north.

Will and Anna stood side by side, grim faced as they watched the noble woman pass by, her hair bound by a silken net and her long blue mantle elegantly draping the hindquarters of her dappled courser. Constance de Warde was visiting her husband whose tent was pitched on the outskirts of the town, surrounded by the encampments of his men and the men-at-arms loaned to him by William de Aune.

"Do you think she'll recognise us?" Will asked Anna.

"Shouldn't think so. That bitch is probably too concerned with where the next stuffed woodcock is coming from to pay attention to the faces of commoners."

Anna's mood was soured by hunger. They hadn't eaten in two days. Their life independent of Robert Hood had not been as plentiful as they had hoped. They had hunted but the deer were skittish from the constant tramp of armed men on the roads and tracks. They had tried robbery but sorely missed the safety in numbers they had enjoyed in Hood's band.

Their first attempt had only resulted in a handful of pennies from a page who had been carrying correspondence from some lord to another. Anna had suggested stripping the youth of his fine garments and seeing if they couldn't sell them at the nearest town but Will thought the risk too great for what small coin they might get for them and so the page had been set on his way fully clothed but with an empty purse.

Then they had tried to rob an inn but had to flee as the elderly barkeep's sudden cry for help had aroused several soldiers who emerged from the upstairs rooms in naught but their braes. They may have been caught in the throes of passion but they were well armed. The objects of their distraction peeped from their chambers in admiration as the soldiers charged downstairs in pursuit of the rogues who had dared to try and rob the inn that was providing them with food and cunny.

Hungry, dejected and feeling vulnerable without their old gang about them, Will and Anna had joined one of the wandering bands of brigands that had been popping up with more and more frequency since the sheriff had put out the call for stout yeomen keen to fight Lancaster.

The brigands had robbed a small hamlet of meat and ale on their way to Barnsley where it was said the sheriff had set up a recruitment post but the meagre victuals did not go far in satisfying the hunger of the dozen-strong band. By the time they had assembled at Barnsley along with the other thieves and outlaws drawn from every corner of Yorkshire, their bellies were aching and their blades thirsty for the fight.

Will watched Constance de Warde's face as she surveyed the ranks and averted his eyes as she passed over him. Had she recognised them?

His fears were confirmed later that evening when they were trying fruitlessly to scavenge some food from one of the cook fires. A burly man-at-arms approached them, his kettle helmet under his arm.

"Somebody wants a word with you two," the soldier said.

"Who?" Will asked.

"Lady de Warde."

Will considered taking Anna by the hand and making a run for it but there were several other men-at-arms in the vicinity. They wouldn't get far if this fellow should start bellowing orders for their seizure.

They found Constance de Warde alone in her husband's tent sipping wine with a capon and fine white loaf on the table before her along with a pie of some sort that filled the tent with its tantalising smell.

"Will Shacklock and Anna Cawthorne," she said with a smile at her own ability to remember the names of outlaws.

The man-at-arms left them with a frown and Constance bade them sit before her. They eyed the food ravenously.

"You may as well tuck in," she said. "My husband will not be back until late and this is far too much food for me alone."

Will and Anna did not need asking twice, trap or no, and they wolfed down bread, bird and pie which, to their delight, they found to be stuffed with partridge, dates, honey and cheese. The wine was also offered and gulped down with equal gusto. Constance waited until they were picking their teeth before she began to speak.

"I looked for the others in my husband's ragtag army out there but I saw only you two. Tell me, are you still in the company of Robert Hood?"

Will's face turned sour. "Did you invite us here to jest with us, lady?"

Her face looked genuinely hurt. "I do not follow."

"You must know, as all Yorkshire does, that our old master was slain by the bounty hunter your husband hired to hunt us down. Every inn is abuzz with talk of how Guy de Gisburn slew Robert Hood and carried his body to your husband."

Constance shook her head and spoke with urgency. "Hood lives. It was he who slew de Gisburn and dressed his corpse in his own Lincoln green. He tricked my husband with this ruse and freed your companions who were in his custody. They all escaped and I assumed they met up with you, although how you escaped my husband's trap is beyond me. Are you now telling me that you have not seen Hood or the rest of your band?"

"We thought they were all slain or captured," said Will slowly. He willed it to be true but dared not believe it.

"It's another trick," said Anna, rising. "Come, we've filled our bellies, let's away."

"It is no trick, my girl," said Constance. "Have I given you reason to distrust me in the past?"

"You're the sheriff's woman!" said Anna.

"And I risked all in betraying him to you! Was it not I who saved you from capture and I who then arranged for my husband's ransom to be paid? I risk much now in consorting with outlaws in my husband's own tent…"

"What would you have of us?" Will asked.

"I had hoped that you knew of Hood's whereabouts, even if you no longer ran in his company."

"You found the band once before with little trouble."

"Yes, by crying all the names I could remember at the top of my lungs on the Great North Road. I do not have the luxury of time or freedom to do so again."

"What do you want with Hood?" asked Anna. "If he truly lives."

"You can see about you that my husband is desperately rallying Yorkshire on the king's orders. He is assembling an army of undisciplined rogues who may yet be the saving of the north and thus England. I would aid my husband and our king in their task and what better boon to their army than the fearless Robert Hood and his band of outlaws?"

"Rob would never work for the sheriff!" said Will, almost laughing at the notion.

"Pardons will be given once this war is over. I know you have little reason to trust a laurel wreath from my husband at this stage, not after he so cruelly used you last year but these pardons will come from the king himself."

"I think we've wasted enough time here," said Anna but Will remained seated.

"Can you guarantee a royal pardon if I should lead you to Rob's camp?" he asked.

"Of course not. Few things are guaranteed in this war. Can you guarantee that Hood will serve his king? Or that you can even find him for me?"

"No."

"Then we can only trust in each other and pray that our trust will be rewarded."

Simon de Warde returned to camp late in the evening. The lights of the cook fires were as glow worms on the banks of the River Dearne. He was tired and sore from riding all day in his armour and longed for a cup of wine, a good meal and Constance's soft hands massaging his shoulders.

She had anticipated his wishes and the soft light of the candles filled his tent with a warm glow. She even had a basin of warm water ready to bathe away the sweat and dust of the day.

"What news?" he asked her as an attendant helped him out of his armour.

"Your army grows," she replied, pouring some wine into a pair of goblets. "Lancaster's brutality will be his undoing for the starved and the dispossessed from across the shire rally to your standard eager to deal the final blow that will rid the north of him forever."

"Good, good. De Aune has sent envoys to the Coterels and bidden them block the roads through their manors. If the king defeats Lancaster he will have to retreat north between Tickhill and the Peak District. It will be a thin bottleneck that will slow him down."

"Slow him, yes, but he will be strong enough to push through and then what?"

"Then we will deal with him. I have strengthened my position here considerably since his departure south."

"Why not strengthen it more?"

"How so?" Stripped to his braes, he dismissed the attendant and accepted a goblet from Constance. She had begun to act coy and that was never a good sign.

"You have recruited so many rogues and wretches, why not recruit one who might be a standard bearer to the downtrodden and the outlawed? One who might train these undisciplined peasants into a fine body of archers and forest fighters."

"Good God, you're talking about Hood, aren't you?"

"Two of his followers are here in your camp. They thought he was dead after the debacle at Adwick-le-Street. I informed them that their master lives and they have agreed to take me to him. I require only your permission."

"Ah! Shacklock and his woman have shown themselves at last! But why do you ask for my permission now? You have never required it in the past. Yes, I know it was you, Constance. I know it was you who foiled my plans to steal that chest of silver last summer. Need I even wonder how it is that you came to recognise their faces in my ranks? It is because you met with them again, didn't you? It was your actions that saw me a hostage of that scum!"

"I only sought to save your soul from the tarnish it would have received if you had gone through with your plan. You intended to use those outlaws for your own gain and then betray them. Their lives would have been on your head."

"I am the High Sheriff! The lives of outlaws are always on my head!"

"But these are different, Simon. Hood is different. You would know that if you only met him under more congenial circumstances."

"I don't need to meet with every outlaw in Yorkshire before I make my mind up about their character. The man's a hardened criminal responsible for countless robberies in the past two years."

"And it is his stealth and quick wits that I am asking you to recruit, not his character. Admit it, husband, this army of yours is a rabble. They're just as likely to lay Yorkshire to waste as defend it."

"And Hood isn't?"

"No. He robs, yes, but he is a man of honour and his band follow his orders without question. All Barnsdale is his manor and it is through those shady tracks that Lancaster must pass if he is to reach Pontefract. With Hood and his band on your side, you cannot fail to defeat our enemy."

Simon sighed and collapsed into his camp chair. This was not the relaxing evening he had hoped for. He sipped his wine thoughtfully. He hated to admit it but Constance had a point. The thought of Lancaster returning to Pontefract had been a worry to him. He hated to think that the fate of England rested in his ability to stop the rebel earl from raising a new army against the king. Constance was right, he needed all the bows and blades he could get. He looked at her solemnly.

"Make it happen."

THIRTY-SIX

The battle of Burton Bridge had lasted a mere three days. The king's forces crossed the Trent at Walton and came upon Lancaster from the south. Abandoning his wounded follower, Roger Damory, to be captured along with Tutbury Castle, Lancaster fled north.

Skirting Tickhill, his army endured assaults by men raised by the Coterel family who swept down from the Peak District to the west. Hungry and defeated, the rebel army eventually pushed through and entered the shadows of Barnsdale.

Bowstrings thwacked against leather bracers as the outlaws sent another volley into the baggage train struggling to ford the foaming River Went. Several men-at-arms and a knight tumbled from their saddles into the water while their mounts reared and thrashed in the reddening foam.

"Fall back!" Robert cried as the enemy mustered a punitive force to deal with the attackers and the band turned and fled deeper into the woods.

Lancaster's men would never catch up with them. The outlaws were fleet on foot and the lumbering armoured soldiers and their mounts would struggle to push through the foliage and thick undergrowth. This had been the way of it since Lancaster's army had entered Barnsdale. Robert and his band had waged a ceaseless campaign of hit-and-run warfare on the rebel earl, instructed in their tactics by Old Stephen who had done the same to the old King Edward's forces in the Weald in the days leading up to the Battle of Lewes.

To the east, a dark haze could be seen over the treetops. As a final blow to Lancaster's progress before the cover of the woodland petered out, the outlaws had torched the bridge over the Went. The smoke and flames had driven Lancaster east in search of a passable fording point and the outlaws had peppered them with arrows every step of the way.

The offer of a royal pardon in exchange for fighting Lancaster had come as much as a surprise to the band as the sudden reappearance of Will and Anna. Nobody had really known what had happened to them when the sheriff's men had come upon the outlaws by the burning bridge to Adwick Hall and the general assumption was that they had both been slain. Their deaths had been mourned by all but Robert who could not dispel the sneaking suspicion that they were alive.

Anna.

Robert was convinced she was the traitor. They had met up with the Bradburn brothers after the disaster at Adwick-le-Street and the brothers had been as disappointed as anyone at the failure to secure the treasure. They had never had anything to gain by betraying Hood and had skulked back to James Coterel in the Peak District, fearing his fury.

It had to be Anna.

Robert longed to squeeze the truth from her. There could be no closure until he had it from her lips. But it would never do to challenge her in front of Will. That would just lead to another row. Robert needed to get her alone somehow and that would have to wait until Lancaster and his army had marched on.

It hadn't been easy to convince the band to fight for the king and he couldn't blame them. They had been betrayed before and the brutality of de Gisburn still stung them deeply, especially Simon. But Robert believed in Constance and his belief gradually swayed the opinion of the band. Even after all that had happened, he was still their leader and he thanked the Holy Virgin for their trust in him. It also helped that Lancaster was an easy man to hate.

If the sheriff was no friend of theirs then the same could be said for Lancaster. Yorkshire had lived under his boot for too long, its people bullied and robbed by his barons and driven to starvation by burned crops and looted granaries. Outlaws across the north were eager to rise up against him, either in the king's service or not, and Robert reminded his band that it was due to Lancaster that most of them were outlaws in the first place. It made sense to strike a blow against the man who had taken everything from them.

The band split into two groups as was their wont whenever they were chased and the majority of the pursuers followed Little John, Much, Simon, Wat and Rob Dyer. A pair of soldiers on foot kept after Robert, Katherine, Will and Anna. Robert turned to face them, nocking an arrow.

The shaft flew true and struck one solider in his belly while his companion dove for cover. Realising that he was outnumbered, the solider rose and turned to flee but an arrow from Will's bow caught him between the shoulder blades and felled him. The sound of men moving through the undergrowth could be heard as a distant hiss like that of a viper concealed by long grass.

"Katherine, Will, you go back to the river and see how the others fare," Robert told them. "Anna and I will draw Lancaster's men deeper into the woods. Go, now!"

If there was any question in the minds of Will and Katherine as to why Robert had chosen Anna to join him in his diversion there had been no time to properly address it for Lancaster's men were close now. They took off, leaving Robert and Anna staring at each other.

Neither made a move. The sounds of their pursuers drifted away as the movement of Will and Katherine drew their attention, just as Robert had hoped it would. Anna said nothing.

She knows I know, he thought.

"You knew de Gisburn from before, didn't you?" he said. He couldn't read her eyes. She had spent a lifetime hiding her soul from the world. "He told me that you betrayed us," Robert continued. "And you have not yet denied that you knew him so I know that it must be true. There is no running from this, Anna. I shall tell the others what I know and you will be forced out of the band. You may as well tell me your reasons."

"Aye, I knew de Gisburn," she said. "A lifetime ago."

"How did he convince you to turn on us? On Will?"

"I never turned on Will! Whatever I may have done in my life I would never turn on him!"

"You truly love him, don't you?"

"God help me, yes." And he thought he saw tears welling in her eyes. Her tough mask was beginning to crack. "I've never loved a man until him. Not my husband, not even Ralph de Gisburn."

"*Ralph* de Gisburn?"

"I was the wife of an inn landlord when Ralph came into my life. My father was an alderman who had too many daughters but not so much pride that he wouldn't make a tavern wench of one to avoid a hefty dowry. I was thirteen when I was sent to that grubby inn on York's riverfront. My husband was a score of years older than me and, although he was not cruel, I knew that I could never love him.

"As we know from robbing ale merchants, they often employ gangs to transport and deliver their swill for them. As well as protecting the shipments, these gangs also pressure landlords to buy their ale and no one else's. Ralph de Gisburn and his brother Guy headed one such gang.

"Ralph was a good-looking villain with a wicked charm and he regularly convinced a landlord to do what he was told just by using his sliver tongue. If that failed there was always his brother's violence to fall back on. My husband was no fool and he knew to buy the de Gisburns's ale when they told him to.

"I liked Ralph for he used to come in as a customer and lay his charms on thick with me. I was young, trapped in a loveless marriage and desperate for excitement so it wasn't long before I fell for his graces. We began courting. I fancy my husband knew for he grew sour and quarrelsome but lacked the guts to stand up to the de Gisburn brothers, even when one of them stole me from him."

She spoke of her husband's cowardice with such poison in her voice that Robert understood why only a man like Will Shacklock would do for her. She despised any weakness in a man and could only ever love one who was as bitter and ill-served by life as her.

"I killed him eventually," she said and her eyes were fixed on some far-off point in the greenwood. She was revealing everything to him now, however much it hurt her, for reasons he could only guess at. "He eventually summoned the courage to refuse the de Gisburns their business. I urged him to it. It was my only way out. They would kill him and I would be free to love Ralph openly.

"I told my husband that I had set up a meeting with another brewer and we set off to meet him five miles outside of York. It was the de Gisburn brothers who met us by the banks of the river according to my arrangements. Guy slew my husband and threw his body into the water. We thought we had planned it perfectly; I would inherit the inn and bring Ralph in as a partner. Through his connections to the brewer, we would purchase ale at a discount. I had everything I had ever dreamed of; love, my own business and a life of comfort.

"But somehow we were found out. Somebody got suspicious and did some digging. The sheriff's men came for me one night but Ralph and I managed to escape. We fled to the greenwood and met up with Guy and some other rogues who ran in their company. We were soon outlawed and became a band of robbers to survive.

"I won't go into all the details of what happened. Suffice to say that Guy killed Ralph over some quarrel too petty to bother remembering. The rest of the band turned on Guy and he fled deeper into the greenwood. He was always half-mad and I think living in isolation drove away any vestiges of sanity he may have had. I truly believed he was dead until I saw him at that inn at South Elmsall."

"So why betray your companions for a man you thought dead?" Robert asked her.

She regarded him with a look of confusion "How long do you think Will would love me if he knew that I betrayed and murdered my husband? Guy threatened to destroy all I have with him."

"Much as I love him as a brother, Will doesn't value human life as much as some men," Robert said. "He would have understood. And, although he tries his best to hide it, he has a forgiving heart. But even if he forgave your past crimes, I think he will have a hard time swallowing your betrayal of him and his companions. We have become his family; more than his real family ever was."

Anna looked as if she had been struck by a thunderbolt. She leaned her back against a tree. "My

God," she whispered. "I've been a fool. I could have avoided all of this had I just told him of my past."

"Yes, perhaps."

Her eyes fixed on his. There was a panic there that made Robert pity her despite her crimes. "Will you tell him?"

"I don't know. I can't allow a traitor to remain in my band, no matter what your reasons were."

"I'll leave. Will and me. *We'll* leave. That was always the plan anyway."

"Aye, after you left us to the sheriff's men."

"My apologies for that will never change anything. But I beg you, do not tell Will of my treachery! We'll leave and you'll never hear from us again."

"And you'll rob me of my best fighter and the closest brother I've ever known."

She was silent. She had nothing left to offer. She had thrown it all before him and now it was up to him to decide what to do with the pieces. She didn't beg. She didn't try to convince him further but rather waited for him to make up his mind. Despite her villainy he respected her for that.

"Let's meet up with the others," he said. "I don't know what is going to happen but it is not going to happen until we are all together."

The foray did not last long. Lancaster could not spare the men and time was of a limited supply. The troops eventually crossed the Went and moved out of Barnsdale. It would not be long before the king himself would pass through the greenwood and the outlaws did not want to hang around to see if they would be rewarded or arrested.

They met back at camp and Robert said nothing of Anna. Both remained silent while the food was served up and the ale jug passed around.

"I say we head north tomorrow," said Little John. "There'll be a siege at Pontefract no doubt and the king won't be going anywhere for a while. I want to see about getting that royal pardon!"

"Do you really trust this king you have never met?" Old Stephen said. "On the word of a man who betrayed you once before?"

"On the word of a woman who has proven to be nothing but faithful!" John said in a voice that advised caution where Constance was concerned.

"Yet her word will only go as far as her husband's actions," Old Stephen continued. "And even if the sheriff agrees to leave us alone, he made that bargain without the king's consent. If the king should decide to flush all outlaws from Barnsdale as part of his reclaiming of Yorkshire, then whose side do you think the sheriff will take?"

"You don't trust anyone, old man," said John.

"He has little reason to," said Robert. "He has told us of the villainous ways of the old King Edward. Why should Longshanks's son be any different? Besides, what chance do we have of making our way to an audience with the king when betrayal so easily comes from one of our own?"

Everybody's gaze turned to him and he could feel Anna's eyes burning holes through him.

"What's this all about, Rob?" Much asked. "The Bradburns?"

He shook his head. "The Bradburns didn't betray us, I figured that out long ago. I wasn't sure who it was until de Gisburn told me himself."

"And you believed that serpent?" Will demanded and Robert saw the desperation in his eyes. He knew where this was going. *Perhaps he has always known.*

"I only half believed it. I had to get the truth from the lips of the traitor and she confirmed what de Gisburn said but a few hours ago."

The band looked from Robert to Anna.

"Anna, no...," Katherine said in a small voice.

"This nonsense again?" Will said, his voice dangerously close to anger. "Why do you persist in this? After Anna and I returned to you? Why should she sell us out to de Gisburn and then come dancing back into camp?"

"Think, Will," Robert said. "Did she seem reluctant to return? Did you fight hard to persuade her?"

Will looked sheepish but still defiant. "We had... plans of a life together."

"Look at her, Will. She denies nothing."

Will looked at Anna, his face pleading, willing it not to be true. She could not return his gaze. Her eyes were fixed on Robert and a hatred burned there that turned him cold. But he could not stop now. He had to tell them everything.

And he did.

Anna said nothing while Robert told them of her past, her crimes and her betrayal. Her face remained impassive. She was like a ghost to them now, barely there.

When Robert was finished Will knelt down and leaned forward as if he was going to be sick. There was no denial in him now. He knew Robert had spoken the truth.

"Anna, how could you?" Katherine asked.

"Because I loved a man and couldn't bear to lose him," Anna said.

"If you loved me you would not have betrayed my companions," Will replied, not looking at her.

"What do we do with her?" Old Stephen asked.

"We kill the bitch," said Little John.

"Aye," Much agreed. "String her up like her friend did to those monks."

Anna showed no fear at her looming fate. She looked at Will as if only his words mattered to her.

Slowly, he lifted his head to look at her. "She means nothing to me now," he said. "Kill her."

"No," said Robert. "Too many lives have been lost because of de Gisburn. I'll not have another on my hands, even if it is the life of a traitor."

"Then what?" Old Stephen asked again. "You can't just let her go, surely?"

"She will remain here with us tonight, under watch, and in the morning, we will take her to Kirklees Priory. I will induct her into their care and there she will remain for the rest of her days."

"As a nun?" Much scoffed. "The Good Lord would surely strike down that poor priory if this woman should cross its threshold."

"She is to be given a chance at repentance and we will have washed our hands of her," said Robert, his voice final. "It is the only way."

It happened as he said. Anna was bound to a tree and did not speak the whole night. Will's renouncement of his love for her had broken her. Nothing could hurt her now.

The next morning, Robert, Katherine, Little John and Much took her towards the River Calder. Will did not wish to come and Robert could see that his heart was broken. For that he hated Anna more even than her betrayal.

They took her to Kirklees and Domina de Scriven accepted her and the silver Robert handed over for her upkeep gratefully. Still Anna said nothing but as she was led away to be stripped, cleansed and given her lay sister's gown and wimple, she shot a look over her shoulder at Robert that made him feel cold for many days after.

By the time they had returned to camp news had reached the band of the king's passing through Barnsdale. There was a charge in the air as before a thunder storm. Lancaster was finished and the north would soon be returned to the control of the king. What then for outlaws who had fought against Lancaster? Only time would tell. As it was, Robert was content to sit by the fire on a warm spring evening with the girl he loved in his arms.

"Why did you give Anna a chance at redemption?" Katherine asked him, her freckled face wrinkled into a frown. "Not but a few weeks ago you would have killed her without question, or so you claimed."

"Things have changed, lass," he told her.

"De Gisburn?"

"Aye. I saw in de Gisburn my own dark reflection. We were similar men once; shoots from the same branch that grew along different paths. I now know that the greenwood can corrupt a man just as it can free him. And I don't want to veer that close to damnation ever again."

She kissed him and he felt as if he had returned home from a long journey in foreign parts.

By the end of the month they learned of Lancaster's defeat. Fleeing Pontefract before the king even arrived to lay siege to it, he had continued north, presumably to make contact with his allies in Scotland. But Andrew de Harclay, the Sheriff of Cumberland, headed him off and shattered his army at the banks of Boroughbridge. His followers deserting him and outnumbered by the arrival of fresh troops brought by Simon de Warde, Lancaster surrendered and was taken to Pontefract to await the king's judgement.

The judgement came swift and was without mercy. Lancaster avoided the brutal hanging, drawing and quartering that was due any traitor not of royal blood. On an overcast morning in late March, he was led from the castle to a grassy knoll, pelted with snowballs by the commoners all the way. There he was made to kneel facing Scotland as indication of his treasonous correspondence with Robert de Brus, and then beheaded in front of a baying crowd. It was a similar fate to that of Piers de Gaveston which Lancaster had played a hand in ten years previously and the symbolism was lost on nobody. The king had taken his vengeance.

The following day saw the executions of John de Mowbray and Roger de Clifford. The tyranny of Lancaster and his friends was over. The north was back under the king's rule and for Robert and his companions the promise of home beckoned.

FITT VI
THE DISINHERITED

"When they had him told the case
Our King understood their tale,
And he seized in his hand
The Knight's lands all."
- A Little Gest of Robin Hood

Derbyshire
Spring, 1266

THIRTY-SEVEN

If I could pinpoint one event that marked the end of the war for us then it would be the Battle of Chesterfield. It is true that the war continued in various parts of the country for the rest of 1266 and 1267 but Chesterfield marked the end of our involvement and Roger's patience with the barons and their Ordinances.

It had been a grim winter. The Isle of Axholme is a gloomy location at the best of times but the hard weather turned those fens into a frozen and bitter wasteland. The so-called 'isle' is formed by the river Trent to the east, the Idle to the south and the Don to the north and west. This rectangle of land is mostly marsh connecting a series of settlements, effectively islands in themselves, navigable only by local knowledge.

We built our camp in the woodlands between Haxey and Epworth and were in regular contact with John d'Eyville's manor at Adlingfleet where he and Simon the Younger had taken up residence. They spent the winter there eating sweetmeats by a wide fireplace while we froze and starved in the wilderness. We robbed the local settlements for victuals but they yielded little to feed a rebel army so we took to riding out as far as the Great North Road to rob travellers of coin.

Naturally our boldness drew unwanted attention and in December Longshanks laid siege to our island haven. Leaving half of his forces to besiege Kenilworth, he travelled north and attempted to penetrate our watery holdfast. He sent ferries of men down the waterways seeking a way through to us but he lacked local knowledge and his men often got lost and fell to volleys of our arrows.

We were under siege as much as those at Kenilworth Castle were although we did not have the luxury of a keep, mere and curtain walls to cower behind. Longshanks was as cunning as he was persistent and he eventually found a way in. He built a series of wooden pontoons that connected the areas of dry ground and pushed us ever eastwards until our backs were against the Trent.

It was Simon the Younger who gave out in the end, fearful that Adlingfleet manor would fall to Edward's troops and he would suffer a similar fate to that of his father. His heart for the baronial movement had died with his brother and father in the bloody vale of Evesham. He didn't want to fight anymore. He wanted out and took the opportunity as soon as it was offered.

The parley was signed at an artificial diversion of the River Idle called the Bycar Dyke. We were offered life, limb and liberty on the condition that we attended parliament the following Easter to submit to the king's judgement. A swifter attendance was required of Simon who journeyed to Northampton that January to face trial. We never saw him again although the word was that he departed England for France where an annual pension from the king's coffers kept him out of poverty for the rest of his days.

Simon may have trusted Longshanks and the king enough to do their bidding but the likes of John d'Eyville and his fellow rebel leader Baldwin Wake were more cynical. They had no wish to eke out the rest of their days in France on a pitiful pension and we knew that no such quarter would be offered to common soldiers. For us the fight would continue.

A condition of the parley was that we leave Axholme immediately but with Longshanks returning to Kenilworth to oversee his siege, there was little haste on our part to break camp.

People began to slip away in small groups and the army grew smaller and smaller. When we finally did leave Axholme it was with no sore heart. We were glad to be out of those stinking fens and waterlogged islands. John d'Eyville took us with him to his northern properties and we spent the rest of the winter at Hode Castle near Kilburn.

In spring we received word that changed everything. That January, our old lord, Robert de Ferrers, had been released from the Tower where he had been incarcerated by Simon de Montfort since their falling out after the Battle of Lewes. He had purchased his freedom and his lands from the king for 1,500 marks and a golden cup studded with precious stones.

I knew this meant a great deal to Roger. His lands had been confiscated from him after the Battle of Evesham and he had become one of the many known as 'the Disinherited'. Swannington lay in the demesne of de Ferrers and the possibility of a home to return to beckoned temptingly. Roger had proved himself to be a loyal servant of de Ferrers and had lost Swannington as a result of that loyalty. We all knew he flirted with the idea of holding it for de Ferrers once again.

"If only I could make him know that I still live and that my sword is still his," I remember him saying when he was in his cups one night by the hearth at Hode Castle. I understood his desire to return to the way things were before the war. For all his efforts, the rebellion had won him nothing.

Despite the return of de Ferrer's freedom and his lands, the parliament that spring had been as ashes in his mouth. His response had been to break every oath he had sworn to the king and begin marshalling his forces at Duffield Castle. The north of England was on the cusp of rebellion once more.

John d'Eyville immediately began outfitting his men for the march south. This was the moment d'Eyville had been waiting for. He had never really surrendered at the Bycar Dyke. That parley had been Simon the Younger's surrender. Barred from Axholme, d'Eyville had been champing at the bit all spring for a chance to stir up another hornet's nest for the king.

It was learned that de Ferrers had met up with Baldwin Wake who had been aimlessly roaming Lincolnshire after leaving Axholme. The pair had set up camp in the manor of Chesterfield which had previously belonged to Wake before Longshanks had gifted it to his wife. Their occupation was a deliberate act of defiance intended to raise Longshanks's ire.

As it was, Longshanks was busy securing the Cinque Ports which had been infested by rebels and had sent his cousin – Henry de Almain – to deal with de Ferrers and Wake. With our foe based at Tutbury Castle, we headed for Chesterfield to re-join de Ferrers and herald the start of a glorious new era of freedom for the north, or so we thought.

We marched to the small town of Sheffield that lies ten miles north of Chesterfield. The men had been sitting on their arses since December and were hungry for food and loot. John d'Eyville was the very essence of the robber baron but even so, I was shocked by the rapidity and rapacity of our army in securing wine, bread and meat.

Every house and shop was looted and, when we experienced opposition from Sheffield's wooden motte-and-bailey, we burned it along with the men inside. This act of arson soon spread to the town itself and we left that afternoon limned in the fug of burning thatch and timber.

The York Road grew thickly wooded as it approached Chesterfield. We should have been prepared for an ambush but most of the men were still drunk from our debauchery at Sheffield.

They came from a clearing screened by a bend in the road; dozens of knights with mounted squires and men-at-arms. We saw Henry de Almain's sigil among others and knew that our tardiness had dashed our plans to meet up with de Ferrers. We were too late and the royalists had driven a wedge between us.

The knights and their entourages slammed into us head on, lances splintering against shields and armour, seeking the chinks in plate and soft flesh below helms. D'Eyville himself was unhorsed in that initial foray and we galloped to his rescue, swords drawn to retrieve our fallen leader from the churning dust.

It was a ghastly melee on that wooded road. We held our ground as best we could, regrouping and charging at the enemy in waves, but it was hopeless. They had the superiority in numbers and we were forced to fall back. D'Eyville was given a fresh mount. He wheeled around and bellowed for a full retreat.

They pursued us north almost back to Sheffield, biting at our heels every step of the way. Before the smoking ruins of the town could be seen, the royalists turned back and returned to Chesterfield.

"The bastards got there first," said Roger as we gulped water and soothed wounds and sores. The heat of the day added further discomfort to our plight. "They probably have de Ferrers in captivity or his head on a pike."

I was alarmed by Roger's melancholy. It was a recent side of him I had hitherto not seen. It was borne of the failure of the rebellion and his own private desperation. But d'Eyville instilled a flicker of hope in us. He was not about to return to Yorkshire and leave his friend in such dire straits.

"We skirt the town and come upon it from its eastern side," he said. "We'll be screened by the woods and they won't see us coming until we are upon them."

"Will we be able to overcome such odds?" one of his knights asked.

"They had the edge of surprise, that's how they beat us," he said. "This time surprise will be *our* ally."

We headed back south and turned off the road before Chesterfield came into view. The trees offered cool shade as we passed into the dimness. It was slow going but eventually our scouts reported that we were at a level with Chesterfield. It was late afternoon and if we were to attack we would have to make our move soon.

"Men approach!" called a scout as he ran through the trees towards d'Eyville's hastily erected pavilion.

"How many?" he demanded.

"Between twenty and fifty, some on foot some mounted. I saw no sigils."

The camp was kicked into action and we formed a hasty battalion with pikemen at the front. We moved forward to the edge of the woods and could see the column of soldiers heading in a southerly direction. D'Eyville squinted, shielding his eyes from the dying flare of the sun.

"By God, its Baldwin!" he exclaimed.

The news that the men belonged to our ally Baldwin Wake raised our spirits and d'Eyville led a detachment to greet the fleeing army. As night fell we found our numbers increased. Wake had informed us that de Ferrers was still in the town but if he was captured or indeed alive was unknown. We filled our bellies with the last of the looted stores we had brought from Sheffield and prepared our attack.

We struck a little before midnight. The royalists mustered some small defence but they were unprepared for our attack on the east gate. Roger, the others and I took up position by an overturned hay cart and covered the battering ram with our bows.

After we broke down the gate the royalists fell back and we pursued them as far as the market place. Then we realised that we had stormed right into a trap. The thatched roofs of some of the nearby buildings had evidently been soaked in oil for they went up at the touch of a flame and we found ourselves engulfed on both sides by hot fire and thick smoke.

Henry de Almain led his troops in a flanking manoeuvre to our rear and tried to pen us in. Desperation fuelled our fight out of that hellhole and we hacked and slashed our way out of the market place. The royalists decided that we were not worth the bother and let us escape. We quickly put as much distance between us and the blazing town as we could.

When dawn broke we apprehended some of the fleeing townsfolk and interrogated them. They said that Henry de Almain had lain all the dead out in the smouldering ruins of the marketplace but had been unable to identify the body of de Ferrers. Then, a local woman had approached the royalists with information of his whereabouts. It was said that her husband had been hanged the previous day by de Ferrers for offering some small resistance to the earl's occupation of the town. She led de Almain to a storage hut by the church where they found de Ferrers cowering under sacks of wool much to their amusement.

It was useless. Our lord was captured once more and there was nothing we could do about it. There was talk of heading back to Yorkshire to regroup and plan our next move but Roger's morale had reached rock bottom.

"No more," he said. "I can't do it anymore."

I glanced at Wyotus and Richard. We had seen this coming.

"First, we serve one lord, then another," Roger continued. "We are rebels and then we are soldiers then rebels again and on and on it goes. It ends here, now."

We were silent. What choice did we have in the matter? Roger was as good a lord to us as de Ferrers or d'Eyville. What he decided more or less went for us too.

He seemed to sense our thoughts and sought to makes things clear. "I ask no man to follow me if he be not willing. All I can promise you is that we are a strong fighting unit with experience in war and robbery. Our bows, blades and horses stand us in good stead for an independent life."

"Independent?" Richard asked.

"Aye. We're not the first and we won't be the last. There are plenty of roving bands across England and why not? Why traipse across the land in the service of some earl or baron who can no more promise a living than I can?

"Aye, d'Eyville's own cousin Nicholas heads such a band in Sherwood and does very well at it by all accounts," said Walter d'Evyas. Walter was a young man who had come under Roger's command during our time on Axholme. His family held land in Yorkshire and he had an uncle who was close to John d'Eyville. We liked Walter. He was a born thief and a good fighter.

"Nicholas d'Eyville is more interested in profit than the provisions despite his cousin John's attempts to recruit him to the cause," said Wyotus.

"Sounds alright to me," said Walter with a grin.

"Sherwood Forest is wide enough to shelter a dozen such bands," Roger said. "With venison and travellers enough to keep us all fat and wealthy for a good long time to come."

"You wish to go to Sherwood?" Wyotus asked.

"I wish to go home," Roger replied. "I plan to take back my manor and embrace my children again before it is too late. I grow no younger and I fear the winter of my days when my babes will no longer have need of me. I've wasted too much time fighting the wars of others. It is time I fought the only war that matters to me."

There was no doubt in our hearts. Indeed, we had yearned for his decision to break from the rebellion. He was our leader and he inspired loyalty more than any man could and so it was decided. A dozen of us agreed to leave with him that night and those who didn't were still loyal enough to say nothing of our desertion.

We left before dawn broke, loading our horses with food and weapons. We struck in a south-easterly direction and before the sun had fully risen we had entered the wooded fringes of Sherwood Forest.

THIRTY-EIGHT

Those first few weeks in Sherwood were days of glorious freedom for us. We were so hard-bitten by war and marching and sieges that to be suddenly master-less and without duty in the tangled woodlands and rolling heaths was like breathing fresh English air after a long confinement in the dankest dungeon.

We made our camp in the woods near the eastern banks of the River Leen which flows south towards Nottingham. We were not far from the fields between Bulwell and Bestwood where we had poached game while serving in the garrison at the castle. I still thought of my brother William, rotted away with no gravestone to mark his passing. I thought of looking for his remains and giving him a decent burial but as I could not pinpoint the exact spot he died, I had no hope of finding them.

Our camp was well outfitted with workshops and stables and we never went hungry thanks to the king's deer and the travellers that passed along the Nottingham Road. We robbed merchants, messengers and clerics alike and amassed a large pile of goods and supplies not to mention silver. It was too easy. We were a dozen men skilled in fighting and used to skulking about the woods unseen. But we were not strong enough for what Roger had in mind. We had heard from nearby villages that Swannington Hall and its demesne had been given to Hugh de Babington after Roger's disinheritance.

"We need to be stronger if we are to take Swannington," Roger said to us.

"Taking it is one thing," said Wyotus. "How are we to hold it?"

"It is a small demesne," he replied. "And Longshanks and his father are too busy to bother sending soldiers to take it from us. Besides, my family has held Swannington for generations. I am bound to its fields as a branch is to an oak. I raised my children there and I mean to reclaim it, disinheritance or not. But I can't take it without help."

"There is always Nicholas d'Eyville," said Walter d'Evyas.

"Why would he help us?" I asked. "He's as likely to kill us as rivals than throw in his lot with us."

"Then I shall have to convince him," Roger replied. "More to the point, I shall have to convince his men."

We eventually learned that Nicholas d'Eyville operated near his home of Caunton which lies on the eastern edge of Sherwood. We rode east, galloping over rolling heaths and through bubbling brooks as we moved from wood to wood, spanning the breadth of Sherwood.

Caunton is a small manor and its village is little more than a hamlet of poor thatch and warped wood. We torched it and drove its inhabitants into the woods. It is one of my more shameful acts and I still dwell on it. I am a changed man now but back then, we were men hardened by constant contact with brutality. Every lord seemed to be burning and looting and to tell you the truth we did not think too much of putting a village to the torch. We killed none. We were making a statement and casting a lure. Nicholas d'Eyville and his band roved close by and the burning of a village presumably under his protection was a deliberate act to draw his attention.

It took several days for Nicholas to find us. We made camp nearby and robbed a couple of travellers on the Great North Road just for good measure. He found our camp one morning. We were barely done with breakfast when we spotted a score of men approaching through the bluish smoke of our campfire.

They were heavily armed although on foot. They wore the maille and helms of soldiers gone rogue; mismatched equipment that was battered and repaired. It was like looking into a mirror.

"Which of you is Nicholas?" Roger demanded, not giving them the chance of speaking first.

"I am he," said a youngish man of about my age. He had a thick head of black hair and good armour that signified a lad of minor status. "And this is my manor so you'd best state your business."

"Roger Godberd. I fought under your cousin, John."

"Why aren't you still with him?"

"He's back in Yorkshire. Perhaps you've heard of our defeat at Chesterfield."

"Aye, I heard of it. My question is, why did you desert him?"

"Why should you care? You've never heeded his call to arms yourself."

"I'm doing my bit to disrupt the king's lines of communication and we keep d'Eyville lands in these parts safe. Which brings me to my next question. Was it you lot who burned Caunton?"

"Didn't do a very good job of protecting that, did you?" Roger said with a smile.

Nicholas d'Eyville drew his sword slowly. "Take your time with this lot, boys. No need for quick deaths."

I looked to my comrades nervously. Roger's cockiness was a strange way of winning support from a rival band. He may well have led us to the slaughter.

"Look at the situation," said Roger. "You may have almost double our numbers but we are veterans. We slaughtered Longshanks's men in the Weald by the dozen. We fought at Lewes and won. We lorded it over the Isle of Axholme with your cousin. And all this while you lot were robbing yeomen not ten miles from the place of your birth. Face it lad, it would be a bloody battle and not half of you would survive it."

Nicholas grimaced. His pride had been bruised but he saw Roger's point. "What then? Do you think I'd let any scum settle in my manor, veterans or no? It may be a bloody battle but I am a d'Eyville and I have my family's name to uphold."

"Oh, aye. I've no doubt. But you see, it may not have to come to a battle. Perhaps we could come to some sort of agreement."

"You wish to join us?"

"More lead you than join you."

Nicholas scoffed. "These are my lands, Godberd. D'Eyville's name rules here and none other. You lot may remain in my lands as my vassals or you fight me as my enemies."

Godberd looked at us and grinned. *We have him scared*, his face signalled. "Very well. Then it looks like we are your men. We've served the d'Eyvilles before and will gladly do so again. You won't regret it."

"But you may," said Nicholas through his teeth.

We spent a couple of weeks in eastern Sherwood, plundering the Great North Road. We found that our new companions were not as organised as we were and lacked discipline when it came to ambushing large parties. As Nicholas's new lieutenant, Roger whipped them into shape and none bore him a grudge for we began to haul in prizes the like of which they had never dreamed of. We were a strong band of thirty or so and often split into groups to pursue different targets which increased our profits even more.

The only one who resented our arrangement was Nicholas. We knew that he only tolerated our presence because he had no other choice. Most of his band had come to welcome us as comrades and appreciated Roger's instruction in particular. This angered Nicholas even more. Eventually Roger felt that he was in a strong enough position within the band to make his challenge and put his plan into action.

Most of the band was intrigued by Roger's suggestion that they move west to look for larger pickings. Nicholas, of course, was alarmed by the suggestion, recognising at once that Roger was trying to wrestle control of the band from his hands.

"We're doing well enough here," he protested. "Why up sticks and move into unknown territory?"

"It's not unknown to us," Roger said. "There's plenty of traffic through Chesterfield on account of the wool trade and the road to Nottingham is a rich thoroughfare. If you think we've done well here, wait until you see what we can do in my part of Sherwood."

"Is it really that good then?" asked a member of Nicholas's band and Nicholas shot him a venomous look.

"Aye," Roger replied. "And what's more, I hold a manor – Swannington – not twenty miles from Sherwood's western fringes. It was taken from me during the war and I mean to take it back. The royalist who was given its custody still resides there and is a snivelling coward. It will not be a difficult fight and we can split whatever loot we find there. We will be fighting from a position of considerable strength with a manor to our names."

"To *your* name," said one of Nicholas's men with some scepticism.

"I'll hold Swannington, aye, but think of the supplies and shelter a whole manor might give a band of Sherwood robbers!"

"It does sound promising," said another of Nicholas's men.

"It doesn't matter how promising it sounds, we're not leaving and that's final," said Nicholas.

"Maybe you ought to let your men speak for themselves," Roger said. "They're all freemen and owe you no service."

"Are you trying to steal my band from me, Godberd?" Nicholas asked.

"It's not stealing if they come with me of their own freewill."

Nicholas's men said nothing and it was their silence that confirmed their view on the matter.

"Very well," said Nicholas. I can see that you lot have let yourselves be tempted by this man's wild tales of treasure on the other side of Sherwood. But I am still leader of this band and if we are to move westwards, then a leader must make that decision. I've let you join us, Godberd and I'll not deny that you have been useful. But you've challenged my authority from the beginning. It's time we settled it. If you want the position of leader then you fight me for it."

I respected Nicholas for that. Roger was a big man and a skilled fighter. Nicholas was visibly nervous but he had enough pride not to give up his band without a fight. His self-respect would not let him.

"Weapons?" said Roger.

"Quarterstaffs," Nicholas replied.

It was a smart choice. The quarterstaff could inflict horrific injuries but was generally not as lethal as bladed weapons. I pitied Nicholas then, for I knew Roger to be a fine quarterstaff fighter.

Four wands of ash were laid down on the grass to form a square and the combatants stripped to the waist and began limbering up. Quarterstaffs were fetched and bets were placed. We couldn't help it. Gambling is one of the few pastimes left to outlaws in the wilderness and such a fight between leaders was an opportunity not to be missed.

Roger started in strong, swinging his staff with mighty 'thwacks' against Nicholas's defences. I was immediately worried that he was overexerting himself so early on. It was not unheard of for a weaker opponent to win a fight by wearing the other out but Nicholas had a desperate enough fight of it as he fended off Roger's powerful blows.

Roger's quarterstaff clipped one of Nicholas's fingers and smashed the knuckle. There were hisses from the spectators as that was considered a move lacking in honour but I honestly believe it was an accident. Nicholas howled in agony but, to his credit, did not release his injured hand from his weapon.

His pain seemed to awaken the fight in him and he suddenly lashed out at Roger with a cunning move that slid past his defences and caught him in the middle, winding him.

Roger followed up with a mighty overhead swing that Nicholas dodged and he caught him again with a blow to the side that must have cracked a rib for Roger bellowed in agony.

The odds had changed. Nicholas apparently made up for his slight stature with cunning. I bit my knuckles as I realised that this fight could go either way.

Roger proceeded with more caution, now having the full measure of his opponent. He let Nicholas go on the offensive for a while, each crack of the quarterstaff accompanied by cheers from his men. They had forgotten that if their leader won there would be no move west but all that was irrelevant as the two sides were swept up in the heart-pounding joy of sport.

Nicholas's strength began to waver. Encouraged by his early victories he had grown overconfident and had wasted his reserve. I saw it before it happened and thanked God for backing my man. Roger sidestepped a blow from Nicholas and brought his own quarterstaff around in a circular arc that connected with Nicholas's skull. It was a sickening blow that sent the younger man sprawling, blood gushing from his opened temple. He tried to rise, stumbled and fell outside the square of ash wands, forfeiting the fight. It was over. Roger had won.

We roared our victory and Roger raised his quarterstaff over his head in triumph. I saw the pink bruise on his left side that was gradually turning purple; a sign of cracked ribs to be sure. Nicholas was attended to by his men who poured cold water over his head and stitched his wound up with needle and cat gut. He was barely conscious but he was alive and we were glad of that.

We waited until the following day for the decision to be made. Nicholas was sorely ill but still had his senses. His body had borne the beating that his pride could not have endured. It was this that allowed him to tell Roger that he was the new leader of the band.

THIRTY-NINE

Swannington Hall lies in the manor of Whitwick and is surrounded by fine farming country with good black soil and plenty of woodland. A rich seam of coal is quarried northwest of the village and many assarts of gorse and scrub border its fields. It was desirable land and upon seeing it for the first time I did not wonder at Roger's ongoing quest to retain it for his family.

The hall itself lay north of the village. It was a modest building but sturdy and looked like it would stand for many generations to come. A timber causeway led across a moat to an inner courtyard surrounded by uncrenulated walls. The windows at the rear overlooked low fields that dissolved into patches of woodland called Charnwood that continued all the way to the southwestern edges of Sherwood.

It was from those trees that we emerged; a band of thirty warrior-thieves. Many of us were mounted as we had stolen some more horses on the journey west. We halted at the tree line and looked across the dew-cloaked fields that lay heavy with the morning mist. Swannington Hall was like a ghost in the distance, almost as if it wasn't tangible but the look in Roger's eye as he gazed on his family home told us that it was anything but in his mind.

"We need to strike them before they know we're here else they'll send to Whitwick for reinforcements," said Geoffrey.

"Aye," Roger agreed. "I want archers covering our battering ram. Those walls are low but de Babington will post his own bowmen over the gatehouse as soon as we are within spitting distance."

The ram was a felled tree with its branches hacked off and its end sharpened into a tip, blackened by fire. Leather handles had been riveted to its sides. I wasn't overly confident that a team of ten men could use it to break down Swannington's gate but I trusted that Roger knew how to break into his own house.

Those of us who were most skilled with a bow were formed into an archery unit while the mounted men accompanied the ram team at a fast trot across the fields. We were within an arrow's flight of the walls before somebody noticed and a horn could be heard bellowing within.

The mounted escort drew up at the foot of the causeway and we nocked arrows as the ram team pelted across the moat. Helmed heads appeared above the gatehouse and we loosed, sending a volley that shattered against the walls or flew over and into the courtyard beyond without hitting any targets.

"Come on, you men!" Roger bellowed from his saddle, whirling a singlehanded axe around by its leather strap. "I've taught you better than this! Shoot the bastards!"

He cut a heroic figure astride his prancing courser, framed against the barred gates of the stronghold, oaths roaring from his bearded lips and I was put in mind of Richard the Lionheart who made a name for himself by always being amidst the slaughter. I then remembered how a lucky shot from a French cook atop the walls of Châlus-Chabrol had ended that particular monarch's life and determined to hit somebody with my next arrow.

I did not let myself down and neither did somebody else in my group as two of de Babington's men tumbled back down into the courtyard with arrows protruding from them.

The ram team were making good progress on the gates which had begun to cave in. We could see the courtyard through the splintered wood and Roger called his mounted troops to form up and prepare for a charge as soon as the ram team were in.

The gates came down and, yelling bloodcurdling cries, the horsemen thundered across the causeway, nearly trampling the ram team who swiftly stumbled aside, dropping their victorious tool and drawing short blades for the fight.

We set down our bows and drew our own blades, eager to assist our brothers who were now under attack within the walls. By the time we got there it was mostly over. De Babington had few men and those who had resisted lay dead in the courtyard, their blood seeping into the hardpacked earth. The rest had surrendered and were being disarmed and herded together.

Roger dismounted and strode towards the door of the Great Hall. It was unlocked and we followed him in leaving Nicholas and his men to guard the prisoners and man the walls against a possible counterattack from Whitwick.

We found Hugh de Babington cowering in the Great Hall wearing a maille shirt over not much else. He held a wavering sword in his shaking grip. A woman's weeping from a chamber beyond told us he had been in female company until we had so rudely awoken him.

"Who in God's name are you?" he demanded and I fully expected him to piss himself he was that frightened.

"That you do not recognise the true owner of this hall is proof that you have no business here," Roger snarled, his axe dangling from its strap in his hand.

"Godberd!" de Babington stammered. "These lands were stripped from you! You have no claim here, not after your disinheritance for treason!"

"Are you a fool as well as a coward?" Geoffrey asked. "To dare to insult the man who returns to claim his family home with axe in hand!"

"I have done nothing wrong!" de Babington cried, suddenly realising his precarious situation. "I was given custody of this land by the Lord Edward himself!"

"I have long grown tired of men quoting the law at me," said Roger. "First the king, then de Montfort, then the Lord Edward. I have come to the conclusion that the only true law is the law of the sword and the axe. He who takes what he wants, rules. Do you think to stand in my way, de Babington?"

The sword clattered from de Babington's hand and he looked relieved to have been given the choice of surrender. We stripped him of his maille and bustled him out to join the rest of the prisoners in the yard along with his woman and any cowering servants Roger did not recognise as old family retainers. A mounted guard was sent to lead the prisoners to the outskirts of the manor where they left them to find their fortunes elsewhere.

We spent the rest of the day repairing the gates, refortifying the hall and feeding well on the meats, cheeses and wines de Babington had left behind in Roger's cellars. It was as nectar in comparison to the coarse fare of the greenwood. Wyotus, Richard and I along with a few others accompanied Roger to the market town of Whitwick a little after noon to make contact with some of his old associates. We had expected hostility but instead found the town largely ignorant of the invaders in their midst. We visited an inn and a guild house where Roger met with friends and told them to spread the word that the Godberds had returned to Swannington Hall.

On our way back, we took a detour through Swannington village and found it barricaded. Nervous faces peered above ramshackle barriers. Farming tools and ancient weapons were brandished without much conviction.

"The poor buggers think the manor has been overrun by brigands," said Wyotus.

"Aye, they probably think we're set on looting and raping," Richard agreed.

Roger rode ahead of us until he was well within bowshot of the barricades. He paraded his mount back and forth so all the villagers could see him.

"I am Roger Godberd!" he called to them. "You know me and you know my family. I have been gone too long and I return home to find my place usurped by royalist pretenders! Hugh de Babington was no friend to you and now I have kicked him out! Let it be known that Swannington is Godberd's once more!"

There was muttering behind the barricades and men tentatively emerged from behind them. One, who was braver than the rest, approached Roger, peering curiously at him.

"Aye, it is you!" he said. "No lie! It's Osbert, master! You remember? My father was your father's steward. We used to play together as children."

"God's teeth, did you think I'd forget you, Osbert!" Roger cried. "It's only been three years since I left!" He dismounted and the two men embraced. "Your father is still steward of Swannington Hall as far as I am concerned, and I have sore need of him now."

"Alas," said Osbert. "De Babington booted him out when he took over the hall and my father did not survive that winter. He was old. It was his time."

"I am sorry, Osbert. I should have been here seeing to my lands, not charging around with de Ferrers and de Montfort. The barons' rebellion was a fool's errand and all the while my home was squashed under a stranger's boot. Ride back to the hall with us and you can tell me all that I have missed."

As we rode back, Osbert related the extent of de Babington's depredations.

"He cut down the oaks northwest of the church," Osbert said. "And sold the timber to folk in Loughborough."

Roger snarled at this but said nothing.

"And he enclosed common ground in the Red Hills. A villein was flogged for letting his pigs graze for acorns there last autumn."

"He dares to treat the land and tenants of another so?" said Roger bitterly. "I should have killed him, not cast him out."

"It may be for the best that you did not kill him, lord, said Osbert. "De Babington has powerful friends with royal connections."

Roger said nothing.

We spent the next few days entrenching ourselves at Swannington Hall in preparation for a retaliatory attack. We posted watches on the walls and stabled a detachment of mounted men in the village and at the inn in Whitwick. That way we would be easily warned if anybody approached from the south or east.

Roger employed Osbert as his steward and filled the vacant posts in his staff with locals from the village. He paid them with the loot we had stolen in Sherwood. There was a little silver de Babington had amassed in his coffers but even I could see that Roger would have financial problems in the near future.

There was no treasure to pay back Nicholas and his men for their aid besides the cups and crucifixes from the family chapel but, to their credit, they did not demand any. They looked to Roger as their leader now and for the moment were content to help out around the hall in return for good food and ale and warm beds by the hearth.

After a couple of days Roger's brother William, whom I had not met before, brought Roger's children to him. It was an emotional meeting for the Godberds; three brothers reunited and a father with his two children whom he had not seen in three years.

Roger's son and namesake was a sturdy lad of twelve. We all took to him immediately after he boasted that he had practiced with his bow every day since his father's departure, just as he had promised. He was eager to show off and we all agreed to have a friendly tourney the day after. Roger's daughter Godiva – referred to affectionately as 'Diva' by her family – was a striking girl of about twenty. Tall and willowy, she had her father's thick, nutbrown hair. I couldn't understand why such a comely girl had not been married years ago but that night, Walter d'Evyas set me straight.

"She was married once. Must have been about eight years ago. Roger married her to a cordwainer. He was a decent man but died after a year leaving the poor child a widow. She had her dowry which was a nice plot of land west of here with a wood on it. Godiva's parents in law took it upon themselves to rule the roost after their son's death and took over the land, relegating Godiva to the position of a mere tenant."

"I can't imagine Roger took that lying down," I said.

"He didn't, but he was a different man in those days, more trusting in the law than in the sword. They went through the courts and Godiva brought an assize of novel disseisin against her in-laws. Would you believe the sheriff backed them?"

"And Godiva lost her dowry?" I asked, astounded.

"And Roger damned near lost his life or his liberty. He took that land back by force and drove his late son-in-law's parents off it. They took their own legal action and Roger was fined heavily. He had to take out a debt and lease a good portion of his land to Garendon Abbey as surety. He hadn't a hope of paying it off and the church swallowed up much of his demesne."

"So that is why he went to war," said Wyotus.

"And that is why he hates the church," I added. All the missing pieces of Roger's mysterious past were fitting together.

"How do you know so much about it all?" Richard asked Walter. "We've been with Roger since our time in Nottingham's garrison and he's never told us anything about his past."

"My uncle, Richard de Foliot of Grimston, was a custos of Nottinghamshire back when de Montfort was appointing his own rivals to the king's sheriffs. He knew first-hand of Roger's transgressions."

FORTY

Two weeks passed before any sign of retribution for our actions came our way. The men we had billeted in Whitwick galloped across the causeway as if they were trying to outrun the devil himself. They clattered into the courtyard and bellowed for Roger.

"Armed men approach from the east!" they cried. "We counted fifteen men-at-arms on horseback."

"Any sigil?" Roger asked.

"None."

"The sheriff, perhaps," said Geoffrey.

"Old William de Bagot?" said Roger. "He has always been a friend to us. A darn sight better than his predecessor at least. But even if he feels compelled to oust us, why has he waited two weeks to do so? Surely word reached him of my return before now."

A rider was dispatched to the village to recall our men there. Roger needed as much of a show of force as he could muster. We were ordered to the walls and Roger seized me as I started to ascend the ladder. "On my signal, give them a warning arrow," he told me.

The gates were barred after the men from Swannington had galloped in and we strung our bows. All eyes were on the road to Whitwick and we could already see a cluster of mounted men moving along it. But as they came into view we saw that it was not William de Bagot, High Sheriff of Warwickshire and Leicestershire who approached. I heard a sharp intake of breath from both Wyotus and Richard beside me at the sight of the man's face. I did not hear my own breath for I had none in that moment.

The man who now approached us was the very man who had caused us to flee Nottingham a lifetime ago. We had heard that Reginald de Grey had been made High Sheriff of Nottinghamshire, Derbyshire and the Royal Forests and to tell the truth it hadn't surprised us. His father had been made constable of Nottingham Castle after the king had taken it and the weasel had clearly profited from his betrayal of his former comrades to the previous sheriff. That betrayal had cost my brother his life.

My fingers tensed and I drew my arrow back a little, unsure if I was capable of a mere warning shot should I be called to make it.

"You're out of your jurisdiction, de Grey!" Roger called down from above the gatehouse. "This isn't your shire!"

"And this isn't your demesne!" Reginald called back. "It belongs to my good friend Hugh de Babington who has informed me that brigands from Sherwood have invaded his lands and driven him off them. It is only due to the lacklustre efforts of that old bumpkin de Bagot that I must ride here to do his job for him!"

"The king had no right to take this land from me! It has belonged to my family for generations!"

"No right?" Reginald scoffed. "You fought under de Montfort! You are a traitor! Every man who betrayed their king at Lewes has been disinherited!

You are a brigand and a thief, Godberd, nothing more."

"And yet I hold the high ground. I have twice as many men as you. You are welcome to try and oust me, but you will all lose your lives in the attempt."

We all jeered at our would-be attackers. It was true; we were twice as many as they were. Reginald's face paled as this sunk in.

"Would you dare challenge royal authority in such a brazen manner?" he demanded. "You have no woodland to hide in now. You are in plain sight and you think to defy the king?"

"The king is not here," Roger replied. "His stoat-nosed errand boy is."

We roared with laughter and Roger gave me the signal.

I took aim at the causeway beside Reginald's horse. I ached to aim a little to the left and up an inch but I obeyed my lord. I loosed and the thud of the arrow a few feet away caused Reginald's horse to rear up in panic. He was unprepared and nearly tumbled from his saddle which provoked more mirth from the walls.

"Take heed, brigands!" he roared once he had regained control of his mount. "The king is within a week of cracking Kenilworth. I have heard that they die by the score daily behind those stinking walls, starving and filthy! Once those walls are breached, your friends will be butchered like lambs! And then the king will march north to sweep away the last vestiges of de Montfort's dogs!"

We did not laugh at that. The siege of Kenilworth had lasted longer than any siege anybody had ever heard tell of and I had thanked God more than once that we had followed d'Eyville to Axholme rather than remain in that hellhole.

Reginald led his men off the causeway, not wanting to outstay his welcome and risk more than a warning shot. Once the small troop had vanished in the direction of Whitwick, we descended the walls and went to our meat and ale. I heard snatches of bravado from the men but Roger was silent. He wore that worried frown that I had come to recognise as a sign of a keen mind deep in thought.

It took him two days to formulate his worries into a plan and while we were at meat in the Great Hall he broke his news to us.

"De Grey is right," he said suddenly. "Kenilworth will fall and when it does the king will turn his attention north."

We said nothing.

"It is possible that pardons will be offered but only at great cost. I need to solidify my foothold here and that requires an expedition."

"Where to?" Nicholas asked. "And what sort of expedition?"

"I once lost a wood and an assart of waste to Garendon Abbey," Roger said and I knew he spoke of the assurance for the debt he had been unable to pay after he was fined for driving Diva's in-laws off his land. "The Abbot of Garendon still holds those charters and I mean to take them back. These churchmen are like leeches, sucking at the misfortune and misery of others."

"I don't disagree with you, lord," I said, "but how do you intend to convince the abbot to hand the charters over to you?"

"My sword point will convince him," Roger replied and there were grins from the men at the benches. "Garendon Abbey is large and will contain other treasures. We could do very well from such an expedition."

"But robbing an abbey?" I asked. "The clergy and the law take a dim view of such antics..."

"Damn the clergy and damn the law!" spoke up Walter d'Evyas. "Neither has served us in the past. Roger is right, the law of the man holding the sword is the only true law."

There was a cheer at this and the only other person in the hall who seemed to share my misgivings was Diva.

"Don't leave Swannington again, father," she said. "You have only so recently come back to us. I couldn't bear to lose you now. And Stephen is right, you will make powerful enemies by robbing an abbey."

Roger patted his daughter's arm and poured her some more wine. "Diva, my love, what I do, I do only to preserve what we have fought so hard to reclaim. If the king should offer a pardon I will need the silver to purchase it. It is the only way to truly be free of all that has passed. Think! Swannington could be legally ours once more and nobody could take it away from us ever again!"

"The king may just decide to execute you," Diva grumbled.

Nevertheless, it was decided. We rode out the day after the next. Most of the party was made up of Nicholas's men with the addition of Walter, Wyotus, Richard and myself. Roger's brothers and the rest of his men were left behind to guard Swannington Hall in his absence.

Garendon Abbey is a large building belonging to the Cistercian order. The woodland that once encroached on its southwestern walls was cut down by the monks long ago and is an open space of stumps that provide little cover. We stuck out like sore thumbs as we walked down the road towards the gatehouse but stealth was not our plan. We were to appear as poor pilgrims seeking hospitality for the night.

We wore no armour and what small weapons we did carry were concealed beneath long cloaks. We left our horses with two of Nicholas's men in the part of the woods that was nearest to the abbey.

The porter admitted us and, once we had explained that we wished to impose on the abbey's hospitality for the night as it was fast nearing compline, he led us across the monastic enclosure towards the guest hall.

"Which site do you mean to make your devotions?" said the porter, "for I can see that you are pilgrims, on foot and humble in appearance."

Roger had asked me for advice as to our cover story and I had thought long on it. A pilgrimage to

St. Albans was a good enough reason for half a dozen men to be on the road south.

"Ah! But of course," the hosteller replied. "I once gazed upon the tomb of that blessed man long ago, before I was tonsured."

He questioned us more closely as we passed the barns, workshops and outhouses that sustained the abbey. The guest hall itself was west of the lay brothers' infirmary and dormitory. An abbey is like a ringed fortress with each ring of inhabitants an obstacle to any who wish to gain entrance to the abbey's inner sanctum.

Once we had deposited our travelling gear within the guest hall the porter led us to the church where, according to custom, we were to pray for sins committed on the journey. As we entered he sprinkled us with holy water and I suppressed a smile as I saw Roger and the others sink stiffly to their knees in the choir and bow their heads solemnly. For my part I enjoyed this revisit of a part of my life that felt like it had vanished forever. Once I had rarely been off my knees but in the two chaotic years since my expulsion from the priory of St. Thomas, I had barely prayed at all.

We were then returned to the guest hall and introduced to the hosteller who instructed a lay brother to wash our feet. This strange and uncomfortable ritual over, we were served a meal and shown to our beds. There were no other visitors in the guest hall although somebody of more significance than six shabby pilgrims must have been staying in the better furbished guest house nearby for the hosteller scurried off to attend to them.

"We wait until after dark," said Roger, "and head out with plenty of time before matins. Stephen, you have an idea where the charters might be kept?"

"They'll be in a locked room near to the chapterhouse," I replied, remembering the little room of documents at St. Thomas's priory. "The sacristan will have the keys."

"And where do we find this sacristan?"

"They often sleep in the south transept near the treasury, sacristy or some other special room."

"It'll be like bloody Christmastide!" said Walter, his eyes alight no doubt at the thought of all the fine vestments, gold cups and silver plate the sacristan was the custodian of.

"How will we tell which of the buggers is him?" Richard asked. "All monks look alike to me."

"There can't be too many who kip down in the south transept," said Roger.

We lay down on our pallets and stared at the vaulted ceiling, pretending to doze and willing ourselves not to. We were tired from the journey and the straw was clean and soft but the thought of treasure just behind the west range of the abbey was good company for long hours.

It was left to me to judge when the time was right. My time in the priory had tuned my mind to know more or less how far off a certain canonical hour was. I lifted my head slowly and whispered to Roger that our window of opportunity was open. Like shadows, we rose from our pallets.

We left a further two men in the guest hall to secure our escape should the porter decide to disappear with the keys to the main gate. If an abbey is a ring of defences, it pays to leave a guard at each defence you penetrate so that you might get out again.

The summer night was warm and the sky clear of cloud. The way was well lit by moonlight but we felt extremely exposed as we hurried across the precinct towards the doors of the church.

They creaked horribly and we only opened them wide enough to admit us. As we slipped inside, we felt as if we had entered a tomb; perhaps our own. The moon shining through the windows bathed the place in a weird patchwork of silver crisscrossed by black and the smooth columns that rose up all around us felt like trees in a moonlit forest beneath black skies.

I led my companions towards the south transept and our feet caused soft echoes to ripple across the nave. Two doors led from the transept. The one on the southern wall I guessed led to the chapterhouse and I silently indicated that the door to the left of it would most likely lead to our goal.

Roger tried it. It was open and we slipped into a narrow corridor that contained two more doors. Roger looked to me. I shrugged. Either one could be sacristy, treasury or neither. The exact layout of Cistercian abbeys was not my speciality.

Roger tried the first of the doors. It was bolted. He tried the second. Also bolted. He rapped on it with his fist. We heard movement behind it and

Roger stood back. He drew his knife and, as the door opened, he planted a boot to it and knocked the emerging monk backwards before storming in.

We followed our leader and found him with the terrified monk's robe held in his fist, his dagger pointed at his throat. "Are you the sacristan?" Roger demanded."

"I am!" the poor monk replied. "Who are you and what do you want?"

"The keys to the rooms hereabouts!"

"Robbers!" the sacristan whispered hoarsely. "You'll never get away with it!"

"You'd better hope we do, or it's my knife for you! The keys! Now!"

The sacristan fumbled at his belt for a purse. It clinked as his shaking hand passed it to Roger but its contents were far more valuable than coin. We were already inside the sacristy. A gold crucifix stood on a table that was decked with white linen. Vessels of gold and silver and ceremonial plates glinted from the shadows. There were chests in the room too, hinting at further treasures.

"Away with it, lads!" Walter cried as he shouldered past the sacristan. A sack was produced and my companions began filling it with whatever they could lay their hands on.

Roger emptied a bunch of keys from the purse and examined them. "Which one is for the room where you keep documents."

"Documents?" asked the sacristan. "You mean the library?"

"I mean land charters, deeds, the livelihoods you bloodsuckers squirrel away in your vaults!"

"This one!" said the sacristan, a shaking finger pointing out the correct key. "It's for the records chamber across the corridor!"

Roger turned and made for the other door. I followed him and left the others to their looting. We entered a vaulted room filled with many ironbound chests and shelves that held scrolls of dusty parchment. Roger heaved up the lid of one of the chests and started leafing through the documents within.

"This is it!" he said with excitement. "These are the charters to all the lands this abbey has swallowed up."

I should have stood in the corridor to watch for anybody approaching but we were all caught up in the thrill of our crime. I watched Roger as he rifled page after page, scanning the names of acres and assarts. He jumped up excitedly as he saw his own lands written on parchment.

And then we heard a booming voice of authority in the corridor outside; "What is the meaning of this outrage?"

FORTY-ONE

"Don't these monks ever sleep?" said Richard with a curse.

We had emerged from our respective rooms and stood in the corridor facing a superior monk and one of his lackeys; a pale-faced lad who looked like he would need a clean robe soon. They had evidently glided through the nighted abbey with the purpose of some late appointment with the sacristan and found a robbery in progress.

"Hold your tongues and we'll be out of your beards before you know it," Roger told the two monks.

"Roger Godberd?" asked the senior monk incredulously. "I know that brutish face!"

"Greetings, Abbot John," said Roger with a grin. "You must have thought yourself long shot of me."

"Actually, I had heard of your disgraceful intrusion at Swannington. The king will soon be upon you for your treachery and you will be cast back to the woods and heaths where Satan's imps belong."

"If you had heard of my return, abbot, then surely you must have expected a visit from me. Did you think I wouldn't drop by to reclaim what's mine?"

The abbot's eyes flitted to the papers bunched in Roger's hand. "You handed those charters to the abbey of your own free will!"

"Aye, after I had been robbed and exploited to the point of ruin. A man can always count on the church to kick him when he's down, eh?"

"And so, you broke into God's house to threaten and steal what is not yours? This is abominable sacrilege!"

"Your hypocrisy knows no bounds, does it?" said Roger. He stuffed the charters into his vest and drew his dagger. Seizing the abbot by his robe, he pressed the blade against his throat.

"Your soul will bear the penalty if you shed blood in the holy house of God!" the abbot gibbered.

Before we could stop him, the young monk pelted off down the corridor.

"Stop him, Stephen!" Roger bellowed to me. "He'll raise the entire abbey!"

I took off after the fleeing monk and instantly knew where he was headed. The bell tower lay beyond the north transept. If he started swinging on those ropes we would have every monk in the abbey making their way to us wondering why their sleep had been cut short an hour before matins.

I gained on him as we weaved around the stalls of the choir. He burst through the door of the north transept and I could almost reach the flapping hood of his robe. As we entered the bell tower, I seized him by his neck and hauled him to the ground. He rolled away from me and made a leap for the ropes that would set the bells ringing but I intercepted him and we hit the ground again, grappling and struggling.

I drew my dagger.

As I raised the blade to neutralise the threat to us I felt something stay my hand. I have often wondered if it was God or one of his servants but the older I get the more I believe that it was my own conscience that stopped me from committing what would have been my most grievous sin.

The monk looked up at me, terror in his eyes. I could not kill him. I did not want to. I sheathed my knife and seized him by his forelock. I raised his head just enough to provide momentum and slammed it down on the stone flags. He sank into unconsciousness. He would awake with the worst hangover he was ever likely to suffer or, in the worst case, live out his days as an imbecile. But he would be a live one.

I made my way back to my comrades and, as I crossed the choir, I saw Roger leading them out of the south transept. He propelled the abbot before him, his knifepoint tickling his spine. The sacristan was held in a headlock by Walter.

We left the church and made our way back towards the gatehouse. If Nicholas's men were doing as they had been ordered, they would have the way open for our flight into the woods.

It was as we had hoped. The gate stood open to the wild beyond the abbey walls and the abbot, sacristan, porter and hosteller looked as keen for us to vanish back into it as we were. We pushed the monks into a chamber within the gatehouse and closed the door. There was no way to bolt it from the outside but that was of little consequence. They could ring the abbey bells as much as they liked for they would muster no army to ride out on our heels. As soon as we were beyond the abbey walls, we were free and victorious.

And so we were.

Roger was in the mood for celebrating once we had returned to Swannington Hall and the feasting lasted for several days. Nicholas's men were comfortable; well fed but growing bored. Roger's promises to them of great wealth to be stolen on the Nottingham Road had kindled a fire within them that would not be quenched by wine and ale. Less than a week after our robbery of Garendon Abbey, Nicholas informed us of their decision to leave.

Roger was sorry to see them go for they had proved to be loyal followers and stout men in a fight. A bond had been formed between the two unlikely leaders who had once beaten each other bloody with quarterstaffs.

"You are welcome here any time, Nicholas," said Roger. "If you are ever in need I will offer you whatever shelter I can."

"And the same goes for you," Nicholas replied. "I'm proud enough to know when I've met my match. You are the true lord of Sherwood and while I lead these men, they are yours to command. You only have to send word."

"We have yet to deal with the king," Roger replied gravely. "My repossession of the charters to my lands may all have been for naught if there is no pardon to be given. We may all be outlaws before the year is out."

As it turned out, we were not outlawed by the year's end. In early November, word reached us of the king's proclamation. The Dictum of Kenilworth was designed to offer reconciliation with de Montfort's followers. The deal was sweetened by reconfirming the Runnymede Charter and the Charter of the Forest but these clauses were merely intended to soften the blow. The Provisions of Oxford, for which the whole bloody war had been fought, were discarded. The king and the king alone would decide on the appointment of officials, foreign or otherwise.

Just as Roger had predicted, there was the offer of pardons on the payment of steep penalties. The garrison of Kenilworth rejected the dictum written in the shadow of those crumbling walls. They were mad, Roger said, to not know when they were beaten. There was only one way out of the disaster of the Barons' War and that was through the payment of fines.

We rode for Kenilworth in late November. The trees were bare and the wind was biting and we knew that if Roger failed to get a pardon and the king sought to reclaim Swannington, it was the worst time of the year to go into hiding.

"What if it's a trap?" Walter said as we journeyed south.

"The devil it is!" snapped Roger."

"Do you think you'll go before the king himself?" I asked him.

"Doubt it," he snorted. "I'm sure he has teams of examiners who do all the paperwork for him."

We lodged at an overcrowded inn on the outskirts of Kenilworth. It was bedlam. The siege was still ongoing but the royalists had more or less turned their backs on the trapped rebels. They had more pressing concerns such as the issuing of safe conducts to the swarms of knights, barons and smallholders who arrived with their charters in hand and chests of payment in tow.

There was endless waiting and, when Roger was finally admitted into the king's peace, he was questioned and examined for hours on end. His guilt was weighed and converted into a monetary amount. They were lenient due to their ignorance of some of Roger's greater crimes during the war and set the price of freedom at five times the annual yield of his lands.

To pay this he handed over the charters to the assarts he had so recently liberated from the coffers of Garendon Abbey and made up the rest with the loot we had taken from the sacristy and amassed during our time in Sherwood. It was going to be a hard winter, but we were free.

We returned to Swannington immediately for the town had an ill and feverish quality to it. Two days after we departed, the garrison of Kenilworth, decimated and diseased, finally surrendered and accepted the dictum.

We celebrated Christmastide humbly. Our frugality was a testament to all we had suffered and lost and yet it had the feel of a fresh start. Come spring, crops could be grown, livestock reared and livings eked out. Roger Godberd was lord of

Swannington once more and I was his servant. We were set to live happily ever after.

And for a while we did.

FITT VII
KING'S MEN

"But well you greet Edward, our king,
And sent to you his seal,
And bids you come to Nottingham,
Both to meat and to meal."
- A Little Gest of Robin Hood

Yorkshire
Summer, 1322

FORTY-TWO

The mud began to dry on Robert's hose as he strode towards the house. His arms were weary and his throat was parched. It was a hot summer and the necessity of digging a new latrine, indicated by the smell, outweighed the effort required in the digging of one in such heat. Besides, with seven now sharing the house on Bichill, the facilities were in dire need of expansion.

Robert rested his pick against the water butt and gazed across the rooftops of Wakefield. The sun was setting and the afternoon air was a pleasant haze above the odorous, bustling town. There was an uncomfortable energy there that Robert had grown acutely aware of since his return. It was a constant reminder that a great many people were close to him at all times. Perhaps he had never noticed it until he had turned outlaw but now that he was back in Wakefield, he yearned for the soft sound of the breeze in the treetops, the creak of oak, birdsong and the feeling of being alone.

Little John rounded the house with a huge load of firewood in his massive arms. The blow of his axe was a regular rhythm these days. Robert took some of the wood from him and they went inside where his mother was preparing their evening meal. Katherine and Isabella were helping her, chopping herbs and stirring the pot while Old Stephen tended the fire.

"This must be a feast fit for an earl if it takes all four of you to prepare it!" Robert said. "Katherine, come and help me fetch a firkin from the alewife."

"I'll do it, Rob," said John.

"Simon will be back soon," said his mother. "Why don't you three lads go? Supper won't be for a while and Katherine is a dab hand with the herb knife."

"Simon is helping Walter with the thatching next door," Robert said.

Katherine saw the look in Robert's eye and set down her knife. "Oh, very well. You sit here, John. But hands off the pottage!"

"I wouldn't dream of it, lass," the big man said as he made himself comfortable in the corner.

Robert and Katherine stepped out into the warm dusk and Robert exhaled slowly. He found the house unbearably cramped these days and preferred to spend more time out of it than in. As they headed down the hill they saw Simon climbing down the ladder from the Alayn house. The Alayn family had shown much gratitude for all Robert had done for them during his outlawry. Mary was long gone; married to her merchant in Horbury and Robert was glad of it. He didn't know if he could handle seeing her and Katherine coming into daily contact with each other.

"Don't let my mam press you into being her maid," Robert said to Katherine as they wandered through the closed marketplace towards the alewife's hut. "She has Isabella to help with the cooking."

"I don't mind. Unless it's my cooking you're taking objection too!" she elbowed him playfully but he didn't respond.

"I just never thought of you as a housewife that's all," he said.

"A year ago, neither did I. But a lot has changed." She smiled at him.

"You're really happy here?"

"You aren't?"

He shrugged. "It's good to be back with my family. I've missed them. It's just that I never thought I'd ever come back and now that I have... I'd forgotten how town life is."

"You miss being an outlaw."

He said nothing. After two years in the greenwood, civilisation was a strange companion to them all. And it wasn't as if they had rushed back home after Lancaster's defeat. They had taken their time in emerging from the greenwood, not liking the constant tramp of men and horses on the roads.

Soon after Lancaster's execution in March of the previous year, the king began his third campaign against the Scots. Thousands of men from England, Wales and Ireland heeded the call and marshalled at Newcastle before advancing on England's old enemy. Although keen for their pardons, the outlaws had no desire to get caught up in a war in Scotland so they had waited until the dust had settled in the wake of the marching army before they decided to head back to what was left of their homes and their families.

Robert had brought the larger portion of his band to Wakefield while Wat and Rob Dyer had gone to South Elmsall, Will to his father at Crigglestone and Much to his own father at the old mill.

Wakefield had welcomed the return of its prodigal son with open arms. Lancaster's steward, bailiffs and foresters had all been replaced but staying at Wakefield was still a risk for them all. Although the town was keen to forget the past, no official pardon had been granted and for all Robert knew, he was still an outlaw.

The end of summer saw the return of King Edward and his defeated army as they limped back south. The campaign had been a disaster. Flemish pirates allied to Robert de Brus had blocked the English supply ships from reaching the king's army which was too large and cumbersome to be of much use anyway. The Scots remained un-subjugated.

Winter came and went and as spring blossomed into summer the outlaws began to feel safer. But in late June, Little John climbed Bichill at a jog, the sweat glistening on his wide forehead.

"Trouble, Rob!" he panted. "The sheriff is here and has demanded that we speak with him."

"He waits over a year to have this chat with us?" Robert said.

"Something's not right about this," said Katherine. "Why now? What does he want?"

"Didn't say, by all accounts. I didn't hang about to be seen by him. He's at the inn refreshing his men and demanding that we all be brought to him. Nobody's cooperating and I hear he's beginning to lose his temper."

"We'd better go and see what's up before he starts pushing people about too hard. Fetch the others."

All but Old Stephen left Bichill and wandered down towards the inn. The old man had never technically been outlawed and was a stranger to the sheriff. Robert wanted to keep it that way. They brought no weapons for that would be a provocation and they were outnumbered anyway.

They found the sheriff and his men drinking ale in the shade of the lean-to. The soldiers shambled to their feet as they approached and made customary reaches for their weapons.

"Hood," said the sheriff without a hint of emotion in his voice.

"Sheriff," Robert replied. "Have you come to give us the pardons you promised?"

"The pardons my *wife* promised," the sheriff corrected. "And no. Only the king himself can give you a royal pardon but I have come to take you to him."

"How *is* your wife, sheriff?" Robert asked.

The sheriff's face turned sour. "Dare you show me insolence? I am commanded to bring you to the king by force if you will not come peaceably."

"Why now? The king has long since returned from Scotland."

"The king has been busy since his victory over Lancaster. There is much in England to set to rights, particularly here in the north. It has taken him this long to get to your case and I am to take you to him at the royal manor at Cowick."

"Why should we trust you?" Robert asked.

"Why should you not? Have I not left you all to return to your homes in peace? Have I harassed you, knowing full well the whereabouts of each and every one of you? You aided the king's efforts against the rebels last year and the king wishes to reward you. Do you throw this gesture in his face?"

"Forgive me, sheriff," said Robert, "but trust comes hard from those you set your dogs on."

"As the sheriff I have a duty to apprehend criminals in this shire. Surely you understand this. Your actions may be pardoned in light of your loyalty but the fact remains that you are robbers and outlaws."

"Your bounty hunter butchered my wife and children!" spat Simon. "They were no outlaws."

The sheriff looked at him and there seemed to be a genuine look of regret in his eyes. "De Gisburn was a madman. Had I known the depths of his depravity I would have never had hired him. I am sorry."

"Very well," said Robert. "I suppose we have no choice in the matter. We are to be pardoned whether we will it or no, it seems."

"I have horses beyond the gates so we may reach the king the quicker," said the sheriff. "My men will accompany you to your homes so that you may collect what you want and inform your kin."

They headed up Bichill with an armed escort, heads turning to stare all the way. Robert's mother was none too pleased at the thought of him riding off with the sheriff and Isabella wept but Robert comforted them both with promises of his return with a royal pardon. Old Stephen spoke a word of caution to Robert in passing.

"Don't trust the king," he said. "If he's anything like his father then he'll wring all he can out of you before he grants you your freedom."

Robert nodded. "You know where I've hidden the band's wealth. I leave you as custodian of it. I'll be damned if I'll bring it with us for the king's taking. Keep it safe until I return or a ransom demand is sent in my stead."

Horses was not all the sheriff had waiting beyond the gates. A small group of mounted men loitered about and Robert recognised Much, Wat and Rob Dyer.

"So, you have been prised from your homes too, then?" he asked, smiling to see his old comrades. "But what of Will?"

"As for Shacklock," the sheriff replied, "I decided that he should be picked up last. If he sees you are already obeying the king's summons he may be less inclined to bolt for the trees."

"You mean you want me to talk him into coming so you don't have to," said Robert.

The sheriff did not answer him. "What happened to his mate; the blonde woman?"

"Anna is no longer with us," Robert replied. "She betrayed us to de Gisburn."

"I see. I dare not ask what happened to her for I would then be bound to inform the king and that may influence his decision."

Robert realised that the sheriff wanted the king to pardon the outlaws as much as they did. They had proved to be too troublesome a quarry for him and he wanted to be well shot of them.

Shacklock Hall was a shadow of what it had once been. Will's father had evidently suffered financially since the death of his two eldest sons. The servants had been dismissed and the place was overgrown and falling apart. Will was found mucking out the pig sty and his companions roared with laughter to see the coldblooded killer reduced to a farmhand. Will cursed at them.

"Set down your shovel, Will," said Robert. "We've an audience with the king!"

Will glared at the sheriff. "A pardon at last is it? Took bloody long enough. Or are we to be cast into gaol or hanged? Who's to tell with this double-crossing bugger?"

"We've been through all that already," said Robert. "I trust the sheriff for my part and the others trust my judgement. What of you? You always were the hardest to talk into anything."

Will's father had appeared from the entrance to the hall. He was a grey man, stooped and scruffy. He hobbled on a crutch due to a nasty case of gout. "William!" he bellowed. "See these buggers off my land!"

"It's the sheriff, father!" Will yelled back in a tone that suggested he was well used to being shouted at.

"What's he want?"

"I have come for your son!" the sheriff called. "The king has requested his presence at Cowick."

"So, the boy's to hang, eh?" the old man grumbled. "Can't say he doesn't deserve it but what do I get out of it? He so recently returned to me after leaving his brothers for dead. He is a poor substitute for them but he's all I have, God rot him."

Robert could see Will's teeth clenching and wondered at his old companion's devotion to such a vile old man.

"A summons from the king is not to be quibbled over," snapped the sheriff. "If you're lucky, your son will return to you with a full pardon."

"Lucky?" said Adam Shacklock. "I do not know the word. All I've had is bad luck. Two good sons dead and their wretched bane alive to taunt me!"

"Enough!" Will yelled and he hurled his shovel to the mud. "I'll come with you, sheriff. Either a pardon or the rope would be a blessing in my life at this point."

"Oh, too good for me now, eh?" Will's father sneered. "High and mighty with your outlaw friends and riding in the company of the sheriff himself! I hope the king hangs you!"

Will ignored him, vaulted into the saddle of the offered horse and urged it on. The group left Adam Shacklock raving in his own yard. Robert felt a pang of guilt for having jeered at his friend moments earlier. He reached over and clasped Will's shoulder. "Whatever happens, Will, you'll never have to go back to that old man."

"Aye," Will replied. "I've done all I can for him, for all the thanks I've received. Let the bastard rot along with his filthy hall. I'm done with both."

FORTY-THREE

They headed east and passed through Pontefract before heading on towards Cowick. The closer they drew to their audience with the king, the more nervous Robert became. What if he was leading his companions into a trap? For all the talk of liberating the north from Lancaster's tyranny, the king had developed something of a tyrannical reputation himself.

Punishment for supporting Lancaster had been dealt out swiftly and without mercy. Over a hundred men across the country had been stripped of their lands and possessions. Even their families were not exempt from the king's vengeance. Widows and orphans had been shipped off to castles and convents in their dozens. Lancaster's creditors, desperate for recompense, were told "the king does not pay the earl's debts" and were consigned to bankruptcy. King Edward was clearly not a man to forget a word spoken or an action taken against him and seemed to match the portrait painted by Old Stephen of his father; ruthless, vindictive and lusty for vengeance for even the smallest slight.

When they stopped to water their horses and stretch their legs, Katherine took a knife to her hair and cut off the auburn locks that had grown during their time in the greenwood. She now resembled the boyish youth Robert had first encountered. He gave her a puzzled look.

"If we are to spend any length of time at the king's court then I do not wish to tempt any of those lonely men-at-arms," she explained.

"You need not be afraid of assault, Katherine," Robert told her. "I'd protect you."

"Not all of the time," she said. "You wouldn't be able to. And I'd rather a fight not break out on my account. Life is so much simpler when everybody thinks you are a boy."

"I seem to be the only man who isn't as blind as a mole," he said.

"Are you saying my disguise is no good?"

"Not at all. I'm just glad everybody else is blind to your beauty." He kissed her and looked over to the sheriff who sat on a rock, inspecting his shoe. He drew up Katherine's hood, concealing her trimmed hair. "For the sake of the sheriff. He knows you are no lad. Best if he doesn't see what you've done to your hair."

Cowick Hall lay a mile south of West Cowick and had, until recently, been one of Lancaster's properties. The king had since claimed it as his own and had begun fortifying it in earnest. A dry ditch was being dug around the walls and a stone bridge was under construction. It was clad in timber scaffolding which the sheriff led the outlaws across as they approached the gatehouse.

A pair of men-at-arms studied the group as they dismounted and, upon realising that the High Sheriff of Yorkshire was leading them, hastily sent for grooms.

The courtyard was crowded with pavilions but there were few people about apart from occasional squires and pages dashing about on errands. The bulk of the king's retinue would be at their meat in the Great Hall.

As soon as they entered the antechamber it became clear that they had a long wait before them. A queue stretched the length of the hall from the antechamber to the trestle tables at the far end where the king presumably sat. Servants hurried between the crowded benches bearing platters of meat, fish and bread while soldiers lined the walls, leaning on their spears looking thoroughly bored by the proceedings. Piping from the minstrels' gallery gave the solemn chamber an atmosphere of forced merriment. The sheriff and the outlaws said nothing as they waited patiently in line.

A handsome man in very fine clothes approached them and shared a private word with the sheriff. He regarded Robert and his companions with a look of mild disgust but appeared to be partially appeased by whatever the sheriff said to him.

"The king's chamberlain," the sheriff explained as the well-dressed man sauntered off to examine other parties in the queue. "Nobody sees the king without his say so."

"Hugh le Despenser?" Robert said, awed. The name was spoken with disdain across England. The entire civil war had its root in the king's gifting of the Gower Peninsular to le Despenser which had so incensed the Marcher Lords and caused them to turn to Lancaster's council.

As the latest party was dismissed, they shuffled closer towards the dais and for the first time Robert saw the heads of the people sitting at the trestle table. The king sat in the middle in a highbacked chair. He was tall and handsome with a strong jawline and a clear and hale complexion. Curling locks of light brown hair were bound by a circlet of gold. Far from the glowering tyrant Robert had expected, King Edward had a pleasant face that suggested a man with good humour and he forced himself to remember that this man might mean to execute them all. Appearances could be deceiving.

Next to the king sat a woman of great beauty whom Robert took to be Queen Isabella. She was a petite lady with fair features but there was no denying the maturity in those eyes that looked as if they had seen a lifetime more than the twenty-eight years their owner had walked God's earth.

Further along the table sat the only person Robert recognised; William de Melton, the Archbishop of York. As they approached the dais, the archbishop recognised the outlaws and started suddenly. He exclaimed something in French and turned sharply to the king as if to tell him to order their arrest but then thought better of it.

"Ah yes," the king said, "the mighty Robert Hood and his band."

A silence fell over the hall and the outlaws gazed at the king in stupefaction. He had spoken to them in English and good English at that albeit with a strong French accent. The nobles at the head table clearly knew of the king's mastery of the commoner's tongue but seemed embarrassed for they all looked to their plates and goblets.

"Yes, sire," said the sheriff. "You requested that they be brought to you and so here they are."

"Very good, de Warde. And they came peaceably?"

"Indeed, sire. They hope to gain your pardon for their past crimes. You do remember I told you of how they harried Lancaster's troops as they fled north?"

Robert looked to his incensed companions and shared their anger. From the sheriff's words this was the first time a pardon had been mentioned to the king. Nothing had been decided. The sheriff was presenting their case to the king for the first time after baiting them to appear at court.

"I do remember," the king replied and he looked upon Robert favourably. "I thank you for your loyalty. Would that all in my realm understood their duty as well as you do. I have need of men like you and your followers. During Lancaster's tyranny the north has gone to wrack and ruin. Bands of outlaws, not so loyal as yourselves, infest the forests, plundering the roads and depleting the royal parks of deer. I will clean up Lancaster's mess but I need men like you to help me; men who know the outlaws' ways."

"Begging your pardon, sire," said Robert, biting down on his anger, "but we didn't exactly come here expecting employment."

There was a stir amongst the nobles at this but the king did not seem to mind his frankness. "You were expecting to come here and receive an immediate pardon, no doubt," he said with a small smile. "Well, that shall be given gladly. But what guarantee do I have that you will not return to your thieving ways? Hood, I require your continued loyalty, nay I demand it, as I demand it of all my subjects. We must all make sacrifices if we are to bring the north to heel once more. And, do understand, there can be no pardon without this service."

Robert gritted his teeth. He could not refuse the king in front of the entire court. He had to accept. They all did. "I thank you for your mercy and your offer," he replied.

"Good!" the king clapped his hands together. "You shall enter my service as *valets de chambre* and as such, you will be close to me at all times, to advise and to serve. My chamberlain will instruct you in your duties tomorrow."

They were dismissed and afforded spaces at the benches where they fell to with appetite. The sheriff had other business with the king and evidently felt that he had washed his hands of them for he paid them not a glance the rest of the evening. Later, the outlaws held a private counsel in the courtyard beneath a clear, starry sky.

"I knew the sheriff was tricking us, the conniving bastard!" said Will. He had drunk much that evening and was even quicker to anger than usual. "The king won't let us get out of this service to him. Pardon? Hah! We're being held hostage!"

"It's not as bad as all that," said Little John. "We half expected to be strung up as soon as we entered the gates. We're still alive and the king is offering us pay."

"Pay in captivity!" said Will. "Listen to yourself, John! Are you really considering staying?"

They all stared at him. "You aren't?" Katherine asked.

"Not on your life!"

"Will, you can't very well refuse the king!" said Robert. "There'd be no pardon. You'd be hunted for the rest of your days."

"So be it! Better the life of an outlaw than as a performing bear with the king tugging on your leash!"

"You're wrong, Will," said Wat. "This could be a new start for all of us. A royal valet is a highly regarded position. We'll be in the confidence of the king himself; privy to all that goes on in the realm, trusted with secrets and paid handsomely too."

Robert had to admit that Wat was right. There were many benefits to a life at court. Wealth, intrigue and excitement being at the forefront of them. He would remain, even if some of his band deserted him. "What do the rest of you think?" he asked them.

"You and Wat seem to have made your minds up," said Katherine. "I'm with you, Rob, you know that." She then gestured to her shorn locks. "Though God knows how long I can keep this pretence up."

"I'll stay at court if it keeps me busy," said Simon.

"Aye, I've got mouths to feed so I'll do almost anything for that pardon," said Rob Dyer.

There was only one of them who had not yet spoken.

"Much?" Robert prompted.

The miller's son sighed and ran his fingers through his dark locks. "I can't believe I'm saying this but I agree with Will on this one. The sheriff has tricked us time and again and I'm pig sick of it. Where will it all end? I'm a simple miller. I've no desire for a life at court. And it's the principle of the thing; we earned our freedom fighting Lancaster's dogs and now the king demands service from us or else he'll hang us. It sits ill with me to live under such terms. If Will means to leave then I'm with him."

"If you're caught, you'll be hanged right here at Cowick," Robert warned.

"Better a free death than a life in captivity," said Will.

They found space to bed down by the kitchens and when the sun rose, Will and Much were gone. Robert had no idea how they had managed to get away unseen but he was glad. He made sure to remember them in his prayers for many nights after.

As they broke their fast in the courtyard a valet approached them and told them that their presence was required at the archery butts.

"The king?" Robert asked.

The valet did not answer but asked them to follow him. They crossed the timber scaffold and circumvented the hall to a grassy sward at its rear.

Here several butts had been set up and a crowd watched several men-at-arms show off their prowess.

"Ah, here come the famous bowmen of Barnsdale!" cried a voice and Robert could see the king between the folds and veils of the assembled crowd. He wore a dazzling scarlet cloak lined with miniver and seemed to be in high spirits. "Come, stand by me, Hood and watch our fine archers. You may give them some pointers, eh?"

"These men have not yet sworn an oath of loyalty to you," protested Hugh le Despenser who was dressed in an outfit of blue which nearly matched the king's in its extravagance.

"Oh, nonsense, Huchon!" said the king a tad peevishly. "Hugh here likes to do all things by the books." He considered his words for a moment and then added; "well, all things pertaining to my chamber as befits the royal chamberlain, but you can all swear your oaths later. I must say, weren't there more of you?"

Robert had dreaded this. "Yes, sire. Two of my followers deserted last night."

"And you said nothing until asked by the king directly?" Hugh said.

Robert looked from Hugh to the king and saw that the monarch's mood had turned somewhat. His jaw was clenched as if angry. "My apologies, sire. I knew nothing of their desertion until this morning."

"Very well," said the king. "I suppose men who throw my offer of mercy back in my face are no men I want at court. They shall be apprehended before long and will regret their decision I dare say. Now,

Robert, tell me what you think of de Wodeham's technique here. Roger de Wodeham is a valet in my chamber and my bowbearer. He favours a square stance. What say you?"

Robert watched a valet with ear-length brown hair loose a shaft which sailed in a high arc and struck the target near the centre. "A square stance is fine for shooting on level ground," he said, "but I generally prefer an open stance. It's good for uneven terrain although it does wear the arm muscles and quickly tires archers of small stature or ones who haven't developed the muscles since childhood."

"Good, good!" The king was pleased. "You see, Huchon? This is why I need outlaws to advise me! Tell me, Robert, do you think you could outshoot Roger here?"

"Well, I don't presume to claim that I am equal to the royal bowbearer but..."

"A wager! A wager!" the king called suddenly, "Set up the rose garland!"

Robert had heard of such a competition. A small wreath of rose flowers was mounted on a pole and looked impossibly small. "I have no bow, sire," said Robert.

"Then you shall use mine! I made it with my own hands while campaigning in Scotland with my father. Some Welsh archers under his command taught me how. It took me several tries to get it right, but I'm rather proud of it."

Robert was astounded. Archery was a common skill amongst the nobility for they often shot bows on the hunt if never on the battlefield but the idea of the

King of England smoothing and shaping his own bow was laughable.

The bow was provided and Robert tested it. He was impressed. It was of good craftsmanship and took a deal of strength to bend. The contest was arranged and wagers were placed. Robert and Roger took turns shooting at the rose garland. Roger used three arrows and Robert only two making him the winner. The crowd cheered and clapped although none so heartily as the king himself.

"Bravo, Hood! De Wodeham is my champion archer, although I'd say that position is now a matter of dispute eh, lads?" He winked at Roger de Wodeham and the young valet regarded Robert sourly. "Oh, come now, let us all be friends," said the king, thumping Roger on the back. "Robert and his companions here are to join you as *valets de chambre* and I want you, Roger, to take them under your wing. Show them how we do things, eh?"

"As you wish, sire," de Wodeham replied.

"Now, I yearn for a little light exercise myself," said the king, stretching his long arms until the joints cracked. "My bow, Hood. What say you we have a little contest of our own?"

"Sire, that would hardly be seemly," broke in the Archbishop of York.

"Are you telling me what to do again, de Melton?" said the king as he took the bow from Robert.

"But the king shooting against a common yeoman? And an outlaw at that!"

The king ignored him, strode up to the marker, plucked an arrow from the quiver of a nearby archer, nocked, drew and loosed. The arrow sailed close to the wreath and the crowd broke into an embarrassed applause. "Your turn, Hood," he said and handed the bow back.

Robert accepted an arrow and took aim. His shaft flew closer than the king's had done and the breeze of its passing made the rose petals flutter. The king's next flight overshot the pole and he cursed; a foul English noun no less which caused an intake of breath and a few sniggers from the crowd. Robert was beginning to enjoy himself until his next arrow – second time lucky once more – threaded the garland. His heart fell. He had beaten the king and embarrassed him in front of half his court. He could have kicked himself. *Of course you let the king win.*

The crowd was silent, not knowing how to respond. The king stared at the wobbling garland and his face broke into a grin. "Bravo once again, Hood! You truly are England's finest archer!"

The crowd erupted into a relieved applause but none were as relieved as Robert who turned to glance at his companions sheepishly.

FORTY-FOUR

That afternoon the outlaws swore their oaths of loyalty to the king under the stern instruction of Hugh le Despenser. Cowick was in a state of upheaval. The court was moving to York the following day and all was being packed up and loaded into carts and carriages.

York was Robert's first taste of a big city. He recollected Old Stephen's descriptions of London and Gloucester and decided that, fine storyteller though Stephen was, no one could accurately describe the sights and smells of a city.

"The clerk of the chamber will give you money for clothes," said Roger de Wodeham who had not failed in his promise to the king that he would take the outlaws under his wing. Despite Robert thrashing him in the archery contest, he had been a good companion to them on the journey to York, instructing them in how the king's household was governed and how they were required to behave. "There are a few rules regarding our status in the king's household," he said. "You are to eat boiled meat only, not roasted for that is reserved for men of higher rank. You are not to have the pages serve you and you are not to ride horses."

"What *are* we allowed to do?" Little John asked, alarmed at the sudden restrictions placed on their lives which had previously been as free as the wind.

"Oh, you'll find that there are many privileges afforded to members of the king's household," de Wodeham said with a cryptic wink.

After a visit to the cordwainer and clothier, Robert and his companions found themselves standing in the street outside dressed in matching doublets, hose and shoes. They had laughed at the clothier who had grumbled at having to use more cloth than he had been paid for in clothing Little John's massive frame.

"Not bad, eh?" said Wat as they admired themselves. "Better than the green mantles Old Stephen stitched together, God love him!"

Robert was astounded at the number of servants the king's household required. Every possible function and duty was catered to. In the Great Hall there was one squire to taste the king's food at the table, one to carve his meat and one to fetch his cup. The king's chamber alone employed thirty valets, thirty sergeants-at-arms, a dozen squires, two dozen archers as well as a number of knights, pages, ushers and clerks. All were under the strict management of Hugh le Despenser.

Unless Robert had seriously misunderstood the role of a chamberlain, the administrative power le Despenser wielded seemed to rival that of the king. He sent letters on the king's behalf, administrated in law cases, oversaw petitions and strictly controlled who saw the king and when. Nothing happened at court without his say so. The king seemed more than happy with the arrangement and he and le Despenser seemed to be the best of friends. They sat together at table and talked alone in the king's chamber long into the evening.

One thing Robert quickly learned was that the queen despised le Despenser with a passion. This was made apparent in a dramatic scene outside the king's chamber one afternoon. Robert and the others were disturbed from their duties by a woman's voice raised to anger and much shouting in French. They hustled down the corridor to see what was amiss.

The queen and her handmaidens were clustered outside the door and were engaged in a heated contest of words with the squire who guarded it. The poor fellow dared not meet the queen's eye but remained firm in his instructions which were apparently to deny her entrance.

Queen Isabella raised her hand as if to slap the unfortunate servant but then thought better of it and unleashed a barrage of French which, although incomprehensible to Robert, clearly contained some choice obscenities. With a whirl of her gown, she stormed off, her handmaidens falling in behind her, each of them paying the wretched squire a filthy look.

"He's done it this time," said de Wodeham afterwards.

"Who's done what?" Robert asked.

"Le Despenser. The queen has a wicked tongue and a temper to match. She won't forget this in a hurry."

"What exactly was all that about?" Little John asked.

"I don't rightly know the root of it but it seems to have something to do with the downsizing of the queen's household. The king has seen fit to let some of her servants go in the way of cutting down expenditure. The queen is none too pleased, especially as she knows that it was truly le Despenser's decision. The king rarely says a word in the way of administration these days that has not been put into his ear by the chamberlain. The queen knows this and wished to take her husband to account for it but she was refused admittance to the king's chamber."

"The king refused to see her?" asked Katherine.

"Le Despenser forbade it, more like."

"He wouldn't!"

Believe me, he would. Whether it was to spite the queen, I've no idea. The two don't exactly see eye to eye."

Much of the king's time was spent engaged in administrative affairs with le Despenser ever on hand to suggest and to guide the king. There were escheats to be overseen, inquisitions to conducted, petitions to be heard and orders to be dispatched. This was of little concern to the valets of his chamber who went about a parallel circuit of duties and were rarely idle. They relayed messages, made purchases, prepared rooms and lit torches. The duties were mundane but the backdrop of court made every day exciting.

There was a constant current of gossip in both English and French; the language of court that Robert was determined to master. The valets took great pleasure in flirting with the handmaidens of the queen's chamber and, accompanied by smiles and winks, gossip passed from one household to another more efficiently than any official dispatches.

Robert found that he had extra duties in improving the archery skills of the king's eldest son and heir. Edward of Windsor was ten years old and already a tall and stout youth. He had a pleasant humour much like his father and Robert enjoyed teaching him the finer points of bowman-ship. The queen often watched from afar, ever protective of her son and fearful that he might fall under le Despenser's influence as his father had done. But she was apparently satisfied that her son's military skills be improved and so did not seek to interfere. The king took a great interest in his son's improvement and regularly joined them at the butts, roaring with mirth at a missed shot and proudly clapping his son on the shoulder whenever he hit his mark.

But for all his joviality, the king had not escaped the infamous Plantagenet temper and Robert soon got his first taste of it. At the end of June, John de Stafford was translated to the bishop of Winchester; a decision made by the pope which went against the king's wishes to see his clerk Robert Baldock in the position. The news sent the king into a rage and he hurled a platter of lampreys across the room.

"God's soul!" he roared. "At every move I am thwarted! He cannot expect me to believe this is mere coincidence for it reeks too much of the business with de Orleton!"

Adam de Orleton, de Wodeham explained later, had been appointed bishop of Hereford in 1317; another decision that had incensed the king. The Bishop of Hereford had remained a figure of defiance ever since and the king was convinced he had aided

Roger de Mortimer during the civil war by secretly sending him men.

"Just like de Orleton, de Stafford has abused his position as envoy at Avignon to further his own career," the king continued. The church is rotten to the core; corrupt from cardinal to parish priest! I receive reports daily of parsons taking mistresses and friars fighting over the corpses of the rich like ravens, leaving the poor unburied. Money rules all, not duty to God and crown."

The king dispatched a barrage of letters to Avignon demanding that the pope revoke his decision. He ordered the Cinque Ports to intercept all papal correspondence pertaining to John de Stafford. It did no good. The pope's decision was final and the king had to put up with it.

If the king was quick to anger then he was equally quick to take solace in idle distraction. He loved exercise and outdoor pursuits and could regularly be found in the company of villeins learning some new skill be it thatching, hedging, ditch digging or fishing. It was a subject of some embarrassment for the barons, bishops and earls who felt that their king should pursue more fitting hobbies but for the members of the king's own chamber, who were regularly encouraged by their monarch to join in, it was all a tremendous lark.

The king was on exceedingly, some said vulgarly, familiar terms with the staff of his household. He used first names and affectionate nicknames too. As well as calling Hugh 'Huchon', he regularly referred to Robert as 'Robin'. Little John had chosen his own alias of 'Great Hob' which the king found particularly amusing. John had felt that 'Great John of Holderness' and 'Reynold Greenleaf' were names that had earned too many enemies in his lifetime for them to be used at court. They were all hobs of the woods, he explained, and the mythical creature had proved a good alias for many an outlaw.

There had been a scene of much amusement when they had presented their names to the clerk of the chamber for entry into the payment record. "Great Hob?" the clerk had said, quill poised over parchment as he looked Little John up and down with suspicion. "That's what your mother called you, is it? Great?"

"Aye," Great Hob replied. "When they passed me to her, naked as God made me, she took one look at my enormous spindle and decided no name could be a better fit."

The outlaws had roared with laughter at the clerk's indignation but the name had been scribbled down anyway and Great Hob had received his wages.

The king had heard the tale and joined the outlaws in their mirth. He had slapped Great Hob on the shoulders and said; "Your dear mother's sense of humour aside, you are a magnificent specimen, Hob. Taller than my father even and flatterers regularly tell me that the men of my family are the tallest in England. But with you at court, the country shall know that there are finer studs in England's hills!"

They had called Katherine 'Little Colle' and most assumed her name was a shortening of Nicholas. In her valet's outfit there was no reason to suspect that she was anything but a young, if rather pretty, boy.

Robert was the cause of the masquerade's failure and he could have kicked himself for it. It was during a lull in their duties when le Despenser was attending to some important matter on the other side of the palace. Robert and Katherine found themselves alone in the king's chamber and both realised that this was the first time they had been alone together since they had arrived at court.

Robert desperately missed her touch and the feel of her in his arms. Although they slept near to each other every night, there was never fewer than a dozen other members of the king's household slumbering nearby and they had never dared so much as hold hands beneath the covers. This unexpected moment of privacy was too much for Robert to resist and he grasped her and kissed her on the mouth.

"Rob, stop!" she hissed, wriggling out of his embrace. "Imagine if somebody should walk in!"

"Come on, Katherine," he said, and noticed how good it felt to say her real name. "Everybody else is busy. Where's the harm? Haven't you missed me?"

"Well," she said, "that's beside the point."

He moved towards her and she did not retreat. He placed his hands on her hips and pulled her towards him. Their lips locked and, as if a spell had been broken, the doors to the chamber were flung open and somebody strode into the chamber.

"God's soul, what have we here?" said the king.

The two lovers flung themselves from each other, knowing that it was much too late to salvage the situation. They had been rumbled and by the king no less.

"Sire, I..." Robert began, not having the first clue how he was going to end his sentence.

"You do realise that this is my own chamber?" the king said. "I would think that you might pursue your eh... activities in a more secluded place. Although privacy around here is about as unattainable as Jerusalem, God knows." He looked Katherine up and down. "So, Robin, it's Little Colle for you, is it? That's where your fancies lie? I must admit he is a fine boy."

Christ on the cross! Robert thought. *He thinks we're sodomites!*

"Sire, I fear you have been taken in a deception," Robert said, desperately wanting to erase such a conclusion from the king's mind. He looked at Katherine. "Little Colle here is not quite what she appears to be."

"She?" The king's brow furrowed as he looked her up and down and then understanding dawned. "Good lord, you mean to say you're..."

"A woman, yes, sire," said Katherine and she cut a ludicrous curtsey.

"But why all this subterfuge?" The king demanded.

"My real name is Katherine Colle, so you see, we didn't really lie to you, sire. I never actually said I was a boy."

"Then you've a damned funny notion of truth!" said the king. "But why?"

"Robert is my lover. I wanted to follow him to court. I wanted to be with him at all times and I could never do that as a woman."

"Nonsense! I have female valets in my chamber. Some of them are married to men in my service."

"But their duties are different," Katherine replied. "They serve you as washerwomen for the most part and only see their husbands at the end of each day. That is a life I could not live. And besides, we are not married."

"No, I don't suppose you are," said the king with a touch of disapproval. But then his face broadened into a smile. "Well, Robin and Little Colle, you have my permission to continue as you are."

Robert was not sure he had heard him right. "Sire, you are not going to dismiss us for our deception?"

"Not at all. I think it is really quite romantic. And exciting too! Two lovebirds right here under my nose, deceiving and defying all! It is the stuff romances are made of! I commend your loyalty and your love for each other. It shall be our little secret!"

"Thank you, sire!" said Robert and, once dismissed, he and Katherine could not get out of the chamber quick enough. They left the king in a contemplative mood, gazing out of the window at the lawns where le Despenser could be seen returning to him.

It was only once they had entered the passage that it occurred to Robert that the king had not been at all outraged by the notion of two sodomites serving in his household. Every day, it seemed, revealed more of the king than met the eye.

FORTY-FIVE

The king's attitude deeply affected Robert and he found himself contemplating it day after day. To his knowledge he had never met a sodomite although he was well aware of their existence for the priests regularly railed against such perversions. It was a sin against nature, they said, and was so unspeakable that everybody spoke of it even if they didn't know exactly what it entailed. If such things went on at court, would the King of England really turn a blind eye to it?

It would be much later that Robert came to hear the vicious rumours concerning the king's own sexuality and when he did hear them he was not surprised. He knew nothing of the king's bedchamber activities but his overly-familiar relationship with le Despenser could only ever lead people to draw one conclusion and it was a conclusion he himself contemplated that summer of 1323.

He thought of the long hours le Despenser and the king whiled away behind closed doors late of a night and began to see their relationship in a wholly new light. *Could it be possible?* But he forced himself not to dwell on so scandalous and outrageous an idea. To suggest such a thing would be tantamount to treason. And in early August of that year, suspicion of treason permeated the air like a sickness.

The court was on the eve of moving from Kirkham to Pickering where the king wished to crack down on the rampant poaching which had decimated his deer during Lancaster's revolt. Robert advised the king as best he could on the methods and practices of poachers. They were about to set out for one of the king's deer parks when the king received news which threw him into a panic.

Roger de Mortimer had escaped from the Tower.

De Mortimer and his uncle had been incarcerated since their surrender at Shrewsbury in January of the previous year. As one of the most powerful Marcher Lords and leader of the rebellion next to Lancaster, de Mortimer's capture had been a decisive victory for the king. To now have such a dangerous man on the loose was to risk a rallying point for all the king's enemies.

"He should have executed him after his capture!" de Wodeham grumbled as they walked down the corridor to the king's solar. "Everybody said so!"

"I can't understand why he left him alive," Robert said. "He's as much a traitor as Lancaster was. Why on earth did he spare him?"

"Because our king has a soft heart," said de Wodeham although not unkindly.

They found the king with le Despenser and both seemed on edge.

"You have heard the news, I take it?" the king said. "Gossip travels like wildfire in my court I am given to understand."

"Yes, sire," said de Wodeham. "Most unfortunate."

"Unfortunate? Pah! It's a conspiracy! I should never have let de Mortimer live. He has too many allies, too many treasonous snakes he calls friends. Do you know his gaoler was in on it? Helped ply the guards with drugged wine and then scarpered with him! And we don't need to look too far to see that he had aid from higher places."

"Indeed, one need only look as far as the church," said le Despenser, his face sour. "The loyalties of the bishops do not always lie in the king's favour."

"De Orleton!" said the king as if he had suddenly hit upon the source of all his woes. "That weasel has been friend to the de Mortimers for years and undoubtedly played his part in the escape!"

"He must be dealt with," said le Despenser, "but we must choose our moment well. He has the support of the pope and it would not do to act impulsively."

The hue and cry for de Mortimer was given up and letters were sent to all England's sheriffs, ordering them to pursue him and take him dead or alive. The ports were notified and men were dispatched to ensure he did not escape to the continent. The king and le Despenser were in a constant state of unease that almost amounted to a fear for their own lives. If de Mortimer were to rally an army then all their work since Lancaster's defeat might be undone.

Despite the king's efforts de Mortimer remained elusive until early October. The court was at Ightenhill Manor in the demesne of Clitheroe when the messenger arrived bringing the news that de

Mortimer was in France, enjoying the hospitality of his kin in Picardy.

"He had help!" said the king who had been worked up into another state by this latest piece of news. "All around me is treachery! Whom am I to trust? De Orleton aided in his escape to France, I am sure of it. Just as he aided in his escape from the Tower!"

"Then perhaps the time has come for us to make our move," said le Despenser who was doing a better job of concealing his fear although Robert could see the cracks in his usually ironclad demeanour. "We are going to need proof of his treason if we are to haul him before the assizes."

"We are well aware of his dealings with the de Mortimers," said the king. "Men from his *familia* were seen in de Mortimer's army before Boroughbridge. What more proof do we need?"

"Something documented would be preferable to word of mouth," le Despenser suggested. If de Orleton helped de Mortimer escape then he must still be in contact with him."

"Of course! He must be watched! No letters must be sent by him without my knowledge. He is currently at his residence at Shinfield. I shall dispatch men immediately to intercept his wicked little words!"

It was not until later that evening that Robert and his companions learned of their role in the king's mission to spy on the Bishop of Hereford. Robert was summoned away from his duties to attend the king directly and when he reached the king's solar he found Katherine, Simon, Wat, Rob Dyer and Little John there already. The only other people in the room were the king and le Despenser.

"I am sure you all overheard our conversation concerning the Bishop of Hereford earlier today," said the king. "I have spent the afternoon in deep meditation on how I am to proceed against his treachery. He must be prevented from contacting de Mortimer in France but he must not know that I am directly interfering with his dealings. And so, the idea came to me; why not send men who are used to operating outside of the law? Men who have made careers of thievery and skulduggery?"

"You wish to send us to intercept the bishop's communications," said Robert.

"Exactly that," the king replied. "And who better? You shall be licensed thieves and no suspicion will fall upon the crown."

"Meaning that we run all the risk with no guarantee of your protection," said Little John.

"What risks are you afraid of?" said the king. "You evaded my Sheriff of Yorkshire and his agents well enough and you are required only to rob a few messengers of some letters. Hardly dangerous work for England's boldest band of outlaws."

As with any decision the king made there was no way the outlaws could refuse. They were to leave early the following morning and the king arranged for fast horses to be placed at their disposal.

"It's alright being robbers if it suits the king," grumbled Little John as they changed from their brightly-coloured doublets and hose back into their dull, coarse garments which they had kept in their bundles since joining the king's service.

"Orders are orders," said Wat. "And the king's orders are good enough for me."

"I'm surprised you're so keen to charge off on a mission," said Robert. "That chambermaid giving you grief?" Wat had begun a romance with one of the queen's maids and relished court life more than any of them. He seemed to thoroughly enjoy his new purpose in life although Robert wondered how much of that was down to frequent tumbles in the stables.

The skies were grim as they galloped south and rain threatened to fall in torrents. By the time they had reached the wooded ridge of Alderley it was lashing down. The lowlands of the Cheshire Plain stretched for as far as the eye to see; open and empty, promising nothing but cold nights and wet days.

They stopped at towns and inns whenever they could but were sparing with their use of coin. They had not been paid in advance and none of them could guess how long they would spend in the south on the king's errand. They may well be hungry before winter was upon them.

"The king never said we weren't to make a living along the way," said Katherine.

"You mean thievery?" Robert asked.

"What we're doing isn't legal anyway," she replied with a grin. "Robbing a bishop's messengers?"

"Whatever the king says is legal *is* legal," said Wat.

They reached Berkshire as autumn entered its death throes. The wind was strong and the rain ever more frequent. Mud and decay was all they could see against a backdrop of leafless trees.

"This is no time of year to be robbing folk," said Robert. "There's bugger all cover and the weather is foul."

None of the outlaws could read much beyond their own name and so the king had seen fit to set up a contact who would determine if they had found sufficient evidence to be levelled at the Bishop of Hereford. A messenger had been sent ahead of them to inform the clerk in Reading of their arrival. They met him at an inn and were glad of the fire and a tankard of ale to warm them.

"You are to watch for the bishop's messengers on the wooded trackway between Shinfield and the bridge that crosses the River Lodden at Twyford," said the clerk. "All messages are to be brought to me for my inspection."

They slept at the inn that night and luxuriated in their hot meals and pallets of dry straw for they knew that the weeks ahead were to be ones of hardship and discomfort. The following morning, they stabled their horses and paid for their upkeep several weeks in advance. They headed south on foot, skirting Shinfield for fear that the bishop would hear reports of strangers abroad in his tithe.

The trackway followed the River Lodden northeast to Twyford and a good deal of it was not as wooded as Robert had been led to believe. They spent the rest of the day travelling its length and they met no one.

"At least when we do see someone it'll be a good bet it's one of the bishop's men," said Wat.

Robert said nothing. The loneliness of the place was a worry to him. Few travellers meant few pickings and empty bellies.

They made camp roughly halfway between Shinfield and Twyford where the woods were the thickest. It was a modest camp; nothing like their winter camp in Barnsdale. Robert remembered those months of inactivity with nothing but Old Stephen's stories to keep their minds busy and missed the old man's company. He hoped he and his family were well. He also hoped their stay in the south would be a short one.

They made good progress for that very first week a youth came trotting down the track way, a messenger's satchel hanging from his saddle. Robert, Katherine and Little John stepped out onto the track ahead of him, their weapons drawn while Simon, Wat and Rob Dyer emerged from the trees to his rear. The rustle of their movements made the messenger turn in his saddle in fright and his horse sidestep nervously.

"Hand over the satchel, lad, and you'll receive no ill-treatment," said Robert.

"Not from you perhaps," said the messenger. "But my master'll give me a thrashing."

"Cheeky bugger, isn't he?" said Little John. "We'll give you worse than a few stripes across your hide if you don't drop that satchel right now!"

The youth gave in and untied his satchel. It fell to the track and the outlaws moved aside to let him pass before seizing the satchel and rifling its contents.

"It's from the bishop, no doubt about that," said the clerk at Reading when they presented the letters to him the following day. "But there's little of use here. An order for cloth, some correspondence regarding rents and a letter to a friend in London. Nothing the king can use against him. Keep trying."

"Keep trying?" said Robert. "How long are we supposed to be sitting on our arses down here?"

The clerk blinked at him. "As long as it takes."

"To think we gave up warm beds and regular meals for this," said Rob Dyer as they left the inn.

"You've got soft!" said Little John. "We all have! We once wintered in Barnsdale! This southern climate isn't half as bad."

"We had the king's deer to hunt and fat merchants to rob in Barnsdale," said Robert. "Face it, John, we won't survive much more than a few weeks if we don't start broadening our horizons. Katherine is right, the king never said we weren't to return to our old habits. We may be down here for the long haul and I don't know about you, but I've a hunger for venison and some coin in my purse!"

FORTY-SIX

The following day Robert sent Little John, Wat and Rob Dyer into the woods south of Shinfield to see if they couldn't shoot a deer to keep their bellies full. He, Katherine and Simon remained by the trackway in case another messenger came up from Shinfield Hall.

Little John and company returned at dusk bearing a roe buck between them which raised their spirits immensely. But after several days, when the buck was little more than bones and the taste of its roasted flesh a distant memory, the gang began to lose hope once more. No more messengers had passed by.

"We're worse off than when we were outlaws," said Rob Dyer. "At least then we were in familiar country and had the Great North Road to rob."

"We can't keep this up," Robert agreed. "We need to find out if the bishop is communicating with de Mortimer some other way. Only then can we return to court."

"If we could just get our hands on him we could squeeze a confession out of him," said Little John, his mighty fists making a wringing motion in the air before him.

"Assault a bishop?" said Wat. "As well tie our own nooses! The king's sanction has its limits, I fear."

"If we could only get inside his house," said Katherine. "That way we could see if there was any correspondence from de Mortimer."

"There are too few of us," said Robert. "We can't assault his manor house nor can we break in like we did at Adwick-le-Street. It's too well guarded." He rubbed his chin thoughtfully. "There must be some way..."

Over the next couple of days Robert formulated a plan. It was a risky one but risky plans had served them well in the past. For the first step, the outlaws shot and dressed a deer at the edge of Shinfield woods; well within the bishop's tithe. Then they approached some shepherds and paid them handsomely for their staffs and sheepskin cloaks.

Robert, Katherine and Simon donned the sheepskins and left Little John, Wat and Rob Dyer with the dressed deer and small campfire before setting off towards the bishop's residence.

"Are you sure this will work?" Katherine asked Robert.

"No. But we have no better plan. Anything beats sitting around here while the weather gets worse, waiting for a messenger who probably won't show up."

The bishop's residence was a country manor a mile from the village of Shinfield. It had no moat but a wall ran head-height around its precinct. As they approached the gatehouse the porter poked his face out as if to tell them to clear off.

"We wish to speak with Bishop de Orleton," said Robert, mustering his best southern accent and hoping that his Yorkshire brogue would not betray him.

"His excellency has far more pressing concerns than passing the time of day with three shepherds," the porter snapped.

"What we have to tell him concerns his lands and the king's deer that roam in Shinfield Woods," Robert persisted.

The porter's eyes widened. "Poachers is it?"

"Aye," said Robert.

"Where?"

"They have a camp not half a mile within the woods. We can take his excellency straight to them if you let us speak with him."

"Follow me," the porter said and he unlocked the gate to admit them. They were led to the Great Hall where the bishop was engaged in some administrative affairs beside a cosy fire.

He was a tall, slender man of about fifty years of age with a sanguine complexion. Small, clever eyes peered out from beneath long brows that were touched with grey as if a frost had just set in. The porter told him their story while the three outlaws were subjected to an intense looking over from the bishop.

"This is very loyal of three shepherds to come to me with this news," said the bishop not without a touch of suspicion in his voice.

"Well, your excellency," said Robert, scratching his ear. "We folk who live off the land and have flocks to safeguard don't take too kindly to outlanders. One minute it's poaching deer the next it's stealing sheep and robbing families."

"Quite right," said the bishop. "Lawlessness must not be tolerated, especially within the bounds of the church's land. Wait here and I will prepare. I have a mind to deal with this scum myself."

The bishop floated away to some solar and the porter returned to his post. The three outlaws basked in the heat of the fire and looked around at the expensive furnishings. De Orleton's wealth was renowned. A small arch led off from the Great Hall to a parlour that seemed well stocked with shelves and documents.

"What if the bishop sees fit to kill John and the others instead of bringing them in?" Katherine said to Robert in a low voice.

"He may be clergy but he can't afford to be that corrupt," Robert replied. "They can't just string up poachers. Not without involving the law."

"Things may get rough though," said Simon. "You know John will put up a brave front for the sake of appearances."

Robert did not have time to answer for two men in maille entered the hall.

"You are to come with us," said one as he placed a helm on his head. "The bishop wants you to lead us to these poachers."

They left the hall and waited in the yard while horses were readied and a small host of the bishop's men assembled around them. At last, the bishop himself appeared astride a grey palfrey wearing travelling clothes which were by no means rude or unrefined.

They set off at once and cut a straight line towards the woods. The outlaws led the way and walked briskly, ever mindful of the impatience of the mounted men at their back.

As they entered the treeline, Robert halted and raised his hand for caution. The campfire could be seen a little distance through the trees. He turned to the bishop and pointed at it.

"They dare camp so openly?" said the bishop incredulously.

There was a soft rasp as one of his men drew his sword from his scabbard. The bishop gave the order and the men fanned out, approaching the camp from several sides.

Robert and the others remained with the bishop and watched with concern as their comrades were apprehended. They couldn't see much and heard no more than angry shouts. Before long, Little John, Wat and Rob Dyer were led through the trees. To their credit, they did not so much as pay their leader a glance.

"Caught red handed," said one of the men to the bishop. "With a fine buck dressed and hanging."

"The sheriff will deal with them," said the bishop. "Good work, you fellows," he said to Robert and the others. "We shall take it from here."

"Begging your pardon, your excellency," said Robert, "we are but poor shepherds and, well, one good turn deserves another, that's what my mam used to say…"

"Oh, very well," sighed the bishop irritably. "I suppose it is too much to ask that the commoners do a good deed for its own sake. Come back with me and I shall see that you are suitably recompensed for your time."

They trooped back to the bishop's residence and Robert, Katherine and Simon had a job to keep up with the mounted men who bore the prisoners between their horses at a fast trot. When they arrived, they were ushered into the kitchen and told to wait while the bishop interrogated the poachers in the Great Hall. Food and ale were provided and they wasted no time in filling their empty bellies.

When they were done Robert rose and said softly; "Katherine, when we enter the Great Hall, you secure the door while Simon and I deal with any resistance from the bishop and his men."

Silently they filed out into the screens passage. Two arched doorways led into the Great Hall; one closed and the other ajar. The outlaws drew their long knives which they had kept concealed beneath their cloaks and rushed the hall.

The bishop stood up from his table in alarm. Little John, Wat and Rob Dyer spun on their heels and the two guards who stood on either side of them drew their swords.

An elbow from Little John sent one of them sprawling, his sword clattering to the flags and the other threw down his own blade as Robert and Simon advanced on him, their keen knives glinting in the light from the high windows. The sound of bolts sliding home behind them confirmed that Katherine had secured both doors.

Little John picked up the discarded swords and handed one to Wat. The hall was secure and the bishop was at their mercy.

"A conspiracy?" said the bishop, his face red as a beet. "You'll hang for this, all of you!"

"Not if you hang first, your excellency," said Robert. "We know about your communications with traitors and we are here for proof of it."

"I don't know what you're raving about," said the bishop.

"Do you deny that you are de Mortimer's friend?"

"I do not answer to common ruffians. As it happens I have no clue as to de Mortimer's whereabouts, much less the inclination to write to him."

"We'll see," said Robert. "Wat. Rob. Ransack that little parlour back there and see what you can find. We'll make sure his excellency continues to be such a good host."

The bishop seethed in silence as Wat and Rob headed into the chamber beyond the dais and began looting it of every document they could find. They stuffed rolls, parchments and letters into a sack they had brought for the job before emerging, grins on their faces.

"You checked every shelf, every chest?" Robert asked.

"Aye," Wat replied. "The good bishop doesn't have a scrap of paper to wipe his arse with now!"

"Then we shall take our leave of you, your excellency," said Robert, throwing the bishop a wink.

The outlaws headed into the recently ransacked parlour and booted a window out, bending the leading and smashing the glass before pushing through it, one by one. By the time they were all standing in the yard at the rear of the building, the bishop and his men had unlocked a door in the screens passage and had roused every member of the household. They could hear shouts on the other side of the building and the tramp of running feet on both sides.

"We're going to be hemmed in!" said Simon.

"Over the wall, now!" said Robert.

He and Little John stood by the wall, facing each other, and gave each member of the band a leg up. When it was his turn, Little John needed no help for he was taller than the wall itself and he sat atop it, one leg dangling on either side. He reached down to help Robert up and together they tumbled down into the fern bushes on the other side. The bishop's men rounded the corner of the hall and found that the intruders had vanished into thin air.

The outlaws cut through the woods and joined the trackway that led down to the river. They could hear horns bellowing in the distance as the bishop's men rode out to scour the countryside. They made for their camp and retrieved their gear before striking out northwest towards Reading.

They met with the clerk the following morning and he spent several hours examining the haul of documents they had pilfered from Shinfield Hall.

"I'm not sure that robbing the bishop's private residence was quite what the king had in mind when he sent you down here," he said as he leafed through the reams of documents. He pulled out an account roll.

"Bugger what he had in mind," said Little John. "Have we accomplished our mission or not?"

"Difficult to say," the clerk muttered. "There is nothing here from de Mortimer's hand, although of course de Orleton may well have burned any letters from the traitor to be on the safe side."

"Is there anything at all that can be used against him?" Robert asked desperately.

"I don't know if much can be used against him," said the clerk as he examined the account roll, "but this is very interesting nonetheless."

"Interesting?" snorted Little John. "Interesting doesn't get us home."

"What is it?" said Robert, looking at the roll with its indecipherable scrawlings.

"The Peruzzi..." said the clerk. "Hmm."

"What's that?"

"They are an Italian banking society based in Florence. Le Despenser has placed huge deposits with them and so too, it seems, has de Orleton."

"Is that illegal?" said Katherine.

"No, but it shows that de Orleton has some very lucrative private affairs."

The clerk continued examining the papers and finished late that evening. He concluded that there was nothing of use in what the outlaws had stolen from Shinfield Hall.

"Our time is up," said Robert. "Either de Orleton has no contact with de Mortimer or he is too careful about it. Either way we can do no more good sitting by the road to Twyford. It's already November."

It was true. The mornings were frosty and the nights bitter. They spent their last night at the inn and then fetched their horses first thing in the morning before heading north in search of the king and his court.

FORTY-SEVEN

As they entered Warwickshire they began asking at inns and inquiring of travellers on the roads if anybody knew the whereabouts of the king's court. They were met with ignorance and the further north they went the more lost they felt.

"We could wander around the Midlands for a year or more and not find the king," grumbled Little John. "We've no idea if we should head into Staffordshire, Leicestershire or up through the middle into Derbyshire."

"The king's court shouldn't be too hard to miss," said Robert.

"Although England is a big place," said Wat.

"Still, somebody must know something."

Eventually somebody did know something and an old cowherder informed them that the king was currently residing at Nottingham Castle.

It was with a tingle in the hairs on Robert's neck that the outlaws passed through the very barbican gate that Old Stephen and Roger Godberd had patrolled nearly sixty years previously. Robert looked about at the grim curtain walls and mighty keep and thought back on all the tales Old Stephen had told them. With a thrill he considered that somewhere below their feet was the storeroom and secret passageway.

They were immediately called before the king who was most eager to hear of their mission. They told him all and handed over the bundle of documents which were immediately squirreled off by one of le Despenser's clerks for closer inspection.

The king was gravely disappointed that nothing had turned up that could be used against de Orleton and he dismissed them with a wave of the hand.

"Things have gone from bad to worse in your absence," said Roger de Wodeham at table that night.

"How so?" asked Robert.

"War is brewing, put simply."

"War?" asked Little John. "Who with? The Scots?"

De Wodeham shook his head. "The French. Not long after you left, the king received word of a dispute in the Duchy of Aquitaine. Some boneheaded French sergeant erected a stake in a small Gascon village called Saint-Sardos bearing the arms of the king of France."

"Why make such a bold insult to England now?" Robert asked. "Gascony is still part of the duchy, is it not?"

Roger nodded. "All that is left to our king of the mighty Angevin Empire of his ancestors. You know the French have been constantly eroding England's foothold there. Well, it took another bonehead to complete the disaster. The lord of nearby Montpezat stormed into Saint-Sardos the following day, hanged the French sergeant from his own stake and burned the village to the ground. Naturally King Charles was outraged and the situation grew even more sticky when it became known that Montpezat met with the Seneschal of Gascony but two days before. The

French king is convinced it's all a plot on Edward's part."

"Bloody hell," said Katherine. "Do you think it will be war?"

De Wodeham shrugged. "The king is sending all sorts of desperate promises and excuses to King Charles but it's all too little too late. His tardiness in paying homage to the French crown for the Duchy of Aquitaine has not stood him in good stead. The French believe he slights them at any excuse and, in turn, will not hesitate to punish him for it."

"What does the queen think of all this?" Robert asked. "Being King Charles's sister and all."

"The king's relationship with his queen has soured further too. She's in London with the young Edward. They barely speak these days and all letters between them are intercepted by the chamberlain's agents."

"He dares to do that?" asked Katherine in an appalled voice.

"He does as he pleases," said de Wodeham. "And who is to stop him? The queen? Hardly. The king?" his eyes turned to the dais at the head of the hall and Robert saw that the king and le Despenser were deep in discussion about something that caused lines of worry to crease the king's face. Every so often le Despenser would place his hand on the king's arm as if to reassure him of something.

They were to spend Christmastide at Kenilworth and stopped off at Duffield Castle and then Tutbury along the way. By the time the great red keep of Kenilworth hove into view Robert felt as if he had done a walking tour of Old Stephen's youthful adventures.

Christmastide was a busy but merry time for Robert and his companions. They were rushed off their feet but had never eaten nor drunk so well and the games and entertainments provided by the king created a riotous atmosphere. But throughout it all Robert could not help but feel that things had changed. It was not just the pointless errand they had been sent on in the autumn. The king's attitude towards them had changed. He never outwardly expressed any disappointment with their failure to secure damning evidence against de Orleton but he had developed something of a cold shoulder to them that was in stark contrast to his jovial embrace they had enjoyed before their departure.

"He is a fickle man," said Katherine to him one night. "We learned that of him within our first days at court. We were a novelty to him but now the year has turned and we are dulled in his eyes. He has found other diversions."

With the new year came a new parliament and the court journeyed to Westminster. In late February they rolled up to the palace in a great procession as the city greeted their long-estranged monarch with much celebration. But even Robert could see that much of it was staged and when the king and le Despenser walked up the steps, arm in arm like schoolboys enjoying a jape, he even heard some booing.

Despite the lack of concrete evidence, the king went ahead with his prosecution of de Orleton and the bishop was summoned to appear before him. He had already stood before the royal justices at Hereford that January and had refused to answer the charges of collusion with de Mortimer on the grounds that he, as a man of the church, could only be judged by his peers. It was a defence he used again when the charges were read out at Westminster and, as the king's temper began to flare dangerously, the Archbishop of Canterbury stepped in to claim de Orleton for the church.

The king threw up his hands in exasperation but he knew he had to abide by the rules of the clergy. He ordered the archbishop to produce de Orleton at a later hearing in March.

Robert and the other valets attended to the king as he exited the hall. Up ahead they saw the archbishop and de Orleton making for the doors. De Orleton turned to pay the king a passing glance. His eyes roved over the assembled company and froze when he saw Robert. Understanding crossed his face and he looked like a man who has suddenly realized that a great prank has been played on him.

"Sire, you count villains in your household!" he called to the king.

"My household is chosen by myself and my chamberlain," the king retorted. "Their quality is a reflection of mine."

"I would not think to compare our king to hedge robbers and poachers," de Orleton continued," but these men of yours robbed me in my own home. They poached your deer and held me at knifepoint!"

"Clearly you are mistaken," said the king. "These men are my attendants and never leave my side. But if you wish to press your allegations in a more official capacity then by all means I will answer to them."

De Orleton said nothing but cast Robert a gaze of hatred he had not thought possible on the face of a man of the cloth before departing.

The bishop remained in London for a short while at his house on the Strand. Nothing came of his accusations against the outlaws except a savage beating dealt out to Rob Dyer when he was returning alone from an errand in the city one night.

"Bastards left him bleeding in the mud," said Wat after they had visited their comrade in the infirmary. "He recognised one of them as de Orleton's man."

Little John ground his teeth. "Let's pay the good bishop's men a visit."

"What will that achieve?" Robert asked. "A brawl on the Strand? A few broken noses and loose teeth? De Orleton deserves a meatier justice. And he'll get it sooner or later."

The further proceedings against de Orleton provided some consolation as this time the king had his day. The bishop was found guilty of having given aid to de Mortimer and was stripped of his properties. He returned to his home in Hereford a broken man. Word had it that the king's agents had turfed all his belongings out into the street to be picked over by the commoners. Most at court felt like justice had been served but Robert found himself unable to agree.

"Come on, Rob," said Little John, noticing his sour face over the rim of his ale jack. "That bugger got what was coming to him, just as you said he would."

"Despite our not finding any evidence that he had colluded with de Mortimer," Robert replied.

"Since when have you been so keen to see fair treatment of corrupt clergymen?" Katherine asked.

"Whether or not de Orleton is guilty is irrelevant now," said Robert. "But we were used as the king's hatchet men and don't think he won't use us so in the future."

"Well, it's a job isn't it?" said Wat.

"Maybe a job isn't what I want out of life," said Robert. "Robbing folk is something we can do on our own. We don't need the king's sanction for that."

They ignored him and continued with their drinking, all except Katherine who was worried by the gloomy turn he had taken. "What's really up?" she asked him.

He shrugged. "It's not been the same since we got back. Court life stifles me and I miss the old days when it was just us and the greenwood. And I miss you..." he placed his hand on hers.

She pulled it from him. "Don't," she said.

He sighed. "This is what I mean. Why should we have to hide? We were once king and queen of the greenwood! How much longer do you want to stay here?"

"I don't know," she replied. "What choice do we have?"

She had spoken the irrevocable truth. They were trapped in their new lives as valets. The novelty of their first months at court had peeled away to reveal their true circumstances. Will and Much had been right. Although they lived in comfort, it was a gilded prison.

By high summer their situation had not changed. They were staying at the Tower and Robert had been shooting at the butts with the king and his son. Afterwards the king took them to see the leopards and lion in the menagerie.

Robert found the leopards curious beasts but it was the lion that struck him the most. It was a melancholy old thing with mangy fur and few teeth left so that it had to gnaw at the meat it was thrown on one side of its mouth. Robert stared into those sad, rheumy eyes and felt a kinship with it. He knew what it was to have once been free and wild and how it was to yearn for those things from a prison.

They returned to the lawns and saw the queen and her handmaidens strolling in the sunshine by the wall. "Run to your mother, boy," said the king. "Tell her you fed the lion yourself. She will believe that you are ever so brave."

Young Edward went jogging off and the king smiled in his wake. Robert knew how proud he was of his eldest son.

"Do you think she still has any feelings for me at all?" the king said and for a moment Robert did not know of whom he was speaking. In the distance the queen kissed the young Edward on the cheek.

"I couldn't say, sire," Robert replied, wondering why on earth he was being asked to comment on the queen's feelings.

"Sometimes it as if all the current turmoil between us is but a forgotten dream," the king went on. "Take last night for instance. As we seated ourselves at table she told me that I looked very handsome in my new gown. In turn, I told her how beautiful she was and we actually discussed trivial things throughout dinner. She even laughed once. We used to be very much in love, did you know that? That's not always a given in royal unions, you know."

"Sire?" Robert said, not sure where all this was coming from or where it was leading.

"I don't know where it all went wrong for Isabella and me," the king continued. "We used to be united in all things and our love for each other foremost. Now it seems that every word we speak to each other gets swept away by the winds of politics and the whims of others. A wall has been built between us a wall which I had a hand in building, I have no doubt – and I do not know how we can ever break through it again. But every once in a while, like last night, we both pass by a small hole in that wall and catch a glimpse of each other and in that one moment, we see each other as we did all those years ago."

Robert didn't know how to respond but fortunately the king had sunk into one of his melancholies and seemed to forget he was there. But his words had struck a dull chord in Robert's soul and all he wanted in that moment was to run to

Katherine and embrace her and never let her go. The year they had spent at court had torn them from each other's arms and he knew that the longer they remained at court the further they would drift from each other. He was terrified of losing her as he had lost Mary. He wanted her. He wanted the greenwood and the free life they had once led. So, what had once been only a whisper of an idea, began to grow in his mind and take the shape of a plan.

FORTY-EIGHT

The opportunity Robert's plan required did not come along until November of that year. They were staying at the Tower once again and the court was preparing to travel north with the intent of keeping Christmastide at Nottingham. It was late in the evening and most of the valets, squires, porters and other members of the king's household were bedding down for the night, their last duties for the day carried out. Robert summoned all his old outlaw comrades. They met at the foot of the Tower wall where the shadows were deep enough to conceal them.

"I'm sure you all know why I've brought you here," Robert said to them.

"Not really," said Wat. "What's up?"

"The point of the matter is that we have been at court for a year and a half now. Whatever duty we owed the king, if indeed we owed him anything, is done. By rights we should be free."

"I think you are forgetting that we are criminals, Rob," said Simon. "Our accepting of the king's employment was not a duty but a forfeit. It was the only way we could keep our necks from being stretched."

"Was it the only way?" he replied. "What if Will and Much had the right of it?"

"God knows where they are now!" Wat said. "Dead or worse perhaps. We've had it good here. Good food, good clothes and coin in our purses."

"But at what price?" Robert said. "Don't you yearn for the free air, the smell of the greenwood and the unknown path? Here we live in comfort but are ever on call to do this or fetch that. And who knows how long it will be before our master sends us off on another fruitless errand into unknown parts?"

"Aye, this war with France will drag us into it sooner or later," said Little John. "The king won't let his brother-in-law hold onto the Duchy of Aquitaine without a fight, though he is taking his time in getting to it. We might find ourselves fighting in Gascony in the spring."

"John speaks the truth," said Robert. "We need to get out before it's too late."

"We can't keep running forever," said Katherine.

"You want to stay and play king's hound?" said Robert

"No. I want to be free. But if we run, we'll never be free again. You know the king never forgives an insult. The sheriff will be on our heels again. It will never be over."

"Yes it will," said Robert. "There is only one way to be free. Truly free. And this is how we are going to do it." He reached under his tunic and pulled out a roll of parchment. He opened it and tossed it down on the ground. The outlaws recognised it, despite not being able to read it.

"De Orleton's account roll!" said Little John.

"The one that details his deposits with those Italian bankers," said Simon. "You kept this from the king? Why?"

"Let's just say I put it by for a rainy day. And now that day has come, you all feel it, I know you do. We're going to make one final score. We're going to rob the Bishop of Hereford of all he has and then disappear. Forever."

"Stop," said Wat. "Whatever it is you are planning, you must not reveal any more of it to me."

"Why?" asked Robert.

"I'm not with you. I love you all as kin and I wish you the best of luck but I cannot go with you."

"It's that handmaid of yours isn't it?" Robert replied. "You would really turn your back on us, on freedom, for a pretty maid?"

"I love her," Wat replied. "And furthermore, I like it here at court. Before this I was a fish trader and then an outlaw. Now I have a sense of purpose and no fear of the future. Oh, I may be called upon to fight for the king but even that is preferable to spending the rest of my life fighting for food and shelter. I am sorry, but it is best that I know no more."

He turned and slunk off to his bed, leaving the five outlaws – all that was left of Robert's ten-strong band – staring in his wake.

"What about the rest of you?" Robert asked them.

"Sorry Rob," said Rob Dyer. "I've got my kin to think of."

"And I don't?"

"I'm better suited to legal employment. You have a fire burning within you that I just don't have. I want to earn my money and support my family without the law on my tail. I'm sorry, but I'm out too."

"And me," said Simon.

Robert gazed at his cousin in disbelief.

"What have I got outside court life? I lost everything when de Gisburn killed my family but the king has given me some purpose. I'm happy enough here at court, surrounded by people, always having something to do."

Robert swallowed. This was not the response he had expected from his band. "Very well," he said. "You must all do as you see fit."

Simon and Rob turned away and followed in Wat's footsteps. Robert looked from Katherine to Little John. "What about you two?"

Neither said anything committal. They just stared at the parchment on the grass, unsure of it.

"How can it be done?" said Little John after a while.

Robert smiled. "I'll show you," he said.

The Bishop of Hereford was in London that November to meet with the papal nuncios who had arrived in England to take up his case with the king. It was his return to the capital that Robert had been waiting for and he had paid a local street urchin to spy on the bishop's residence and to bring him word of any sign that the bishop's business in London was at its end.

The court made to leave the city on the 23rd of November where they would overnight at Puckeridge before continuing north. Time had run out for the outlaws and, with de Orleton showing no signs of leaving, Robert cursed as he realised he would have to find some way of staying behind in London while the king travelled north.

"Feign sickness," Little John told him. "You'll get a reprieve from service and probably a little something to tide you over if you catch the king in a generous mood. We can sneak off while the court is on the road, double back and return to London."

"He'll never believe it," Robert said. "He'll think I'm deserting."

"You've been in his service a year and a half, Rob," said Katherine. "Why should you desert now? Besides, if John and I stay with the court at least until London is behind us, the king won't suspect anything is up."

Robert allowed himself to be convinced and sent his excuses to the king. Fortunately, the king's attention was so distracted by the move and the visit of the papal nuncios that he waved aside Robert's excuses and ordered the clerk of the chamber to gift him five shillings and a demand to come to Nottingham when he was better.

Robert took up residence at an inn in the city and kept a low profile. He did not want to run the risk of being seen in full health by any other member of the king's household. All was set to proceed when a further hitch turned up in the form of Robert's street urchin who brought him news of the bishop's plan to depart London on the 28th.

"That gives us just under a week," he told John and Katherine. "You won't make it back to London in time so you will have to cut westwards from the king's progress. I will follow the bishop and meet with you on the road."

Robert remained at the inn as the king and his train flooded out of the city. He whiled away the next five days at the inn, preparing himself. He discarded his valet's doublet and hose for the last time and donned his patched tunic, grey woollen hose and a hooded travelling cloak. On the 28th, he purchased a horse and left the city.

He waited in the fields by the hamlet of Charing Cross and spent the rest of the morning trying to keep warm for it was a frosty day and his breath was a fug on the chill air. Eventually the bishop and his entourage passed by. Robert could see the bishop astride his palfrey, bundled up in warm furs and decided that those would be the first things he would have off his back.

He waited until they had passed into the distance before following at a slow trot. He continued in this manner until they neared the Crown Crossroads where the road from Westminster split into two; one leading to Windsor and the other to Bristol. Beyond it was a small hamlet called Slough and before that a wooded rise overlooked the road.

Robert urged his horse up the rise and galloped along it to the point he had spotted nigh on a year ago. He dismounted, hobbled his horse at a point well screened by the trees and strung his bow. Before long, the bishop's retinue tramped past and Robert drew three arrows from his quiver. He shot all three in quick succession; his fast hands making it appear that the bishop's entourage was under attack by more than one man.

Panic struck the procession of monks, clerics and soldiers and there were cries of alarm and confusion. Two soldiers fell from their saddles, struck by Robert's arrows while a third reeled, his horse wild, an arrow jammed in his shoulder.

The bishop cried out orders. Blades were drawn and crossbows loaded. Eyes searched the embankment for their attackers but Robert was too well screened.

Three more arrows sailed out of the trees, striking men and horses. The bishop and his monks and clerics galloped towards the crossroads leaving the soldiers to deal with their attackers.

Robert took off through the trees to where his horse was hobbled. Below him the bishop's archers and men-at-arms were climbing the rise, pushing their way through the foliage, curses and taunts on their fevered lips.

Robert scrambled up into his saddle and rode hard and fast in a south-westerly direction, passing through the northern edge of Windsor Forest to an inn near the market town of Wokingham.

He stabled his horse and entered the establishment. There were few travellers which was as Robert had hoped. He looked to the innkeeper who seemed to be expecting a visitor matching his description.

"Looking for your companions?" the innkeeper asked. Robert nodded. "You'll find them upstairs. They came in not an hour past. They've paid for the room several days in advance so you won't be disturbed."

Robert climbed the stairs and knocked on the door of the room indicated by the innkeeper. It opened a crack and Little John's face peered out.

"Well, let me in then," said Robert. "Did all go to plan?"

"Aye," said John admitting him to the room and bolting the door behind him.

In the centre of the room two men sat on chairs, their hands bound and their faces pale and sweating. Katherine leant against the wall, sharpening her knife.

"Hood!" said Bishop de Orleton. "By Christ's beard you've gone too far this time! The king will not stand up for you now! Not after you've abducted a bishop, by God!"

Robert strode forward and struck the bishop across the mouth savagely. "I no longer have business with the king," he said, "and you are a fool if you look to him for protection."

"They took the Windsor road as you predicted," said Katherine. "A great clutter of monks and clerics it was. The bishop was easy enough to spot so we made off with him and one of his underlings as you said."

"Did the rest of his followers give you any trouble?" Robert asked.

"Nah!" John replied. "They just about soiled their robes when they realised your attack was a diversion intended to drive them into our arms!"

"What are you going to do with us?" the bishop asked in a quiet voice. "Murder us? Torture us?"

"It would be no more than you deserve," said Robert. "We know it was you who ordered the beating of our companion in London."

"Nonsense! I ordered no such thing!"

"You just greeted me by name," Robert continued. "A hedge-robber you knew only by sight. You've been making inquiries, my good bishop."

The bishop said nothing, knowing he was entirely at the mercy of three outlaws in some wayside tavern and nobody in the world knew where he was.

"You have dealings with the Peruzzi society," said Robert.

"What of it?" the bishop replied, his nervous eyes flitting from one outlaw to another.

"Vast wealth squirreled away no doubt."

"Yes, yes! How much do you want?"

Robert leaned in close to him and smiled. "All of it."

FORTY-NINE

It had been almost a week since the bishop's clerk had been sent to the Peruzzi's representatives in London with a mandate to pay signed by the bishop. The terrified clerk had been assured that should he return with anything but the cart bearing the bishop's withdrawal then it would go very hard for his master. The bishop also had been informed of a similar threat should his mandate, which none of the outlaws could read, contain anything but a request to withdraw a thousand pounds of silver.

The outlaws had no idea how much wealth the bishop had deposited with the Peruzzi and they could not trust him to give an honest answer so they had decided that a thousand pounds, split three ways, would be a nice sum of money to ensure that the rest of their lives would be spent in comfort.

"How much longer do you reckon?" Little John asked Robert on the fifth day since the clerk had been dispatched.

"Even the Peruzzi society needs a little time to drum up a thousand pounds," he replied. "They keep their wealth in property, land and treasure held in abbeys and monasteries across England. But I should think that our man will return to us within the next day or so."

"I hope so." John glanced at the bishop who was still tied to his chair. Katherine was spoon-feeding him some pottage the innkeeper had cooked up downstairs. "People tend to notice things like missing bishops."

Robert's prediction proved true for the clerk returned a week to the day since he had been sent. He rode atop a wicker cart loaded with barrels.

"Welcome back," Robert said as the outlaws greeted him in the stable yard. "Your journey went without a hitch, I trust?"

"It's sheer madness travelling alone with such wealth," the clerk spluttered although he was visibly relieved to be back with his master and to have washed his hands of the loaded cart.

"We could hardly have asked you to hire some guards in London," said Robert. "The risk to us – and your master – would have been too great."

Little John scrambled up onto the cart and prised off the lid of one of the barrels. He let out a whistle at its contents. Robert and Katherine joined him and together they opened up all of the barrels to make sure the clerk had not tried to cheat them. A thousand pounds worth of silver plate and coin winked at them. They recovered the barrels and took the clerk upstairs to be reunited with his master.

"Now that you've robbed me to ruin will you release me or kill me?" the bishop asked.

"Neither, as it happens," said Robert as he tied the clerk back to his chair.

Little John produced a couple of gags made from torn cloth and he and Robert bound up the two men's mouths so securely that the most noise they could muster was a frightened and muffled moaning.

"Sorry to leave you in such dire straits, your excellency," said Robert. "But we really must be moving along with our new fortune. I expect the innkeeper will let the room to somebody else sooner or later. He might even send his maid up to clean the place first in which case I should think you'll only be tied up in here a day or so."

The eyes of the two restrained men bulged in their reddened faces and Robert couldn't tell if the bishop was pleading with them or cursing them.

The innkeeper was given a handsome reward for his cooperation and was advised to keep it hidden lest the bishop or the authorities ever suspect he had profited from the unfortunate episode. If he wondered whatever happened to the two extra men he had seen entering the room upstairs he did not ask.

They journeyed north at a slow pace for the cart was heavy and the roads muddy. It was December and the weather was bitter. It was something of an irony that the outlaws were now richer than they had ever been but also more sodden, cold and hungry than they ever remembered.

They joined the Great North Road and followed it through Nottinghamshire and into Yorkshire, ever wary of bandits. But it was late in the year and any robbers destitute enough to still be plaguing the Great North Road in such weather were put off by the sight of three hooded rogues, each of them armed with blade and bow.

It was decided that they would winter at Wakefield. Robert was desperate to see his family and the sheriff would not hear of their desertion from the king's service for many weeks. They each took a little of the treasure from the cart and buried the rest at a marked spot in Barnsdale. Come spring they would retrieve it and then decide what to do.

They found Wakefield much as they had left it and it pleased Robert to think that some places remained the same while the world whirled and shifted around them. His mother wept and Isabella yelped with joy as the three outlaws shambled in from the cold, their hose and boots sodden and their cloaks dusted with snowflakes.

"You're home!" Robert's mother said. "Praise God, you're home!"

A meal was hastily prepared and ale poured out as they sat down by the fire and told of all that had happened to them in the year and a half since they had left.

"Where's Stephen?" Robert asked.

His mother's face turned grave and Robert prepared himself for the worst news. "He's sick, Rob. Very sick. The winter has been hard on him. He's upstairs. I gave him your bed."

Robert climbed the ladder to the sleeping quarters. Old Stephen lay on the straw pallet with a blanket up to his chin. Sweat stood out on his brow which told Robert he was running a high fever.

"Ma used the coin you left us to fetch the best doctors in the West Riding," said Isabella who had followed him up. "But they couldn't fix him."

"Only God can fix an old wastrel like me," came a weak voice from the pallet. "And He has long since washed his hands of me."

Robert knelt beside him and felt his forehead. He was burning from the inside out. "You survived your king's service, I see," said Old Stephen. "Did he let you go or did you desert?"

"What do you think?" said Robert and the old man managed half a smile.

"I suppose I'm to blame. My life hasn't exactly been a shining example for a young rogue such as yourself."

"I think it's been a fine example," said Robert with a small smile.

"But you haven't heard the last of it," Old Stephen replied. "And I should so very much like to tell it to you before I die."

"Now is not the time for storytelling, old friend," said Robert. "And you're not going to die. You survived the Second Barons' War, a life of outlawry and much more besides. What's a simple fever to you?"

"It's my time, Rob. And what better time for storytelling than the final days of a man's life? I won't manage it all in one go but, God willing, I have enough evenings left to tell you all."

It took three nights for Old Stephen to tell the final chapter in his tale and Robert was his sole listener. He would tell the others when the time was right but for now the final details of Stephen's life and the conclusion of Roger Godberd's tale was for his ears alone.

Old Stephen died two days before Christmastide. They buried him on a plot of waste behind the house and marked his grave with a simple wooden cross; an outlaw's burial. Robert knew that Stephen would have considered it appropriate for a man who had drifted so far from his beginnings as a novice in the clergy.

As always, Robert awaited spring eagerly. It wasn't just that the sheriff would soon come knocking but he wanted to find out what had happened to Will and Much and, if necessary, avenge their fates.

"There was a rumour that Will had returned to Crigglestone," said Robert's mother, "But nobody knows where he is now, nor Much. The sheriff is looking for them, that much is certain. And now you're back, he'll be looking for you too. Be careful, won't you Rob?"

"Of course, mother," he replied. "It's the greenwood for us, probably for the rest of our lives but we have enough wealth put by so that we will never want for anything. And I'll be dropping by to see you whenever I can."

They headed for their old haunts in Barnsdale. They found their old camps deserted; the rings of charred stones like ghosts of the happy times they had spent there.

They encountered a cattle herder on the road and gave him a coney Little John had shot. The man took it gratefully. "Best to keep bow and blade at hand," said the cattle herder. "Things are worse than ever since Boroughbridge. The king has made life hard for the north by way of punishing those who supported Lancaster. What about the villeins and yeomen, that's what I say! We had no say in where the likes of de Clifford and de Mowbray cast their allegiances. Poverty and hardship are worse than ever and bandits plague the roads worse than in Robert Hood's time, God rest him. Take the Scarlet Men for example; they'd sooner cut your throat as rob you and they don't just pick on merchants and clerics the way Hood used to. Everyone is fair game as far as they're concerned."

"The Scarlet Men?" Robert asked. "Who are they?"

"Some new band of rogues that have sprung up in the last year or so. Most of the young outlaws seek them out and join them for it's better to be with them than against them."

"It seems we have been usurped," said Robert as the old cattle herder disappeared into the distance.

"Hardly surprising," said Little John. "With us gone who was there to stop other gangs taking over?"

"I've a mind to seek out these Scarlet Men," Robert said. "If what that old man says is true then it's a good bet we might find Will and Much in their ranks."

It took them two days to find their quarry or rather, it took two days for their quarry to find them. They stuck to the road and had almost reached Doncaster when three ragged-looking men stepped out onto the road ahead. They brandished poorly oiled blades and crude bows and around the left arm of each of them was bound a length of red cloth. Four more rogues emerged from the trees behind them; each also wearing the red mark.

"The Scarlet Men by any chance?" Robert said to them.

"Aye, that's us," said the leader of the group. "Who wants to know?"

"The name's Robert of Wakefield," Robert replied. "Me and these poor souls have been ousted from our lands and outlawed. We heard that the Scarlet Men run things in these parts and were hoping to join their company."

"We don't just take in any landless wastrels," said the lead robber. "You have to have an iron spirit, good skill with a blade and no qualms about bloodshed. And you have to prove it to our leader."

"Well, as you can see, we are all armed," said Robert. "And as for our skill and spirit, I can only vouch for it. But by all means, take us to your leader so we can prove it to him."

The robber smiled. "Aye, you may be some sport at least. Follow us. We'll take you to Will."

"Will?" Robert asked.

"Will Scarlet. He's our leader and you won't find a more bloodthirsty rogue than him. Know why he calls himself Scarlet?"

"Isn't it his real name?"

"Nah, he took it when he turned outlaw on account of his bloodthirsty ways. Time was when his hands were rarely any colour but scarlet. Heh-heh!"

As they were led through the woods to the Scarlet Men's camp, Robert turned to Little John.

"*Will* Scarlet?" John said to him softly.

"Aye," Robert replied. "I don't like the sound of this."

The old cattle herder's words were no exaggeration. The camp was huge and judging by the number of shelters it was home to at least forty outlaws. It was a sprawling, dirty collection of lean-tos and smoky campfires. All eyes were on them as they were led to the largest of the fires.

"New recruits for you, Will," said the lead robber. "Leastways they think so."

Will Scarlet wore a fine tunic and cloak which had clearly been pilfered from some passing franklin. He had a long, jewelled dagger at his belt and well-made boots. He looked at the newcomers incredulously. "I'll be buggered," he said.

Robert looked Will up and down and shook his head. "You never did learn to blend in with the greenwood," he said.

Will laughed and strode forward to throw his arms around Robert. "You came back after all! And Little John and Katherine too! And what of the others?"

"Not all of us yearned for the outlaw's life," Robert said. "They remained at court."

"Ah, well. Good for them. But what of your adventures? What has our tyrant had you doing this year and a half you've been away?"

"Never mind that," said Robert. "What's all this I hear about the Scarlet Men ripping up the countryside and robbing honest yeomen? And where is Much?"

"I'm right here!" called Much from the other side of the campfire.

"Much is my highest lieutenant," Will said.

Robert peered at the miller's son. "And this sits well with you, Much? This robbing and killing of honest folk?"

Much gazed at the ground and said nothing.

"Oh, that's all blown out of proportion," Will said. "We always used fear to our advantage in the old days, eh, Rob? It's no different now. There's just more of us!"

Robert considered the possibility that there was some truth in what Will said. He may have put it about that his name was due to his red-handed ways but it was in fact a clever play on words. Shacklock was an old Saxon name meaning 'shear-cloth', hinting at the trade of Will's ancestors. Scarlet, while meaning the colour red, was also the literal translation of shear-cloth in Norman-French. It was a pun Robert had not thought Will capable of.

"Friends!" Will called to the entire camp. "Welcome our newest members led by none other than Robert Hood!"

"Hood?" they cried. "That Hood?

"The same Robert Hood who ransomed the sheriff and sent his wife a white palfrey?" somebody said.

"The same Robert Hood who slew Guy de Gisburn?" asked another.

"Aye! Aye!" said Will. "The very same! Rob and I used to run together in the old days and now he's back to lend his bow to our efforts!"

There were cheers of at this and Robert faced them with a forced smile. It was true, he was back, but things had changed dramatically. Not only was he part of a band of outlaws much larger than before but now Will was the leader. He had been usurped by his best friend.

Although Will was as a brother to him Robert knew that he was not always a moral man and he didn't know how he felt taking orders from somebody he had disagreed with so often in the past. He had returned to Barnsdale expecting to lead a band of outlaws once more and here he was playing second fiddle to one of his own men.

But all that could wait. It was spring, the year was young and there was a reunion to celebrate. The campfires glittered in the woods that night like rubies spread across dark green velvet. Mead, ale and wine flowed freely and Robert and his companions feasted as they had not done since they had left for the king's service.

"So, it was all for nothing, eh?" Will asked after they had related the events of the past year and a half. "You should have come with Much and me. We've done very well for ourselves."

"I wouldn't say it was all for nothing," Robert replied. "And we've done far better for ourselves than you give us credit."

"How do you mean? You lot are so ragged you look worse off than when you left!"

"What would you say if we told you that we robbed the Bishop of Hereford of over a thousand pounds of silver plate and other treasures?" said Robert with a grin.

"I'd say you were a bloody liar," Will replied.

"Well, then we might have to take exception to that," Little John replied. "Eh, Rob?"

Will gazed at Robert.

"It's true," Robert said. We buried the loot not far from here. You'll share in it too. There's enough there to keep us all in comfort for many years to come."

Will eventually let himself be persuaded that it was not all a jape and let out a hoot of laughter. "Then we celebrate the more tonight! Open another barrel! If only Old Stephen was here to regale us with another one of his tales. Have you looked in on him since you returned? We have not dared go near Wakefield."

"Stephen is dead," said Robert. "The winter took him. It was his time."

Will's face fell. "That's too bad."

"But he did reveal the last of his tales to me," Robert went on. "I could never do him justice as a storyteller but I will try to relate his own words to you, so far as I can remember them."

"Aye!" they all cried, raising their cups and horns in salute of a fallen comrade. "Let's hear Stephen's last tale!"

Robert cleared his throat and began.

FITT VIII
THE HOB IN THE GREEN

"Robin bent a full good bow,
An arrow he drew at will;
He hit so the proud sheriff
Upon the ground he lay full still."
- Robin Hood and the Monk

Leicestershire
Summer, 1269

FIFTY

You may be forgiven for wondering where all the stories of Roger Godberd defying the High Sheriff and escaping Nottingham Castle came from as, by the winter of 1266 we were all set to live out the rest of our days in peace as free men. I promise you that those stories have their kernels of truth and that I was very much involved in all that made Roger Godberd the legendary Hobhood of Sherwood.

Nearly three years had passed since we had settled in Swannington and those were the three finest years of my life. Never have I known such peace, companionship and boards of plenty. After that first spartan winter we began planting crops and rearing livestock, soon to reap the benefits. We all had our roles to play; some of us were farmers, others builders and craftsmen. Myself, I was a purchaser of goods such as salt, leather, wool, iron, pots and wine. My errands took me to villages in all of the three manors that bordered on Charnwood but most of my purchases were made in Shepshead.

It was on my return from Shepshead that I saw the heralds of our ruin. As I approached Whitwick from the northeast I could see a trail of dust kicked up by many horsemen approaching the town. By the time I entered Whitwick the visitors had taken residence in the wooden motte-and-bailey. Whitwick manor was the property of Alexander Comyn but its small castle belonged to the Lord Edmund, younger brother of Longshanks.

I hurried to Swannington to bring my lord the news.

"The Lord Edmund?" Roger exclaimed after I had told him of the horsemen I had seen. "Did you see his sigil?"

"No," I admitted. "The castle is bare of banners."

"Then he has not come in person. I wonder why he sends his men to us now. Perhaps he intends a visit."

Lord Edmund had been made Earl of Leicester after Simon de Montfort's defeat although he had been too young to play a part in the war himself. Whitwick Castle came with the title and was little more than a small wooden fort. That the earl paid it any attention at all was surprising and worrying.

I found Diva in the chapel at prayer and knelt beside her. We were alone and the echoing silence was pleasant. After crossing myself I withdrew the amulet from my tunic and passed it to her.

"Another present?" she said, the corner of her mouth betraying a smile. She examined the bubbles in the amber and the thin copper wiring. "Thank you."

"Had we still been robbers I would have given you something much prettier," I said. "Gold, silver. Those were the days!"

"I would rather you and my father were free men than have gold and silver trinkets. It's beautiful."

I made a point of bringing Diva a present every time I went away and, though she was right about the merits of freedom, I did miss wealth and the sport of its pursuit. We were well fed and slept warm but we were not rich.

My relationship with Diva had blossomed steadily in the spring of 1267. I had been wary of women ever since Margot had broken my heart but I could not help my growing feelings towards Diva. She was bold, clever, and had a heart of gold. And she was beautiful.

I knew my feelings were reciprocated although we had never uttered our love for one another. It was an unspoken pact borne from our need for secrecy. I knew as well as she did that her father would never tolerate me as a son-in-law. I was his servant – a valuable and well-loved one – but his servant nonetheless. Roger, for all his rough ways and colourful past had a strong sense of pride reserved for his family name and only a wealthy and noble-born man would suit his daughter.

That afternoon we received visitors. They wore the livery of the Earl of Leicester and had come from Whitwick Castle. Roger received them in private and they departed, touching none of the refreshments that had been brought from the kitchens.

"God's teeth what new treachery is this?" Roger exclaimed as we entered the hall to see what our guests had wanted. "They say de Ferrers has been dispossessed of all his estates but Chartley in Staffordshire. The whole lot of it – Derby, everything – has been signed over to the Lord Edmund."

"How can that be?" we asked. "De Ferrers paid his dues and was released from the Tower!"

"There is something foul afoot and I smell Longshanks all over it!" said Roger. "The Lord Edmund could not have cooked up something like this without his big brother's help."

"Well, what did Edmund's men want with you?"

"I have been summoned to Whitwick tonight. This bodes ill. Don't forget that Swannington is de Ferrers's, despite lying within Whitwick Manor."

"But you are merely its tenant," I reminded him. "Why should the Lord Edmund care who tills his land?"

"He may not think well of a baronial supporter like myself running one of his estates," Roger replied.

We accompanied Roger to Whitwick Castle that night and were admitted to the Great Hall which was not much bigger than the one at Swannington. It was filled with people, many of whom we recognised from the Charnwood manors. They sat at meat or stood in groups discussing matters of clear and grave import. A long trestle table was set up at the dais and a man with a grey pointed beard and a black leather cap sat at it flanked by clerks and other assorted officials. Roger recognised William de Bagot, the High Sheriff of Warwickshire and Leicestershire.

"I am Godfrey de Oadby," said the man in the pointed beard as Roger was announced and ushered forward. "Castellan of Whitwick. You are Godberd, the same rebel who fought under de Montfort at Lewes and then under John d'Eyville at Axholme?"

"You are well informed, my lord," said Roger. "Perhaps your information on me also includes my pardon which I purchased from the king under the Dictum of Kenilworth."

"It does indeed. And it too includes an account of your removal of Hugh de Babington from Swannington Hall under force of arms and of your occupation of said hall and plundering of its demesne."

"Your information is faulty, my lord. Swannington Hall is my family's tenancy and has been so for generations. Hugh de Babington took advantage and occupied it unlawfully during my absence. I merely reclaimed it for Robert de Ferrers."

"During your *rebellion*," de Oadby corrected. "You are no doubt aware of my lord Edmund, Earl of Leicester's acquisition of Robert de Ferrer's lands, including Swannington."

"Your men made me aware of it this morning."

"De Ferrers is a traitor and he is lucky to still have one manor to his name. As for Swannington, it is now my lord Edmund's and he has reappointed Hugh de Babington its lord. Young Hugh is the nephew of the Archbishop of York and has performed many fine services in Derbyshire. My lord Edmund thinks he will go far and wishes to reward him."

Roger ground his teeth together. "This is why you called me here? To tell me that you mean to evict me from my own land? You have no right!" His eyes glanced to the sheriff who paled under his glare and shifted uncomfortably in his seat.

"Well, um, legally speaking, the Earl of Leicester can appoint whomever he chooses to run his own manors," the sheriff said.

Roger said nothing but the sheriff wilted under his stare.

"You have until tomorrow to clear out of Swannington Hall and seek your fortune elsewhere," said de Oadby with an offensive little smile. "I'm sure your rebel friends in Yorkshire or wherever will open their doors to you. While they still have doors to open."

I was prepared to restrain Roger from striking either the castellan or the sheriff and exhaled slowly as he turned, face like thunder and strode from the hall. I caught the look of Wyotus and Richard and saw that they shared my relief.

"We have until tomorrow," said Walter d'Evyas as we rode back to Swannington. "That is enough time to reinforce the gate and call in as many favours as we can. I can have Nicholas and his men here by daybreak."

Walter had become Roger's contact with the outlaws in Charnwood and regularly relayed messages to them. They had successfully evaded the authorities for the past three years despite a couple of close shaves. In April of 1267 they had fought a pitched battle with a patrol sent by Roger de Leyburn, castellan of Nottingham Castle. They had robbed the soldiers of their horses, forcing them to return to Nottingham on foot. In September of the same year they had been routed from their Charnwood camp and fled to Sherwood. De Leyburn had since joined the Lord Edward on his crusade to relieve Acre from the Saracens and Walter said that the outlaws had now returned to Charnwood.

"It is pointless," said Roger, his face set. "We can't hold out against the Lord Edmund. He'll descend upon us with all the might of his family if we defy him. I should have known it was futile to think I could keep Swannington. I should have known the law would never be on my side."

Diva was distraught when we told her the news. The happiness we had all so recently found was on the verge of being swept away. "Where will we go?" she said. Who can we turn to now?"

"There are those I would turn to who would offer some path to recompense though our home may never be ours again, I fear," Roger said.

"Who?" she asked hopefully.

"Nicholas d'Eyville."

"The outlaws? You'd become a robber again? Father, please! You'll be outlawed too!" Her worst nightmare of her father's freedom going up in smoke had suddenly been rekindled.

"The law has shown itself to be no friend of ours," Roger said. "What difference does it make if we live within its bounds or without them? I had the right of it once; the only true law is the law of the sword. We are for Charnwood and you, my girl, will be well provided for."

"What do you mean?" she asked, suspicion creeping into her voice.

"I am sending you to Langley Priory. They are good nuns there, better than most the church has to offer. You will be looked after and, when I have amassed a sufficient dowry for you, we will look into finding you a husband. Your fate will not be the same as ours."

I felt my heart sink though I was powerless to object. I could not let Roger know of my feelings for his daughter nor my misery at his plans for her but she spoke for the both of us.

"Father, I'm coming with you! I'll not be shunted off to some priory to live in despair not knowing if you are alive or dead!"

"It's far past time you were married, girl. I will return for you, that I promise."

"You can't promise that! If you are killed then I'll die all alone behind those priory walls. No! I won't go!"

"You'll do as you're damn well told!" he roared. "God's breath, do I not have enough on my plate that I must quarrel with my own daughter too!"

"So, I'm a nuisance you wish to be rid of?" she snapped. "There lies your true reason for sending me away. You don't want to be tied down by a daughter as you pursue your life of crime!" She stormed from the room leaving us all a little red-faced at having witnessed a family dispute.

"What about me, father?" asked Roger the Younger who was on the cusp of manhood now. "Am I to be sent away too?"

"And me lose my best archer?" said Roger, mustering a small smile. "Not on your life. Run now and pack your things. We leave tonight."

"And Diva?" I ventured.

He glanced at me. "She is to go to Langley. You take her, Stephen. She has a fondness for you and I trust no man more with the safety of my daughter."

And so it was decided. In a cruel twist of fate, I was to be the one to escort the woman I loved out of my life and to a future of misery for the both of us.

Diva was no happier than I the following morning as we saddled up in the stables. She seemed peevish with me as if it was my fault for escorting her. I could not bear for her to be angry with me so I whispered in her ear; "trust me, it will be alright."

I could see that she wanted to ask me what I meant but was smart enough to hold her tongue for the stables were crowded with activity. The whole hall was being stripped of anything of value. Roger wasn't about to leave a single cup or plate for his usurper.

We trotted out into the morning sun and left Swannington for the last time. We did not speak as we headed north and I could tell Diva was still angry with me. As we approached Shepshead, I led her off the track and into the shade of Charnwood.

"Where are we going?" she asked me at last.

"I know a crofter out here who will put you up at least for a while."

She regarded me with suspicion although a touch of the old fondness had returned. "You don't intend to take me to Langley?"

"No. You wouldn't be happy there and I wouldn't be happy knowing that I might never see you again. Your father intends to marry you into a good family once he is able to raise a good dowry. If you enter that priory you are as good as gone for me."

She smiled. "Stephen de Wasteneys, are you abducting me?"

I tried to share her humour but I was sick to the stomach with fear. Fear of what Roger would do if he found out and fear of what I would do next. I had no plan beyond ensuring that Diva did not reach the priory. I knew the crofters well for I regularly traded with them on my trips to Shepshead and knew that they would look after Diva. I had some coin in my purse which was more silver than they had ever seen for they were poor folk. It would cover her upkeep and buy their loyalty.

I left Diva with a kiss and a promise that I would return to her as soon as I was able. I didn't know how far we would stray from Charnwood but prayed that it would not be too far. I was confident that I could occasionally slip away from Roger and visit her.

There were no tears as I departed. Diva was grateful that I had spared her a nun's life but she must have shared my trepidation for what the future held. In a day we had gone from contented farmers to landless wastrels. All had changed but I was determined to ensure our love for each other would hold strong.

FIFTY-ONE

I had tarried with Diva long enough to make Roger think I had been all the way to Langley and back before heading for our arranged meeting spot in Charnwood. Roger did not question me, he merely nodded; a gesture which I returned to signify that his orders had been carried out. I caught Wyotus and Richard looking at me and ignored them.

We set out before nightfall and followed Walter who knew the way to the outlaws' camp. We could see their campfires twinkling through the trees and received a welcome fit for princes. Nicholas seemed genuinely pleased that we had returned to the greenwood.

"Always knew a farmer's life wasn't for you, Godberd!" he said.

There is little to relate of the year that followed. We moved through a succession of camps and robbed so many travellers that folk in the surrounding manors began to swear that Charnwood was haunted. Our greatest threat was from Roger de Leyburn who had cut short his trip to Palestine and had resumed his position as castellan of Nottingham Castle. He and his son regularly led large patrols into Sherwood and Charnwood but they were never able to find us.

I visited Diva only a couple of times during the year which were the only occasions I could get away. I found her well but bored and lonely. My heart ached for her and I longed to be with her. Roger was amassing a small fortune through our thievery but still had not found a husband for her. I was glad but knew it was futile to get my hopes up. Roger was clearly hoping to marry her into the very best of families and I still had no idea what I would do when he deemed the time was right to fetch her from Langley.

In September we robbed a group of monks from Stanley Abbey who were passing through Charnwood on their way to Nottingham. We had come to expect little resistance from the clergy although on this occasion the train included a brawny young monk who carried a quarterstaff. We immediately pegged him as a potential troublemaker and gave him a wide berth while we dealt with the prior who seemed eager to hand over his purse and be on his way.

As the pouch of silver passed from the prior's hand to Roger's, the big monk strode forward, pushing his brethren aside. "You don't have to give this scum your money, prior," he said in a deep voice laced with anger.

"We'll not have trouble, Brother Thomas," said the prior. "Let's just pay these men and, God willing, we shall survive the day."

"Get back in line, oaf," said Walter, pointing his sword at the big monk. "Listen to your prior and he might yet live."

The monk's face turned thunderous. "No one threatens Prior John," he growled.

"Thomas! Let it go!" said the prior and I could see the fear in his eyes. This Brother Thomas was clearly a loose cannon.

"I'll not tell you again," said Walter and he prodded the big man in the belly with the tip of his sword. This snapped what was left of the monk's patience and he swung at Walter with his quarterstaff.

"Thomas, no!" the prior cried but it was too late. Walter was a devil with a blade and he sidestepped the swing of the quarterstaff and thrust his sword through the monk's belly. It tore through habit and flesh and emerged on the other side, red and dripping.

The monk's face was pale and horror-stricken and it mirrored everybody else's. His knees buckled as he gurgled for air. Walter withdrew his blade and the monk vomited blood, collapsing to lie face down on the road. He twitched occasionally.

"For Christ's sake, Walter!" Roger barked.

"There lies a man of God!" said the prior, his ashen face twisted with outrage. "His blood is on your hands! May God forgive you!"

We had what we needed and made a run for it, vanishing into the greenwood and leaving the distraught party of monks with their fallen comrade. We were all angry at Walter and few spoke to him at camp that night. Although he was one of Roger's highest lieutenants, he had become something of a loose cannon himself. In the February before we had left Swannington he had killed a man in a tavern fight. That had nearly cost him his head but for the intervention of his uncle, Richard de Foliot, who had friends in high places. It had been Longshanks himself who had sealed Walter's pardon. Such was the judicial system in those days that even a former rebel could be excused of murder if he knew the right people.

If Walter's actions set in motion the series of events that brought about our downfall then it was my actions that saw them to fruition. It had been nearly two years since we had been driven from Swannington. We had long since been declared outlaws but Roger had never given up on his ambition to see Diva married into respectability. The dowry he had amassed was more wealth than we had ever seen during the civil war and eventually, unbeknownst to me, he had decided upon a husband.

Also unknown to me was the errand he had sent two of Nicholas's men on to fetch Diva from Langley Priory and bring her to him in Charnwood. Why he didn't go himself, I have no idea. The accumulation of wealth seemed to consume him in those days and all else was irrelevant.

Nicholas's men returned bearing the news that not only was Diva not at Langley but she had never been received there. Roger turned to me, his eyes demanding an explanation. I had none.

"Where is she?" he said in a low voice.

"Safe," I said.

He seized the front of my tunic in one fist and slammed the other into my face, knocking my head back and sending stars flashing before my eyes. "Where is she?" he roared.

"Shepshead," I mumbled, tasting blood.

"What the hell have you been playing at, de Wasteneys? Why is she at Shepshead and not Langley?"

"Because... because I love her." I felt all eyes in the camp on me. I no longer cared. The secret had run its course. There was nothing more I could do either for Diva or myself.

"You love her?" Roger's brow furrowed, trying to comprehend the events of the past few years. He had known that we had been fond of each other and had used it to his advantage but he had still not *known*.

"Yes, love," I said, "rare though it is these days. I did not take her to Langley Priory for I knew that she dreaded such a fate. She wants to be free, free to love me so I hid her away with a crofter's family in Shepshead until I could convince you that I am the one to marry her."

"You? Marry my Diva?" He drew his knife slowly and I felt sure that my life had reached its pathetic conclusion. It was then that Wyotus and Richard came to my rescue and proved themselves to be my lifelong friends.

"Roger, stay your hand," Richard said. "Stephen has only ever been your loyal servant. Don't kill him for this. Not *this*."

"Aye, he's a fool and a liar but a lovesick one," Wyotus added. "What he did was out of love for your daughter. We all love Diva, just as you do. But Stephen's love is a wild stallion. He has no more control over it than he does over his beating heart. Surely that warrants a lesser punishment?"

Roger was silent for a long time, his blade drawn. I waited, anticipating a sudden thrust to the gut or a sharp draw across the throat. It never came. He sheathed his blade and released me from his grip with a shove that sent me sprawling.

"I don't want this waste of space near me from now on," he said. "In the morning I ride to Shepshead to fetch my daughter. Nicholas is in charge in my absence."

I was pulled out of Roger's sight by Richard and Wyotus.

"Christ's beard, Stephen!" said Richard, "but you're a lucky son of a whore!"

"Why on earth did you do it?" Wyotus asked.

"Why?" I said. "Didn't you just tell Roger why?"

"Aye, I said what I had to to save your neck but I can't believe you are that foolish!"

"How did you think you'd get away with it?"

"I didn't," I replied. "I never thought to. I just did what I had to."

Within two days Diva was back with us but, agonisingly, I was not allowed to approach her. She saw me from a distance and I could see in her eyes that she was pained too but it was more than our lives were worth to attempt to speak with each other.

Roger had found a minor lord of some manor in Nottinghamshire whom he intended to marry Diva to. I could not listen to the details for they were too painful to me. He wasn't about to keep Diva at camp, witness to our thievery and coarse lives. He wanted to squirrel her away in some new hiding place until the wedding could be arranged and it was Walter who provided a suggestion.

"There's always my uncle," he said. "He holds Grimston manor which is well fortified and close to Sherwood."

"The same uncle who helped you avoid the gallows for killing that fellow in a tavern?" Nicholas asked him.

"Aye, Richard de Foliot married my father's sister and bequeathed my family lands in his Yorkshire manor. He's a generous man and would welcome us with open arms."

"He's also a royalist," said Roger.

"What?" Nicholas exclaimed. "You'd place your daughter in the care of one of the king's supporters?"

"He may switch allegiance whenever he stands to gain from it," said Walter, "but he has no love for the king and would never betray family or friends."

"Then we make for Grimston," said Roger. "Will your uncle be there or at his estates in Yorkshire?"

"He'll be at Grimston this time of year."

We broke camp and headed to Sherwood. Grimston Hall resembled a small castle rather than a manor house for it was crenelated and surrounded by a ditch and wall of stone and lime. Richard de Foliot was a roaring, gluttonous man the like of which I had seen before in de Ferrers and d'Eyville. He seemed inordinately pleased to be visited by his prodigal nephew and his uncouth friends. Roger placed Diva in de Foliot's care with promise of much loot to pay for her upkeep. De Foliot beamed while making a pretence of refusal but I could see the glint of greed in his eyes. I loathed the man and trusted him not at all. How could I trust so obviously greedy a man who had been a baronial Sheriff of Nottinghamshire under de Montfort only to switch his loyalty to the king when de Montfort's luck ran out?

Roger wasn't about to draw attention to Diva's location by remaining at Grimston with his band so we made camp in Sherwood. De Foliot introduced us to the monks of nearby Rufford Abbey whom he was on good terms with and they occasionally lent us the use of one of their granges. The monks of Rufford had no love for the current authorities in Nottinghamshire. Reginald de Grey had since moved on to become the Justice of Chester and the new High Sheriff of Nottinghamshire was Walter de Giffard, the Archbishop of York. De Giffard's undersheriff was none other than his nephew, Hugh de Babington. De Babington had proven himself to be a craven and vindictive man and tales of his ruthlessness circulated Nottinghamshire. The monks of Rufford had some axe to grind with him and saw in Godberd an enemy of their enemy and so welcomed us.

It was a nice grange with fish ponds and bee hives for the making of honey and brewing of mead. We slept in the barn and it was good to have a roof over our heads after two years in the greenwood. We helped out around the grange as best we could, farming, fishing and transporting goods to the abbey itself.

It was upon one of these trips to the abbey that I saw a monk whose face looked familiar. Looking back, I cannot believe I was so stupid as to not recognise him or even mention the incident to the others. He was standing with several other Cistercians in the abbey precinct and looked like he had either just arrived or had spent the night there and was preparing to set out. He saw me and his head nearly unscrewed from his neck as it followed my passing. I knew I had seen his face somewhere but all I could think of was my days at St. Thomas's Priory years before and could not place him.

The attack came after dark. It was the monks who warned us and we awoke to their cries of outrage. I sat up on my pallet and saw the heads of my comrades stirring. A monk burst in through the doors.

"They've surrounded the grange! They know you're here! You must flee!"

"Who knows we're here?" said Roger, scrambling to his feet.

"Hugh de Babington and his troops!"

"How the devil...?" exclaimed Walter but nobody was listening. We were all too busy seizing our weapons and bundling together our meagre possessions. We rushed the door, not wanting to be penned inside the barn and spilled out into the grange's precinct. We could see movement in the trees on all sides. Moonlight reflected off plate and naked blades.

"Bows!" ordered Roger.

We bent our bows and formed a tight unit facing the part of the woods that lay closest to the grange. Men on horseback thundered into the precinct and I could see Hugh de Babington amidst them, his grinning face gleeful at his chance of capturing Godberd. He wasn't the only once keen for revenge.

"Break through and make a run for it!" Roger said to those of us with bows. "We'll hold them off and follow after!"

We let arrows fly as the horsemen engaged Roger and his men. There were screams from the treeline as our arrows found their marks. The perimeter was broken and de Babington was too foolhardy a commander to be prepared for such an event.

"Draw blades!" Nicholas shouted and, as one, we ran for the treeline.

Soldiers closed in on both sides but they were too late. We were free of the grange and were making good distance through the trees. Our pursuers hacked and slashed and cursed behind us, unused to the woods at night. I knew we could lose them but Roger and the others would have a hard time finding us without running into de Babington's soldiers.

We made for a place we called the trysting tree which was a large oak tree not far from the village of Edwinstowe. We often used this spot as a meeting place. The sun had risen fully by the time the stragglers from the grange made it to us.

"By Christ we had to take a roundabout way to lose them!" said one of the approaching men as we hailed them. "We think they've doubled back now to re-join de Babington. Godberd's been taken. Walter too and four others besides."

"They'll be on their way to Nottingham by now," said Wyotus. "What an evil slice of God-cursed luck! How do you think he found us?"

"Christ knows," said our man. "It'll be the rope for Godberd now. He's had his luck."

We had no choice but to make for Grimston to bring Diva the bad news and hope that Richard de Foliot was able to pull some strings to secure Roger's release.

"Can't do it, lads," he said once we had related the events of the previous night. "Godberd's a hardened outlaw. There's outrage over his killing of some monk or other and the clergy are demanding he swing."

The monk had been slain by de Foliot's nephew but as Walter had been captured along with Roger there was little point in mentioning it to him. It was then that I suddenly remembered the familiar monk I had seen at Rufford Abbey. It had been Prior John of Stanley Abbey whom we had robbed in September. The piece of the puzzle slid into place and it was clear who had told de Babington of our presence at the grange.

It mattered little now for none of us had any idea how to save our comrades. Diva suddenly exploded.

"Are you so content to give up on my father – your leader – at the drop of a cap?" she demanded, her eyes spitting fire at us all.

"He's taken, lass!" said Nicholas. "He'll be in the dungeons of Nottingham Castle by now."

"And you are too craven to attempt his rescue?" she said. "You men who do naught but cry for the good old days when you were rebels under de Montfort! You, who sup ale and recount tales of bravado and recklessness! Where is that spirit now? Dulled by years of farming and robbing monks?"

"My sister is right!" said Roger the Younger. "What good are we if we so easily leave six of our men to the likes of de Babington?"

"You do not know of what you ask!" said Nicholas. "It would be suicide to try and storm Nottingham Castle!"

"Aye, you'd never manage it," said de Foliot. "Even if I lent you every man I can spare."

"I do not speak of storming the curtain walls," said Diva. "But there has to be some way, some other way we can help him."

"There is," I said in a quiet voice which was almost drowned by the cries of frustration around me.

Diva looked at me. "What did you say, Stephen?" she asked.

All eyes turned to me. "There is a way," I repeated.

FIFTY-TWO

I, of course, was thinking of the tunnel. Of the entire band, only Roger, Geoffrey, Richard, Wyotus and I were left of the Nottingham garrison and none of the others knew of the existence of the secret passageway through the castle rock.

"What if it was discovered years ago and blocked up?" said Nicholas once I had explained my idea.

"Yes," agreed Wyotus. "The tunnel was known not only to us. Reginald de Grey, for example, knows of its existence."

"De Grey is no longer sheriff," I said.

"Even so, he may have told somebody."

"And what if someone has inadvertently placed a barrel over the trapdoor?" said Richard. "We'd be on our arses if we made it that far only to find our way blocked."

"It has to be worth a try," I said, catching Diva's grateful smile.

"It's pointless even talking about this tunnel," said Nicholas, "for even if we get into the castle we still have to get past the guards, into the dungeons and out again with Roger and the others without being seen. It's hopeless!"

"Not if we plan a diversion," I said.

"How do you mean?" asked Diva.

"We aren't enough to storm the castle, true," I said, "but we are enough to cause a ruckus in the town that might draw the garrison out. There'd still be a few guards within the castle but it would be a lot quieter, that's for sure."

The band was silent as they considered this. I could see that I was winning them round.

"Roger de Leyburn may even show his ugly face if he learns it's us," said Nicholas and there were hopeful murmurs from his men.

As soon as I saw that the promise of a showdown with Nottingham's castellan who had plagued Nicholas's men for so long was a temptation I knew that they would agree to my plan.

We returned to the grange and found that our horses had been taken by de Babington and his men. The monks were not as warm to us as before for their beehives had been burned and their stores looted as punishment for harbouring outlaws. It wasn't difficult to see why they despised de Babington.

We walked to Nottingham and split up before the town hove into view. Nicholas and his men camped in the woods near the Mansfield Road while Wyotus, Richard and I headed west, approaching the castle through the trees that grew close to the rock.

We found the cave and waited until dark, reminiscing about the days we had used it for dressing and skinning the deer we had poached. It all seemed a lifetime ago. Once night had fallen we entered the tunnel and made whatever prayers we could think of for our safe passage.

Richard tried the trapdoor at the end of the tunnel and found it thankfully open. As silently as possible we climbed up into the cellars below the Great Hall. We could hear much activity on the other side of the door that led to the courtyard.

"Looks like Nicholas has started his attack," said Richard.

We could hear shouts and many pairs of feet splashing through the mud as the garrison marshalled itself. We waited until the noise had died down, indicating the departure of the garrison for the town.

We found the courtyard deserted and only a few guards patrolling the walls. Weaving between the buildings, we kept out of sight. The guards were all looking outwards in any case, wholly taken up by whatever was going on in the town.

The way to the dungeons was an arched doorway cut into the sandstone at the foot of the keep. A steep stair worn smooth by the passage of many prisoners over the years led down to the guard room. We paused at the threshold and whistled to attract the attention of the gaoler. We hoped it wasn't anybody we had known before.

As he emerged from the guard room we were relieved to see that he was a total stranger. Richard swung his sword low and drew it across the gaoler's belly. As he doubled over in agony I swung at his head and almost sliced the top of his skull off. He tumbled forward, dead before he hit the floor.

We seized the keys from his belt and made for the locked door beyond. It opened into a wide room with several pits dug into the rock floor. These oubliettes held those unfortunate enough to be held indefinitely at the castellan's pleasure and could only be accessed by ladder or rope.

"Roger?" I called. "Walter?"

"Down here!" a familiar voice cried out from some depth below us. We found the correct oubliette and held a torch over its black circular entrance to illuminate the dirty, bloodied faces of our comrades looking up at us.

"The ladder!" I said, indicating a rickety old thing in the corner of the room. Wyotus and Richard brought it over and lowered it down into the pit.

As our comrades emerged, one by one, we could see that they had been illtreated. Broken noses, swollen cheeks, black eyes and split lips spoke of rough interrogation.

"We have Hugh de Babington to thank for our appearances," said Roger, seeing our appalled faces. "By God, I shall have a reckoning with him, I swear it!"

"And de Leyburn, for that matter," said Walter. "He was looking on."

"How the devil did you get inside the castle?" Roger asked.

"The tunnel," Wyotus said. "It was Stephen's idea."

Roger looked at me and briefly seemed to reassess his opinion of me. "Where are the others?"

"They are launching an assault on the town as we speak. It was necessary to draw the garrison out."

"Then we don't have much time," Roger said. "We must be out of here and re-join the rest of the band. They will need our help in cutting a retreat."

We hurried out of the dungeon and made for the cellars of the Great Hall. As we crossed the courtyard the main gates opened and a host of mounted troops flooded in with Roger de Leyburn at their head. Foot soldiers and crossbow men jogged to keep up. They looked worn out and spattered with mud and blood but their arrival boded ill. Not only did it signify a defeat over Nicholas and the others but they now stood between us and our escape.

We desperately looked for cover but there was none. It was de Leyburn who first spotted us, flinging out his finger, fire in his eyes. "The outlaws! It was a diversion! Seize them!"

"The walls!" I said. "Quick!"

There was still a minimal guard on the walls and, although it was a long drop on the other side, it was our only chance.

We dashed up the steps. Horns blared about the courtyard and Richard tossed Roger his blade. Roger caught it and used it to split the skull of the first guard who charged at us. Walter picked up the fallen man's spear and pushed his body over the edge into the courtyard below.

"Make for the postern gate!" I cried. Not only was it the lowest part of the wall but it also faced the woods that grew close to the castle rock.

"But how are we to get down?" Richard asked as we ran, single file, along the wall top, trying to keep up with Roger.

Crossbow bolts sang through the air, making us duck and wishing we had bows of our own. Another guard ran at us from the direction of the postern gate and I had to admire his bravery in the face of nine hardened outlaws hellbent on escape. Roger deflected his spear thrust with his sword and Walter struck with his own spear beneath Roger's arm, skewering the man under the armpit. He grimaced and Roger seized him by the shoulders, kneed him in the groin and hurled him over the battlements to shatter on the rocks below.

The postern gate was close and, peering over the crenulations, I judged that we had reached the lowest point of the wall.

"Here!" I cried and we took cover, shielded from the crossbow men by the thatched roof of one of the courtyard buildings.

"It's a bit of a jump!" said Walter, peering over the wall.

"Wait here!" I said before scuttling along the wall, thankful that it was dark and the crossbow men had difficulty picking me out as I ran. Eventually I found what I was looking for; a bucket dangling on a rope for the hauling up of rocks during a siege. I pulled the rope up and severed it where it was tied to the wall. As I hurried back to my companions I could see an orange glow beneath the clouds over the town. Dead or alive, Nicholas's assault had been more than successful; Nottingham was burning.

My companions watched me with slowly dawning comprehension as I looped the rope, bucket and all, around a crenulation and tossed the rest of it over. It did not quite reach the ground meaning that we still had a bit of a drop but it was at least a vast improvement.

"Get yourselves over," said Roger. "Walter and I will hold them off."

We could see that the soldiers were climbing a ladder further along the wall and it would not be long before they were upon us.

It was an agonizing wait as our companions clambered over the crenulations, one by one, and abseiled down the wall, the rope straining and groaning with their weight. Eventually it was just Roger, Walter and I left. The soldiers were running along the wall towards us. Roger looked at me. "Get over, de Wasteneys. Hurry!"

I didn't need telling twice. I had done more than my bit in this escapade and so I squeezed through the crenulations and grasped at the rope. It was a slippery climb and the rope was so thin and threadbare that it chafed my hands and threatened to snap at any moment. When I reached the end of it I dangled precariously, not knowing how far I had left to drop. My heart in my mouth, I let go and fell several feet, crying out as pain shot through my ankles on impact with the rock below.

I looked up and saw Walter sliding down the rope at an impressive speed. Below me I could make out the shapes of my other comrades climbing down the castle rock. It was a steep and terrifying descent but it would not be long before crossbow bolts would start sailing out from the walls and I for one did not want to be clinging for purchase on the cliffside like a sitting duck when they did.

As I made my descent I looked up and could see that Roger was making his way down the rope but already helmeted heads were catching the moonlight on the wall above. I quickened my descent, slipping and sliding as the dusty sandstone crumbled beneath my grip. At last I made it to level ground and ran for the woods, fearful of a bolt in my back at the last moment.

The bolt never came and the darkness of the trees swallowed me whole.

I found my comrades after some hallooing and we waited for Walter and Roger to catch up with us. Once reunited, we circumvented the castle rock towards the town. Even from the woods we could see that the town gates were burning and the flames had spread to the thatch of several nearby buildings. Townsfolk were desperately trying to put out the flames, dousing them with pails of water and beating at them with blankets.

There was no sign of Nicholas and the others so we headed deeper into the woods towards our temporary camp. When we reached it, we were overjoyed to see that Nicholas and a good portion of our band was still alive.

"By Christ, we pulled it off!" Nicholas exclaimed upon seeing Roger. "Though it was a hard fight of it! Did you see the mess we made of the town gates?"

"Aye, half the town will be ablaze if they don't quench those flames," Roger said. "I am indebted to you all, especially you, de Wasteneys." He patted me on the shoulder. "Your resourcefulness saw us through."

I beamed at my return to favour but I did not fool myself into thinking that I had earned Roger's full forgiveness nor his blessing. Somehow, I knew it would take more than saving his life to win him around to the idea of letting me marry his daughter.

"We'd best strike camp," said Nicholas. "We have a head start but de Babington and de Leyburn will be out in full force looking for us. We don't have long."

"We're not going anywhere," Roger said. A silence fell over the camp. "Our feud with de Babington ends here. I'm going to kill him for what he has done to my family."

"Roger, there are too many of them," Nicholas said.

"We have the forest," he replied. "That gives us the advantage. But we must split up and wage woodland warfare on them the like of which they have never seen."

He was met with an uneasy silence. I knew the others must have been feeling the same as me. This feud with de Babington was Roger's feud, not ours. We had the chance to slip away and yet he would have us stand our ground for no reason other than revenge.

"Well, damn you all?" cried Walter, drawing his blade. "Do you not see our faces pounded black and blue by de Babington's thugs? Do you not remember the good times at Swannington which was stolen from us by him? Are you so craven that you would flee now when justice is right within our grasp?"

There were murmurs of assent. We may have been unsure but when it came down to it we were loyal to the end. We had recovered our leader and were not about to turn our backs on him now.

FIFTY-THREE

The following day was one of relentless cat-and-mouse pursuit. As dawn broke over Sherwood, patrols led by Hugh de Babington delved into the woods to sniff out our trail. We used the very same hit and run tactics we had used in the Weald seven years ago; luring them close and then riddling them with arrows before vanishing.

The final battle took place at a small ford sometime after midday. De Babington had been worn down to his last party and led them himself through the shallow water. We loosed a volley on them and, while the horses were rolling and men were screaming, we ran at them with blades drawn.

The battle was brief but bloody. The ford ran red by the time we had whittled the patrol down to de Babington and two of his men. We hauled them ashore and made them kneel, hands on their heads, while we encircled them, triumphant. The terror in their eyes showed us that they truly thought their lives were over but Roger, as much to our surprise as theirs, had other plans.

"Where is de Leyburn?" he demanded.

"At Nottingham," de Babington replied.

"He did not ride out with you? Strange for one who has made such efforts to hunt us before."

"He fears a counterassault by you and your wolves," de Babington said. "He and half the garrison are dug in for a siege."

"A wise move but I am not interested in the castle or its castellan. It is you I am after."

"Well, you have me. What now?"

"Don't think I'm not tempted to hang you from the nearest oak as you have done to many good men before. But I am not finished with you yet. You and your remaining two followers are to return to Nottingham as fast as you can."

"Why? What message would you have me carry?"

"None. Your survival is the only message I wish to convey."

"I do not understand."

"You are not required to. Now get moving. Tarry and you'll find our arrows in your backs. Go, now!"

The three men scrambled to their feet and took off in the direction of Nottingham.

"What's the jest, Roger?" Walter asked. "We should have run them through on their knees!"

"De Babington will get what's coming to him," Roger said. "But not here. I want his death to be a thing long remembered. Come! We follow!"

None of us understood but we took off after our leader. We chased them all the way to the fringes of Sherwood, never letting them get too far ahead. It was a hard run and as dusk approached we felt our strength flagging. None of us had slept in the last forty-eight hours. The pursuit was hard on our enemy too for they were slow despite having cast off their plate and maille to give them more speed.

Before the trees petered out Roger nocked an arrow to his string and let it loose into the back of one of de Babington's men. He cried out and fell headlong. His death spurred the other two on and they quickened their pace, knowing that Nottingham was almost in sight.

As the town hove into view Roger felled the second man. Night had fallen and the Trent floodplain was silver beneath the moon. It had begun to rain. In the distance we could make out the lone figure of Hugh de Babington, staggering and stumbling towards the charred remains of the town gates. The fires had been doused and torchlights indicated a renewed guard at the entrance to Nottingham.

"We'll be seen out here in the open," Walter said to Roger.

"I know," he replied.

The guard had indeed spotted us and, apparently terrified of a second assault on the already destroyed gates, retreated into the town. The torches winked out as de Babington slipped between the charred posts of the gates.

"Hurry!" said Roger, breaking into a run.

We found the town ghostly quiet but for the drumming of the rain on thatch and mud. Further down the long street we could see de Babington hammering on the door of a tavern. A light in an upstairs window faded and went out. De Babington turned and saw us striding down the street towards him. We must have looked like wraiths borne of mud and mist, hooded as we were against the foul weather.

Our quarry panicked and ran across the street to the doorway of some merchant. He began hammering on its bolted door, wailing for admittance. Nobody answered.

The town voiced its displeasure of the undersheriff. The unjust punishments he had meted out were well remembered by those who now barred their doors to him and ignored his pleas. He turned this way and that, seeing no escape. The castle lay up ahead but was too distant to save him from the hooded figures that grew closer with every step.

Roger nocked another arrow. De Babington turned and fled up the street, his boots splashing in the mud. Roger drew and loosed. The arrow cut through the rain and struck de Babington in the back, knocking him forward to land face down in the mud.

He groaned and rose on shaking limbs. Slowly, he found his feet and, with the arrow protruding between his shoulder blades, staggered onwards.

A second arrow from Roger's bow felled him once again. I began to see lights appearing in high windows as shutters were eased open. Dark faces peered out, squinting in the downpour at what was unfolding in their streets. Nottingham was not nearly as asleep as it pretended.

De Babington gasped for air as he lay on his belly, unable to rise once more. Roger strode forward and seized him by his hair. He hauled him up to his knees and I saw that more people were watching now. They clustered in porches and leaned out of windows, craning their necks to see.

Roger unslung his singlehanded axe from his belt and raised it high in the air. He brought it down once, twice on de Babington's neck, hewing through bone and sinew with great spurts of blood. The head came loose and the body slumped forward into the mud. Roger held up his grisly trophy for all to see and hurled it as far as he could down the length of the street.

Without a word we retreated from the town and vanished back into Sherwood. Roger had taken his revenge and had left Nottingham with a memory they would speak of for generations to come.

We made our way back to Grimston, walking through the night and much of the next morning. We were sodden, starving and so tired that most of it passed as a hazy dream. Richard de Foliot admitted us and called for Diva who ran into her father's arms, joyful at seeing him alive. We toasted ourselves at the hearth while servants brought us spiced wine, meat and freshly baked bread.

"The king himself will be after us for this," said Wyotus as we sat with full bellies, swimming heads and steam rising from our slowly drying clothes.

I sat alongside Diva. Roger did not seem to care anymore. He was deep in one of his thoughtful moods.

"So what if he does?" Walter replied. "We'll just kill more of his men. He can't touch us in Sherwood. It's too big."

"Not for the king's army," I said. "He'll tear this forest apart to find us."

"Should we have let de Babington live, is that what you are saying?" Walter snapped.

"No, not at all," I replied. "But we need to have a plan. We can't hide forever."

"Stephen is right," said Roger. "Our days of robbing the roads are over. We are too exposed here. We need somewhere to lay low until this all quietens down a bit."

"But winter is coming," said Richard. "And we are ill-prepared."

"Then you must winter at my manor of Fenwick!" said de Foliot. "I will gladly travel with you. It is time I saw to my Yorkshire manors and Fenwick is a fine place to spend Christmastide!"

It was not too hard to sway us with the thought of wintering at a manor house with a roaring fire and plenty of food and drink. It was agreed and we made plans to travel to Yorkshire within the month.

The following day, after we had all slept a dozen hours each, Roger took me to one side and persuaded me to do the most difficult and painful thing I have ever done.

"Our future is uncertain," he said to me. "I don't know how long we can remain at Fenwick undiscovered but I do know that before long we will be forced to leave and make our way in the world once more, sustaining ourselves by robbery and skirmishing with the king's agents. I hope that you can see that such an existence is no life for my daughter."

"You do not mean to take Diva with us to Yorkshire," I said. My heart sunk at the prospect but I knew that Roger was right. He couldn't protect her and I certainly couldn't.

"I want to go through with my plans to marry her to Walter de Akney. She will be safe with him and well provided for. She may even find some degree of happiness which I can never give her."

"I might," I said. I knew I was pushing my luck with him.

"A common thief?" he said with a frown. "It's not that I don't love you as a brother, Stephen and I am sorry for my treatment of you, doubly so after you organised my escape from Nottingham. But you must see that Diva is in the gravest danger every day she remains with us. I have had my chance at a peaceful life and I now accept that God had different plans for me. I am content to fight and live rough for the rest of my days but Diva still has a chance to escape this nightmare we have all been living in since the war."

I could not speak. Every word he said was true and I knew it.

"Will you help me?" he said. "Will you help me help her?"

"How can I help you?"

"She loves you, I know it. And I know that I will break her heart by sending her away but her heart will mend and so will yours. It would be much easier if you helped her see."

"You want me to convince her?" I said.

"If you truly love her then you will do what is best for her."

He had me. I could not refuse him for I saw it all as he did. Diva would never be safe if she stayed with me. If I or Roger were killed, as we might well be, where would that leave her? Alone and homeless and entirely at the mercy of strangers.

Later that day I severed my ties to Diva and tore open a wound that has never healed to this day. She stared at me uncomprehending as I told her that I no longer loved her and that she should do as her father asked and marry this Walter de Akney.

"You do not speak the truth," she said, pale-faced. "You do not speak with your heart. This is cold loyalty to my father and I never thought it of you!"

"Diva," I said, "we shared a dream and it was a nice dream while it lasted. It was a dream suitable for youthful innocence, for summer days when Swannington was ours and we did not live in fear for our lives. But the world has changed now. We are outlaws and must scratch and fight to stay alive. Your father does not want that for you and neither do I. Go to your new husband and know that I loved you once but that love is no more."

She shook her head, her eyes brimming. "If you ever loved me at all you would not ask this of me. I still love you and I will always love you though it humiliates me to say it. You have torn my heart out and I fear that it is lost to me forever."

She turned from me and walked out of my life.

That night I got horribly drunk and passed out in my own vomit. When I woke I found that Roger had left with Diva and I never saw her again. I often wonder if I did the right thing. My mind has always been as a pendulum on the matter, swinging from one side to the other but in my later years, after having seen what fine outlaws women make; women such as your Katherine who possess hearts of fire and wills as strong as any man's, I lean more to the idea that I should have thrown Roger's words back in his face and absconded with his daughter. But I was still young and foolish and stayed with Roger rather than follow my heart.

As the year turned, we set out for Fenwick.

FIFTY-FOUR

Fenwick Hall is a large manor house surrounded by a rectangular moat not far from the eastern fringes of Barnsdale. We were less than a score of men after the skirmishes of that summer so de Foliot wasn't too hard pressed in finding us accommodation or stabling the horses he had lent us for the journey north.

Yorkshire was uncharted territory for us and we didn't know what to do with ourselves besides help out around the manor hall, get drunk and keep our martial skills honed in the yard. I missed Diva terribly but was forced to see her as part of my past. I feared for my future as much as the rest of us. We didn't know what the following months or years would bring. One thing we were sure of; it would take a long time for the murder of an undersheriff and the nephew of the Archbishop of York to die down.

Sure enough, although unknown to us at the time, things were stirring in the Midlands and the hand of justice was balling itself against us. A small army had been formed of men from Leicestershire, Nottinghamshire and Wiltshire and placed under the command of none other than Reginald de Grey. Still the Justice of Chester, he had been charged with scouring the Midlands and the north for a trace of us. To this day I do not know how he found us but, while we were preparing for winter, de Grey and his men joined forces with the High Sheriff of Yorkshire and marched on Fenwick Hall.

We awoke on a cold morning in October to find an encampment of pavilions under the shade of Barnsdale's treeline. We hurried to the walls as we had done at Swannington as the delegation approached and when we saw Reginald de Grey's odious face we were struck with an uneasy sense of déjà vu. Surely, I thought, I would not be denied my reckoning with de Grey this time. After all, what had we left to lose?

The man who rode at de Grey's side did the talking and introduced himself as Roger le Strange, High Sheriff of Yorkshire.

"Is the knight Richard de Foliot resident?" he called up to us atop the gatehouse.

"Aye, I'm here, le Strange!" said de Foliot.

"It is known that you harbour the outlaws Roger Godberd and Walter d'Evyas and many more besides," the sheriff replied. "These men are known to my associate Reginald de Grey here and he sees them in your company! Open your gates, de Foliot, and give up the king's enemies!"

"I would be a poor knight if I did that," de Foliot replied. "These men are my kin and companions. They sought refuge with me against those who bear them prejudice."

At this, de Grey spoke up. "Have you taken orders, good knight, and declared your hall an abbey to offer sanctuary to criminals? I know these men of old and they are no friends to true subjects of the king. But then, your loyalty has always been in question, has it not?"

De Foliot's face reddened. "My loyalty is not in question here, only your authority to take men from my land."

"I am the king's justice and this here is the High Sheriff of this shire! No authority is higher save that of God! Open your gates, de Foliot or we shall break them down and you will be declared traitor!"

Roger turned to de Foliot. "I am afraid we have brought trouble to your doorstep in return for your generosity."

"Not at all," said de Foliot. "I don't know this weasel, de Grey but I know his family and it does not strike me as odd that one of them should ride in arms with le Strange. He and I have business that goes way back. This is about more than the handing over of a few outlaws."

"Very well," said Roger. "We have come to the end of our course and will fight to the death if need be. You have only to give the signal."

De Foliot smiled. "Consider the battle standard raised," he said.

We strung our bows and made to send a volley at the men below but de Grey and le Strange saw what was coming and turned tail and fled back to camp. We loosed a few arrows in their wake for good measure. It was done now. We had stood our ground and possibly sealed our own death warrants.

The small army mustered at midday and began their attack. De Foliot ordered the drawbridge raised and we hunkered down against the fire arrows they sent over the walls, dousing the flames they kindled in the thatch. We sent a few arrows in return and even struck some of the attackers but it was a poor afternoon's battle.

"This could turn into a bloody siege," said Roger once the attackers had returned to their camp for the night. "And we do not have victuals enough to last for long. There is a postern gate in the wall of your home, is there not?"

"Aye," said de Foliot. "It opens about a foot from the moat at this time of year. I have ladders long enough to stretch across the water so you can sneak out unnoticed from the south. You can be away before dawn."

"We're not thinking of fleeing?" I exclaimed.

"You want to stay here and hold off the king's men?" Walter asked.

"What about making a last stand?" I said. "What about our reckoning with de Grey?"

"I'm sorry, Stephen," said Roger. "You, more than any, deserve revenge on that man. But they've run us to ground here and we have a way out. I'll not prolong our host's inconvenience when he has been so hospitable to us. We must take this chance and leave him to explain our absence in the morning. We've been more than he's bargained for already."

"Don't you worry about me, lads," said de Foliot. "I'll make good with the king. It's been an honour to know you, one and all. Best of luck and Godspeed."

I felt betrayed. Roger had taken the woman I loved from me and now he had taken my chance at avenging my brother. It was only then that I realised that I had given everything for Roger Godberd and now I had nothing left.

We slid the sturdiest of de Foliot's ladders out of the postern gate and it only just reached the other side of the moat. It bent terribly in the middle and would only allow the passage of one man at a time but eventually, with the cover of darkness still impenetrable, we made it across and cut our escape through the woods.

We struck south in the direction of Sherwood and it was here that Walter took his leave from us. Roger expressed plans to make for Derby where he hoped to find some of Robert de Ferrers's old supporters who might show us a degree of sympathy. Walter wanted none of it. He wanted the thief's life in Sherwood and was determined to stay close to his uncle and to repay him for his kindness if he could.

We tried to persuade him that it was folly; that he was the most wanted member of our party second only to Roger for his killing of the monk of Stanley Abbey but he had made up his mind and stayed while we took the road south. I never saw him again and I later heard that Roger le Strange ran him down near Perlethorpe and beheaded him without trial.

While Roger le Strange occupied himself with the pursuit of Walter and whatever new brigands he assembled, it was de Grey who came after us with a hot vengeance. Our escape from Fenwick did not fool him for long and he was on our trail like a master huntsman. He knew our haunts and we were forced to leave Sherwood.

Derby offered little in the way of shelter. De Ferrers's name had grown unpopular and those we did know from the war were reluctant to shelter a band of grubby outlaws wanted by the king.

We moved on after only a couple of days and cut a south-westerly direction, passing through muddy market towns like Birmingham and Worcester. Roger had a mind to make for the Forest of Dean which could potentially conceal us for the duration of the winter. It would be a hard one but we had grown used to hardship. The nearby town of Hereford was known to us and we could purchase supplies to keep us going.

We reached the Forest of Dean without incident and found a likely spot for a camp. Roger set most of the band to work building shelters and collecting firewood while he led an expedition into Hereford. He took his son with him and Richard, Wyotus and I came along to help carry our purchases back to the forest. I had noticed that he rarely let Roger the Younger out of his sight since Diva had left.

Richard and Wyotus were allowed to enjoy a few ales at a nearby tavern while we purchased the goods at market. I enjoyed the market. The hustle and bustle of civilisation was something I had grown unaccustomed to during my outlawry and a nostalgia for the smells and stenches of humanity had developed deep in my breast.

"We need arrows," Roger said to me, handing over a pouch of coin. "Take this and purchase as many barbed heads and small broadheads as you can carry. I'll see to the leather from the tanner's." He gave me charge of his son and we left him in the market place, crossing the open space towards the small fletcher's shop.

We made our purchases and left the shop with an armful of arrows each and headed towards the tanner's booth. As soon as we entered the market place I could see that something was up. It was the silence that hit me first, then the motionlessness of the crowd. The bustle had slowed to a standstill and the marketplace was like a frozen image.

A cluster of helmed heads could be seen crowded around a figure kneeling in the mud, his hands on his head. I would have thought a thief had been apprehended were it not for the size of the military presence. I did not need to see Roger's face to know that it was him who had been captured.

We dropped our bundles of arrows and reached for our daggers. We had a futile fight ahead of us and we would be run through within seconds but Roger's love for his father was not bound by logic and I could not flee and leave him to die.

A gap widened in the crowd enough for me to see Roger's face. He sought us out, knowing that we would come charging in an ill-fated rescue attempt. My eyes met his and I saw the warning in them. He shook his head slowly as he held my gaze and seemed to be telling me something.

"Come on, Stephen!" Roger the Younger said.

I had halted in my tracks. "No," I said. "He doesn't want us to."

"What?"

"He wants us to leave." I could see the look intensify in Roger's eyes. It was the usual steely look of defiance I had always seen in them but there was something else there too. There was a pleading there; a desperate request of me. He was saying 'keep my son safe. Do not let him throw his life away for me.'

A man slid out of the saddle of a nearby horse and strode over to Roger. It was Reginald de Grey. Once again, he had found us. I suppose we had left something of a trail since Derby. People had seen us passing through and it could not have been hard to pick up our scent in Birmingham or Worcester. De Grey struck Roger across the mouth with a mailed fist, knocking his head to the side and drawing a nasty wound across his check.

Roger the Younger cried out and made to charge the market square, dagger drawn. "No!" I cried, grabbing him around the middle to restrain him.

"What are you doing?" he cried, squirming in my grip.

"He doesn't want this!" I said. "He doesn't want you to die for nothing! He wants me to protect you."

Roger, his face bleeding, looked our way once more. His son saw that same look in his eyes that I had seen and went limp in my arms. "No...," he said in a weak voice.

"Come, let's away while we still can," I said.

Before the crowds obscured our view once more, we saw two burly soldiers haul Roger up by his arms and lift him into the saddle of a nearby horse. We picked up our bundles of arrows and headed for the inn where Richard and Wyotus were drinking, blissfully ignorant of what had happened.

There is very little left of my tale to tell. With Walter dead and Roger captured the heat on the rest of the band cooled off. De Grey wasn't interested in us and neither were the local sheriffs as we had committed no crimes in their shires.

Roger was taken to Bridgnorth Castle and don't think we didn't consider rescuing him. But we had been whittled down to less than ten men and Bridgnorth's great square keep was impenetrable. We had no choice but to return to our old haunts in Sherwood and Charnwood where we continued to live as outlaws.

Over the next few years Roger was moved between Bridgnorth, Hereford and Chester and trial after trial was postponed. King Henry had died the November after Roger's capture and, with Longshanks still in the Holy Land, England's administration was in chaos. It seemed that Roger would be doomed to remain a prisoner forever.

Longshanks eventually returned to England in the summer of 1274 and, for the first time since the Saxon Confessor, England was ruled by an Edward again. The date for Roger's trial was eventually set and he appeared before the king in London in April of 1276. I joined his brothers in their journey to London to see the final outcome. We were on tenterhooks. Would we see Roger swinging from the gallows before our return trip?

God smiled on our companion. Roger's answer to the accusations of homicide, robbery and arson was that all of his depredations had been committed while England had been in the throes of civil war and he had been in the service of Robert de Ferrers. As he had already been pardoned under the Dictum of Kenilworth, he could hardly be tried again for the same crimes. This did not answer the more recent allegations but, in a rare display of mercy, King Edward took Roger's part and pardoned him.

We were ecstatic. It had taken nearly five years but our beloved companion and leader was finally free. Our jubilation soured as we met Roger upon his release from Newgate Gaol. He was a shadow of the man who had led us through so much. Years of imprisonment had left him emaciated, pale and feverish. He seemed pleased to see us but his face told of many hardships he would never recover from.

We were determined to nurse him back to health as best we could and the first step of that treatment was to return him to his ancestral home of Leicestershire. Swannington was forever lost to him but the silver we had managed to save from our days as outlaws was enough to purchase a modest holding near Shepshed. I stayed on as part of Roger's household while the rest of the outlaws dispersed on their separate ways. Nicholas d'Eyville returned to his home at Caunton and William to his own family nearby. Wyotus disappeared and the last I heard of Richard was that he had become the parson of Shirland which was a remarkable achievement in the eyes of anybody who knew him.

I had no such pretentions myself and was content to live the life of an idle country bumpkin. It reminded me of those days when Diva and I had loved each other, free from war, lawmen and hardship. I missed her terribly but told myself that I could hardly complain when I had seen so much and survived it all while so few could say the same.

Roger died in 1293 and his son and namesake inherited his lands. I was well into my forties by then. I liked the younger Roger Godberd well enough but I had begun to tire of service and wished to wander the trackways and roads I had roamed during my youth. I wanted to be my own man once more and so, foolishly perhaps, I set out with my belongings in my pack and my intentions set on earning bread and board any way I could.

I steered clear of robbery for it is a poor enterprise for an old man. I did odd jobs here and there but I found that what people appreciated most was my stories. I told them whenever and wherever I could so long as I could get something out of it; a jack of ale or a bed for the night. I talked of the war, of Simon de Montfort and of love but people mostly wanted to hear about Roger Godberd; the hobhood of Sherwood.

I obliged them and, after several years, I began to hear my stories told back to me by people who were wholly ignorant of my role in his saga. I heard exaggerations of them and outright lies too but one thing became clear to me; Roger Godberd's adventures had captivated the north and his name and deeds had taken on a life of their own. Roger Godberd's story was out of my hands and belonged to the people who would remember him forever.

FITT IX
THE LAST ADVENTURE

"Sir Roger of Doncaster,
By the prioress he lay,
And there they betrayed good Robin Hood,
Through their false play."
- A Little Gest of Robin Hood

Nottinghamshire
Autumn, 1330

FIFTY-FIVE

The inn heaved with people. With parliament already at the end of its third day up at the castle every inn, merchant's house and hostel was jampacked with petitioners, clerics and merchants who, business concluded for the day, were well into their merrymaking. Nottingham was bursting at the seams and for the two hooded figures who pushed their way through the press of sweating, drunken revellers, even this inn on the town's outskirts could be full of spies.

"They have a room on the eastern face of the building," said William Eland to his companion, daring to raise his voice over the raucous singing.

"Good. As long as it's private," William de Montagu replied. He eyed the inn's patrons nervously. He and Eland were playing a dangerous game and failure would mean certain execution. Time was of the essence now.

Eland led him up the stairs to the landing that ringed the great common room and they followed the grubby cob-plastered wall around to the inn's eastern side. Eland knocked on an unassuming door and they waited. After a time, the door creaked open and a large, brutish face peered out at them.

De Montagu had never seen a man so tall for the face hovered at least two feet above Eland who was no dwarf himself. It was greatly scarred and bristled with a thick, dark beard.

"Let us in, John," said Eland. "There have been developments and we need to accelerate our plans."

The giant called John grunted and opened the door wide enough to admit them. A single candle illuminated the pokey room and by its flickering light de Montagu could make out the faces of the other two outlaws. One was a handsome if rugged man of about his own age and the other was a petite but fierce-looking woman with tawny hair.

They wore rough-spun woollen cloaks rather than the green livery Eland said they had worn on his first encounter with them. They were trying to blend in but to de Montagu they reeked of the forest as if they were somehow part of it. He half expected them to have leaves for armpit hair.

"You are the man they call Hood of Barnsdale?" de Montagu asked the youngish man.

"Aye, that I am," Hood replied. "This is Little John and Katherine Colle."

"And you three are all that came from Barnsdale?"

Hood nodded. "That I am here at all is as a favour to an old friend. John and Katherine came with me as they are the most loyal of my following. The rest of my band have no business in Nottingham and I cannot ask them to risk their lives for a cause not their own with no promise of reward."

"If this goes to plan there will be ample reward for all involved," de Montagu said.

Hood smiled. "*If*. And by your own admission, there have been developments."

"We were betrayed, it is true," de Montagu said. "John Wyard, damn his soul, reported our activities to de Mortimer. We were each of us hauled before him earlier today and interrogated. None said a word for all are committed and devoted to our king."

"I'm surprised de Mortimer let you live," Hood said.

"He had no choice. I am the king's closest friend and he cannot execute me without proof. But our flight from the castle only piles more suspicion on us. There can be no turning back now. We must move tonight."

"How many men do you have?"

"A score of mounted knights left the castle with us and await our coming south of Nottingham. All are the cream of England's nobility and fiercely loyal to the king. Robert de Ufford, William de Clinton, the de Bohun brothers; fine men all."

"What is your plan?" Hood asked.

"The very same as Eland discussed with you. De Mortimer is ignorant of it for none of us betrayed our goal. We need only strike while the iron is hot."

"You are to take us to the tunnel's entrance tonight," de Eland said to the outlaw. "As agreed. We leave immediately."

"As far as I know the cave is located on the western side of the castle rock, above the deer park," said Hood. "We'll have to give the town a wide birth to avoid detection."

"Are you telling us you've never used this passageway yourself?" de Montagu said.

"Never had a need to," Hood replied with a shrug. I've been inside the castle but we used the barbican gate when I was with the old King Edward.

De Montagu was confused. "Then the tale of you escaping Nottingham's dungeons is false?"

"Ah, that was a different hobhood," Hood said. "The one who used the tunnel died years ago. I know of it from a mutual friend."

De Montagu threw his hands up in despair. "Then all rests on thirdhand information! We follow a man who no more knows the location of the tunnel than I do!"

"Fear not, de Montagu," Eland said. "All is not lost. This fellow is confident of the tunnel's location. And besides, we have run out of time and options. We *must* follow him."

De Montague was forced to agree. The events of the day had thrown all into turmoil and they had little else to do but to press on with their plans and hope for the best. He regarded the three outlaws critically. "Can we count on you to accompany us into the castle and to lend your aid in arresting de Mortimer?"

Hood returned his gaze. "I knew the king when he was a lad and I knew his father too. Both were good men. Now you tell me that de Mortimer has, among his other crimes, murdered the father and means to do away with the son too. Aye, I'll follow you into Nottingham Castle and help set England to rights. And when it's over I'm done with kings and their wars for good."

De Montague sighed. "Very well. I suppose an outlaw's promise will have to do."

"Good," said Eland. "Then let's get moving."

"How many men does de Mortimer have?" Robert asked as they rode west after having met with the king's friends south of Nottingham.

"Hard to give an exact amount," said Eland. "Most are billeted in the town but there will be patrols along the walls."

"It doesn't much matter how many men de Mortimer has," said Little John. "This whole plan goes to shit if we are detected entering the castle. We won't survive an open battle with the garrison."

"Then you'll have to be quiet then, won't you, you big oaf?" said Katherine.

"With luck, this tunnel of Rob's might even muffle your chattering gob," John replied.

Robert loved his companions for coming with him. When he had put Eland's request to his band, John and Katherine had been the only ones who had agreed to it without question.

"To think," Eland said, "That a tunnel such as this exists in my own castle without my ever knowing of it. The king was most intrigued when I told him. I truly think it made up his mind on removing de Mortimer now rather than later for it offers some small chance of success."

"*Some* chance," Robert replied. "If we find the entrance blocked then we will have to give it up. There will be no other way into the castle."

"I unlocked the door to the cellars beneath the Great Hall personally, just as you said," said Eland. I found the trapdoor too and ensured that it is free of obstruction. I did not open it in case anybody goes down to the cellar for a new cask of ale. It has no lock but we will just have to pray that the tunnel is clear of detritus."

Four years had passed since King Edward II had been deposed by his wife and her lover. The war with France over the Duchy of Aquitaine that had been brewing when Robert had left the king's service had dragged on through 1325 without any end in sight. As Queen Isabella was the sister of the French king, it had fallen to her to smooth things over with her brother.

The queen's arrival at the French court did little to pacify her family. They were furious over her husband's and le Despenser's treatment of her and demanded King Edward's atonement. Edward could have ended it all by travelling to France in person and kneeling before King Charles in homage for the Duchy of Aquitaine but here he was presented with a conundrum. Hugh le Despenser had become so unpopular that the king feared to leave him in England that he might return to find a rebellion and his beloved companion's head on a spike. But he could hardly bring him with him to France for the French hated le Despenser almost as much as the English did. Only one solution presented itself.

He sent his twelve-year-old son, Edward of Windsor, in his stead.

It was after the young Edward had joined his mother and uncle at the French court and paid homage for the duchy on his father's behalf that word reached England that Queen Isabella had no intention of returning to her husband or of letting their son return to England. She had become something of a rallying point at the French court for the enemies of the English king. Exiles, traitors and contrariants who had fled after Boroughbridge flocked to make her acquaintance. The emergence of one in particular threw the king into a rage. Roger de Mortimer.

Rumour had it that de Mortimer and the queen became lovers during their time at King Charles's court. It may have begun as a simple alliance of two people who loathed le Despenser but their relationship grew into something far more dangerous. A plan began to take root; a plan to save England from le Despenser and to save the king from himself.

The invasion fleet landed in September of 1326. To the king's outrage they were met with more support than resistance and the bishops of Lincoln, Ely and Norwich threw their lot in with the queen and de Mortimer. The Bishop of Hereford also sided with the invaders, which surprised no one, and publicly accused the king of being a sodomite.

Abandoning London in October, the king desperately tried to muster some opposition. He emptied the gaols and sent word to his allies in Wales but it was to no avail. Edward of Windsor was appointed regent in place of his father who, Isabella and de Mortimer claimed, had abandoned his kingdom.

The king and le Despenser took up residence at Caerphilly Castle but they were eventually captured while trying to rally support in the countryside. Le Despenser was taken to Hereford where a mockery of a trial saw him hanged drawn and quartered. The king was taken to Kenilworth and forced to hand over his great seal to the Bishop of Hereford. It was over. For the first time in England's history, a king had been deposed.

As news of the upheaval trickled into the countryside, Robert had been proud to hear the names of several of his former associates remaining loyal to their king to the end. Roger de Wodeham – his fellow valet of the king's chamber – had stormed the manor of Isabella's supporter John de Giffard with fifty armed men and had stolen some horses to ride against the invading force while Wat Coward had been one of the last men standing in the garrison that held Caerphilly Castle against Isabella.

The parliament of January 1327 saw the king's fourteen-year-old son crowned Edward III at Westminster although his rule was to be governed by his mother and de Mortimer. The former king was removed to Berkley Castle where the details of his fate were clouded by rumour and speculation. A rescue attempt by those still loyal to him failed and less than a month later it emerged that he had died.

The official cause of his death was sickness but there were many who suspected foul play on the parts of the queen mother and de Mortimer. He was buried at Gloucester Abbey, though his body was curiously obscured by a wooden effigy atop the casket dressed in his coronation robes. This lent support to the rumour that the rescue attempt had in fact succeeded, that the king was living somewhere on the continent and Isabella and de Mortimer had covered up the embarrassing escape of their prisoner with the false story of his death. Others claimed that the king had been murdered on their orders and, as the years passed with no sign of his re-emergence, most gave up hope of his survival.

Edward II had never been a popular monarch. His reign had been disastrous and Isabella and de Mortimer had presented a clean slate for England; one that many rejoiced in. But as time passed it became clear that de Mortimer was more the tyrant than Edward had ever been. His appetite for land and wealth rivalled le Despenser's and appalled the nobility while his scandalous love affair with the queen mother was not something easily forgotten by the commoners. Edward III, still a boy, was entirely under the thumb of his mother and her lover and, as the list of depredations increased, many began to wonder when the youthful king would start to assert his own will.

None of this meant anything to the outlaws of Barnsdale. The north was still as wild as ever and it mattered little to them who sat on the throne. The Scarlet Men were no more; Will was as poor a leader as Robert had suspected and eventually the entire band came back under his leadership. He had thought little of the political upheaval until they had robbed two Benedictine monks passing up the Great North Road.

Robbery was rarely a necessity for Robert and his band anymore. The silver they had stolen from the Bishop of Hereford still held out and their lair in Barnsdale had become more of a village than a camp. Sturdy, well-thatched accommodations were capable of withstanding the worst winters and a bakery, smithy, fletcher and brewery provided all of their needs and ensured that they never needed to visit the towns or villages.

But life in the greenwood was very isolating and months could go by without any contact with other people. Robert liked to maintain some connection to the outside world and had taken to accosting the occasional traveller on the road, leading them blindfolded to camp, and providing them with a good meal and good cheer. If the visitor supplied the band with entertaining gossip, a humorous tale or some music or song, then they were permitted to leave the following day with full purses. If, however, they proved to be poor company or told obvious lies then Robert would demand that they pay for the hospitality provided. It was a good game and allowed the outlaws occasional entertainment as well as news and commentary on current affairs.

There had been something strange about the two black monks from the get go. They did not act like monks and showed none of the outrage and anger the band was used to seeing in the men of the cloth they accosted on the road. In fact, the monks appeared to be rather pleased with themselves. They accepted their blindfolds willingly and even looked smug as they were led through the trees. Robert pegged them as imposters before they had even reached camp.

It was only after they had finished their meal and the two monks were picking their teeth with the bones of a devoured pheasant that Robert demanded a tale from them. They looked to each other and then one of them told a story so outrageous that Robert would have sent them away with empty purses had they not seemed so in earnest.

"You no doubt know that our king is currently at residence at Nottingham Castle where parliament is about to be held," said one of the monks. "He is on the very cusp of manhood and his will, bolstered by his friends, has grown stronger every day. The time has come for him to overthrow de Mortimer and hold him and his mother to account for his father's murder."

"Then it is true that they are guilty of the old king's death," said Little John.

"Undoubtedly. The king himself accuses them although not publicly. That is about to change."

"You speak as if you know the young king yourself," said Robert.

"Aye, I know him," said the monk. "My name is William Eland and I am Nottingham's castellan."

"Then it is as I suspected," Robert said. "You are no monks."

"No. I apologise for our deception but it was necessary to leave Nottingham in disguise. And we figured that the best way to run across your path was to appear as travelling men of the cloth. They are your preference, are they not?"

"You wished for me to rob you?" Robert asked.

Eland nodded. "In a manner of speaking. I am close to the king and he is preparing to put his plan into action. He requires the support of his loyal subjects and has spoken of you in particular. He seems fond of you and bade me seek you out."

"Aye, I remember the young Edward well. I taught him archery. He was a good lad and I do not doubt that he will make a fine king. Better than his father at any rate. But he sent you to recruit my help? How might I help him? We may be a sizable band of hardened outlaws but we are too few to storm Nottingham."

"How it is to be done, he did not say," Eland replied. "But times are getting desperate. The young king must make his move now. He has begun to fear for his life."

"Surely de Mortimer would not go so far as to harm the king?"

"De Mortimer murdered the old king. He wants England and will even murder his lover's son to get it. He must be stopped."

"Just a minute," said Much. "How are we to trust you? We've been tricked before."

"The king thought of that too," said Eland and he looked to his companion who had remained silent so far. With a nod, the second monk drew an object from his robes and handed it to Robert. It was a large seal, the type used to imprint its image into the wax on documents. The image was of an enthroned man holding an orb and sceptre. Latin ringed the figure and all Robert could make out was the word 'EDWARDVS'.

"The king saw fit to send with me Richard de Bury, his Lord Privy Seal along with the great seal itself. Is this proof enough that I speak the truth?"

"Aye," said Robert, examining the youthful face of the king on the seal. "I believe you. And I pledge the king my support. But how is it to be done?"

"Leave the planning to us. We shall return to the king tonight before our absence is noticed. I will tell him that his loyal friends in Barnsdale will heed his call and travel south to Nottinghamshire. I suggest you move to Sherwood so that you can be nearby when the time comes. The king has some other friends and we shall rally them all to attack the castle on the king's word."

"That would be folly," said Robert. "Nottingham is too hard to crack for a ragtag army. But there may be another way."

He felt the eyes of his band on him as he said this, knowing that they knew of what he was thinking. The eyes of Eland and de Bury regarded him with hopeful expectation. It was a mad plan but a far better one than attacking the castle itself.

FIFTY-SIX

It was a cold night and the clear sky was starry. The knights left their horses under the cover of the trees before approaching the castle rock on foot, wary of the torches on the walls above that passed slowly back and forth in the darkness.

Could it work a second time? Robert thought as he led de Montagu and the rest of the king's friends towards the castle rock. Old Stephen had been nervous at using the tunnel to rescue Roger Godberd and that had been sixty years ago. Who knew what changes the castle had undergone in that time? Would the tunnel still exist or had it been filled in with rubble? These questions had been asked a generation ago but the hope of their predecessors had been ultimately rewarded. Robert could only hope and pray to the Virgin that some things had been untouched by time.

He was not sure of the exact location of the cave but he was willing to bet that it would not be visible from the foot of the rock. He still wasn't sure why he was doing this. He had decided long ago that he wanted no part in the kingdom's troubles. Old Stephen's tales had served as a warning and all he wanted was the solitude and freedom of the greenwood. He couldn't keep coming to the rescue every time some king or other found themselves in trouble. But there was something about Edward of Windsor that just made him like the lad. He would feel safer knowing that England was in his hands.

One last time, he told himself. It was the same thing he had told Little John and Katherine although he had not really needed to. In truth they had relished the idea of an adventure outside the greenwood. 'Just like old times', was one of the things John kept saying. Robert did not think it was a coincidence that the only members of his band who expressed an interest in helping the young king were the same two who had served his father.

The ground levelled out into a thin, grassy strip that ran several yards along the rockface. The sandstone was pockmarked with nooks and crannies, some small, some large and Robert inspected each of them. Several were large enough to admit entrance and, after poking his head into a few dead ends, he eventually found one that went deep into the rock.

"I think this is it," he said to the others in a hushed tone so as not to attract the attention of the passing guards above.

William de Montagu pushed his way forward and peered into the cave. "Black as pitch," he said. "But we can't risk a torch. Hood, you'll have to lead us in."

Robert felt like pointing out that he knew about as much as any of them about what they might find at the end of the tunnel but decided that it would be futile. He had offered his services to them as a guide and so naturally it fell to him to guide them.

Katherine drew her blade at his side. "Whatever we face at the end of this tunnel," she said, "I'll face it with you, same as always."

"I wouldn't have it any other way," Robert replied with a smile and drew his own sword.

The tunnel was narrower than he had ever pictured it from Old Stephen's descriptions. The ground was uneven and curved making passage along it difficult especially in the dark. He felt his way along and could hear the nervous breathing of the score or so men behind him shuffling and scraping along in the blackness. Eventually the ground rose up and Robert stumbled over the first step. He crawled up on his hands and knees until he bumped his head on a wooden ceiling.

"The trapdoor," he whispered to Katherine.

He sheathed his sword and pressed his palms against the old wood. It didn't budge. He strained and Katherine joined him but even together they could not lift it.

"Let me try," said Little John, shouldering his way between them. He squeezed himself into the cramped space and set his broad shoulders to the trap door and pushed up with his legs. They could hear him groaning and straining and then, suddenly, the trapdoor loosened with a dry grating sound. The passage had gone unnoticed for so many years that time had almost welded the hinges shut.

Little John clambered into the chamber above and the others followed quickly, immediately drawing their weapons. They stood in the cellars beneath the Great Hall and all was silent above. There would be soldiers slumbering on the rushes of the hall, a floor's thickness above their heads. De

Montague assumed the position of leader and beckoned them towards the door to the courtyard.

Peering up at the torchlit walls, de Montague waited for the time to be right and, when the guard had passed, they were off, slipping out of the cellars and hurrying across the courtyard towards the upper bailey gate.

"The gate should be open," said Eland as they ran. "I saw to that myself."

Nobody had interfered with Eland's plans and they gained the upper baily without incident. De Montagu led them towards the queen's tower and they hurried up the stairs to the quarters above. As they exited the stairwell there came a shout from the end of the corridor and a richly-dressed man emerged from the doorway to some inner hall.

"De Turpington the steward, damn him!" said de Montagu.

"Traitors!" the steward cried. "Down with the traitors!" He drew a dagger and charged at them.

It was a brave attack but futile. One of de Montagu's knights dodged the steward's desperate swipe and brought his mace down on his head with an awful crunch that knocked him lifeless to the ground.

Two more men hurried from the hall. These were men-at-arms and they rushed the group with drawn swords. While the clash of steel rang out in the corridor, Robert followed the rest of de Montagu's retinue into the hall where they found several nobles gawping in terror at what was unfolding around them.

The long oak table that stood before the great hearth was strewn with maps and documents. As soon as the intruders entered the hall, two more chamber guards ran to halt them. In the ensuing fray, most of the gathered nobles managed to flee. Only two remained. Robert recognised one as Queen Isabella and the other he took to be de Mortimer. De Montague stepped over the bodies of the fallen guards, avoiding the blood that pooled around them on the flags and demanded that de Mortimer be seized.

"De Montague!" de Mortimer yelled as two knights grabbed his arms and held them behind his back. "Eland! You traitorous bastards!"

"Gag the son of a whore!" de Montagu said and a rag was shoved into de Mortimer's outraged mouth.

"Fair son!" the queen mother cried. "Have mercy on gentle Roger!"

Her head and begging hands were raised upwards as if pleading with God and it was only after Robert followed her gaze that he realised somebody else had entered the hall.

On the stairs that led up to the chambers above stood a youngish man dressed in the very finest of garments. A jewelled sword was belted at his waist and his hand hovered over its hilt as if he was considering drawing it. Robert looked at the youth's handsome face and recognised it. He had known it in its younger phase and saw in it the same fine features of the old king.

"Your tyranny is over, de Mortimer, said King Edward. "Never again shall your poisonous words have a say in the ruling of my kingdom. Take him down to the courtyard and await my orders."

"Sire," said de Montagu. "The plan has succeeded. The castle is yours. As is the kingdom."

"Good work, William," said the king. "Well done, all of you. You have proven to be my most loyal friends." He then noticed Robert. "Hood," he said, his face cracking into a smile. "My old tutor!"

"Sire," said Robert, bowing.

"Your days of outlawry are over, old friend. I will reward you with land and titles as I will reward all here tonight."

"Sire, I..." Robert began but the king was not listening. There was much still to be done and a search began in earnest for de Mortimer's supporters. The king led the expedition himself, going from room to room, leaving no chamber unsearched. De Mortimer's two sons, Geoffrey and Edmund, were apprehended while the Bishop of Lincoln was found trying to exit the castle via a privy.

By dawn the entire castle was roused and assembled in the upper bailey. The king addressed the crowd from the Bridge of the Tower. Robert and the rest of the rescuers flanked him while de Mortimer and the queen mother were held under armed guard, high up for all to see.

The king informed the assembly that the rule of his mother and her lover was over and that he was now assuming total control of England. There was a muted applause and Robert guessed that many in the crowd were quickly assessing their future liberties and pondering how they might creep into the favour of the new ruler after years of supporting his captors. It was then that he spotted Adam de Orleton. The former Bishop of Hereford had been translated to the Bishop of Worcester under de Mortimer, presumably in return for his scathing denunciation of the former king.

When it was all over, the queen mother was escorted to her apartments where she was kept confined. De Mortimer was hurried out of the castle via the secret tunnel lest any of his supporters attempt his rescue. Where he was taken Robert did not know.

Later, the king summoned Robert to a private audience in the courtyard and, as they walked around the vegetable plots, the king began to speak once more of his reward.

"Sire, with the greatest appreciation for your generosity," said Robert, "I require no reward from you. I want no lands or titles. I have my own realm where I am king, begging your pardon. I speak figuratively of course, but Barnsdale is my home and I have no desire to leave it."

"King of the greenwood you may be," said the king with an amused smile, "but there you are an outlaw. And leafy bowers must provide poor comfort in comparison to the feather beds of a manor hall."

"It is a coarse life, I cannot lie," said Robert, "but it is a humble and satisfying one. We want for nothing and we enjoy each other's company. We don't even rob folk anymore."

"Really? My castellan and Lord Privy Seal tell me a different story..."

"Oh, we occasionally invite passing travellers to dine with us," said Robert, "but really, we are quite self-sufficient. We have no need of the world beyond the greenwood and the world has no need of us."

"Have you no family? No kin who miss you?"

He shook his head. "My band is my family. My mother died two winters ago and my father long before that. I have a sister who married a good yeoman last year."

"You provided her with an adequate dowry I trust?"

"More than adequate. She is happy and will have her own children to think of before long. There is nothing left for me in the towns. The name of Robert Hood has no place there anymore. It has been entirely consumed by the greenwood and there it must stay."

"My father loved you, you know," the king said after they had walked in silence for a bit. "He never understood why you deserted his service. But I think I do, a little, now." He placed his hand on Robert's shoulder. "I don't suppose I'll be seeing you again, Hood. But I will be forever in your debt. Not just for your aid in the overthrow of my mother's lover. I still look to your teaching whenever I shoot a few arrows at the butts. You gave me such a respect for the bow as a weapon that far surpasses the opinions of others."

"Keep that stance steady and always place your feet well, sire," said Robert, "and you can't go wrong."

"Good luck, Hood," the king replied. "And Godspeed. Rule your kingdom well with my blessing."

"And you yours, sire."

FIFTY-SEVEN

In the seventeen years that followed, Robert and his outlaw band remained in Barnsdale and, as Robert had told the king, they had little to do with the outside world.

There were occasional exceptions. In addition to a new gang called the Folvilles making incursions into Yorkshire, James Coterel, the gang leader they had briefly served when they had attempted to rob the manor house of Adwick-le-Street, had grown in power and influence. The Coterel family were known throughout the Midlands for their robberies and ransoming of churchmen and even the Folvilles paid them their dues. They even came down from their lairs in the peak district and sought to expand their territory to Sherwood and Barnsdale.

Robert and his band defended their greenwood fiercely and those wars with the Folvilles and the Coterels did not lack for casualties. One of them was Much whom Robert had buried with a heavy heart. As one of the original members of the band, his death hit Robert hard and he was overcome by a feeling that England had moved on without them. What little they heard from the outside world suggested that it had become a more dangerous place than ever before. King Edward III had proved to be a strong and successful king but the same problems that had plagued his father dogged his reign.

The French king had died childless and, as his nephew, Edward pursued his claim through his mother. War consumed England and the outlaws got wind of the king's victory at Crecy in 1346 and of how his archers had decimated the French with their arrows. Robert could not resist feeling a little pride when he heard that, remembering the king's words to him on their parting.

That year Katherine succumbed to a sickness and died. Robert was ruined by her passing. Of all his band she was the one he felt he could not live without. She had become his other half, his good half, and had remained his loyal and loving companion to the end. He regretted that they had never been blessed with any children but, as she had always said herself; two outlaws living in sin could never expect to receive God's blessing in such matters.

Robert refused to bury her in their small, sad cemetery alongside Much and the other few who had fallen over the years. He found a high spot near a bubbling brook where he could visit her grave and be alone with only the sound of the water and the birdsong for company. He did this almost daily and it was after one of these visits that he did not return to camp.

Little John was the first to grow worried for he and Robert had become the closest of friends in recent years and he knew how tormented their leader was by the loss of Katherine. He went to her grave and, when he did not find Robert there, he began a wider search. It was near dusk when he found the small bower between two whitebeams. A trickle of smoke seeped through the piled-up briar.

He found Robert inside sitting on a pallet of bracken, staring into the flames of his small fire while a coney roasted on a spit.

"What's this? Finally sick of us?" John asked.

Robert looked up at him, his face devoid of all humour. "I'm sick, John. It's better I do not remain at camp. I may smite you all."

"Sick? What's wrong with you?"

"The same Katherine had. I ache, deep in my bones and I sweat at night and have awful visions. Who knows how many of us may be affected?"

"You've just got a fever is all," John said. "We all come down with something once in a while. You need a bit of Maud's nettle broth, that'll fix you up, or at least it'll make you forget you're sick."

"No, it's more serious than that," Robert replied. "My time is up. It's better this way. You should go back to camp."

"And what will you do? Wait for death out here on your own?"

Robert shrugged. "I have nothing left to live for anyway."

"At least seek help," John said. "We hold our freedom and independence so highly that we often forget how isolated we really are. We have no healers, save Maud, bless her, but there are others beyond Barnsdale who have knowledge of herbs and cures. The nuns of Kirklees for example."

"We sought no such help for Katherine," Robert said. "What right do I have to seek it for myself?"

"Katherine's sickness came on too fast for anything to be done. We would not have left the greenwood before she would have passed. But you are still hale. We can make for Kirklees. The prioress herself cured Much when he was at death's door, do you not remember?"

"That was many years ago. My cousin may be long dead."

"Well, what if she is? There's bound to be some nun there who can help you."

"I do not have the strength, John. It is best I remain here."

"I'll take you," said John, setting his jaw. "I'll carry you if I have to."

"It's too dangerous."

"Then I'll fetch Will. The three of us can journey to Kirklees and it will do you good to ride in our company. We three are all that is left of the old gang."

Robert gave a small nod and that was all the permission John needed. He hurried away from the bower and back to camp where he drew Will to one side for a private counsel.

"Rob's sick, or at least he thinks he is."

"You've seen him?" said Will. "And what do you mean he *thinks* he's sick?"

"I don't know. He looked all right to me but he's miserable. He has been since Katherine died. I truly think he wants to die himself."

"Surely you don't suspect him of doing anything stupid? Not Rob!"

John shrugged. "He's made himself a bower a mile from here. He's just sitting there, waiting for death. I convinced him into letting us take him to

Kirklees Priory. Maybe the nuns there can see if there is anything wrong with him. And if it's all in his mind then maybe the change of scenery and our company on the road will get him out of this rut."

"You want me to come?"

"Aye, us two have known him longest. We're practically his family. Who else is better to protect him and bring him out of his gloom?"

"What will we tell the others?"

"The truth. That Rob is sick and we've taken him to Kirklees to be bled and whatnot. They'll understand."

It was the work of a few moments for John and Will to gather a few provisions for the journey, fetch three garrons from the camp's stables and give their instructions to Robert's lieutenants. They rode for Robert's bower and coaxed him onto a horse before setting out.

Robert found that his spirits lifted somewhat despite himself as they left Barnsdale and headed northwest towards the River Calder. The greenwood had been a home to him for as long as he could remember but since Katherine's death he had felt that it's jades and emeralds were less vibrant, it's comforting embrace and earthy smells now stifling. The open fields between the villages of Nostell and Crofton were wide and refreshing in contrast. He even enjoyed seeing the villeins at work in the fields after going for so long without seeing any new faces.

They followed the river west and passed within sight of Wakefield on its other side. Robert gazed at his old hometown with conflicted feelings of homesickness and revulsion. It had grown since he had last seen it and seemed ugly to him. He knew that there would be precious few people left within its walls who would remember him.

Upon arrival at Kirklees, Little John did the talking and explained that, many years ago, the prioress did a poor outlaw a good turn and now that outlaw sought her help once more.

They were allowed entrance to the hostelry where a low fire glowed in the hearth of the hall and a couple of other guests sat at benches, sipping something from clay mugs. The hostler bade John and Will to sit in the hall while Robert was taken upstairs.

In a bay by a window there stood a crude wooden bed with a hearth nearby and Robert realised, as the hostler motioned to him to lie down, that it was the same bed Much had recovered on all those years ago while he and Katherine had dwelled downstairs. At the thought of those youthful days when he had first got to know Katherine, his eyes nearly welled up and he squeezed them tight to stem the tears.

The hostler set about kindling a fire in the small hearth. "I will send for the prioress," she said once the flames were crackling. "She is a healer and will tend to you herself."

She left him gazing at the eaves where a spider was building a web in the dusty corner. The low murmur of conversation drifted up from the hall below. He must have dozed off because he awoke with a start to see a cloaked figure silently closing the door to the small room. It was dim in the confined space but Robert could make out the white wimple that surrounded the concealed face.

"I understand you run a fever," said the nun as she set down a basin, a silken blood-band and some bleeding irons by the fire. She passed a hand over his forehead. "You burn, sir. You have a sweating sickness and it is best that I let the bad blood out."

"Thank you, mother," Robert said. "You saved the life of my companion once before."

The prioress said nothing. She rolled the sleeve of his tunic up and fastened the blood-band around his bicep. She then began feeling around for the choicest vein and, upon finding it, made a small incision with one of her irons.

Robert felt the warm blood trickle down his arm and pool in the dish below. The prioress drew up a chair and waited by his bed. He could not see her face for it was obscured by her wimple and cast in shadow. He looked down at the hands which were folded in her lap. They looked like the hands of a woman in her early forties. He remembered his cousin as a woman approaching her forties back in 1321. *She would be, what, sixty-five by now?* A grand age for a prioress. *But this is not the same woman.*

"When did Alice de Scriven die?" he asked.

"Domina de Scriven passed some twenty years ago," said the prioress. "did you know her?"

"She was my cousin. My mother's niece. I suppose she was old. I never really considered that she might not be here anymore."

"Well, your cousin was skilled in herbs and healing and she passed her skills on to me. I will see that you live to return to Barnsdale."

Robert tensed. "What makes you think I come from Barnsdale?"

"I know the great Robert Hood when I see him."

Robert began to feel that he was in danger and tried to rise but his body was too weak. He looked down and saw that the basin at the foot of the bed was overflowing with his blood. *How much was this prioress planning on taking?*

She turned to him and, for the first time, the glow of the hearth illuminated her face. With a start, Robert recognised it. It was lined with the passing of many years, just as his own face was, but the face of his old follower showed through the quarter of a century that had passed since he had seen it last.

"Anna!" he gasped.

"Aye, Anna whom you betrayed and sent to Kirklees to live out her days in confinement. Anna who goes by Domina Cawthorne now. I'll bet you never saw that coming, eh?"

"Betrayed you?" Robert said. "It was you who betrayed us! I had to send you away. The others wanted to hang you..."

"You could have kept your mouth shut. You could have spared us all of this. You told Will. You made him hate me. And then you cast me out, stripped me of all I had and put me away in here and left me to rot. I thought of running away many times but where would I go? I was an outlaw and my only protection was the band. My only protection was Will, but you turned him against me. I even thought of suicide for life here under that bitch of an old prioress, your cousin, was like Hell only colder. All I had to warm me was my burning hatred of you.

"But then I realised that considerable power lay just within my grasp and that this place might not be so bad if I was in charge. I learned that these nuns are no more than dumb sheep in wimples and easily led. So, I began to play their game, saying my prayers and doing my duties like a good bride of Christ while was also playing a game of my own. In a few years I was close to the prioress and became her student in medicine. I was ready to succeed her but I knew the old goat wouldn't give up the ghost anytime soon. Good thing she taught me so much about the properties of herbs."

In a panic, Robert reached over and clamped his hand over the opened vein in his right arm. It was clear that Anna had murdered his cousin and now meant to kill him too. Was it too late? *He felt so weak...*

Anna rose and smiled down at him. "I'll leave you to your rest now. Don't worry, I'll see that you are not disturbed." She withdrew an iron key from her habit and turned to leave the room. She closed the door and Robert sighed in despair as he heard the key turn in the lock.

He had to escape. He had to warn John and Will that their old enemy was in the vicinity and possibly meant them all harm. *What a fool I was to forget about her!* He looked about the room. *The window?* No. He was too weak to scramble out without falling and killing himself. His eyes rested on the chair opposite the bed. From it hung his father's horn from its worn green baldric.

Slowly, his head spinning, he slid out of the bed and landed heavily on the floor, overturning the basin of blood. His own cool blood spread out beneath him, soaking his clothes and making the floorboards slippery beneath his palms and knees. He slithered about for purchase and was able to drag himself out of the pool of gore and closer to the chair.

He had no strength left in his limbs. Every inch was a strain as he dragged himself closer and closer. The room was reeling. He had to reach his horn! *He had to reach it...*

FIFTY-EIGHT

"I know what you're thinking," John said to Will opposite him.

"Oh? And what am I thinking. Do tell me," replied Will in a surly tone.

"You've barely said a word since we set out from Barnsdale and I know what's been preying on your mind. So what if she is here? The nuns aren't allowed outside their cloisters except the prioress. You won't see her here in the guesthouse."

"It's been twenty-five years since I saw her last," said Will. "Believe me I couldn't care less if I saw her now. Probably wouldn't recognise her anyway, nor her me."

"I still reckon Rob should have hanged her."

Will nodded but said nothing. They drank weak ale and looked around the hall. A large man with fiery red hair was watching them from the corner of the room. He got up and walked over to them.

"Care for some company?" he asked them.

John felt like telling him to piss off but the big man looked quick to anger and he didn't want to get into a fight or do anything that might compromise Robert's recovery. "Feel free," he told the man.

"The name's Roger de Doncaster," said the big man, "but folks round here call me Red Roger. What brings you fellows to Kirklees?"

"Our companion is upstairs receiving the attention of the prioress," said John.

"A fine woman, that prioress," said Red Roger. "A personal friend of mine."

"What is your business here?" Will asked him. It felt odd for them to make small talk with a stranger and John realised how long they had gone without contact with the outside world.

"I bring supplies to the priory; beef, mutton, pork, eggs, salt fish, you name it. The prioress lets me sleep here and occasionally lets me into the cloister. Ever been in a nunnery?"

John and Will slowly shook their heads.

"You've never seen so many young women so innocent of the ways of the world! And not another man in the vicinity! I tell you, it's like being the only cock in the henhouse here. But you have to be on good terms with the prioress, like I am."

Little John began to wish he had told this oaf to piss off. He was clearly a braggart. He wondered when the prioress would be finished with Robert.

"You two seem a likely pair," Red Roger went on. "I've taken a shine to you and wouldn't say no to putting in a good word with the lady of the house. If you put fourpence each my way I can put in a *very* good word and you can have your pick of the cloister, as it were."

Good God, thought John. *He's running a brothel. Is the prioress in on this?* He didn't much care what went on inside a priory's walls but was overcome by an urge to get away as soon as Robert was able. Healers or no, they were hardly in the midst of Christian charity here.

"I think I shall go and check on our companion," John said, rising.

"Why?" Red Roger asked. "He's in the very best hands. Why not sit and drink with me a while? I shall fetch us some more ale."

John looked at Will and nodded in the direction of the door. Will rose and they made to leave the table. Red Roger's hands shot out and grabbed each of them by the wrist. "It's best not to disturb the prioress. You wouldn't want her hand to slip while bleeding him, would you now?"

"What the devil are you prattling about?" John asked him.

There was a low, eerie sound above them. It sounded mournful and fragile.

"Rob's horn!" said Will.

The two outlaws charged for the door and dashed up the stairs that led to the first floor. They entered the apartments and found one with its door bolted.

"Here!" said Will.

Three mighty stamps from Little John's foot broke the lock and they spilled in to find Robert lying on the floor, his clothes soaked with blood and his horn raised to his lips.

John ran to his side and cradled his head on his knees. He looked up and cried out a warning to Will. Red Roger had ascended the stairs after them and charged at Will with a drawn dagger.

Alerted by John's cry, Will sidestepped Roger's lunge but slipped on the pool of gore by the bed. He came crashing down and Red Roger threw himself at him.

John set down Robert's head and leaped over the bed to his friend's rescue. A mighty blow from his fist sent Red Roger reeling across the room to strike the wall by the door. The dagger fell from his hand and clattered across the floorboards. Before Roger could gather his senses enough to retrieve it, John had seized it and driven it deep into the villain's side.

Red Roger gasped and looked up at John with bulging eyes. John withdrew the dagger and drove it once more into his body. Roger sank to the floor and bled out.

Will and John lifted Robert up and carried him over to the bed. They set him down and John tore a strip of bedding to fasten around the wound in his arm. He looked at Will. *This is bad,* their expressions said to each other.

"It was Anna," said Robert in a hoarse voice. "Anna is the prioress."

John felt Will stiffen at his side and saw his fists clench the bedding into bunches. "Never mind that now," he said. "Will, run and fetch a nun; any nun. There has to be somebody else here who can save him."

"No," said Robert. "It is done. I am too weak. It grows dark. Fetch my bow."

"Your bow?"

"I have one final arrow to shoot. Please, John. Fetch my bow."

"Stay with him," John said to Will and he ran down the stairs and hurried to room where they had stashed their weapons upon arrival. When he returned he found Will clutching Robert's hand, tears streaking his face. Robert still lived but John had seen enough men die to know that his time was near. As he knelt down by the bed, Will got up and left the room.

"You must help me, John," said Robert, reaching a shaking hand for the familiar grip of his old bow. "Open the window casement."

John did so and then helped Robert fit an arrow to his string.

"Wherever this arrow lands, I want you to bury me there," said Robert with pleading in his eyes.

"Here, in the priory grounds?" John asked.

Robert nodded. "There is a fine wood over there. I want to rest there. Barnsdale is no longer my home. Not since Katherine died. Help me draw."

John sat on the edge of the bed and helped Robert aim the arrow. There was no strength left in Robert's arms and he could barely cope with the weight of the bow. John placed his fingers on the string and drew it back as far as he could which was some distance past Robert's pale cheek. He released and the string brushed Robert's fingers as it sent the arrow sailing through the window casement, high, high across the priory precinct to fall and disappear into the woods that encroached upon it.

Robert sighed. "Thank you, old friend," he said.

John took the bow away and let Robert sink back onto the mattress. He began to wonder where Will had gone when he noticed that Robert's eyes had glazed over and his chest had stopped labouring for air.

Then Little John wept like he had not wept since he had been a child.

Anna led her garron off the beaten track and cut across country in a north-easterly direction. She would make for York, she decided. It was her hometown and, although she had not visited it in decades, she would know its streets and could start a new life. Maybe she would buy a tavern and pick up where she had left off before Guy de Gisburn had ruined her life and set her on the outlaw's path. No one would recognise her and she would change her name so that she could never be linked to the Prioress of Kirklees or the outlaw of Barnsdale. Once more it was time to reinvent herself.

The saddlebags of her garron bulged with the plate and cups she had pilfered from the priory before fleeing. Deserting her position and the priory which had been her home for twenty-five years had never been part of her plan but when Sister de Stainton had brought her word of violence in the guesthouse she knew that Roger had bungled the whole thing, God rot him. He only had to keep Hood's companions in the hall.

She didn't care if Roger was alive or dead although dead may be tidier. The last thing she needed was him coming looking for her. The damn fool loved her. She had done her best to encourage his love of course for he was a useful contact with the world beyond the priory. She didn't even mind the business he conducted under her roof. She got her cut from his dealings. It had been a good racket while it had lasted.

But now she no longer needed Roger or the priory. Flight was a necessity. Hood would be dead, she was sure of that, but the companions who had accompanied him to Kirklees were undoubtedly the ones who had caused a ruckus in the guesthouse and they would come looking for her. She wondered who they were. Probably Katherine. John too if that big oaf was still around. *Will...?*

A twig snapped behind her and she spun, suddenly aware that somebody was following her. The day was fading and the light was poor but she could make out a hooded figure between the trees, watching her. He held a bow with an arrow nocked to its string. Her heart hammered in her chest and she broke out in a cold sweat at the thought of Robert Hood's ghost pursuing her through fields and woods on the edge of dusk. The figure walked slowly towards her and lifted a hand to draw back its hood.

"Will..." she said, her heart torn in several directions by conflicting emotions.

"You go no further, Anna," said Will. "It's over for you now."

She looked at the arrow, its fletching gripped by Will's two forefingers. He only had to draw it. "I know you hate me," she said, "but I hated Robert so much more. That hatred never died even after all these years. I buried it deep inside me but when I was told that he had turned up at Kirklees and was sick, it rose in my gut. I had to kill him. I had to do it for us."

"Don't pretend that any of this was for me!" said Will. "He was my friend. My *brother*."

"You loved him, I know. It was that love that ruined us. You never had the courage to put him aside, not even for me. I suppose you loved him more than you ever loved me. That's why you are going to kill me."

She saw his fingers tense and the bowstring was drawn back a tiny fraction.

"I'm just glad it was you who came for me," she said. "It was good to see your face again, despite the circumstances. You were the only man I ever truly loved, I hope you know that. That's why I never left the priory. I had nothing left after Robert turned you against me. It was always all or nothing for you and I."

"I had to see you too," Will said. "I don't know why, but I had to prove it to myself that it was over."

"And is it?"

"Yes. Leave. Go north and never come back. If we ever see you in the West Riding again I'll kill you myself. Go now, and don't look back. There can be no looking back for us."

She couldn't believe it. *He's actually letting me go. Why did he bother coming out here after me? He couldn't kill me back then and he still can't!*

"Goodbye, Will." She tried not to smile. His face was stony and she turned from him, leading her garron by the bridle.

Don't hurry, she thought. *Take it slowly. Just make it to those trees over there and you will be out of each other's lives for good.*

She gasped as the arrow struck her between the shoulder blades, the force of it making her stumble. She fell headlong into the long grass and moved no more.

Little John stood by the fresh grave, the salt drying on his bearded cheeks. A simple wooden cross marked it and he wished that he was an educated man so that he might carve Robert's name in the wood. But he could no more mark the wood with his friend's name than he could say a sermon over the grave. Old Stephen should have been here to say a few words in Latin. *They should all be here.*

But he was alone, here at the end of all their adventures, the sole witness to their leader's passing. He waited until dusk and then turned his back on Kirklees and returned to Barnsdale, carrying the devastating news back to the rest of Robert's band.

The band began to dissolve after Robert's death with most members going their own separate ways. Little John and Will were among the last to leave Barnsdale and when they did they found the world very much changed. A pestilence had gripped the land, smiting villein and nobleman alike. The landscape emptied its population into mass graves and crops went untended, left to rot under the sad gaze of deserted manor houses. It seemed to be the very end of days.

But England weathered the pestilence as it had weathered war and famine and revolution. And the England that emerged from those dark years was a different England; one that demanded change. The depleted workforce demanded higher wages and were readier to challenge authority.

One name became a figurehead for this emerging movement and was known from Yorkshire to Hampshire as if it were a rallying call. *Robin Hood*. Minstrels sang ballads of him and tales of his exploits resounded in taverns and guild halls. Little John recognised many of their own adventures in these romanticised, simplified yarns while some of the exploits seemed to be wholly invented. He even saw some of Old Stephen's tales of Roger Godberd attributed to this new folk hero.

Robin Hood had become a man far greater than Robert Hood of Wakefield or Roger Godberd of Swannington. Both had been flawed men more interested in personal gain than starting some sort of revolution, but their failings were the one thing the tales left out. In their struggles the commoners saw a yeoman who stood up to the nobility and the clergy and struck a blow for the downtrodden. They wanted a hero and so one was created, the truth be damned. As the ballads had it;

> *Christ have mercy on his soul,*
> *That died on the Rood!*
> *For he was a good outlaw,*

And did poor men much good.

AUTHOR'S NOTE

I have tried my best to write a Robin Hood novel as authentic as possible with regard not only to history but to the 15th century ballads in which Robin makes his first appearance. In doing so, many well-known parts of the legend had to be jettisoned as they are much later additions and do not appear in the early ballads.

Maid Marian for instance did not become associated with Robin Hood until the May Day celebrations of the 16th century, likewise Friar Tuck and there is no Prince John trying to snatch the throne while his brother Richard the Lionheart is a prisoner on his way home from the Holy Land. The reign of Richard I was not Robin Hood's backdrop until Anthony Munday's plays of the Tudor period and Sir Walter Scott's 1820 novel *Ivanhoe* cemented the tradition. The ballads are set during the reign of an unspecified King Edward meaning a date of 1272 at the earliest. The ballads do however feature Little John, Much the miller's son and Will Scarlet (variously spelled Scarlok, Scathlok and Shacklock in his earliest incarnations).

Perhaps the biggest surprise to readers of the ballads is the location of much of the action in Barnsdale rather than Sherwood. There is a degree of confusion as to whether Hood was a Yorkshire man or a Nottinghamshire man. He is described as living in Barnsdale but is often pursued by the Sheriff of Nottingham who would be out of his jurisdiction in Yorkshire. In the ballad *A Gest of Robyn Hode*, the action switches from Barnsdale to Nottingham in a single day and it is possible that there were originally two Robin Hood traditions; a Yorkshire one and a Nottinghamshire one that were later blended. To take this further, we might surmise there were two Robin Hoods; one who lived in Barnsdale and one in Sherwood. This train of thought inevitably leads us to the age-old question; 'was there a real Robin Hood?'

Robin/Robert Hood was hardly an uncommon name in medieval England making the search for an historical figure behind the legend a tricky task. In order to be even in the same ball park, we must look at specific Hoods who were known to be outlaws.

The first of these was a Robert Hod identified by L. V. D Owen in the Yorkshire assize rolls for 12251226. His property was confiscated due to debt and he became a fugitive. David Crook identified this man with Robert of Wetherby who was hunted down and executed by the High Sheriff of Yorkshire. Subsequent pipe rolls for the city of York refer to Robert Hod as 'Hobbehod'. While Hobbe/Hob was used as a nickname for Robert/Robin in the middle ages, there is also a possible connection to the figure of 'Hobbe the Robber', an incarnation of looting and thievery in the late 14th century. Hobbe is mentioned in a letter by the priest John Ball who was involved in the Peasant's Revolt of 1381. He warned his co-conspirators against wanton plunder and to 'chastise wel Hobbe the Robbere'.

A hob is, of course, an impish demon or a goblin which recalls the trickster side of Robin Hood in the ballads. There is also 'Hodekin' to consider; an elfish figure in Germanic mythology recorded by the folklorist Thomas Keightley (1789 – 1872). Meaning literally 'little hood', Hodekin's link to Robin Hood was first pointed out by Sidney Lee (1859 – 1926) and it is worth noting that an elf's usual weapon of choice is the bow and arrow. This all suggests that in the search for the real Robin Hood we may be dealing with the mythological as well as the historical.

Various other nicknames for outlaws and fugitives appear in subsequent years that bear a passing resemblance to Hobbehod. In 1261 Berkshire, William, son of Robert le Fevre is referred to as 'William Robehod'. In 1272 'John Rabunhod' is outlawed after a tavern brawl in Hampshire. In the same year 'Alexander Robehod' is charged with theft in Essex. There was also an act of parliament in 1331 that refers to the perpetrators of homicides, robberies and felonies as 'Roberdesman'. A popular hypothesis is that Robin Hood (and its many variants) is a moniker for felons and outlaws that draws upon a folkloric figure; a hooded elf of the forests.

On the other hand, if Robin Hood is indeed a personal name, we need to look elsewhere. One possibility is Robert Hood of Wakefield who lived during the reign of Edward II. Aside from his name and era, there is one other thing about him that makes him a possibility; his hometown.

Wakefield was a manor ruled by Earl John de Warenne until around 1317 when Earl Thomas of Lancaster took it from him as a result of a bitter feud.

The previous spring Lancaster's wife, Alice de Lacy, was purportedly abducted by de Warenne's men (although rumour had it that she and de Warenne were lovers). Immensely powerful and more or less ruler of the north, Lancaster also had a falling out with his cousin, King Edward II. Lancaster drew support from the Marcher Lords who resented the king and his relationship with the hated royal favourites; the Despensers. What began as an attack on the Despensers' lands soon turned into open rebellion and ended with the Battle of Boroughbridge in 1322 and the subsequent execution of Lancaster for treason.

It is interesting to find a Robert Hood living in Wakefield at this time because the forest of Barnsdale encroached upon that very manor and was a natural hiding place for any outlaw on the run. The antiquarian Joseph Hunter was the first to put Robert Hood forward as the real Robin Hood and his findings were largely culled from the Wakefield Court Rolls. What follows is a basic outline of Robert Hood's life according to Joseph Hunter.

Between 1265 and 1295, Adam Hood, a forester in the service of Earl de Warenne had his child Robert christened in the town of Wakefield.

On Jan 25th, 1316 'Robert Hade' and his wife Matilda gave 2 shillings for leave to take one piece of the lord's waste on Bichill (the market place in Wakefield) between the houses of Phillip Damyson and Thomas Alayn.

In 1316, Robert Hood's handmaid was fined for taking wood from Old Park. In the same year, Hood himself was fined 3d for not obeying Earl de Warenne's summons to join the forces of Edward II's Scottish invasion.

After the Battle of Boroughbridge and Lancaster's execution in 1322, his followers were outlawed and their properties seized. One property seized in 1322 was a 'building of five rooms of a new construction on Bichill, Wakefield'.

Hunter's hypothesis is that Robert Hood was outlawed after taking part in Lancaster's rebellion against the king and fled to nearby Barnsdale to begin his life of crime. But that's not all. Hunter found a 'Robyn Hode' serving in the chamber of King Edward II not long after. That these two people could be one and the same sounds highly unlikely were it not for the events in the earliest ballad; *A Gest of Robyn Hode*. In this story, King Edward travels to Nottingham and, furious at the poaching of the deer in his royal parks, tracks Robin and his companions down. Impressed by his honour and skill, the king takes Robin into his service where he remains at court for 'twelve months and three'. Then, longing for the greenwood, Robin returns to Barnsdale and lives there for a further twenty-two years until his death at the hands of the treacherous Prioress of Kirklees.

King Edward II did indeed tour the north of England after the defeat of Lancaster's rebellion and was particularly interested in the state of his forests such as Pickering and Knaresborough which had seen many trespasses during the war. He stayed at Nottingham in November 1323 and Hunter remarks that from April 1324, several payments were made to a porter of the chamber named Robyn Hode (along with others named Simon Hod, Wat Cowherd, Robin Dyer and Grete Hobbe). On the 22nd November 1324 – a year after the king visited Nottingham – Hode is given five shillings as a gift because he is 'no longer able to work' and nothing further is heard of him.

Later research by J. C. Holt shows that Robyn Hode was already in the king's service from June 27th, 1323, a good six months before the king arrived in Nottingham. This has weakened Hunter's hypothesis in the eyes of many but it is interesting to note that around this time the itinerary of King Edward II places him at Cowick; a village roughly ten miles east of Barnsdale.

Hunter calculated the year of Hood's death as 1347; twenty-two years after he left the service of the king according to the *Gest* ballad. Interestingly there is a grave at Kirklees Priory inscribed with Hood's name and the date of 1247; exactly a century earlier than Hunter's prediction. This either means that the Robin Hood buried at Kirklees is not Robert Hood of Wakefield or, he is and a scribal error was made on the part of the engraver.

The early ballads may provide several other clues as to an historical figure. Enter Roger Godberd who hailed from Swannington in Leicestershire. Several people have tried to construct his biography but by far the most readable is David Baldwin's in his book *Robin Hood: the English Outlaw Unmasked.*

The first mention of Godberd is in 1250 where he makes a complaint that his mother and stepfather cut down sixty oaks on his land. He is noted as being underage at this time which would make his year of birth 1229 at the earliest. He appears to have later had a daughter called Diva who is mentioned in a court case in 1258 over disputed land.

Swannington was part of the manor of Whitwick until it became a manor in its own right in more recent times. There is evidence of a moated hall north of the village dating to the 12th century. Godberd appeared to be in charge of Swannington by 1259 as he is recorded handing it over to Jordan le Fleming for a period of ten years but then forcibly booting him off it a year later.

Godberd was a tenant of Robert de Ferrers, the 6th Earl of Derby. De Ferrers – a hot-headed and quarrelsome man – came of age in 1260 and immediately began a campaign to take back his lands which had been held in wardship by the Lord Edward (Longshanks, later to become Edward I, the 'Hammer of the Scots'). One of these properties was Nottingham Castle of which Roger Godberd was a member of the garrison.

Roger seems to have run into some legal trouble during his time at Nottingham as a record included in *The Sherwood Forest Book* (a collection of legal documents from various sources) tells of an episode in 1264 where Roger and several companions are accused of poaching deer in Sherwood Forest. That this accusation arose in 1287 – twenty-three years after the fact – is perhaps indicative of the efficiency of the medieval judicial system.

The delay may have been partly caused by the outbreak of the Second Barons' War; a civil war in which the barons, under Simon de Montfort, attempted to establish a parliament more sympathetic to their demands. Robert de Ferrers threw himself into the conflict but was more interested in pursuing his personal vendetta against the Lord Edward than supporting the baronial cause. He ultimately missed out on the Battle of Lewes which saw the barons' victory over King Henry III.

With the king and the Lord Edward under house arrest, Simon de Montfort became ruler of England in all but name. But while squabbling broke out amongst de Montfort's supporters, Edward escaped custody and rallied an army to his father's cause. The resulting slaughter at the Battle of Evesham spelled the end for de Montfort's movement (not to mention his life) and his followers found themselves disinherited.

Pockets of resistance held out; rebels entrenched themselves on the Isle of Axholme in Lincolnshire and at Kenilworth Castle which endured one of the longest sieges in English history. Roger Godberd was apparently financially desperate and appears in the Close Rolls of 1266 for forcing the Abbot of Garendon to hand over the charters for the lands he had leased the abbey.

In October 1266, Godberd was granted safe passage to attend the Dictum of Kenilworth; the king's offer to the rebels to buy back their lands at rates according to their level of involvement in de Montfort's rebellion. Eventually pardoned, Godberd appears to have moved north to begin a life of crime with his brother Geoffrey and others.

When he was finally brought to trial in 1276, the charges against him vary from burglary, homicide, arson and robbery in Leicester, Nottinghamshire and Wiltshire, the most heinous of which was the robbery of the monks of Stanley Abbey in 1270, one of whom was killed.

Reginald de Grey, Justice of Chester, was given money from Nottingham, Leicester and Derby to raise an army to hunt down the outlaws who were running rampant in those counties. De Grey had recently held the position of High Sheriff of Nottinghamshire, Derbyshire and the Royal Forests (Nottingham didn't get its own sheriff until 1449). Interestingly, de Grey was also one of the accused Sherwood poachers of 1264 alongside Roger and Geoffrey Godberd suggesting that they had previously been comrades in the Nottingham Castle garrison and now operated on opposite sides of the law.

All this about Nottingham and Sherwood may sound more like the Robin Hood of later tradition, not the outlaw of Barnsdale in the earliest ballads. But even in those stories, it is the Sheriff of Nottingham who plays the part of the chief villain despite the fact that he would have been out of his jurisdiction pursuing outlaws in Barnsdale. Not only does this suggest that there were once two separate traditions – a Nottinghamshire one and a Yorkshire one that got blended at some point – but one of the first stories of Robin Hood includes an episode that bears a striking resemblance to what Roger Godberd did next.

In the ballad *A Gest of Robyn Hode*, Robin and his companions befriend a knight called Sir Richard who shelters them at his castle from an assault by the Sheriff of Nottingham. The Calendar of the Close Rolls of Henry III show that a knight called Richard Foliot was accused of sheltering Godberd and his companions at his castle of Fenwick in Yorkshire. Richard was eventually forced to hand over his castle and son Edmund to the Sheriff of Yorkshire as surety until he stood trial for harbouring outlaws.

There is also a record (unfortunately undated) in the Hundred Rolls of Edward I showing that Godberd and a number of his followers were captured at a grange owned by Rufford Abbey in Sherwood and imprisoned at Nottingham Castle. The man who captured them was Hugh de Babington, undersheriff at this time to Walter Giffard, High Sheriff of Nottinghamshire etc. and also Archbishop of York. Another record of Godberd's capture has Reginald de Grey take him at Hereford before conducting him to Bridgnorth. This second arrest suggests that Godberd escaped custody (possibly from Nottingham Castle itself) only to be recaptured by de Grey.

While Godberd spent the next few years in various prisons, his followers remained active. There was an attempt to rescue him from Bridgnorth and Godberd's brother Geoffrey attacked the servants of Lucy de Grey (Reginald's stepmother) while they were en route to Leicester.

Stays at Hereford and Chester gaols are also recorded before Godberd was eventually brought to trial at the Tower of London in 1276. Inexplicably, King Edward I pardoned him and Roger Godberd wandered off the map of history.

So, we have a rebellious outlaw operating from Sherwood, robbing the clergy and defying the sheriffs and justices. He was sheltered by a knight called Richard and eventually pardoned by a king called Edward (as Robin was the *Gest* ballad). Roger Godberd's colourful life may be an intriguing parallel despite there being no record of the Hobbehod moniker being bestowed upon him. Conversely, Robert Hood of Wakefield is an attractive candidate being in the right place at the right time but there is nothing to suggest he was ever an outlaw or to connect him with the Robyn Hode of Edward's chamber records.

We are unlikely to ever know if Robin Hood was a personal name or a moniker given to outlaws who acted like hooded hobs or forest elves. It does seem clear that the legends at least were inspired by the exploits of more than one person and that the ballads alternately switch between Barnsdale in Yorkshire and Sherwood in Nottinghamshire suggest there may have been more than one source for the legend. Perhaps Godberd provided one part of the tale while another outlaw in Yorkshire provided the rest.

We can only conclude that the Robin Hood legend is a mixture of fact and fiction, its roots shrouded in England's mythological past. The popularity of various candidates wax and wane but the tantalising details of their lives provide modern storytellers with enough thread to reweave the tapestry again and again.

There are numerous books, papers and websites which have been invaluable in my research. David Baldwin's book *Robin Hood; the English Outlaw Unmasked* is what first introduced me to Roger Godberd as a possible candidate and is a fantastic introduction to the scholarly research that has gone into discovering the history behind the legend. For the most in-depth work on Robin Hood and the early ballads in particular as well as their historical context you really must read Robert B. Waltz's *The Gest of Robyn Hode; a Critical and Textual Commentary.*

https://www.boldoutlaw.com/ is probably the best resource on the web for all things Robin Hood and its message board in particular – The Blue Boar Inn – is an excellent collection of opinions on all things Robin Hood. A couple of other websites of note are http://www.robinhoodlegend.com/ and http://disneysrobin.blogspot.no/.

I can't praise the people involved in The Henry III Fine Rolls Project enough as it really is a brilliant resource for anybody interested in the nitty-gritty details of that particular monarch's reign and the work of Professor David Carpenter in particular was a big help. And for that other monarch of my novel, you really can't do much better than Kathryn Warner's blog http://edwardthesecond.blogspot.no/and her excellent book *Edward II: The Unconventional King.* Her research has been invaluable in depicting the life of a valet in the king's chamber and her passion for Edward II brings a much-maligned monarch to life.

Printed in Great Britain
by Amazon